Webster Memorial Library
Decatur Michigan

D1130695

continued from front flap

Arthur Miller's Pennsylvania Gothic tale ("The Prophecy"); John Updike's poignant view of a boy's spiritual struggle ("Pigeon Feathers"); Flannery O'Connor's powerful and ironic study of a mother-son relationship ("Everything That Rises Must Converge"). Among the penetrating stories by newer authors are W. H. Gass' "The Pedersen Kid," a stark recreation of madness and murder in a blizzard; George Garrett's "The Old Army Game," concerning a horrendous top sergeant beside whom Captain Queeg might seem a boy-scout leader; Seymour Epstein's "Shed One Honest Tear," a bitter-sweet story of love and illusion lost in an off-Broadway world; E. Lucas Myers' "The Vindication of Dr. Nestor," in which a poultry psychiatrist abroad causes an uproarious furore.

As William Peden stated in **The New York Times,** praising the writers in a previous collection, "One thing they have in common is artistry." It is this artistry that makes THE BEST AMERICAN SHORT STORIES both entertaining and illuminating.

Jacket design by Ivan Chermayeff

THE

Best

AMERICAN
SHORT STORIES
1962

THE

Best

AMERICAN
SHORT STORIES
1962

and the Yearbook of the American Short Story

Edited by

MARTHA FOLEY and DAVID BURNETT

HOUGHTON MIFFLIN COMPANY · BOSTON

The Riverside Press Cambridge

1962

813.08
B
1962 2d

IN MEMORIAM
Edwin Grant Skinner
"Swing low, sweet chariot"

FIRST PRINTING

COPYRIGHT © 1962 BY HOUGHTON MIFFLIN COMPANY

ALL RIGHTS RESERVED INCLUDING THE RIGHT TO
REPRODUCE THIS BOOK OR PARTS THEREOF IN ANY FORM

LIBRARY OF CONGRESS CATALOG CARD NUMBER: 16-11387

"The Light of the Sea" by Frieda Arkin. Copyright © 1961 by *The Colorado Quarterly*.

"The Sound of Waves" by Wayson S. Choy. Reprinted from *Prism,* Summer, 1961. Copyright © 1961 by Wayson S. Choy.

"Because I Was Flesh" by Edward Dahlberg. Reprinted from *Prairie Schooner*. Copyright 1961 by the University of Nebraska Press.

"Antaeus" by Borden Deal. Reprinted from *Southwest Review,* Spring, 1961. Copyright © 1961 by Southern Methodist University Press.

"Criers and Kibbitzers, Kibbitzers and Criers" by Stanley Elkin. Copyright 1961 by *Perspective,* Inc.

"Wheat Closed Higher, Cotton Was Mixed" by Seymour Epstein. Originally published under the title "Shed One Honest Tear." Copyright © 1961 by McCall Corporation, Redbook Magazine.

"The Old Army Game" by George Garrett. Copyright © 1961 by George Garrett.

"The Pedersen Kid" by W. H. Gass. Reprinted from *MSS*. Copyright *MSS,* 1961.

"The Model Chapel" by Sister Mary Gilbert. Copyright 1961 by *The Virginia Quarterly Review,* The University of Virginia.

"A Day on Ragged" by Donald Hall. © 1961 by The New Yorker Magazine, Inc.

"The Last Day" by Henia Karmel-Wolfe. Copyright 1961 by The Reporter Magazine Company.

"In the Middle of the Fields" by Mary Lavin. © 1961 by The New Yorker Magazine, Inc.

"Hanging Hair" by Jack Thomas Leahy. *The Kenyon Review,* copyright 1962.

" 'To Hell the Rabbis' " by Ben Maddow. *The Kenyon Review,* copyright 1962.

"Déjà Vu" by Miriam McKenzie. Reprinted from *New World Writing 18*. Copyright © 1961 by J. B. Lippincott Company.

"The Prophecy" by Arthur Miller. Copyright © 1961 by Arthur Miller.

"The Vindication of Dr. Nestor" by E. Lucas Myers. From *The Sewanee Review,* Spring, 1961. Copyright © 1961 by The University of the South.

"Everything That Rises Must Converge" by Flannery O'Connor. Reprinted from *New World Writing 19*. Copyright © 1961 by J. B. Lippincott Company.

"The Education of a Queen" by Thalia Selz. Copyright 1961, *Partisan Review*.

"Love on a Dark Street" by Irwin Shaw. © 1961 by Esquire, Inc.

"Pigeon Feathers" by John Updike. Originally published in *The New Yorker*. © 1961 by The New Yorker Magazine, Inc. Reprinted from *Pigeon Feathers and Other Stories,* by permission of Alfred A. Knopf, Inc.

THE RIVERSIDE PRESS
CAMBRIDGE MASSACHUSETTS
PRINTED IN THE U.S.A.

ACKNOWLEDGMENTS

GRATEFUL ACKNOWLEDGMENT for permission to reprint the stories in this volume is made to the following:

To the Editors of *The Colorado Quarterly, Esquire, The Kenyon Review, MSS, New World Writing, The New Yorker, Partisan Review, Perspective, Prairie Schooner, Prism, Redbook, The Reporter, The Sewanee Review, Southwest Review, The Virginia Quarterly Review;* and to Frieda Arkin, Wayson S. Choy, Edward Dahlberg, Borden Deal, Stanley Elkin, Seymour Epstein, George Garrett, W. H. Gass, Sister Mary Gilbert, Donald Hall, Henia Karmel-Wolfe, Alfred A. Knopf, Inc., Mary Lavin, Jack Thomas Leahy, Ben Maddow, Miriam McKenzie, Arthur Miller, E. Lucas Myers, Flannery O'Connor, Thalia Selz, Irwin Shaw, and John Updike.

FOREWORD

THE first collection of short stories ever to be published in the United States was *Tales of the Northwest,* by Joseph Snell in 1820. In the same year, Washington Irving's first work, *The Sketch Book,* also appeared and made him famous as "the father of the American short story." The actual credit for the first real collection seems to belong to Snell, as despite Irving's superior literary ability, his volume was composed of essays as well as stories. The year 1820 also marked the appearance of Sydney Smith's famous attack on American writing, "Who Reads an American Book?" How quickly Smith was to be discredited!

As the title and date of *Tales of the Northwest* indicate, they were stories of adventure in what was then a wild and far-off place, the "frontier." Apart from its adventures and setting, *Tales of the Northwest* pioneered in a literary sense. It was the first settler in what was to be a realm of thousands of books by thousands of authors, many of them so important they were to encircle the planet with the kind of writing Americans love most — short stories.

The English of the period were to have their great novels as were the Russians and other nations of Europe. But in the short story it was America that was to have the greatest literary influence and the greatest — sleazy word though it has become — popularity. The list of the great modern short story writers who were to follow Snell and Irving is too long to repeat here. There is no doubt, however, that the short story in modern literature has been predominantly American-influenced. That is why a book, like *The Best American Short Stories,* which tries to give a sampling of the most outstanding short stories of each year, fulfills a need for the serious reader.

Why is the short story so important in the United States, which

publishes so many and reads them so avidly? No completely satis-
factory reason has been given. Some have said it is because Americans are always in a hurry and want their literary satisfaction
fast. Others have said it is because we are the newest of countries
that we have latched on to the oldest of literary forms. Whatever
the reason, we certainly do take short stories seriously, no matter
how humorous those of a Mark Twain, Ring Lardner or James
Thurber may be.

How seriously authors themselves take them is shown by an
anecdote of a New York publisher. He was spending the evening
with a celebrated author who suggested they go to his apartment
for drinks. The author was not expected home so soon. When he
opened the door he found his wife in the arms of another well-
known writer. "I was scared stiff," the publisher, a very short man,
said. "Here were two big six-foot guys and how could I ever
separate them?" He need not have worried. The outraged husband
yelled at the intruder, "I always *knew* you were a lousy short story
writer!" "And you know," the publisher commented, "if he had
kicked him in the solar plexus, the other guy would not have
looked more wounded!"

That first book of American short stories dealt with a tangible
frontier, the Northwest, but there are figurative frontiers in any
kind of writing. There are the changing frontiers of character-
ization and emotion, of style and language. Reading a good new
short story becomes an adventure in itself.

And just what is a short story? Poe, who certainly knew how
to write one, said a requisite was that it could be read in one
sitting. An encyclopedia defines it as writing "usually not more
than ten thousand words in length." Probably one of the closest
approximations is that a short story writer *suggests* more than his
space allows him to say.

The foreword to last year's volume in this series — a series now
forty-seven years old — stated that the year had been an unusually
rich one in good short stories. This year has been the same. Its
lavishness makes it difficult to select the stories a reader should
not miss. With a few exceptions (notably *The New Yorker*) most
of the finest stories appeared, as they have for years, in the "little
magazines." It is unfortunate that they have acquired that label

of "little." They should be called the literary magazines, or the serious magazines or, perhaps simply, the good magazines.

Having sounded what might seem like a chauvinistic note on the importance of the American short story, it is only fair to add that a great many excellent short stories from Europe and the Orient have been published in the United States this year. This has been especially true of the *Atlantic Monthly, The Literary Review* and *The Texas Quarterly*. Since this book has to be devoted to American and Canadian authors, those stories cannot be reprinted here.

We are grateful to the editors who have kept us supplied with their magazines and to their authors for generously granting reprint rights. The editor of any new magazine is invited to send it along without waiting for permission to do so.

The editors and staff of Houghton Mifflin Company are also entitled to gratitude for their help. Finally, tribute is paid to Edward J. O'Brien who founded this anthology.

MARTHA FOLEY
DAVID BURNETT

CONTENTS

THE

Best

AMERICAN

SHORT STORIES

1962

(From The Colorado Quarterly)

THE LIGHT OF THE SEA

BY FRIEDA ARKIN

*S*HE OFTEN thought it strange, herself, that a woman of her past energies should take such pleasure now in sitting. Pleasure was hardly the word. Reduced at last to a handful of proud old bones, she still held herself in a kind of stiff readiness as she sat in the spread-winged wicker chair looking out at the crumbling sea wall. She spoke little when there was any listening ear about, and then quietly, half aloud, sitting there on the veranda, knowing Raphael's young wife Angelina was safely clicking about upstairs in her sharp high heels. She faced unblinkingly the glancing lights on the wind-crisped waves, scarcely aware of the fishing boats pulling out from or coming into the bay, or the red-and-black-flannel-shirted men in their outboards, with their ceaseless setting and emptying of lobsterpots. Sometimes the sky was gray as lead, and the bleached stones of the wall and the white swooping gulls and the sullen water combined, in their absence of color, to make the prospect before her into a dreary etching of a seascape. It was at such moments that her mood was worst and her low spoken words savage.

But this morning the gulls wheeled in screaming glee, and the water glittered with such brilliance that it shot pain into her eyes and she closed her pale lids against it. Thoughts that had been recurring for the past months danced in her head, and she tightened her thin mouth and listened for Angelina's steps.

"It's time I got the boys down," Jessica Packard said aloud, and continued to sit with her eyes screwed up and her brain a fever of thought. It was not as though she noted clearly that her nephews had not been to see her for ten years, not since their last journey eastward to witness their Uncle Izaak being lowered into the rocky soil; that aside from due notification of certain major events in their lives (two marriages, two births, one divorce), Christmas and Easter cards of the traditional sort had been the only thin link she had with them through the widowed years. Her thoughts were not discrete. But there was a look about her mouth as though she were tasting lemons.

She grasped the chair arms and brought her thin body upright, like a bird alert for flight. She turned and walked stiffly into the parlor to the dainty-legged escritoire, warped and cracked now from fifty years in an atmosphere of sea spray. There she extracted two limp vellum sheets and wrote off the letters, one to Abel, one to Mark.

Once her trembling hand, with the pen grasped tight in it, was pressed against the paper the words came sharply, smoothly, as authoritatively as they would dropping from her own lips. And the stiffly regal look of them, she saw grimly, lacked the quaver of age which, thwarting the efforts of her amazing will, ran through her spoken words like a thin ragged string. "Please come down as soon as you conveniently can," the upright letters stalked from the broad-nibbed pen, "I have an important matter to discuss with you." To Abel: "I am afraid there is not much to amuse small children here. I should be obliged if you could make other arrangements for your daughters. You may stay as long as you wish, of course, but if arranging for the care of the girls must take time into account, I think a day or two should be enough to finish our business in." To Mark: "Please give my regards to Myra."

She signed the letters quickly, stamped them, and placed them on the hall table for Raphael to mail in town. Then she went back to the wicker chair and resolutely adjusted her eyes to the glare on the water.

"My nephews will be coming down," she said that evening as Angelina brought her dinner into the dining room, the whole meal on a vast linen-covered tray. She looked at the girl speculatively from eyes which had paled with the years; from the early evening lights of them which had first startled Izaak to look at her in an uncousinly way, they had faded to a near-absence of color which had, possibly from her constant looking at the water, something of the light of the sea in them.

Angelina placed the tray on the table and with a flick of dark wrist drew off the cloth. She smiled, and the teeth gleamed in her beautifully modeled olive face. "That will be so nice for you, Mrs. Packard," she said. Her voice was ripe and full and her teeth flashed again in Sicilian brilliance before the warm curved lips met and her mouth settled in repose.

"Um," said the old lady, and brought her eyes down to the tray. "You remember them, I suppose?" She glinted suspiciously at the dish before her: "Blowfish. I hope Raphael bought them whole."

Angelina stepped back, her eyes roaming the tray for omissions. Then she looked at the old woman again, her eyes calm.

"Yes," she said, "I remember that they came here every summer. I used to play with the older one sometimes, when he'd let me. Abel?" The name fell with lazy affectionate remembrance from her lips. For an instant the old aunt felt something indefinable flash through her smile. She would have said triumph. Then Angelina turned and with an easy grace walked toward the kitchen.

Jessica Packard lifted her head and followed the retreating figure, her eyes resting nearly closed on the unself-conscious rise and fall of the rounded hips. For a moment she held her face to the empty doorway; then she snorted and groped for her fork.

There's no greater catastrophe in the universe, she reflected dourly, impaling tender green beans on the silver fork, than the dwindling away of a family. Procreation, expansion, proliferation — these are the laws of living things, with the penalty for not obeying them the ultimate in punishments: oblivion. When the fate of the individual is visited on the group, then (the warm sweet butter dripped from her raised trembling fork and she pushed her head forward belligerently), ah, then the true bitterness of existence could be tasted. And indeed the young garden beans were brackish in her mouth.

She was the last living of the older generation. What had once been a widespread family — at one time, she knew, there were enough Packards to populate an entire county — had now narrowed down to the two boys, Abel and Mark. She swung her eyes up to the blue of the window, her jaws gently mashing the bitter beans. What hope lay in the nephews, she asked the intensifying light out there, with one married to a barren woman and the other divorced, having sired two girl children, with none to bear on the Packard name?

She ate. It seemed to her, as it seemed each night, that the gloom drew itself in and became densest at the table's empty chairs, giving her the frequent illusion that she dined with shadows. Here, too, she talked low, quirking her head at one or another of the places, most often at Izaak's armchair which faced her across the long table. Or it might have been the absent nephews she addressed, consciously playing with the notion that this was one of the summers of their early years.

She thought again of her children, those two who had died young, before the later science which might have saved them could attach even a label to their separate malignancies. The girl, her first, she barely remembered. It could have been anyone's infant, for it had not survived the bassinet. But the boy . . . the boy had been alive yesterday. Each successive movement in his growing was recorded on the unreeling film inside her. He ran on his plump sticks of legs, freezing now and again into the sudden startled attitudes which the camera had caught and held on the paling photographs, all carefully placed and glued and labeled, resting in the fat plush album in the bottom drawer of the escritoire. In the cruel clearness of her memory the boy remained unchanged, quick with the delight of laughter, and the pain with which she recalled that short destroyed childhood was still unendurable to her. It was one with the desolate rocks and the alien water on those days when she hated the sea.

The brothers drove down together in Mark's small red sports car, Mark at the wheel. They rarely spoke. Abel sat and regarded the farm country which, spreading out from both sides of the road, rolled greenly up to where the silent white houses and long barns and silos nested into the tilled fields. He saw the land with a stranger's eyes, all the old familiarness gone. And it presented itself to him as it would to any stranger, impervious, complete in itself. There was stability there, too — a color which his life had had once. That is what childhood is, he told himself. Solid, settled . . . lost. In the stiff neutral lines of the telephone poles he saw the no-nonsense pen strokes of Aunt Jessica's letter. What bad grace, what incredible selfishness he and Mark had shown. The boyhood summers preceding their uncle's funeral might never have been. They had closed over, absolutely, with the sealing of old Izaak's grave. The small car flew on relentlessly. The old woman, stubbornly reigning in the house above the crashing waters took on an ominous reality. Abel moved and adjusted his long legs.

"I suppose it has to do with the property," Mark had said over the telephone when they had discussed their receipt of the letters. Not until the words had been spoken did Abel suddenly see the old house and the insistent sea, and feel his contrition blotted out in one shameful moment of covetousness. He and Mark were the last of the family, and there lay the Cape Ann property which had seemed to have no end, stretching from horizon to horizon, in those golden days of summer.

Now Abel turned his head to look at his brother. Mark held the wheel loosely, but his fingers curved around it in a purposeful way and the deliberate set of his body spoke plainly of the figure he'd make in the years to come. His sandy hair was already beginning to thin and recede at the sides, and Abel looked quickly away. Mark easily looked years older than himself, settled, his world comfortably categorized.

The vacation traffic was becoming heavier as they approached the sea. "She didn't mention bringing Myra," Mark said, maneuvering the car into the next lane. "She's probably getting old — crotchety, I mean — and we figured uh-uh, better not. They've never met, you know. But Myra wouldn't budge without an express invitation. I feel kind of bad about it." He gave Abel a quick glance and moved closer to the wheel, hugging it to him, and Abel caught this briefest of allusions to guilt.

"I imagine the old girl hasn't missed us much," Mark added, his eyes on the road. Abel ignored the half-expressed bid for confirmation. He smiled. It was barely possible that his brother was right.

He could tell they were approaching the sea. The air took on a special strength now that they'd left the fecund warmth of the farmland behind. There was the smell of the coast, like a primeval memory, composed of equal parts salt water, clams, seaweed and northern air. He turned from the flying trees to look ahead and saw with an inward boy's eye again the great fieldstone house which, built on one of the many acres of ancestral land bordering

the west harbor, had been Izaak's bride-gift to his cousin-wife as
the last century ended.

Mark's thoughts must have been keeping silent pace beside his
own, climbing the same crags in dirty white sneakers, clambering
out on top of the headland and coming upon the sudden glinting
water at the same instant. "Remember the *Starbird?*" Mark asked,
and Abel lifted his eyes from the double lines in the middle of the
road, the twin white ribbons which the car swallowed rapidly as it
ascended the crest of the hill and came down.

"The *Starbird*," Abel said. There was the day Uncle Izaak had,
in an unexpected grandiose gesture, handed over the pretty sloop
to Abel for keeps, on condition that he never fail to let his brother
accompany him whenever the younger boy wished. The two of
them had developed into a remarkable sailing team . . . all of this
happening in a time of their lives when their youth and their
brotherhood knitted them together as no other time or circum-
stance could. They seemed then to have had a single mind and
body, a mutuality which had been accepted with the fact of their
youth, casually. He saw the *Starbird* as she lay, her slender mast
up and gently turning, its point describing constant languid circles
against a cumulus sky. Both of them had known the feeling of the
small life in her waiting, ready, for the two of them to run up her
sails. The *Starbird* had been long at the bottom of the bay.

They came unexpectedly upon the sea. Meeting it without preparation as they did, robbed of anticipation, a common disappointment seized them. They were climbing the hill in the night when
the headlights abruptly probed solid blackness, became two parallel
luminous tubes which broadened out into a faint mist of light and
ended. Mark stopped the car and switched off the lights and they
sat looking at the water, which, there being no moon out, at first
could be distinguished from the sky only by an absence of stars.

Abel sat forward in absolute astonishment at the chill which
swept through him, the feeling was so like an experience he'd had
as a boy, right here below, where the aunt's house was. He had
been lying in the field at night, staring up into the heavens (why
are the stars so bright over the sea?), losing himself in the thousand lights. At first near, they sank farther and farther back and up,
became galaxies, distant flaming suns drawing him with them, and
with a shout of terror he had felt himself falling, whirling upward.

He recognized the fear now as one common to his later nightmares, in which he found himself receding from earth in a balloon which had become unmoored, up, up, the earth falling rapidly away, and even now an ancient sweat started out on his forehead and in his armpits.

They saw the hall light flash on, rose-colored behind the narrow mullioned windows, as Mark brought the car to the steps at the top of the curving drive. Abel got out and stood in the chill night, the sound of the water suddenly about him. His ear, practiced again, heard the tide going out. There were the sounds of the inward rush where the small water hit the breakwater nearby, and the receding swish as it ran back, dragged reluctantly over the stones and pebbles. It was only at high tide that the waves crashed, even in good weather and in spite of the breakwater, against the sea wall which formed the boundary of the property. When I wake in the morning, he thought, I shall hear those other sounds.

Jessica Packard had come out and was standing at the steps. She called, "Come up, come up, children," and they both noted how her voice was cracked, like a dry reed. But she held her body straight against the warm light behind her.

Not until they had entered the hallway and she had closed the heavy door did she turn and allow herself to greet them as individuals, and her keen old eyes took their measure, one by one. Mark, she saw, had become rounded, not much taller than she remembered him at sixteen. She had no knowledge of the kind of thing he worked at, but saw at a glance, from the near-effeminacy of his hips, that it must be a sitting job, a desk job. And for the first time in years she saw Izaak with an axe in his hand, wearing the heavy dun-colored old jacket that had always reminded her of a horseblanket, the breath in clouds about his face in the icy air, and her lip curled as Mark laughed a high laugh and pushed his hand quickly backward through his thinning hair. "Hello, Aunt Jess. Wonderful to see you!" The laugh was overboisterous and the old lady thought immediately: a customer's man.

Abel listened to his brother's voice and waited, standing back, to see whether the old woman was going to make their greetings easier for them. But she stood still, turning her head quietly so that for an instant she and Abel looked at one another like newly-met strangers.

"Well, Abel?" she said, and with the force of boyhood suddenly upon him Abel stood forward and surprised himself by stooping to put his arms around the old aunt's thin shoulders. He kissed her cold soft-wrinkled cheek. "Well, Aunt Jessie," Abel said. Round pink spots flamed in her face. "If you can forgive a ten-year absence, here we are to beg it."

His aunt turned abruptly and grasped the white points of her dress collar together at her throat as though she were pulling a shawl close about her shoulders. "Come into the parlor," she said, her voice tight, "there's a fire going."

He had imagined what it would be like to wake in the third-story bedroom — to think perhaps that with the first stirring from sleep, before the years between should penetrate his senses, he might have the illusion that here they were at the start of another Cape summer. But Abel had come awake instantly, without a thought of heading for the window to glimpse the *Starbird* bobbing on the water, or to read from the motion of the leaves of the catalpas below from what direction the wind was coming. Instead, his first thought of the morning was of Celia. He could not say why he placed her here, in the house where she had never been. And then, his eyes seeking the crack-filled ceiling, he remembered how his last summer here had been filled with thoughts of her. She had been in college then, shining-haired, serious, always carrying one of the Great Books with her, bound in library green . . . and later, in flowing graduation black, nun and goddess in one . . . they had stopped in the middle of the field and she had laughed softly at the intensity of his announcement that he was marrying her. He had kissed her and drawn his shaking fingers like a comb through her long silk hair. (Her mortarboard had fallen and lay in the purple thistles.) Celia, who gave him Alice and Sue, who held him somehow responsible for the pain and the diapers and the cryings in the night.

He felt the ten years heavy on his body as he pushed himself from bed and walked to the window to look down, after all, on the flat catalpa leaves, here below. Alice and Sue would love to dance on the green mowed lawn, and he imagined he caught a glimpse of twirling skirt beneath the nearly motionless leaves. Seeing that he had disobeyed his aunt's request that he leave the girls at home, he smiled. They were everywhere, in and out of the house, where he was now and where he had ever been.

He heard Alice's voice out there. He straightened at the absurdity of the notion and then it came again: the excited high querying of childhood, Alice's intonation, surely. Grasping the window sill he bent far out to scan the lawn below. Two figures stood there, an old man and a boy. The boy, a good bit older than Alice, he saw, was holding something in one hand and gesturing rapidly with the other, forefinger darting back and forth like a humming-bird. The old man was bent in low rumbling explanation over the object, and again the high ring of boy's laughter floated up to him. Almost now, but not quite, Alice's laugh. Abel recognized Raphael then, his aunt's old gardener, appearing from here to be at the same point of ancient agelessness as when he'd last seen him. He pulled back from the window and started hastily to dress.

"Mark is out reliving his childhood," Aunt Jessica told Abel dryly, and she picked up and set the glass of orange juice before his plate. "I hope you slept well. Both of you were always late sleepers." There was strain in her voice, and Abel stayed his hand on the glass and looked at his aunt for a hint of her state of mind. Some small war was going on inside her. Perhaps she feared to allow them to recapture the hold they'd had on her affections in those long-gone summers. Well, he thought, and raised the juice glass to his lips, she had right on her side. The casual accepting barbarians they'd been had developed into a couple of graceless nephews. She had a perfect right.

"Who's the little boy I saw out on the lawn just now?" he asked her. Jessica settled herself at the head of the table, where he remembered Uncle Izaak's having sat, and folded her hands in her lap, looking toward him in an oblique way.

"That's Angelina's boy. She's married to Raphael. You must remember him. He does all the work around here now. Angelina cooks and cleans for me. Surely you haven't forgotten Angelina?" There was the same twist of the lips he'd seen last night, but the words evidently covered some confusion in her, for she began to busy herself with the butter, a knife, and abruptly popped a piece of bread into the toaster and pushed down on the little black handle. For a moment he allowed the rhythmic ticking to fill in the silence between them, and then Abel said wonderingly, "The boy looks to be about nine or ten."

Her name, thrown out like that in the clear morning light, hit him strangely, like a clap of chimes. He remembered the dark-eyed Italian girl with hair like glistening black seaweed streaming about her bony shoulders. Abutting the property, nearby, was the settlement of Italian and Portuguese fishermen's families from which she came, and which he and his brother had so many times passed, skimming by in the *Starbird*. Seen from the water, the agglomeration of wooden huts straggled along the extension of the sea wall like disarrayed gray matchboxes, their tarpaper roofs gray-white, encrusted with gull droppings. He recalled how silently, incessantly she used to follow the two of them until in rare moments of youthful magnanimity they allowed her to come up to them, join in a game or two . . . he tried to recall her last name, remembering only that it was like a phrase of music. And another memory, tumbling hard against the tangle-haired image of the girl, the day she had come scrambling upon him looking at the heaving sea as he stood alone on the promontory of rock. Her dark, thin alien hands reached to him, her mouth open, her black avaricious eyes sweeping the landscape, then fixing him with passion. "Can I come live in your house? Oh please? I have a bed, my own bed, they will send it up to me. I like your house so much." He had stared in disbelief, in horror, even — the words had poured in a hissing fury of entreaty from the small foreign mouth, agonized as a woman's. His own answer he could not recall . . . only that, standing masterful on the great rock, he threw his boy's head back and laughed hysterically into the sea wind. Her little face grew wild like a gypsy's and the white lightning that flashed through the skies could have had its origin in her eyes. "You will see! I'll have a house someday just like that. A bigger house! A bigger house!" She turned, spinning with hate, and fled in her printed tatter of a dress, and he continued to laugh crazily into the storm as it broke, the world fixed in a sudden sheet of white light and the thunder bursting on his eardrums. And the last summer here, when he and Mark had returned to find her completed in a tall quiet beauty — unaware, apparently, that she had emerged from childhood. So had he, too, unknowingly come out from the chaos of the minor years.

(The winters between visits were always magically sloughed off when they came here.) They had accepted the girl in her new emergent body in the same old careless spurts of pity, and had the *Starbird* still been above water, might even at last have allowed her aboard.

"Where is she?" Abel asked, and his aunt smiled. There was no friendliness in the stretched lips. With a short movement of her head she indicated the door which opened to the kitchen, and in a stride Abel had reached it and swung it open.

The woman at the sink turned her head to the doorway, and Abel saw that the flamboyant splay of hair had been caught, smoothed back, folded into a gleaming mass at her neck. The tiny gold rings in her ears were gone. Surprise and instant recognition filled the radiance of her face and he stood there, confusedly aware of her full Italian beauty.

"Abel!" She spoke his name as naturally as an expelled breath and he walked to her and smiled down into the warmth of her dark eyes and the serenity of her face. Quietly he took her two hands and they walked back to the dining room. Angelina gave him a quick smile, then turned her head to the old woman sitting there in silence.

"Raphael is going into town now and you haven't completed the list, Mrs. Packard. Shall I tell him what you need?"

Jessica Packard pushed herself from the table with a grunt. "I'll tell him myself," she said and swept them both with a lightning appraisal before she took her stiff, straight body through the door.

Angelina withdrew her hands gently from Abel's and slipped them into her apron pockets. She leaned back against the side of the door and smiled again, but somehow removed, shy. "It's good that you boys got down at last," she said and looked down at the floor. The words fell simply from her lips, with no reproach. "She's been lonely up here, with no one around the place but Raphael and me."

Raphael and you. You and old Raphael. Abel looked at her, seeing the old man as he had seen him in the garden earlier. Angelina smiled faintly, and it was then that he recalled his insistent foolish desire to remember her full name, that name which was like the sound of a brook running. He asked her.

Her eyes opened at him, surprise in the dark irises, and then her lips curved into her lovely smile, and she said, "Mannolini, my maiden name was Mannolini."

"Angelina Mannolini." He lingered on the cadence of the words and she stared at him, startled. They both laughed suddenly.

"Angelina Buffo, now," she said demurely, and the oddly opposed words were a discordance in his ears. He heard the sound of his aunt's steps in the kitchen and turned back toward the table as Jessica Packard marched in, nodded curtly at the girl, and returned to her seat at the table. Angelina withdrew quietly and closed the kitchen door behind her.

His aunt renewed the conversation from the point where they had left it. She folded her sharp arms before her and looked into Abel's face as she talked.

"I imagine you didn't know Angelina was in what we used to call a family way when you boys left, the summer before your Uncle Izaak died." The look from her pale eyes became determinedly neutral, and quickly she began to butter the cold toast. The hand which held the knife shook in what looked to him like withheld anger. It could have been the tremor of age.

He leaned toward her: "Surely she couldn't have been married to Raphael then!"

His aunt's face was stony and reflected nothing, but she closed her eyes and held the lids down over them as though gathering strength to say more. Then she opened them and regarded him steadily.

"No. She came to me with her news, and we talked about it, and I thought a bit. Finally I advised her to marry Raphael to give the child a name and to work here in the house until her time came. Soon afterward Izaak died, and she stayed on here with Raphael."

Abel felt the smile tight on his face. Jessica sat in complete stiffness but for an infinitesimal shaking of her head, and they looked at one another in silence, like two enemies gauging the distance between them. He saw how the irises of her eyes widened and narrowed spasmodically, the perfectly normal muscular movements seeming to measure out the seconds, waiting for him to speak.

"She came to you . . ." Abel said. But her statement and the fact itself seemed completely natural, and he wondered why he spoke.

"Could you have been the father, Abel?" The question was asked so gently, against the look in her eyes, that he sat back instantly. She had taken up between her hands the little golden honeypot, and turned it, first to the right, then to the left, but her eyes never left his face.

Was it possible, could it have been, that in that phantasmagoria of wind and sea and waves, of youth and the past, he had indeed once embraced the slight dark Angelina . . . he seemed to hold the memory of the smell of her hair in his nostrils, a musky sea-salt odor, and at that moment Abel could not have said yes or no to the old woman. He shook his head against this memory that was not a memory. Their eyes held, locked, and he felt a massive tender pulse in his body as he wrenched his look from her. "I think it is not possible," he said, speaking against the quasi memory, but the hesitancy in his voice brought a smile, almost malicious, to his aunt's lips.

"Or might it have been Mark," she said, and the changed timbre of her voice, dry, amused, quickened a remembered anger in him. ("Did you break the mainmast of Uncle's clipper ship?" she asked him in the summer of his eighth year as he faced her, the fragile model on the dining table between them, appearing severed at midpoint where the tiny white sails hung forlorn and low on the dipped black threads. His stricken silent eyes looked up at her, and, tall as a lighthouse, with the hooded eyes of an eagle, she smiled cruelly as she touched the splintered stem lightly with one finger. "Or was it the Old Man of the Sea?")

Far out the sea broke with a muted crash against the breakwater. He slept through the high tide, and it was again beginning to ebb. Swiftly he moved his chair back, rose and walked to the open window. The water was clear and sparkling, young. And there below, the unpruned thickets of wild rose which grew rampant throughout the area splashed themselves in abundance along the wall. Each forgotten thing fell into place, each bringing with it a rich surprise that it could ever have left his mind. He had the sudden illusion that he was viewing from this window each detail as it was when last seen, and the abrupt engulfing of memories, miraculously vivid, held him again in the triumph of his youth. Then the void in time began swiftly to fill and the years rolled in against one another like a rush of water. He had a sense of being time-washed, as though more had changed within himself and with his life than ten years warranted. "Listen to me, Abel," Aunt Jessica said, and he turned back to the dimmed and present room.

There was no pity in him now for her age, nor self-rebuke for the solitude they had left her to. He was aware only of a presence in the room with them, a blow gathering itself in for the strike; this he knew as insistently as his broad eye-sweep from the window had revealed to him how furiously he burned to claim this place, this land, this house, this sea. He looked at her as she sat, her age-palsied hands gripping the edge of the table.

She was smiling bleakly. "I suppose the foibles of old people can't ever be explained to the young. Perhaps we become more tradition-bound as the years pass. But I have always held with our family's traditions. I grew up with them, Abel. And one of them has been to leave the Packard property in trust for the eldest male child in the last of the family line. That is how it came to Izaak." She turned her smile down on the table. "That is why I am leaving it now, to Angelina's son."

From a distant numbness Abel said, "The child is not mine, Aunt Jessica."

He thought she laughed. "I believe I have always known that." But her eyes attacked him coldly, and she folded her hands into a knuckled ball on the table before her. "I have decided to accept Angelina's declaration. The boy is Izaak's."

My girls! Abel instantly thought, and the butterfly feet took immediate and final leave of the lawns they had never crossed and the sands they had never sent flying into the wind. His clear and profound loss removed the old woman's voice from the realm of shock. He said only, "And if the child is none of ours . . . ?"

She sat up and turned her entire body to him. "Have you seen him?" she asked fiercely. "Go look into his face and tell me he is not a Packard! Do you think I cannot see my own boy in him? My son? My baby?" She huddled into the chair, the flesh hanging grayly from her face as though the bones had collapsed inward. Then, slowly, she began to chafe her hands in her lap. The sound was like rustling paper in the dead room. She lifted her face, and her eyes, indistinguishable from the color of water, swam at him, two pale circular universes.

"Izaak, Izaak," she whispered hoarsely, and Abel knew that the words came unaware from her. He could not tell whether malevolence rang in them, or rage, or sorrow, or ravaged pride.

"You had better go out and find Mark," Jessica Packard said. Without transition her voice had become completely passionless. "Tell him what I have just told you. As my nephews, you will each figure in the will, but this matter of the property I wanted you to hear from my own lips."

Abel rose at once and walked to the door, feeling the eyes bright and hard on his back. He left the house and took the graveled path down to the sea. Some instinct — defensive, self-preserving — kept his eyes from the wide lawn and the trees and bushes quiet in the near-noon heat, and he continued on straight to the sea wall. His brother was nowhere in sight. Abel stood looking at the glittering sun-points on the surface of the water. Experimentally, he closed his lids down hard on the scene. It was like the ringing down of a red-brown curtain.

(From Prism)

THE SOUND OF WAVES

BY WAYSON S. CHOY

*S*UNDAY, a warm spring day by the Moira River. I remember
how Bob suddenly stood up. That year he was seventeen and
I was almost fifteen. Bob was a good-looking guy, always full
of energy and surprises; he was two inches from being six foot and
looked taller because he was thin and tautly muscled. We had
been sitting silently on the Moira's rock-cliff banks for almost an
hour. Feet dangling, our eyes meandering across the bright horizon, when all at once Bob gave me a shove and pushed himself up.
Naked to the waist, now warmly tanned by the late April rays, Bob
stood with his head thrown back; then, expanding his chest, he
gulped the damp river air and laughed to feel the warm sun on his
back. In the distance the glowing clay hills seemed to undulate,
to shift like a red wave against the blue sky. Whenever the wind
blew from these northern Ontario hills the river air tasted sharply
of evergreen, of stunted pines and moist, swaying grass. The wind
sang and spiked the warm afternoon with a dreamy restlessness.
Bob's laugh echoed and died.

I stirred reluctantly, swore a casual goddam and threw a handful
of pebbles down the limestone scarp. The stones made a chattering
sound as they tumbled the twelve feet of steep embankment and
then were lost in the swiftly flowing brown water. At the moment
it seemed I had nothing better to do than yawn — to yawn very
slowly, reluctantly, to emerge from my dream world. A world in-
habited by blondes and brunettes: long-legged, full-breasted girls I
had yet to touch.

The sun rose higher in the April sky and the afternoon grew hot like a late summer morning. The breeze caressed our bare backs with sudden changes of warmth and tickling coolness. We could hear the persimmon tree stirring behind us. The persimmon grew at the top of the hill, beside the gravel road that led nowhere; the tree was ugly and tall, and when the sun shone against it the entangling branches threw shadows on the ground that stirred like a knot of snakes. The wind now drifted down the steep hill, swirled dust around Bob's '47 Ford, rattled the persimmon branches above the car, and swooped gently down around us. The tree smelled sweet and dusty: gasoline and perfume with an almost perverse appeal. Funny, the tree always smelled sweet. I started talking like this to Bob. But he only jammed his big hands into his jeans and laughed impatiently: "What'd you take at school this week — Wordsworth?" "What's wrong with — ?" He threw a small stone at me and I ducked in time to hear it whizzing past my right ear.

"C'mon kid, clam it!"

I shrugged, looked at the Moira twelve feet below, then turned around as if nothing had happened: yet, in spite of myself, sweat moistened my palms.

Bob stretched, pushed his hands against the sky and gave a wild hog-calling yell that sent a flock of sparrows fluttering to the sky. The sun mingled with the light yellow of his hair, and his roguish laughter roared with the early Moira. Then the wind shifted, blew from the west the pungent odors of the river; the wind now raced along the limestone cliffs and blew wet with river spray. Wet and chilly, with the sun warm on my back and Bob suddenly dropping to one knee, his pitch eyes darkly surveying the Moira.

"Think you can swim that?" Then he laughed loud and wild to see me gape with surprise. He threw his head back and shot out a half-jeering laugh. White straight teeth gleamed in the sun and his dark eyes danced in the light. Quickly he flashed down on his other knee, held his tightly clenched fists in a mock pose of John L. Sullivan, grinned, and started to wag his head like a punch drunk: ludicrous and threatening. "C'mon kid, fight me." The first punch slammed into my left shoulder.

"Hey you bastard!"

The second punch slammed into my chest.

"Cut it! I'm going over!"

His fists blurred with speed as he kept slashing at me. I started shifting, blocking his jabs, ducking, threw a left that connected. My feet tensed; my legs dangled precariously over the scarp. "I'm going over!" The fall was only twelve feet, but the distance down the sharp limestone with its blade edges would have split a guy's skull. There was nothing I could do. I let my hands down and gripped the ledge. The last punch landed sharply on my left shoulder, burned for a second and then, just as I felt myself going over, Bob feigned a last blow and started to laugh again. A weak layer of limestone chipped under my shifting weight. I made another move and it slipped from me, crashing down the steep embankment.

Bob was still laughing. I guessed I looked pretty comical sitting there, afraid of falling in and then, too, trying to defend myself, my feet dangling over the ledge: I guessed it only looked funny and silly. I realized I was pretty scrawny. Sometimes I became awkward and nervous. My legs were too lanky for my size and I had ribs that bulged ridiculously from pale flesh. Beside Bob I felt like the Oz scarecrow. Maybe he saw that I was hurt, because he stopped laughing and touched my shoulder. He smiled, gently gripped me. I was aware of his hand; the weight of his hand felt strange. I said nothing. Finally he turned away, tossed his hair back, and started looking for something to do.

Bob lowered his head. Strands of light brown-yellow hair dangled over the ledge while his ear almost touched the sharp rock. Looking up, Bob's eyes widened with surprise and he waved his hand for me to bend down. I did, arching my back until my ear almost scraped the limestone. I listened. A noise like a rumbling earthquake drew my head lower. Then the Moira exploded with a freakish dynamite intensity. Slamming roars, wild macabre roars penetrated the ear like shrapnel. Here the miniature canyon shot the air with the sound of waves. The din rose and fell and thundered. I felt myself being drawn away; my head, unreal, detached, now tumbling in the chaotic current. Rising; falling; whirling . . . A touch. Bob's hand. A firm, gentle grip on my right shoulder. *Don't be startled.* I jerked awake. *Careful.* Getting up, I moved too quickly. There was a tightness in the nape of my neck. Then nothing. Now every noise was dull and guttural. The sound of the river was as before: a low, monotonous rumble, a softly palpitating sound like the tense breathing of a trapped animal. The sky grew blue and radiant; the rays of the sun shone white. Shading my eyes, I pulled myself from the razor ledge. Bob picked up a hammer-shape limestone and started chipping his initials on the scarp. He looked up, then flung the limestone into the Moira.

"I'm going to try it," he said. "I'm going to swim across."

The sun slanted warm on my back. I took off my shoes and socks and put them beside my shirt. I glanced at my left shoulder and found it bruised. The sun gently eased the pain but the heat felt uncomfortable and prickly.

"Think we'll tan, Bob?"

But Bob didn't hear me. He was looking at the river on my right side, his pitch eyes bright and hard and their light focused straight ahead. Watching him I heard the rustle of dead leaves mingle with the sound of the river.

"Boy, bet you I'll tan before—"

"Shut up, kid."

The voice was harsh. I withdrew, felt something wither inside me. Look down: twelve feet below the Moira raged with a spring fever. Here and there the river splashed noisily onto a dark patch of winter leaves; gurgling brown water broke into the bubbles of green algae, and waves of glassy liquid rose and shattered against the miniature canyon walls. Bob nudged me.

"Sorry kid . . . Look, you think anyone can swim that?"

Look up: the Moira, eighty feet across, pushing violently between the bend of limestone walls. Sun-slashed, wild and surging; and now suddenly to the right of that bend, beneath the twisting shadows of a stunted fir, extending from there and beyond into the sunlight: a strange watery calm, a flat, almost perfect circle fifty feet in diameter; a watery plateau muddy with gold and raised like a giant penny by the illusory light. But it's calm, that's the main thing — it's temptingly calm.

Bob smiled, extended his hand and jerked me to my feet. He yanked and my arm jerked involuntarily. The pain tightened my mouth.

"Didn't know I hit you that hard; sorry kid."

Against the bright April sky Bob stood like a fiery shadow. I turned away, surveyed the fifty feet of calm. Surrounding it on each side was fifteen or twenty feet of vicious, swirling brown water. Now I wanted to laugh. No one could swim across. It was too early in the year. Anyways, how can a guy get into that calm and then swim out of it? I said this out loud. Bob smiled, but offhandedly, barely twisting his thin lips, a smile that said plainly you didn't know what the hell you were talking about.

"Nuts," I said.

The wind blew down from the hills in the north, slithered down the slope behind us, raising a yellow cloud of dust around our feet: warm and gritty and whispering.

"No one can do it," I said.

But Bob was facing the Moira. He stood with his hands in his back pockets, silent, shifting his feet. "Bob?" Now he stood stock-still: eyes hazy with thought: already thinking the things I had yet to understand. For a moment I felt alone, and then, as the wind died, I thought about him and Jim Whitney.

Last September Bob decided to hop a freight because Jim Whitney, the coal man, who was also his buddy, had done it in 1949. Bob didn't give a damn where the train was going, just so long as he could hop on and see what it was like. Jim was twenty-eight years old, and he and Bob were close buddies. They were so close they even went whoring together in Toronto, in one of those leaning houses along Jarvis Street where naked children still run out and ask you unashamedly for chocolates or ten cents. I remember Jim Whitney sitting on his coal sacks in that old garage on Gibson Drive. The garage was very cool and murky, lit only by the bluish slants that came through the cracked walls and leaky roof. Bob had just asked him how to hop a train. Jim looked like a guy who had just hopped one himself. The lines on his face were black as pencil and his brown hair was streaked with coal dust. If it was a moving train you were supposed to run hard and fast. "If you don't you'll wrench your arm off," Jim said, and then casually picked up a long stick and told us about momentum and inertia, drawing diagrams and arrows in the coal dust. I remember Jim breaking into one of his coughing fits. His face went dark, his cheeks grew red; he gripped the pile of coal sacks he was sitting on, his fingers twisting and pulling the fiber. His cough always ended in a hoarse choking sound. Jim would shake his head, wipe the sweat from his forehead, then go on talking as if nothing unusual had happened. "Hey kid," he said to me. "You'd better not fool around with the trains. Wait till you're taller." I guess he didn't mean to make me feel bad, but I was hurt. Quickly I said to Bob, "Let's do it together," and Bob laughed. Jim laughed, but suddenly in a funny wheezing way. The tight wheezing soon gave way to hard choking sounds, and Jim clutched his sides. Bob sat up, looking like he would run to Jim. Wiping his forehead, Jim glanced up, saw Bob, and quickly, as if he were hiding a pain, took out a bottle of whisky from underneath the coal sacks. He offered a swig to Bob, talking all the while about the whisky being good for colds and stomach flu. I noticed Jim's hand was shaking when he lifted the bottle to his lips. He didn't offer me any because he knew I couldn't take the stuff. Besides, he said, you're too young to be drinking. By next Wednesday Jim's coughing got pretty bad. Thursday afternoon he was admitted to the hospital. It was lung infection, and the poison was spreading through his body. The following Monday, at two o'clock in the morning, Jim was dead.

The day Bob got the news he tore off from work and broke into Jim's garage. The garage was near the woods. He knew no one would disturb him. He dug under the coal sacks and found the bottle of whisky. Bob gulped until his stomach burned; he started laughing and singing and taking swigs that seared down his throat. Then he smashed the brown bottle on the floor and pissed over the broken glass. There was an axe leaning against the coalbin. Bob ended up by pitching it against the garage door; pulling it out, then pitching it again, until the old door splintered and collapsed. I went to see Bob the next day. He told me what he did. I didn't say much. He was moping around like he wanted to hit someone. On the third night, without telling anyone, he got on a CNR train leaving the Belleville Station.

The train chugged along in the dark; the passenger section threw small squares of light on the ground. Bob started trotting beside it, taking deep breaths like a swimmer fighting a current. The train picked up speed and the boxcars started passing him by. The tracks were silver in the moonlight, like luminous antennas, and the window-lit section was now vanishing in the distance; now the black train was gobbling up the light. Bob sprinted hard and fast, like Jim told him to, running carefully, measuring his steps so that he would not trip on the ties and get sucked under the razor wheels. Bob reached out — quickly — and snatched onto a side ladder, felt a slight jerking pain as the momentum of the train whipped him up, banging him roughly against the boxcar. He must have felt exactly as Jim felt: hanging on to the ladder, feeling the wind and the cool night air rushing past his face, everything below his feet moving in a soft grayish blur, and only the stars and the moon pin-pointing the earth . . . I looked at the Moira, heard the water breaking in the wind, and imagined the sound of its waves like the rattling pandemonium of a swaying boxcar.

Bob thought he would jump off at Steven's Junction where the train stops for water and mail. His hands had grown numb from the cold and the tension of hanging on. He was just about to jump when the train gave a violent jerk and threw him off balance. Hurling in the dark, Bob slammed against a barbwire fence, tumbled over the needle-sharp wire, and then cracked his head hard against the iron post. My mother told me how it happened, how the railroad detective, who was also my uncle, discovered Bob beside a fence post, his body torn and bleeding. "Isn't that the boy Mr. Morley thinks burned down his warehouse?" It was, but I said nothing. "He's in a coma." My mother wiped her hands on her apron. "What a strange boy. He woke once in the hospital and asked if Jim Whitney's funeral was over. You know Bob, don't you? His last name is Heskite, isn't it? Were he and Jim related?"

I said nothing. I went upstairs to my room and locked the door behind me. I leaned against the door and felt like crying: I didn't want Bob to die. As I was thinking this a gull started circling the April sky and the sound of the river was rising in my ear. Now I wanted to laugh, to ease the tension, to feel the warm wind on my back and hear the river's roar. The idea of swimming across was funny. It was too early in the year. No one could do it now, not in April . . . I wanted to smile but my lips froze.

"Look at that calm," Bob was saying. "All I have to do is dive hard and fast . . ."

I stared at the river, at the swift surge of water that rounded the bend. I must have looked unbelieving. Bob turned angrily to me and said, "You dare me?"

I shrugged indifferently, felt uneasy.

"Think I can make it, kid?"

I kicked a stone into the river, shrugged awkwardly.

"Don't think so, eh?" he persisted, peeved with my phony non-chalance. "Hell man, have you ever tried it?"

He stood before me, stopped me from walking away. He roughly ran his fingers through his hair and pointed to the freak calm, just beyond the river's bend. I sat down, dangled my feet over the scarp.

I looked to my right, beneath the twisted fir, where the tree's shadow fell on the river like a blob of black ink. There the calm began to stretch away from the shore, twenty feet away, and only phantom shadows touched it. The edge of the calm cut across the bend's terrific undercurrent; here the muddy flat surface broke like a fluttering curtain. And here ripples swirled with foam and tiny whirlpools gaped with bayonet tongues. A dangerous network of crude stones and contrapositing sharp branches poked out of the brown water where the bend narrowed to forty feet, then widened, and finally blossomed to calm: north of that bend, a month ago, I had seen the carcass of a police dog impaled on a sharp branch. The flesh was a putrid gray and the head had swollen and decomposed. I remember how the Moira was slowly shredding the body, slowly tearing the dog apart . . . I looked at Bob: strong, yes, but the river's current, the undertow . . . I sat up, conscious that Bob was expecting me to say something. I turned around. The wind swiped my face.

"Don't try it."

"Why?"

"Just don't."

I took the hand he offered me; a strong yank and I was standing with my face too close to his. Bob wasn't smiling but merely stretching his lips mockingly. He tightened his grip.

"Give me one goddam good reason."

He was six inches taller than me, and I had the uncomfortable position of looking up and into his eyes. The bruise on my left shoulder began to throb. I looked back at him and didn't flinch. Now his face was a mockery of himself, the eyes were too intense, the lips were forced and the nostrils flared with a subtle violence. The wind rose and blew some winter leaves over the rock cliff; the fragments lifted into the air like brown moths, and then, as they sank, one leaf tumbled onto Bob's shoulder. I turned away. Bob, you can't swim across. I felt myself wanting to sink, to fall away, to become nothing. You *can't*, goddam, you *can't* . . .

My mind started to drift, to think of the time when nothing like this seemed possible: this tension, this annoying silence. Don't push me, Bob. Don't push me. And I thought how I worked at my father's café, and of how Bob often ate there after his job at the garage. I got to know him better and we started talking about school sports. Eventually he started coming in around ten o'clock after his work. Bob always took the stool by the cash register. He would have his coffee while I swept the floors and stocked the cigarettes, then we would both go for a drive in his jazzed up '47 Ford. One night he told me he stole some parts from his boss, Cal Lewis. I laughed and told him I always stole smokes from my father. Usually we drove to Jim Whitney's place for coffee, and whisky when he had it, but after Jim died we drove to the cemetery and would sit there for a long while just smoking and listening to the night. Once Bob started to ask me about Jim's funeral. "Were there a lot of flowers?" he said. But the way he asked me it didn't seem like a question anyone could answer. His voice was cold, toneless, and he just stared out of the car not looking at me. "What was the coffin like?" he said. The cigarette burned my fingers. I threw it out and looked into the night, at the tombstones and their long gray shadows. There was nothing I could say. Bob tapped my foot. There was a pause.

"I . . . I used to have a little brother like you." He began slowly, cautiously, and then his words came out in a rush, as if he was compelled to tell a joke that was going to fall flat. "The little guy was crazy about poetry and sunsets. Every time I saw him he was scribbling things down. Only he was younger than you. The things he wrote down he never showed anyone except maybe his teacher. Because he knew if he did you would laugh at him. He was only ten and his spelling was horrible. One day I swiped a piece from his notebook and read it aloud to Mom. It was a sonnet about a lollipop from Heaven. The little guy walked into the kitchen and grabbed a knife from Mom and wanted to kill me. Isn't that crazy? He wanted to kill me."

"What happened to him?"

"He died three years ago." And then, as if he were telling a lie: "Caught polio."

In the night stillness the answer sounded too abrupt; and the sudden cry of a hawk made everything seem unreal and blurry: the tombstones, the shadows . . . I wanted to say something, to say I was sorry.

"You know kid," he interrupted. "Sometimes I think . . . I feel . . ."

But he said no more, and we drove home in silence.

When Bob started training for the spring track meet he dragged me up in the mornings at six thirty so I could clock his speed on the school field. The first time I saw him run he tore against the wind until his lungs burned and he collapsed. "First time . . . first time you give it all you've got." Then between gasping and spluttering he vomited his breakfast. The school nurse said he almost ruptured his lungs. He had to rest, she said. "For a week at least." Three days later Bob was out running again. I stared at the river and my heart went cold.

I stared at the river, at the deceptive calm, at the rage surrounding it, and the sharp branches . . . Maybe in two or three weeks when the waters slowed down . . . But suddenly I saw him racing the train, running in the school field, the muscles of his leg bursting in the dust: the river was a blur of fine mist. Bob moved nearer to me.

"I'm going to try it," he said.

I sensed his brooding coming over me like a moist summer fog, rising from somewhere within me, choking things in me which I could not name, could not understand. His brown-dark eyes began to flash and he tightened his fists till the knuckles went white.

"I'll make it," he said, and his voice was uneven, strained.

"It's stupid," I said.

Turning away I gestured a last *no* with the wave of my hand and began to pick up our shirts to go home. The wind grew chilly on my bare skin. My jeans felt uncomfortably rough on my thighs. As I bent down for the plaid shirts Bob grabbed my arm. I twisted my head angrily and saw the smile disappear from his lips. Impatient, restless, Bob's hand like a vice: "Cut the fooling!"

"To hell with you," he shot back. "I can do it!"

He pinched his lips together; his grip tightened painfully on my arm. The rugby scar, the thin curving line over the corner of his left eye, began to redden as the blood rushed to his cheeks. The lines of his face were tautly drawn, the square jaw, the wide fore-head — but his eyes, brown-dark and small, seemed to draw into their sockets against the skull. I felt a chill, as if an icy hand had gripped my stomach. Then a sudden warmth surged to my cheeks. I began nervously to laugh.

I laughed in his face.

"I can do it!"

I writhed in his grip. He pushed me away. I fell, cutting the palm of my hand. I sucked at the blood that oozed from the small wound. It didn't hurt much but I had to turn away. I found myself staring at a jutting ledge that hung with the dry tendrils of morning glory, gray vines crinkled with winter sleep, so strangely mocking the life now stirring in its roots. Everything was hard and real and suddenly mocking. You're a goddam nut, Bob Heskite, a god-dam ass. If you weren't so fuckin' big, I'd . . . I'd . . . Angry humiliation welled inside me and I put my head on my knee so that he could not see me want to cry. I fumbled with my shirt.

"I didn't hurt you, did I, kid?"

I put my arms through the shirt.

"Let's see your hand first."

I buttoned up my shirt. He held his hand out, in a gesture for me to get up.

"C'mon kid."

I wanted to spit in his palm.

"Take it easy, kid."

I shrugged his hand off, put my cut hand down on the ground and pushed myself up. I stood before him. I wanted to slash his face with a sharp rock I held in my uncut hand. I wondered what he would do. You think you're too big, I thought; and then feigned a quick slashing blow, clearly revealing the pointed rock that would dig out his eyes. Bob only looked at me, not moving, not even de-fending himself. There was a distant sadness in his eyes. He put his hand on my shoulder and asked if anything was wrong. His hand felt heavy on me. There was a deliberate pause, a tone in his voice that was as gentle as wind, that crumbled all my fury, my an-ger . . . The rock slipped from my hand, falling to the ground with a despondent *clack*. My arms hung impotent, useless, as if I could never move them again.

Bob took his hand off my shoulder and then ruffled my hair.

"Look," he said. "I'm going to try swimming that narrow section, that part near the bend."

A sudden seething and burning tightened my gut; my throat went raw. My head spun for a moment, and then suddenly I felt I had to know, to be absolutely sure. Something perverse twisted inside me. I looked at Bob and caught myself smiling.

"Look," he muttered. "Will you help me?"

I thought his voice shook, but his eyes glistened. It was no joke. Surely if he had smiled, if he had only laughed, turned everything into a joke . . .

"I'm going down to that ledge to strip. Put your shoes on and help me. C'mon kid, quit worrying."

I bent down to lace up my shoes. Bob started walking to the overhang, there by the fir tree where the dry tendrils of morning glory hung like shriveled snakes. I finished with my shoes and caught up to him. He took off his watch. The sun shone yellow as gold. "Christ, it's hot," I said.

"When I get down there," Bob said, "I'll take my clothes off and hand them up to you. Here, take my watch and time me."

I took his watch and slipped it on my wrist. The metal felt cold and slippery.

"If anything happens to me, kid, you can keep it." He ruffled my hair.

"Yeah sure."

Bob walked away, paused inches from the scarp, then hopped over and felt for a foothold. I saw how the shadow of the fir tree fell over the river, pointing to the calm. It was then I said, "Bob, come back if —" He did not hear me. He descended slowly, his arms and shoulders flinching each time he made a careless move over the sharp rocks. I remembered how at that level the sound of the river exploded. All at once I felt the chill in my stomach grow to fear. I wanted to speak, to cry out; yet, strangely, I put my hand on his watch and uttered not a sound.

Water slapped against the ledge as Bob climbed down, brushing the dead vines. Finally he jumped onto an overhang that kids in the summertime used for diving. A heavy tree trunk floated by us and disappeared down the lower bend. It bobbed and danced, leaving behind small whirlpools where it had spun with the surface current.

Bob stood on the overhang and started to unbutton his jeans. I put his shoes down beside me, and then he handed me his jeans. He cupped his mouth:

"If it's too strong," he shouted, "I'll make my way back to this side." He pointed south.

Three hundred feet away. There the gray ledges vanished under reddish clay soil. The rock cliffs sloped suddenly into the clay and the Moria spilled onto the land and lapped small, foam-flecked waves onto the desolate beach. Lonely trees jabbed the air with their twisted arms. If Bob didn't make it he intended the current to spill him onto that sloping embankment of clay, on that embankment already cluttered with driftwood and acrid swamp smells. There was a back current that held pieces of wood and weed swaying between the shore and the down current. The shore was muddy with gold, and dragonflies hovering everywhere glinted in the sun like metal. Three hundred feet away. Bob, you'll make it, I thought, and suddenly smiled.

The air was tense, annoying. I wrapped his jeans around his shoes and looked to see if anyone was near. There was no one in sight. The limestone cliffs were bare. The clay shore was deserted. The sky stretched over the emptiness hot and bright, and a solitary tree shook in the warm wind. I looked down at Bob, saw the wind stir strands of his hair, the quiver of a muscle on his shoulder. And when he finally dipped his feet to feel the icy temperature of the water, the thick muscles of his thigh reassured me of his strength. If the current swept him away I could run down the river with him. Bob was an excellent swimmer; he could make the shore where the river was not so swift: he could swim into the back current. Bob knows what he's doing. He won't make it, but he won't get hurt, he won't get hurt. I looked behind me, at the top of the hill between the branches of the persimmon tree. The blank sky silhouetted the '47 Ford, and the dent on the roof reflected the sun.

Two weeks ago Bob overturned the car on Coleman Street, a block away from Sharon's house. Sharon was a high school girl he wanted to make that night. As he turned off Bridge and Everette he misjudged the road and at forty-five miles an hour pitched down a sharp incline, swung into Coleman Street: braked: screeched past a telephone pole and overturned the Ford. Bob told the cop he had slipped on the rainy road. No witnesses. Bob got off with a traffic ticket and a bill from the towing company. Now the dent reflected the sun, harshly, so that the light pricked my eyes and I had to turn away. Bob, I thought, you might break an arm, crack your head, but you'll come out alive. In my imagination I saw him drenched and running away from the Moira — his body scarred with blood; and in my bitterness I saw him crying with pain, heading toward the car like a shot rabbit. A strange animal compulsion beat in my heart. I stood on the rock cliff to watch, safely secured on land.

Bob carefully hopped from the overhang to a smaller ledge nearer the calm. He raised his arms, readying for a dive in what appeared to be a deep and clear stretch of water. Now and again the surface would ruffle up; nevertheless it was the best place to dive into. The stretch of water led directly to the calm. I looked at Bob's watch. Ten minutes to three. Then I looked down at Bob. As he stood he seemed for a moment petrified, like a statue. A pool of brown water on the overhang reflected his tension.

"Time!" Bob's face flashed at me for a brief second, the pupils white and fearless. "Six to three!" And then he dove magnificently into the ruffled path. The water rushed over his feet and enveloped his body with darkness.

I got up, waited with my eyes hard on a spot where I thought he would reappear. Seconds passed. I began to sweat. More seconds. Then his yellow head bobbed up almost twelve feet away — twelve feet away from where I had judged he would come up. But there was something wrong: he wasn't kicking his feet, stroking his arms. He was limp and the current was carrying him away. Wild, tearing, pulling him along the rim of that strange calm. I clutched at wind, bewildered, shocked, watched his head disappear, then bob up, then vanish. I started running parallel to the Moira.

I remembered the clay shore. Three hundred feet away. The torrent was sweeping him in that direction; if he could get into the crosscurrent, into that clutter of weed and driftwood, stay there long enough for me to reach him . . . I was now rushing down the sloping banks, breathing heavily, my eyes frantically searching for Bob's head: a white dot: there: fifty feet away. He was trying to swim into the back current, but the river held him.

The red clay oozed and sucked at my feet, swallowing a shoe. Now I could see Bob struggling, trying desperately to fight the rip tide, the billow and surge of the Moira. His arms flailed the air and his feet kicked wildly. The rumble of the waves fought him, rising over his head and crashing down as he tried to breathe. Crashing down and choking him with a sandpaper mixture of air and water and clay. I struggled into the water, felt the back current sway my legs. The ground slipped from under me and I was swimming. I swam nearer to Bob. He was twenty feet away. Waves rose and tumbled over him, dashed him onto lethal rocks and then rippled over him as he fought to avoid a spearing branch. I tore strands of weed from my legs. When I looked up, Bob's face was slashed. A curtain of blood covered half his face and then was erased by a wave. I shouted to him, but my voice choked in the muddy water and drowned in the sound of waves. I swam harder, kicked with all my might. As I drew nearer to Bob I could feel the current eddying into the downstream. Bob was still struggling. My feet fought against the Moira; I pushed my hands frantically, blood bulged the veins of my arms: closer . . . closer . . . until I reached within five feet of him. The river taunted him, the current brought him nearer to me only to place him inches away from my hand. Bob saw me and tried to reach out. I swam closer, then found myself being hurled into the wild surge of the river. The undercurrent pushed against my legs, against my whole body until I found myself in a swift whirlpool, swinging away from the shore. But Bob was there before me, so close!

In a vortical current the whirlpool held both of us like aimless driftwood, swinging us now toward the clay embankment. I reached out and grabbed Bob, held him tightly against me. He wasn't moving. I would have to swim out of the whirlpool. I pushed with my free hand and somehow the billow of a tide lifted us out, buoying Bob and me like cork. And like playthings we found ourselves spilled onto the soft ooze and slime of weeds, and finally onto the embankment of wet earth. Then I realized Bob was clinging to me and I was holding him by the back of his neck. Somehow, in the madness of that moment, I found the strength to grab him about the waist and drag him nearer to me. I collapsed beside him. There was a burning taste of vomit in the back of my throat. My arms were bloody and my legs cut. I looked at the Moira and it flashed back a thousand suns. I closed my eyes at the sudden explosion of light. Pain twisted my legs and arms. Lights whirled in my head, spinning me into a growing darkness. My ears began to hum, as if to destroy the sound of the river: for a moment there was darkness and humming and the cold wet flesh of Bob against my arm. Someone was saying *little man . . . little man . . .* with a voice gentle and dying, till suddenly there was only the drone and the darkness. My mind reeled.

I opened my eyes, my hands slipped over Bob's head. His head turned upwards: an eye missing, the nostril ripped. There was nothing else I could do. His face was a heresy to life, a cold and torn and bleeding heresy. I held his head on my lap and gently rocked him. He was dead. There was nothing else I could do.

(*From Prairie Schooner*)

BECAUSE I WAS FLESH

BY EDWARD DAHLBERG

*K*ANSAS CITY had been my Jehovah and parent, but now I
felt I had to leave. I no longer had a hearing soul for the
maple and oak trees, or the Paseo, which had become a seedy
colored section. I heard the locomotives on the tracks, listened to
the coupling of freight cars, and the four rivers of Eden passed
through my soul. I watched the steamboats pasturing on the Missouri River and observed ruminating engines and cabooses. Even
the manure on the boots of cattlemen from Montana I was sure had
been dropped by the heifers of Uz. Lucifer walked around the rim
of the earth alone. Was I to have the same fate?

All my errors came from the rudest of shibboleths, I want to be
free. And yet, we only do what we are. Prometheus suffers every
day in the same manner, though he invented philosophy. The vulture devours his liver for every thought he has, but his liver grows
on again each night so that he can have the same pains for his contemplation the following day. We are the prey of the elements
when we think we amuse God, or if we do not bore ourselves. We
can do nothing unless nature allows it. Oh, what God has made us
that we should be the sport of the fate we think we make?

I had purchased a ticket to Omaha and told my mother that I
was now a salesman on the road for Libby's canned milk. I lied to
her to make sure that I would be an orphan, though poor Hagar
was my sole guardian angel. How could she open the Star Lady
Barber Shop at seven in the morning, shave and cut hair until nine
and ten at night, and have the strength to guide a son? We were

only bound together by the fear of death. Should she die who would protect me?

My mother was as wise as trouble, deserts, waste and error, but she only knew what she had done a generation later. All her wisdom came too close to her death. Were it possible I desired to learn earlier. Whatever she did was not so much an error as unlucky. Nobody cares how many follies we commit so long as they do not fall out ill. Misfortune set her apart from the human race; for who keeps company with disease, grief, indigence and mishap? Sorrow and hardship have no other companions save those they infest.

My mother wept so little now that she was as dry as those deserts near Quito. Her virtues, which were the result of her defects, had not been watered for years. No one's essential nature changes; she had learned, however, to wear her sins in public rather than her heart. She was a wild, stubborn plant; the mountain olive is hardy but barren of those fruits which most people covet. Though there are many who will share our foibles, who can endure anybody else's virtues except his own?

I was fleeing from my mother to find my life. An apprentice tramp, a freight train, cattle car and a caboose were to be my bed, and hunger was to separate me from man. I would be my own sepulcher.

Each person flees from the cobblestones which bosomed his feet, and becomes a wandering tomb. We crave to be homeless, though our souls look everywhere for an abode. I had one purpose and that was to leave her who had mothered my flesh. What had I to hope for from this willful bereavement? The pang is as the root, and the root produces the boughs is an olden fable. I coveted misery, asking nature for more wretchedness than is man's portion. People who have withered spirits do not of a sudden become succulent stalks by going elsewhere. No matter. Passion, that worm that sings as it ravels our flesh, was already spoiling my youth; patience, which I was never to have, could not restrain me. Bunyan counsels us, " 'Tis not best to covet things that are now; but to wait for things to come." I had not one drop of quiet in my whole body, and could not even wait for death to annihilate me. By traveling I believed that I would be the free wind that blows in all lands.

Standing on the platform of the westbound local, I could not take my eyes away from my mother, who took off her pince-nez glasses and re-pinned her watch to her shirtwaist. Her face was broken, and all the rivers of grief that wrinkle human flesh ran over her cheeks and peaked chin. "I will water thee with my tears, O Heshbon," cried out that sherd I called my heart.

I kept my own gaze upon her; did I know that a son can remember what apron his mother wore and how she sat in a rocker in the back yard, but be almost helpless in composing her face again? We see the nose and mouth maimed by the driest of gods, hopelessness, but when we endeavor to assemble the features, our soul fails. It is not only that the human visage disappears, but that we can only perceive the whole physiogonomy when we dream or are prophetic. We only see what we dream of, and this is Chaldean augury.

In Omaha I looked for work though I wanted to be a loafer in Eden. I took a room at the Paxton Hotel, which was the garden of Midas for loungers who slept in the cane chairs on the sidewalk in front of the hotel. I tried to get a job as a drummer on the road, with a large territory and a fine expense account. Menelaus went to Iberia, which Homer calls Elysium, but I would have been just as ecstatic could I have been a traveling salesman. I wanted to work only if I could do so by roving.

The education I had received was unprofitable, and the work offered me made me no less a wastrel than the sons of wealth. Man is an idler when he does useless toil. Could I learn a trade from the vintner, miller, harness maker, fuller or tailor? The land was so depopulated of its artificers that the latter were already as alone as Aecus, who had begged Zeus to change the ants on the island of Aegina into men.

There was no commune in Omaha, or elsewhere, for the houseless and unloved oafs of the nation. Where was the spital house for the kinless with ailing hopes? What could I do that would not sink my faculties and soul? Could I shed Adam's guilt by simply toiling, though the products I made were loathsome and immoral? We have such a Puritan conception of work, as though it were lewd to desire labor that is pleasant. He who does what is agreeable or instructive is regarded as a concupiscent idler by the "niggish penny-fathers" of the commonweal. Was it to be a brute that man is tethered to a machine or a desk to reckon up another's avarice or sloth? He who makes others produce baubles that make the multitude dote "lies in wait to catch the poor." Who can sullenly drudge and be Jacob the Performer in Rachel's bed? The Shulamite stands at the machine and her teats fail and her matrix mourns.

I would rather be Lucifer and go to and fro in the earth and walk up and down in it than go up and down in an elevator for eight hours, or be a footman and push a revolving door until eventide for a dowager who has no other thought in the world except to let her cat or dog excrete.

But there was nothing in Omaha for me, for I was not apprenticed to Shem the tentmaker, or to the master of the harp, Tubal-Cain. I had the liberty I so craved, and also the cruelest fang of all beasts, solitude. What could ease me except pestilence, the desert and the wilderness! A week behind in my rent at the Paxton, I had to find a way of slinking out without paying my bill.

The heels of my parched shoes were run down at the sides, and my one suit was stale in my nostrils. There is no marsh, bog or fen that gives off such a fetid vapor as indigence. We smell as much as we imagine we do; a beggar is sure his drawers are nasty, just as everyone is ready to believe that a rich man is a scented bed of flowers.

I came down the carpeted stairs, and the bellhop gathered my valise in his hand and took it outside as I had instructed him to do. Meanwhile I ambled easily to the desk and examined a Union Pacific pamphlet. I casually bought two packages of spearmint chewing gum, tipped the clerk a dollar, and then walked out through the side door, where I handed the bellhop a half dollar. A block away from the Paxton I caught a streetcar which happened to be going to the railroad depot. I shipped my suitcase, collect, to Los Angeles, where Adam was said to have slept in the sun beneath the eucalyptus trees, or dozed, after he was expelled from his bliss of sloth, in the olive yards at Mamre, now called Pasadena.

For the next twelve months I wandered, passing over the Great Plains, up the Columbia River Valley, through California deserts, through misery, misfortune and solitude. The forests cried out of my body, and I stank like poverty. There was nothing I owned except my will; rocks would crumble, and graves cast out their bones, but my will remained.

Though I traveled almost as far as Cabeza de Vaca, who went naked from the Atlantic to the Rio de las Palmas, and sloughed his skin twice a year, I wore the same stupid and dirty skin for twelve months. I slept in depots, boxcars, and on hotel roofs; I passed through a peopleless region and knew not that I was walking through two thousand leagues of myself. I grew accustomed to a solitude no beast could endure and was as unfit for companionship as the ossifrage. We must live alone with our misfortunes, which often make us better, but not more sociable.

In what latitude did I wander? I was neither in the ice nor in the fire. God help those who are themselves their sole food, for we eat our natures when we do not know our surroundings. Those who remember little are already senile though young. It is said by Humboldt that nothing remains of the lost Guanches at Teneriffe but their sepulchers, and that each skeleton and its ashes weigh six pounds. What would I not have given for six pounds of recollection.

We cannot know our bodies unless we comprehend locality. The Caribs, no less than Homer, were sublime geographers. We are more starved for ground than any Ottomac who ate earth when he was hungry; the Quiche Mayas wept when they lost the corn seeds Quetzalcoatl gave them. The American is beside himself when he is shown a bit of marl, breccia or a piece of wild terrain.

The veins in my flesh are the rivers of the New World, the Winipiseogee, the Squam, the Sewanee. Could I have recognized sorrel, purple saxifrage, or the barest lichens, my days as a vagabond would not have been so peeled. Had I known gneiss, feldspar, sandstone or milky quartz, or what rocks were boweled in a range of sere hills, I could have suffered for understanding. My lack of self-knowledge starved my memory. My eyes were torn, sundered pools, and neither the trumpetwood nor the soapwort gentian was shadowed there. How was I to raise this shamble of rags from the grave? Can *no-feeling* be taken from the ground? Do maggots, sod and tufa sorrow; are igneous rocks mute, and are the waters of Lethe untroubled? Were I not to come to a knowledge of my belly and heart, I would be as old as the age of water upon which neither God nor man can leave one word, thought or impression.

We know nothing, and that alone is certain. The worst misery is not suffering itself, but the pain of not seeing. We are blown abroad; the curlew, willet and the snipe have the learned pinions that man lost before the megatherium grazed on the prairies of North America. The fulmar petrels feed on the frozen carcass of a whale on the shingles of Melville Island; the ranunculus flowers in winter grounds. Was I looking for the fiery clouds of Magellan; was it the Polar seas or the Cross in Southern Antarctica? Was I seeking the burning zones where the Mauritius palm tree grows? What can one do? Ask the larvae of ants, and the polypi, ask the eider ducks flying eastward; would that I could cross the shoals to the windy headlands where the narwhal sports. Oh, whither was I going?

I crept into coal cars, and snow, hail and rain were my roof. When I fled from a brakeman with a club or a plainclothes man in the railroad yards, I slunk into towns that were piles of asphalt taken from the Dead Sea. Trudging over countless guts of cement that ran like slag in Gehinnom, I stuffed my shoes with newspapers. My suit was a sickness, the moth sighed in my shirt and my trousers wept for me. I was threadbare when I was clothed, hungered when I ate, and imprisoned when I was free. I ate sleet, wind and confusion. Was I wandering in a comet without herbs, grass or ocean that was as peopleless as Leibnitz had conceived the globe in its earliest stage? How much suffering can be stored in the body and not corrupt and scab the soul? Could I feed upon my sores and not stink? I was as undomestic as the bison and I smelled because I was separated from the human race. My hair fell out in great clumps, and when I viewed the miserable remains of my youth, vultures appeared. I moaned for my youth, for baldness has come upon Gaza and my bones sang in the cinders and the waste places of Jerusalem.

I had looked for the seven cities of Cibola; but each place was the same as the others. The stores were discharges of mucus, and trade, gain, deceit and money had left their scum and foul breath in the gutters. Wherever I was I cried out, "See, I am clothed in the miserable stuff of the spider and the caterpillar, help me." Where were the pity of Zion and the tender footprints at Capernaum?

The ancient Rabbins divided hell into seven parts, each parcel of slough and darkness piled one on another. Beatrice, Abilene, Greening, Salt Lake City, Reno, Portland, Eureka, all were Cain's sewer. Instead of Tenochtitlan, Mayapan and Chichen Itza, I stumbled into Ogden, Utah, and there was not a street paved with mercy or alms for the poor. I sat on curbstones, or lay in doorways as though I were a dead Tupi doubled up in an earthen pot. Who would hear the cry of my ribs? "My strength is dried up like a potsherd."

The Arctic circle is not the coldest place in the earth; for there are no grounds so bleak or stony as indifferent flesh. A man walked by me and I felt my fingers bleeding between his teeth. Another who had eaten his lips skulked into a festering wound in a wall where the American lunches; there was one whose jowl was filled with great morsels of hymns and fried sermons. They carried in their bosoms the remains of my youth.

The people wore the clothes of death and mourning; the unclean mouse had given its coat to them. The buildings were dead, for avarice, meanness, mammon and hatred had drunk up every drop of Abel's blood. The owl and the bittern were in the mouths of the church-goers. The spider was in the empty rafters, and the termite nested in the barren twin beds; the roach took possession of the plate, the porcelain, the iron pots and tin skewers. These were a young people already in their dotage and carried within their breasts the blood of their neighbors; though their end was at hand they cried out, "I am the alpha and the beginning," and though darkness lay upon their perverse hearts, they proclaimed: "I am the word."

I begged when I was able; at the mission houses I was offered as a guerdon for two hours of dreary, canting piety, coffee and a cruller. At times I would be a scullion, peeling potatoes and scalding dishes for my wretched drink, meat and sleep. Epicurus said, "I feed sweetly upon bread and water, those sweet and easy provisions of the body . . ." but seldom did I have either.

My Delphic oracle was my ceaseless hunger. As long as I was starved I would not be the refuse of the cormorant; for the will that languishes skulks among the melons and the potatoes.

Had the American forgotten the privations of the settlers hoary with suffering? There were mullet and bass in the bay, but the Pilgrims did not know how to catch them. One going to gather shellfish on the Cape Cod beach was found dead, stuck in the mud, having fallen down because he was feeble and starved. Does the American no longer remember how inhospitable and rocky were

Matapamient, Morinogh and Ascap *moysenock?* Apamatuck and Powhatan were viperous rivers. What, too, could he get at Patuxet, Nasuet and Satucket, Indian hummocks, save groundnuts and clams?

Natural affections die more quickly in civilized man than in beasts; there is no climate as polar as the fat, comfortable heart. Human charity is so short-winded that it cannot fetch a second breath before it is weary of the scantiest lees of its pocket and table.

There are hundreds of thousands of raw, scathed beggars whose sole offense is that they are poor and more helpless than the gnu, the quagga and the antelope, who can find food in those vast sterile tracts of ground between the Tropic of Cancer and the Cape of Good Hope. Indigent Lazarus was lodged in Abraham's bosom, but the orphans of America were accursed castaways; every door in the land was shut up like a miser's purse. With Odysseus I cried, "Endure, my soul, thou hast endured worse."

Poverty is fierce, savage water and terrain; Lake Titicaca is in the bitter, windy country of Collao where there is no wood for fuel, and where the aboriginal Indian used the dung of sea birds, as well as his own, to make the soil arable. But who can manure his own flesh and eat of it? The Spaniard, Peter Serano, shipwrecked on the islands of Titicaca, subsisted on cockles, and cut the throat of a turtle and drank its blood. Brave men take such journeys, and in discovering the Andes, and eating grief and want, they learn their own characters. I had walked out into the snowy steppes of my life; though I had puling understanding I feared to sit at home; we seek the bitter peaks or lie in bondage to the leeks, the cucumbers and the melons. I am not unmindful of the admonition of St. Augustine: "Go not abroad, return unto thyself, in the inner man dwelleth truth." I was not ready for the sage rebuke of St. Augustine. There were no books for me, or mentor save my mother, who was herself "shaken in the wilderness of Kadesh." Ruled by an uneasy dread of forfeiting the Cordilleras, since what was remote was my Angel, I had to go.

The books I had read at school, *Tale of Two Cities, Ivanhoe, Silas Marner* and *Pendennis,* were like Sir Thomas More's chamberpots, which, though wrought of gold and silver, contain only slops and excrements. Shallow books are not a Jacob's ladder to angelic

ones. "Why should misunderstanding be the precursor of understanding?" wrote Jean Paul Richter.

How many epochs are there in a man? How many centuries do
the Cordilleras contain? What remains of that boy who walks
through my recollections? I am more familiar with Chryssipus, An-
tisthenes or St. Augustine than I am with him. Where is that vine
in my blood more ruined than Heliopolis or a relic at Borsippa?
Could I meet him face to face I pray that there are yet enough
tears in me to cover his suffering, for he was naked.

Let me rest as Abraham did beneath the terebinth tree and wait
for the angels, for they are the sign of meditation, or tend the goats
of Laban, for Rachel waits for me at night in her tent. A hungry Indian woman will sell her clothes for food and then tie a board
about her naked body; in Cuzco there was a street called The Lady
of Mercy where the poor could exchange their rags with one another. Let me beg for my victuals, or stand in the street of
the pauper, and barter everything that I have, save my heart and
my mind, for the meat and the bed that drinketh up the whole life
of a man.

I will be a hunger gnawing fate in the stony ravines of Collao,
and I shall sit and drink from the cisterns of Lake Titicaca. Angelic bed and pillow are sterile wastes and the bitter winds at Po-
tosi. The musk ox, as odorous around his heart as the spices of the
Moluccas, ranges the polar regions and prefers the crook-backed
herbage of the Arctic; the jaguar roams from the equator to the
Straits of Magellan and Port Famine.

I strive for my will; this is my sole understanding. Only by my
will can I exhume my own tombs. Woe to him who is easy grass
and tepid water. We are worms long before the maggots compose
our epitaphs. Comfort is my false angel; the perpetual snows of
the Andes are my abode and hearth; wind my garment and paleo-
lithic gravel my living bread. Rather the driest sepulcher than the
inert flies.

(*From Southwest Review*)

ANTAEUS

BY BORDEN DEAL

*T*HIS WAS during the wartime, when lots of people were coming North for jobs in factories and war industries, when people moved around a lot more than they do now and sometimes kids were thrown into new groups and new lives that were completely different from anything they had ever known before. I remember this one kid, T.J. his name was, from somewhere down South, whose family moved into our building during that time. They'd come North with everything they owned piled into the back seat of an old-model sedan that you wouldn't expect could make the trip, with T.J. and his three younger sisters riding shakily on top of the load of junk.

Our building was just like all the others there, with families crowded into a few rooms, and I guess there were twenty-five or thirty kids about my age in that one building. Of course, there were a few of us who formed a gang and ran together all the time after school, and I was the one who brought T.J. in and started the whole thing.

The building right next door to us was a factory where they made walking dolls. It was a low building with a flat, tarred roof that had a parapet all around it about head-high and we'd found out a long time before that no one, not even the watchman, paid any attention to the roof because it was higher than any of the other buildings around. So my gang used the roof as a headquarters. We could get up there by crossing over to the fire escape from our own roof on a plank and then going on up. It was a secret place for us, where nobody else could go without our permission.

I remember the day I first took T.J. up there to meet the gang. He was a stocky, robust kid with a shock of white hair, nothing sissy about him except his voice — he talked in this slow, gentle voice like you never heard before. He talked different from any of us and you noticed it right away. But I liked him anyway, so I told him to come on up.

We climbed up over the parapet and dropped down on the roof. The rest of the gang were already there.

"Hi," I said. I jerked my thumb at T.J. "He just moved into the building yesterday."

He just stood there, not scared or anything, just looking, like the first time you see somebody you're not sure you're going to like.

"Hi," Blackie said. "Where are you from?"

"Marion County," T.J. said.

We laughed. "Marion County?" I said. "Where's that?"

He looked at me for a moment like I was a stranger, too. "It's in Alabama," he said, like I ought to know where it was.

"What's your name?" Charley said.

"T.J.," he said, looking back at him. He had pale blue eyes that looked washed-out but he looked directly at Charley, waiting for his reaction. He'll be all right, I thought. No sissy in him . . . except that voice. Who ever talked like that?

"T.J.," Blackie said. "That's just initials. What's your real name? Nobody in the world has just initials."

"I do," he said. "And they're T.J. That's all the name I got."

His voice was resolute with the knowledge of his rightness and for a moment no one had anything to say. T.J. looked around at the rooftop and down at the black tar under his feet. "Down yonder where I come from," he said, "we played out in the woods. Don't you-all have no woods around here?"

"Naw," Blackie said. "There's the park a few blocks over, but it's full of kids and cops and old women. You can't do a thing."

T.J. kept looking at the tar under his feet. "You mean you ain't got no fields to raise nothing in? . . . no watermelons or nothing?"

"Naw," I said scornfully. "What do you want to grow something for? The folks can buy everything they need at the store."

He looked at me again with that strange, unknowing look. "In

Marion County," he said, "I had my own acre of cotton and my own
acre of corn. It was mine to plant and make ever' year."

He sounded like it was something to be proud of, and in some
obscure way it made the rest of us angry. "Jesus!" Blackie said.
"Who'd want to have their own acre of cotton and corn? That's
just work. What can you do with an acre of cotton and corn?"

T.J. looked at him. "Well, you get part of the bale offen your
acre," he said seriously. "And I fed my acre of corn to my calf."

We didn't really know what he was talking about, so we were
more puzzled than angry; otherwise, I guess, we'd have chased him
off the roof and wouldn't let him be part of our gang. But he was
strange and different and we were all attracted by his stolid sense of
rightness and belonging, maybe by the strange softness of his voice
contrasting our own tones of speech into harshness.

He moved his foot against the black tar. "We could make our
own field right here," he said softly, thoughtfully. "Come spring
we could raise us what we want to . . . watermelons and garden
truck and no telling what all."

"You'd have to be a good farmer to make these tar roofs grow
any watermelons," I said. We all laughed.

But T.J. looked serious. "We could haul us some dirt up here,"
he said. "And spread it out even and water it and before you know
it we'd have us a crop in here." He looked at us intently.
"Wouldn't that be fun?"

"They wouldn't let us," Blackie said quickly.

"I thought you said this was you-all's roof," T.J. said to me.
"That you-all could do anything you wanted to up here."

"They've never bothered us," I said. I felt the idea beginning to
catch fire in me. It was a big idea and it took a while for it to sink
in but the more I thought about it the better I liked it. "Say," I
said to the gang. "He might have something there. Just make us
a regular roof garden, with flowers and grass and trees and everything. And all ours, too," I said. "We wouldn't let anybody up
here except the ones we wanted to."

"It'd take a while to grow trees," T.J. said quickly, but we weren't
paying any attention to him. They were all talking about it suddenly, all excited with the idea after I'd put it in a way they could
catch hold of it. Only rich people had roof gardens, we knew, and
the idea of our own private domain excited them.

"We could bring it up in sacks and boxes," Blackie said. "We'd
have to do it while the folks weren't paying any attention to us, for
we'd have to come up to the roof of our building and then cross
over with it."

"Where could we get the dirt?" somebody said worriedly.

"Out of those vacant lots over close to school," Blackie said. "Nobody'd notice if we scraped it up."

I slapped T.J. on the shoulder. "Man, you had a wonderful idea,"
I said, and everybody grinned at him, remembering that he had
started it. "Our own private roof garden."

He grinned back. "It'll be ourn," he said. "All ourn." Then he
looked thoughtful again. "Maybe I can lay my hands on some cotton seed, too. You think we could raise us some cotton?"

We'd started big projects before at one time or another, like any
gang of kids, but they'd always petered out for lack of organization
and direction. But this one didn't . . . somehow or other T.J. kept
it going all through the winter months. He kept talking about the
watermelons and the cotton we'd raise, come spring, and when even
that wouldn't work he'd switch around to my idea of flowers and
grass and trees, though he was always honest enough to add that it'd
take a while to get any trees started. He always had it on his mind
and he'd mention it in school, getting them lined up to carry dirt
that afternoon, saying in a casual way that he reckoned a few more
weeks ought to see the job through.

Our little area of private earth grew slowly. T.J. was smart
enough to start in one corner of the building, heaping up the carried earth two or three feet thick, so that we had an immediate result to look at, to contemplate with awe. Some of the evenings T.J.
alone was carrying earth up to the building, the rest of the gang distracted by other enterprises or interests, but T.J. kept plugging
along on his own and eventually we'd all come back to him again
and then our own little acre would grow more rapidly.

He was careful about the kind of dirt he'd let us carry up there
and more than once he dumped a sandy load over the parapet into
the areaway below because it wasn't good enough. He found out
the kinds of earth in all the vacant lots for blocks around. He'd
pick it up and feel it and smell it, frozen though it was sometimes,

and then he'd say it was good growing soil or it wasn't worth anything and we'd have to go on somewhere else.

Thinking about it now, I don't see how he kept us at it. It was hard work, lugging paper sacks and boxes of dirt all the way up the stairs of our own building, keeping out of the way of the grown-ups so they wouldn't catch on to what we were doing. They probably wouldn't have cared, for they didn't pay much attention to us, but we wanted to keep it secret anyway. Then we had to go through the trap door to our roof, teeter over a plank to the fire escape, then climb two or three stories to the parapet and drop down onto the roof. All that for a small pile of earth that sometimes didn't seem worth the effort. But T.J. kept the vision bright within us, his words shrewd and calculated toward the fulfillment of his dream; and he worked harder than any of us. He seemed driven toward a goal that we couldn't see, a particular point in time that would be definitely marked by signs and wonders that only he could see.

The laborious earth just lay there during the cold months, inert and lifeless, the clods lumpy and cold under our feet when we walked over it. But one day it rained and afterward there was a softness in the air and the earth was live and giving again with moisture and warmth. That evening T.J. smelled the air, his nostrils dilating with the odor of the earth under his feet.

"It's spring," he said, and there was a gladness rising in his voice that filled us all with the same feeling. "It's mighty late for it, but it's spring. I'd just about decided it wasn't never gonna get here at all."

We were all sniffing at the air, too, trying to smell it the way that T.J. did, and I can still remember the sweet odor of the earth under our feet. It was the first time in my life that spring and spring earth had meant anything to me. I looked at T.J. then, knowing in a faint way the hunger within him through the toilsome winter months, knowing the dream that lay behind his plan. He was a new Antaeus, preparing his own bed of strength.

"Planting time," he said. "We'll have to find us some seed."

"What do we do?" Blackie said. "How do we do it?"

"First we'll have to break up the clods," T.J. said. "That won't be hard to do. Then we plant the seed and after a while they come up. Then you got you a crop." He frowned. "But you ain't got it raised yet. You got to tend it and hoe it and take care of it and all the time it's growing and growing, while you're awake and while you're asleep. Then you lay it by when it's growed and let it ripen and then you got you a crop."

"There's those wholesale seed houses over on Sixth," I said. "We could probably swipe some grass seed over there."

T.J. looked at the earth. "You-all seem mighty set on raising some grass," he said. "I ain't never put no effort into that. I spent all my life trying not to raise grass."

"But it's pretty," Blackie said. "We could play on it and take sunbaths on it. Like having our own lawn. Lots of people got lawns."

"Well," T.J. said. He looked at the rest of us, hesitant for the first time. He kept on looking at us for a moment. "I did have it in mind to raise some corn and vegetables. But we'll plant grass."

He was smart. He knew where to give in. And I don't suppose it made any difference to him, really. He just wanted to grow something, even if it was grass.

"Of course," he said, "I do think we ought to plant a row of watermelons. They'd be mighty nice to eat while we was a-laying on that grass."

We all laughed. "All right," I said. "We'll plant us a row of watermelons."

Things went very quickly then. Perhaps half the roof was covered with the earth, the half that wasn't broken by ventilators, and we swiped pocketfuls of grass seed from the open bins in the wholesale seed house, mingling among the buyers on Saturdays and during the school lunch hour. T.J. showed us how to prepare the earth, breaking up the clods and smoothing it and sowing the grass seed. It looked rich and black now with moisture, receiving of the seed, and it seemed that the grass sprang up overnight, pale green in the early spring.

We couldn't keep from looking at it, unable to believe that we had created this delicate growth. We looked at T.J. with understanding now, knowing the fulfillment of the plan he had carried alone within his mind. We had worked without full understanding of the task but he had known all the time.

We found that we couldn't walk or play on the delicate blades, as we had expected to, but we didn't mind. It was enough just to look at it, to realize that it was the work of our own hands, and each evening the whole gang was there, trying to measure the growth that had been achieved that day.

One time a foot was placed on the plot of ground . . . one time only, Blackie stepping onto it with sudden bravado. Then he looked at the crushed blades and there was shame in his face. He did not do it again. This was his grass, too, and not to be desecrated. No one said anything, for it was not necessary.

T.J. had reserved a small section for watermelons and he was still trying to find some seed for it. The wholesale house didn't have any watermelon seed and we didn't know where we could lay our hands on them. T.J. shaped the earth into mounds, ready to receive them, three mounds lying in a straight line along the edge of the grass plot.

We had just about decided that we'd have to buy the seed if we were to get them. It was a violation of our principles, but we were anxious to get the watermelons started. Somewhere or other, T.J. got his hands on a seed catalogue and brought it one evening to our roof garden.

"We can order them now," he said, showing us the catalogue. "Look!"

We all crowded around, looking at the fat, green watermelons pictured in full color on the pages. Some of them were split open, showing the red, tempting meat, making our mouths water.

"Now we got to scrape up some seed money," T.J. said, looking at us. "I got a quarter. How much you-all got?"

We made up a couple of dollars between us and T.J. nodded his head. "That'll be more than enough. Now we got to decide what kind to get. I think them Kleckley Sweets. What do you-all think?"

He was going into esoteric matters beyond our reach. We hadn't even known there were different kinds of melons. So we just nodded our heads and agreed that Yes, we thought the Kleckley Sweets too.

"I'll order them tonight," T.J. said. "We ought to have them in a few days."

"What are you boys doing up here?" an adult voice said behind us.

It startled us, for no one had ever come up here before, in all the time we had been using the roof of the factory. We jerked around and saw three men standing near the trap door at the other end of the roof. They weren't policemen, or night watchmen, but three men in plump business suits, looking at us. They walked toward us.

"What are you boys doing up here?" the one in the middle said again.

We stood still, guilt heavy among us, levied by the tone of voice, and looked at the three strangers.

The men stared at the grass flourishing behind us. "What's this?" the man said. "How did this get up here?"

"Sure is growing good, ain't it?" T.J. said conversationally. "We planted it."

The men kept looking at the grass as if they didn't believe it. It was a thick carpet over the earth now, a patch of deep greenness startling in the sterile industrial surroundings.

"Yes sir," T.J. said proudly. "We toted that earth up here and planted that grass." He fluttered the seed catalogue. "And we're just fixing to plant us some watermelon."

The man looked at him then, his eyes strange and faraway. "What do you mean, putting this on the roof of my building?" he said. "Do you want to go to jail?"

T.J. looked shaken. The rest of us were silent, frightened by the authority of his voice. We had grown up aware of adult authority, of policemen and night watchmen and teachers, and this man sounded like all the others. But it was a new thing to T.J.

"Well, you wan't using the roof," T.J. said. He paused a moment and added shrewdly, "So we just thought to pretty it up a little bit."

"And sag it so I'd have to rebuild it," the man said sharply. He started turning away, saying to another man beside him, "See that all that junk is shoveled off by tomorrow."

"Yes sir," the man said.

T.J. started forward. "You can't do that," he said. "We toted it up here and it's our earth. We planted it and raised it and toted it up here."

The man stared at him coldly. "But it's my building," he said. "It's to be shoveled off tomorrow."

"It's our earth," T.J. said desperately. "You ain't got no right!"

The men walked on without listening and descended clumsily through the trap door. T.J. stood looking after them, his body tense with anger, until they had disappeared. They wouldn't even argue with him, wouldn't let him defend his earth-rights.

He turned to us. "We won't let 'em do it," he said fiercely. "We'll stay up here all day tomorrow and the day after that and we won't let 'em do it."

We just looked at him. We knew that there was no stopping it. He saw it in our faces and his face wavered for a moment before he gripped it into determination.

"They ain't got no right," he said. "It's our earth. It's our land. Can't nobody touch a man's own land."

We kept on looking at him, listening to the words but knowing that it was no use. The adult world had descended on us even in our richest dream and we knew there was no calculating the adult world, no fighting it, no winning against it.

We started moving slowly toward the parapet and the fire escape, avoiding a last look at the green beauty of the earth that T.J. had planted for us . . . had planted deeply in our minds as well as in our experience. We filed slowly over the edge and down the steps to the plank, T.J. coming last, and all of us could feel the weight of his grief behind us.

"Wait a minute," he said suddenly, his voice harsh with the effort of calling. We stopped and turned, held by the tone of his voice, and looked up at him standing above us on the fire escape.

"We can't stop them?" he said, looking down at us, his face strange in the dusky light. "There ain't no way to stop 'em?"

"No," Blackie said with finality. "They own the building."

We stood still for a moment, looking up at T.J., caught into inaction by the decision working in his face. He stared back at us and his face was pale and mean in the poor light, with a bald nakedness in his skin like cripples have sometimes.

"They ain't gonna touch my earth," he said fiercely. "They ain't gonna lay a hand on it! Come on."

He turned around and started up the fire escape again, almost running against the effort of climbing. We followed more slowly, not knowing what he intended. By the time we reached him, he had seized a board and thrust it into the soil, scooping it up and flinging it over the parapet into the areaway below. He straightened and looked at us.

"They can't touch it," he said. "I won't let 'em lay a dirty hand on it!"

We saw it then. He stooped to his labor again and we followed, the gusts of his anger moving in frenzied labor among us as we scattered along the edge of earth, scooping it and throwing it over the parapet, destroying with anger the growth we had nurtured with such tender care. The soil carried so laboriously upward to the light and the sun cascaded swiftly into the dark areaway, the green blades of grass crumpled and twisted in the falling.

It took less time than you would think . . . the task of destruction is infinitely easier than that of creation. We stopped at the end, leaving only a scattering of loose soil, and when it was finally over a stillness stood among the group and over the factory building. We looked down at the bare sterility of black tar, felt the harsh texture of it under the soles of our shoes, and the anger had gone out of us, leaving only a sore aching in our minds like overstretched muscles.

T.J. stood for a moment, his breathing slowing from anger and effort, caught into the same contemplation of destruction as all of us. He stooped slowly, finally, and picked up a lonely blade of grass left trampled under our feet and put it between his teeth, tasting it, sucking the greenness out of it into his mouth. Then he started walking toward the fire escape, moving before any of us were ready to move, and disappeared over the edge.

We followed him but he was already halfway down to the ground, going on past the board where we crossed over, climbing down into the areaway. We saw the last section swing down with his weight and then he stood on the concrete below us, looking at the small pile of anonymous earth scattered by our throwing. Then he walked across the place where we could see him and disappeared toward the street without glancing back, without looking up to see us watching him.

They did not find him for two weeks. Then the Nashville police caught him just outside the Nashville freight yards. He was walking along the railroad track; still heading south, still heading home.

As for us, who had no remembered home to call us . . . none of us ever again climbed the escape-way to the roof.

(From Perspective)

CRIERS AND KIBBITZERS, KIBBITZERS AND CRIERS

BY STANLEY ELKIN

*G*REENSPAHN cursed the steering wheel shoved like the flat, hard edge of someone's hand against his stomach. "God damn lousy cars," he thought. "Forty-five hundred dollars and there's not room to breathe." He thought sourly of the smiling salesman who had sold it to him, calling him Jake all the time he had been in the showroom. "Lousy *podler*." He slid across the seat, moving carefully as though he carried something fragile, and eased his big body out of the car. Seeing the parking meter he experienced a dark rage. They don't let you live, he thought. "I'll put your nickels in the meter for you, Mr. Greenspahn," he mimicked the Irish cop. Two dollars a week for the lousy grubber. Plus the nickels that were supposed to go into the meter. And they talked about the Jews. Greenspahn saw the cop across the street writing out a ticket. He went around his car, carefully pulling at the handle of each door.

He started toward his store.

"Hey there, Mr. Greenspahn," the cop called.

He turned to look at him. "Yeah?"

"Good morning."

"Yeah. Yeah. Good morning."

The grubber came toward him from across the street. Uniforms, Greenspahn thought, only a fool wears a uniform.

"Fine day, Mr. Greenspahn," the cop said.

Greenspahn nodded grudgingly.

"I was sorry to hear about your trouble, Mr. Greenspahn. Did you get my card?"

"Yeah, I got it. Thanks." He remembered something with flowers on it and rays going up to a pink Heaven. A picture of a cross yet.

"I wanted to come out to the chapel but the brother-in-law was up from Cleveland. I couldn't make it."

"Yeah," Greenspahn said. "Maybe next time."

The cop looked stupidly at him and Greenspahn reached into his pocket.

"No. No. Don't worry about that, Mr. Greenspahn. I'll take care of it for now. Please, Mr. Greenspahn, forget it this time. It's O.K."

Greenspahn felt like giving him the money anyway. Don't mourn for me, *podler,* he thought. Keep your two dollars worth of grief.

The cop turned to go. "Well, Greenspahn, there's nothing anybody can say at times like this, but you know how I feel. You got to go on living, don't you know."

"Sure," Greenspahn said. "That's right, officer." The cop crossed the street and finished writing the ticket. Greenspahn looked after him angrily, watching the gun swinging in the holster at his hip, the sun flashing brightly on the shiny handcuffs. *Podler,* he thought, afraid for his lousy nickels. There'll be an extra parking space sooner than he thinks.

He walked toward his store. He could have parked by his own place but out of habit he left his car in front of a rival grocer's. It was an old and senseless spite. Tomorrow he would change. What difference did it make, one less parking space? Why should he walk?

He felt bloated, heavy. The bowels, he thought. I got to move them soon or I'll bust. He looked at the street vacantly, feeling none of the old excitement. What did he come back for, he wondered suddenly, sadly. He missed Harold. Oh my God. Poor Harold, he thought. I'll never see him again. I'll never see my son again. He was choking, a big pale man beating his fist against his chest in grief. He pulled a handkerchief from his pocket and blew his nose. That was the way it was, he thought. He could go along flat and empty and dull and all of a sudden he could dissolve in a heavy, choking grief. The street was no place for him. His wife was crazy, he thought, swiftly angry. "Be busy. Be busy," she said. What was he, a kid, that because he was making up some-body's lousy order everything would fly out of his mind? The bottom dropped out of his life and he was supposed to go along as though nothing had happened. His wife and the cop, they had the same psychology. Like in the movies after the horse kicks your head in you're supposed to get up and ride him so he can throw you off and finish the job. If he could get a buyer he would sell. That was that.

Mechanically, he looked into the windows he passed. The displays seemed foolish to him now, petty. He resented the wooden wedding cakes, the hollow watches. The manikins were grotesque, giant dolls. Toys, he thought bitterly. Toys. That he used to enjoy the displays himself, had even taken a peculiar pleasure in the complicated tiers of cans, in the amazing pyramids of apples and oranges in his own window, seemed incredible to him. He remembered he had liked to look at the little living rooms in the window of the furniture store, the wax models sitting on the couches offering each other tea. He used to look at the expensive furniture and think, *merchandise*. The word had sounded rich to him, and mysterious. He used to think of camels on a desert, their bellies slung with heavy ropes. On their backs they carried *merchandise*. What did it mean, any of it? Nothing. It meant nothing.

He was conscious of someone watching him.

"Hello, Jake."

It was Margolis from the television shop.

"Hello, Margolis. How are you?"

"Business is terrible. You picked a hell of a time to come back."

A man's son dies and Margolis says business is terrible. Margolis, he thought, jerk, son of a bitch.

"You can't close up a minute. You don't know when somebody might come in. I didn't take coffee since you left," Margolis said.

"You had it tough, Margolis. You should have said something, I would have sent some over."

Margolis smiled helplessly, remembering the death of Green-spahn's son.

"It's O.K., Margolis." He felt his anger tug at him again. It was something he would have to watch, a new thing with him but already familiar, easily released, like something on springs.

"Jake," Margolis whined.

"Not now, Margolis," he said angrily. He had to get away from him. He was like a little kid, Greenspahn thought. His face was puffy, swollen, like a kid about to cry. He looked so meek. He should be holding a hat in his hand. He couldn't stand to look at him. He was afraid Margolis was going to make a speech. He didn't want to hear it. What did he need a speech? His son was in the ground. Under all that earth. Under all that dirt. In a metal box. Airtight, the funeral director told him. Oh my God, *airtight. Vacuum-sealed*. Like a can of coffee. His son was in the ground and on the street the models in the windows had on next season's dresses. He would hit Margolis in his face if he said one word.

Margolis looked at him and nodded sadly, turning his palms out as if to say, "I know. I know." Margolis continued to look at him and Greenspahn thought, He's taking into account, that's what he's doing. He's taking into account the fact that my son has died. He's figuring it in and making apologies for me, making an allowance, like he was making an estimate in his head what to charge a customer.

"I got to go, Margolis," Greenspahn said.

"Sure, me too," Margolis said, relieved. "I'll see you, Jake. The man from R.C.A. is around back with a shipment. What do I need it?"

Greenspahn walked to the end of the block and crossed the street. He looked down the side street and saw the *shul* where that evening he would say prayers for his son.

He came to his store, seeing it with distaste. He looked at the signs, like the balloons in comic strips where they put the words, stuck inside against the glass. The letters big and red like it was the end of the world. The big whitewash numbers on the glass thickly. A billboard, he thought.

He stepped up to the glass door and looked in. Frank, his produce man, stood by the fruit and vegetable bins taking the tissue paper off the oranges. His butcher, Howard, was at the register talking to Shirley, the cashier. Howard saw him through the glass and waved extravagantly. Shirley came to the door and opened it. "Good morning there, Mr. Greenspahn," she said.

"Hey Jake, how are you?" Frank said.

"How's it going, Jake?" Howard said.

"Was Siggie in yet? Did you tell him about the cheese?"

"He ain't yet been in this morning, Jake," Frank said.

"How about the meat? Did you place the order?"

"Sure, Jake," Howard said. "I called the guy Thursday."

"Where are the receipts?" he asked Shirley.

"I'll get them for you, Mr. Greenspahn. You already seen them for the first two weeks you were gone. I'll get last week's."

She handed him a slip of paper. It was four hundred seventy dollars off the last week's low figure. They must have had a picnic, Greenspahn thought. No more though. He looked at them and they watched him with interest. "So," he said. "So."

"Nice to have you back, Mr. Greenspahn," Shirley told him, smiling.

"Yeah," he said, "yeah."

"We got a shipment yesterday, Jake, but the *shvartze* showed up drunk. We couldn't get it all put up," Frank said.

Greenspahn nodded. "The figures are low," he said.

"It's business. Business has been terrible. I figure it's the strike," Frank said.

"In West Virginia the miners are out and you figure that's why my business is bad in this neighborhood?" Greenspahn said.

"There are repercussions," Frank said. "All industries are affected."

"Yeah," Greenspahn said, "yeah. The Pretzel Industry. The Canned Chicken Noddle Soup Industry."

"Well, business has been lousy, Jake," Howard said testily.

"I guess maybe it's so bad, now might be a good time to sell. What do you think?" Greenspahn said.

"Are you really thinking of selling, Jake?" Frank asked.

"You want to buy my place, Frank?"

"You know I don't have that kind of money, Jake," Frank said uneasily.

"Yeah," Greenspahn said, "yeah."

Frank looked at him and Greenspahn waited for him to say something else, but in a moment he turned and went back to the oranges. Some thief, Greenspahn thought. Big shot. I insulted him.

"I got to change," he said to Shirley. "Call me if Siggie comes in."

He went into the toilet off the small room at the back of the store. He reached for the clothes he kept there on a hook on the back of the door and saw, hanging over his own clothes, a woman's undergarments. A brassière hung by one cup over his trousers. What is it here, a locker room? Does she take baths in the sink? he thought. Fastidiously he tried to remove his own clothes without touching the other garments, but he was clumsy and the underwear, together with his trousers, tumbled in a heap to the floor. They looked, lying there, strangely obscene to him, as though two people, desperately in a hurry, had dropped them quickly and were somewhere near him even now, perhaps behind the very door, making love. He picked up his trousers and changed his clothes. Taking a hanger from a pipe under the sink he hung the clothes he had worn to work and put the hanger on the hook. He stooped to pick up Shirley's underwear. Placing it on the hook his hand rested for a moment on the brassière. He was immediately ashamed and he straightened. He was terribly tired. He put his head through the loop of his apron and tied the apron behind the back of the old blue sweater he wore even in summer. He turned the sink's single tap and rubbed his eyes with water. Bums, he thought. Bums. You put up mirrors to watch the customers so they shouldn't get away with a stick of gum, and in the meanwhile Frank and Howard walk off with the whole store. He sat down to try to move his bowels and the apron hung down from his chest like a barber's sheet. He spread it across his knees. I must look like I'm getting a haircut, he thought irrelevantly. He looked suspiciously at Shirley's underwear. My movie star. He wondered if it was true what Howard told him, that she used to be a 26 girl. Something was going on between her and that Howard. Two bums, he thought. He knew they drank together after work. That was one thing, bad enough, but were they screwing around in the back of the store? Howard had a family. You couldn't trust a young butcher. It was too much for him. Why didn't he just sell and get the hell out? Did he have to look for grief? Was he making a fortune that he had to put up with it? It was crazy. All right, he thought, a man in business, there were things a man in business put up with. But this? It was crazy. Everywhere he was beset by thieves and cheats. They kept pushing him, pushing him. What did it mean? Why did they do it? All right, he thought, when Harold was alive was it any different? No, of course not, he knew plenty then too. But it didn't make as much difference.

Death is an education, he thought. Now there wasn't any reason to put up with it. What did he need it? On the street, in the store, he saw everything. Everything. It was as if everybody else was made out of glass. Why all of a sudden was he like that?

Why? he thought. Jerk, because they're hurting *you*, that's why.

He stood up and looked absently into the toilet. "Maybe I need a laxative," he said. Troubled, he left the toilet.

In the back room, his "office," he stood by the door to the toilet and looked around. Stacked against one wall he saw four or five cases of soups and canned vegetables. Against the meat locker he had pushed a small table, his desk. He went to it to pick up a pencil. Underneath the telephone was a pad of note paper. Something about it caught his eye and he picked up the pad. On the top sheet was writing, his son's. He used to come down on Saturdays sometimes when they were busy and evidently this was an order he had taken down over the phone. He looked at the familiar writing and thought his heart would break. Harold, Harold, he thought. My God, Harold, you're dead. He touched the sprawling, hastily written letters, the carelessly spelled words and thought absently, He must have been busy. I can hardly read it. He looked at it more closely. "He was in a hurry," he said, starting to sob. "My God, *he* was in a hurry." He tore the sheet from the pad and folding it, put it into his pocket. In a minute he was able to walk back out into the store.

In the front Shirley was talking to Siggie, the cheese man. Seeing him up there, leaning casually on the counter, Greenspahn felt a quick anger. He walked up the aisle toward him.

Siggie saw him coming. "*Shalom*, Jake," he called.

"I want to talk to you."

"Is it important, Jake, because I'm in some terrific hurry. I still got deliveries."

"What did you leave me?"

"The same, Jake. The same. A couple pounds blue. Some Swiss. Delicious," he said, smacking his lips.

"I been getting complaints, Siggie."

"From the Americans, right? Your average American don't know from cheese. It don't mean nothing." He turned to go.

"Siggie, where you running?"

"Jake, I'll be back tomorrow. You can talk to me about it."

"Now."

He turned reluctantly. "What's the matter?"

"You're leaving old stuff. Who's your wholesaler?"

"Jake, Jake," he said. "We already been over this. I pick up the returns, don't I?"

"That's not the point."

"Have you ever lost a penny account of me?"

"Siggie, who's your wholesaler? Where do you get the stuff?"

"I'm cheaper than the dairy, right? Ain't I cheaper than the dairy? Come on, Jake. What do you want?"

"Siggie, don't be a jerk. Who are you talking to? Don't be a jerk. You leave me cheap, crummy cheese, the dairies are ready to throw it away. I get everybody else's returns. It's old when I get it. Do you think a customer wants a cheese it goes off like a bomb two days after she gets it home? And what about the customers who don't return it? They think I'm gypping them and they don't come back. I don't want the *schlak* stuff. Give me fresh or I'll take from somebody else."

"I couldn't give you fresh for the same price, Jake. You know that."

"The same price."

"Jake," he said amazed.

"The same price. Come on Siggie, don't screw around with me."

"Talk to me tomorrow. We'll work something out." He turned to go.

"Siggie," Greenspahn called after him. "Siggie." He was already out of the store.

Greenspahn clenched his fists. "The bum," he said.

"He's always in a hurry, that guy," Shirley said.

"Yeah, yeah," Greenspahn said. He started to cross to the cheese locker to see what Siggie had left him.

"Say, Mr. Greenspahn," Shirley said, "I don't think I have enough change."

"Where's the *shvartze?* Send him to the bank."

"He ain't come in yet. Shall I run over?"

Greenspahn poked his fingers in the cash drawer. "You got till he comes," he said.

"Well," she said, "if you think so."

"What do we do, a big business in change? I don't see customers stumbling over each other in the aisles."

"I told you, Jake," Howard said, coming up behind him. "It's business. Business is lousy. People ain't eating."

"Here," Greenspahn said, "give me ten dollars. I'll go myself." He turned to Howard. "I seen some stock in the back. Put it up, Howard."

"I should put up the stock?" Howard said.

"You told me yourself, business is lousy. Are you here to keep off the streets or something? What is it?"

"What do you pay the *schvartze* for?"

"He ain't here," Greenspahn said. "When he comes in I'll have him cut up some meat, you'll be even."

He took the money and went out into the street. It was lousy, he thought. You had to be able to trust them or you could go crazy. Any retailer had the same problem, and he winked his eye and figured, all right, so I'll allow a certain percentage for shrinkage. You made it up on the register. But in his place it was ridiculous. They were professionals. Like the mafia or something. What did it pay to aggravate himself, his wife would say. Now he was back he could watch them. Watch them. He couldn't stand even to be in the place. They thought they were getting away with something, the *podlers*.

He went into the bank. He saw the ferns. The marble tables where the depositors made out their slips. The calendars, carefully changed each day. The guard, a gun on his hip and a white carnation in his uniform. The big safe, thicker than a wall, shiny and open in the back behind the sturdy iron gate. The tellers behind their cages, small and quiet, as though they went about barefooted. The bank officers, gray-haired and well dressed, comfortable at their big desks, solidly official behind their engraved nameplates. That was something, he thought. A bank. A bank was something. And no shrinkage.

He gave his ten-dollar bill to a teller to be changed.

"Hello there, Mr. Greenspahn. How are you this morning? We haven't seen you lately," the teller said.

"I haven't been in my place for three weeks," Greenspahn said.

"Say," the teller said, "that's quite a vacation."

"My son passed away."

"I didn't know," the teller said. "I'm very sorry, sir."

He took the rolls the teller handed him and stuffed them into his pocket. "Thank you," he said.

The street was quiet. It looks like a Sunday, he thought. There would be no one in the store. He saw his reflection in a window he passed and realized he had forgotten to take his apron off. It occurred to him that the apron somehow gave him the appearance of being very busy. An apron did that, he thought. Not a business suit so much. Unless there was a briefcase. A briefcase and an apron. They made you look busy. A uniform wouldn't. Soldiers didn't look busy, policemen didn't. A fireman did but he had to have that big hat on. Schmo, he thought, a man your age walking in the street in an apron. He wondered if the vice-presidents at the bank had noticed his apron. He felt the heaviness again.

He was restless, nervous, vaguely disappointed in things.

He passed the big plate window of "The Cookery," the restaurant where he ate his lunch, and the cashier waved at him, gesturing that he should come in. He shook his head. He hesitated. For a moment when he saw her hand go up he thought he might go in. The men would be there, the other business people, drinking cups of coffee, cigarettes smearing the saucers, their sweet rolls cut into small, precise sections. Even without going inside he knew familiarly what it would be like. The criers and the kibbitzers. The criers, earnest, complaining with a peculiar vigor about their businesses, their gas mileage, their health; their despair articulate, dependably lamenting their lives, vaguely mourning conditions, their sorrow something they could expect no one to understand. The kibbitzers, deaf to grief, winking confidentially at the others, their voices high-pitched in kidding or lowered in conspiracy to tell of triumphs, of men they knew downtown, of tickets fixed, or languishing goods moved suddenly and unexpectedly, of the windfall that was life; their fingers sticky, smeared with the sugar from their rolls.

What did he need them, he thought. Big shots. What did they know about anything? Did they lose sons?

He went back to his place and gave Shirley the change.

"Is the *shvartze* in yet?" he asked.

"No, Mr. Greenspahn."

I'll dock him, he thought. I'll dock him.

He looked around and saw that there were several people in the store. It wasn't busy, but there was more activity than he had expected. Young housewives from the university. Good shoppers, he thought. Good customers. They knew what they could spend and that was it. There was no monkey business about prices. He wished his older customers would take lessons from them. The ones who came in in their fur coats and who thought because they knew him from his old place that entitled them to special privileges. In a supermarket. Privileges. Did A&P give discounts? The National? What did they want from him?

He walked around straightening the shelves. Well, he thought, at least it wasn't totally dead. If they came in like this all day he might make a few pennies. A few pennies, he thought. A few dollars. What difference does it make?

A salesman was talking to him when he saw her. The salesman was trying to tell him something about a new product, some detergent, ten cents off on the box, something, but Greenspahn couldn't take his eyes off her.

"Can I put you down for a few trial cases, Mr. Greenspahn? In Detroit when the stores put it on the shelves . . ."

"No," Greenspahn interrupted him. "Not now. It don't sell. I don't want it."

"But, Mr. Greenspahn, I'm trying to tell you. This is something new. It hasn't been on the market more than three weeks."

"Later, later," Greenspahn said. "Talk to Frank, don't bother me."

He left the salesman and followed the woman up the aisle, stopping when she stopped and turning to the shelves, pretending to adjust them. One egg, he thought. She touches one egg, I'll throw her out.

It was Mrs. Frimkin, the doctor's wife. An old customer and a chiseler. An expert. For a long time she hadn't been in because of a fight they had over a thirty-five-cent delivery charge. He had to watch her. She had a million tricks. Sometimes she would sneak over to the eggs and push her finger through two or three of them. Then she would smear a little egg on the front of her dress and come over to him complaining that he'd ruined her dress, that she'd picked up the eggs "in good faith," thinking they were whole. "In good faith," she said. He'd have to give her the whole box and charge her for a half dozen just to shut her up. An expert.

He went up to her. He was somewhat relieved to see that she wore a good dress. She risked the egg trick only in a housecoat.

"Jake," she said, smiling at him.

He nodded.

"I heard about Harold," she said sadly. "The doctor told me. I almost had a heart attack when I heard." She touched his arm. "Listen," she said. "We don't know. We just don't know. Mrs. Baron, my neighbor from when we lived on Drexel, didn't she fall down dead in the street? Her daughter was getting married in a month. How's your wife?"

Greenspahn shrugged. "Something I can do for you, Mrs. Frimkin?"

"What am I, a stranger? I don't need help. Fix, fix your shelves. I can take what I need."

"Yeah," he said, "yeah. Take." She had another trick. She came into a place, his place, the A&P, it didn't make any difference, and she priced everything. She even took notes. He knew she didn't buy a thing until she was absolutely convinced she couldn't get it a penny cheaper someplace else.

"I only want a few items. Don't worry about me," she said.

"Yeah," Greenspahn said. He could wring her neck, the lousy *podler*.

"How's the fruit?" she asked.

"You mean confidentially?"

"What then?"

"I'll tell you the truth," Greenspahn said. "It's so good I don't like to see it get out of the store."

"Maybe I'll buy a banana then."

"You couldn't go wrong," Greenspahn said.

"You got a nice place, Jake. I always said it."

"So buy something," he said.

"We'll see," she said mysteriously. "We'll see."

They were standing by the canned vegetables and she reached out her hand to lift a can of peas from the shelf. With her palm she made a big thing of wiping the dust from the top of the can and then stared at the price stamped there. "Twenty-seven?" she asked, surprised.

"Yeah," Greenspahn said. "It's too much?"

"Well," she said.

"I'll be damned," he said. "I been in the business twenty-two years and I never did know what to charge for a tin of peas."

She looked at him suspiciously and with a tight smile gently replaced the peas. Greenspahn glared at her and then, seeing Frank walk by, caught at his sleeve, pretending he had business with him. He walked up the aisle holding Frank's elbow, conscious that Mrs. Frimkin was looking after them.

"The lousy *podler*," he whispered.

"Take it easy, Jake," Frank said. "She could be a good customer again. So what if she chisels a little? I was happy to see her come in."

"Yeah," Greenspahn said, "happy." He left Frank and went toward the meat counter. "Any phone orders?" he asked Howard.

"A few, Jake. I can put them up."

"Never mind," Greenspahn said. "Give me." He took the slips Howard handed him. "While it's quiet I'll do them."

He read over the orders quickly and in the back of the store selected four cardboard boxes with great care. He picked the stock from the shelves and fit it neatly into the boxes, taking a kind of pleasure in the diminution of the stacks. Each time he put something into a box he had the feeling that there was that much less to sell. At the thick butcher's block behind the meat counter, bloodstains so deep in the wood they seemed almost a part of its grain, he trimmed fat from a thick roast. Howard, beside him, leaned heavily against the paper roll. Greenspahn was conscious that Howard watched him.

"Bernstein's order?" Howard asked.

"Yeah," Greenspahn said.

"She's giving a party. She told me. Her husband's birthday."

"Happy birthday," Greenspahn said.

"Yeah," Howard said. "Say, Jake, maybe I'll go eat."

Greenspahn trimmed the last piece of fat from the roast before he looked up at him. "So go eat," he said.

"I think so," Howard said. "It's slow today. You know?"

Greenspahn nodded.

"Well, I'll grab some lunch. Maybe it'll pick up in the afternoon."

He took a box and began filling another order. He went to the canned goods in high, narrow, canted towers. That much less to sell, he thought bitterly. It was endless. You could never liquidate. There were no big deals in the grocery business. He thought hopelessly of the hundreds of items in his store, of all the different brands, the different sizes. He was terribly aware of each shopper, conscious of what each put into the shopping cart. It was awful, he thought. He wasn't selling diamonds. He wasn't selling pianos. He sold bread. Milk. Eggs. You had to have volume or you were dead. He was losing money. On his electric, his refrigeration, the signs in his window, his payroll, his specials, his stock. It was the chain stores. They had the parking. They advertised. They gave stamps. Two per cent right out of the profits and it made no difference to them. They had the tie-ins. Fantastic. Their own farms, their own dairies, their own bakeries, their own canneries. Everything. The bastards. He was committing suicide to fight them.

In a little while Shirley came up to him. "Is it all right if I get my lunch now, Mr. Greenspahn?"

What did they ask him? Was he a tyrant? "Yeah, yeah. Go eat. I'll watch the register."

She went out and Greenspahn looking after her thought, Something's going on. First one, then the other. They meet each other. What do they do, hold hands? He fit a carton of eggs carefully into a box. What difference does it make? A slut and a bum.

He stood at the checkout counter and pressing the orange key watched the NO SALE flag shoot up into the window of the register. He counted the money sadly.

Frank was at the bins trimming lettuce. "Jake, you want to go eat I'll watch things," he said.

"Not yet," Greenspahn said.

An old woman came into the store and Greenspahn recognized her. She had been in twice before that morning and both times had bought two tins of the coffee Greenspahn was running on a special. She hadn't bought anything else. Already he had lost twelve cents on her. Greenspahn watched her carefully and saw with a quick rage that she went again to the coffee. She picked up another two tins and came toward the checkout counter. She wore a bright red wig which next to her very white, ancient skin gave her strangely the appearance of a clown. She put the coffee down on the counter and looked up at Greenspahn timidly. Greenspahn made no effort to ring up the coffee. She stood for a moment and then pushed the coffee toward him.

"Sixty-nine cents a pound," she said. "Two pounds is a dollar thirty-eight. Six cents tax is a dollar forty-four."

"Lady," Greenspahn said, "don't you ever eat? Is that all you do is drink coffee?" Greenspahn stared at her.

Her lips began to tremble and her body shook. "A dollar forty-four," she said. "I have it right here."

"This is your sixth can, lady. I lose money on it. Do you know that?"

The woman continued to tremble. It was as though she were very cold.

"What do you do, lady? Sell this stuff door to door? Am I your wholesaler?"

Her body continued to shake and she looked out at him from behind faded eyes as though she were unaware of the terrible movements of her body, as though they had, ultimately, nothing to do with her, that really she existed, hiding, crouched, somewhere behind the eyes. Greenspahn had the impression that, frictionless, her old bald head bobbed beneath the wig. "All right," he said finally, "a dollar forty-four. I hope you have more luck with the item than I had." He took the money from her and watched her as she accepted her package wordlessly and walked out of the store. He shook his head. It was all a pile of crap, he thought. He had a vision of the woman on back porches, standing silently at back doors open on their chains, sadly extending the coffee.

He wanted to get out. Frank could watch the store. If he stole, he stole.

"Frank," he said, "it ain't busy. Watch things. I'll eat."

"Go on, Jake. Go ahead. I'm not hungry, I got a cramp. Go ahead."

"Yeah," Greenspahn said.

He walked toward the restaurant. On his way he had to pass a National and seeing the crowded parking lot he felt his stomach tighten. He paused at the window and pressed his face against the glass and looked in at the full aisles. Through the thick glass he saw women moving silently through the store. He stepped back and read the advertisements on the window. My fruit is cheaper, he thought. My meat's the same, practically the same.

He moved on. Passing the familiar shops he crossed the street and went into The Cookery. Pushing open the heavy glass door he heard the babble of the lunchers, the sound rushing to his ears like the noise of a suddenly unmuted trumpet. Criers and kibbitzers, he thought. Kibbitzers and criers.

The cashier smiled at him. "We haven't seen you, Mr. G. Somebody told me you were on a diet," she said.

Her too, he thought. A kibbitzer that makes change.

He went toward the back. "Hey Jake, how are you?" a man in a booth called. "Sit by us."

He nodded at the men who greeted him and pulling a chair from another table placed it in the aisle facing the booth.

He sat down and leaned forward, pulling the chair's rear legs into the air so that the waitress could get by. Sitting there, in the aisle, he felt peculiarly like a visitor, like one there only temporarily, as though he had rushed up to the table merely to say hello or to tell a joke. He knew what it was. It was the way kibbitzers sat. The others, cramped in the booth but despite this giving the appearance of lounging there, their lunches begun or already half eaten, gave him somehow the impression that they had been there all day.

"You missed it, Jake," one of the men said. "We almost got Traub here to reach for a check last Friday. Am I lying, Margolis?"

"He almost did, Jake. He really almost did."

"At the last minute he jumped up and down on his own arm and broke it."

The men at the table laughed and Greenspahn looked at Traub sitting little and helpless between two big men. Traub looked down shamefaced into his Coca-Cola.

"It's O.K., Traub," the first man said. "We know. You got all those daughters getting married and having big weddings at the same time. It's terrible. Traub's only got one son. And do you think he'd have the decency to get married so Traub could one time go to a wedding and just enjoy himself? No, *he's* not *old* enough. But he's old enough to turn around and get himself *bar mitzfah'd*, right Traub? The lousy kid."

Greenspahn looked at the men in the booth and at many-daughtered Traub, who seemed as if he were about to cry. Kibbitzers and criers, he thought. Everywhere it was the same. At every table. The two kinds of people like two different sexes that had sought each other out. Sure, Greenspahn thought, would a crier listen to another man's complaints? Could a kibbitzer kid a kidder? But it didn't mean anything, he thought. Not the jokes, not the grief. It didn't mean anything. They were like birds making noises in a tree. But try to catch them in a deal. They'd murder you. Every day they came to eat their lunch and make their noises. Like cowboys on television hanging up their gun belts to go to a dance.

But even so, he thought, they were the way they pretended to be. Nothing made any difference to them. Did they lose sons? Not even the money they made made any difference to them finally, Greenspahn thought.

"So I was telling you," Margolis said, "the guy from the Chamber of Commerce came around again today."

"He came to me too," Paul Gold said.

"Did you give?" Margolis asked.

"No, of course not," he said.

"Did he hit you yet, Jake? Throw him out. He wants contributions for decorations. Listen, those guys are on the take from the paper flower people. It's fantastic what they get for organizing the big stores downtown. My cousin on State Street told me about it. I told him, I said, 'Who needs the Chamber of Commerce? Who needs Easter baskets and colored eggs hanging from the lamppost?' "

"Not when the ring trick still works, right, Margolis?" Joe Fisher said.

Margolis looked at his lapel and shrugged lightly. It was the most modest gesture Greenspahn had ever seen him make. The men laughed. The ring trick was Margolis' invention. "A business promotion," he had told Greenspahn. "Better than Green Stamps." He had seen him work it. Margolis would stand at the front of his store and signal to some guy who stopped for a minute to look at the TV's in his window. He would rap on the glass with his ring to catch his attention. He would smile and say something to him, anything. It didn't make any difference, the guy in the street couldn't hear him. When Greenspahn had watched him he had turned to him and winked slyly as if to say, "Watch this. Watch

how I get this guy." Then he had looked back at the customer outside and still smiling broadly had said, "Hello, Schmuck. Come on
in and I'll sell you something. That's right, jerk, press your greasy
nose against the glass to see who's talking to you. Shade your eyes.
That-a-jerk. Come on in and I'll sell you something." Always the
guy outside would come into the store to find out what Margolis
had been saying to him. "Hello there, sir," Margolis would say,
grinning. "I was trying to tell you that the model you were looking
at out there is worthless. Way overpriced. If the boss knew I was
talking to you like this I'd be canned, but what the hell? We're
all working people. Come on back here and look at a real set."

Margolis was right. Who needed the Chamber of Commerce?
Not the kibbitzers and criers. Not even the Gold boys. Criers.
Greenspahn saw the other one at another table. Twins, but they
didn't even look like brothers. Not even they needed the paper
flowers hanging from the lamppost. Paul Gold shouting to his
brother in the back, "Mr. Gold, please show this gentleman something stylish." And they'd go into the act, putting on a thick Yid-
dish accent for some white-haired old man with a lodge button
in his lapel, giving him the business. Greenspahn could almost
hear the old man telling the others at the Knights of Columbus
Hall, "I picked this suit up from a couple of Yids on 53rd, real
greenhorns. But you've got to hand it to them. Those people
really know material."

Business was a kind of game with them, Greenspahn thought.
Not even the money made any difference.

"Did I tell you about these two kids who came in to look
at rings?" Joe Fisher said. "Sure," he went on, "two kids. Dressed
up. The boy's a regular *mensch*. I figure they've been downtown at
Peacocks and Fields. I think I recognized the girl from the neighborhood. I say to her boy friend — a nice kid, a college kid, you
know, he looks like he ain't been *bar mitzfah'd* yet — 'I got a ring
here I won't show you the price. Will you give me your check for
three hundred dollars right now? No appraisal? No bringing it
to Papa on approval? No nothing?'

" 'I'd have to see the ring,' he tells me.

"Get this. I put my finger over the tag on a ring *I* paid eleven
hundred for. *A big ring*. You got to wear smoked glasses just to

look at it. Paul, I mean it, this is some ring. I'll give you a price for your wife's anniversary. No kidding, this is some ring. Think seriously about it. We could make it up into a beautiful cocktail ring. Anyway, this kid stares like a big dummy, I think he's turned to stone. He's scared. He figures something's wrong a big ring like that for only three hundred bucks. His girl friend is getting edgy, she thinks the kid's going to make a mistake, and she starts shaking her head. Finally he says to me, listen to this, he says, 'I wasn't looking for anything that large. Anyway, it's not a blue stone.' Can you imagine? Don't tell me about shoppers. I get prizes."

"What would you have done if he said he wanted the ring?" Traub asked.

"What are you crazy? He was strictly from wholesale. It was like he had a sign on his suit. Don't you think I can tell a guy who's trying to get a price idea from a real customer?"

"Say, Jake," Margolis said, "ain't that your cashier over there with your butcher?"

Greenspahn looked around. It was Shirley and Howard. He hadn't seen them when he came in. They were sitting across the table from each other — evidently they had not seen him either — and Shirley was leaning forward, her chin on her palms, which she had made into a cup to hold it. She looked, sitting there, like a young girl. It annoyed him. It was ridiculous. He knew they met each other. What did he care? It wasn't his business. But for them to let themselves be seen. He thought of Shirley's brassière hanging in his toilet. It was reckless. They were reckless people. All of them. Howard and Shirley and the men in the restaurant. Reckless people.

"They're pretty thick with each other, ain't they?" Margolis said.

"How should I know?" Greenspahn said.

"What do you run over there at that place of yours, a lonely hearts club?"

"It's not my business. They do their work."

"Some work," Paul Gold said.

"I'd like a job like that," Joe Fisher said.

"Ain't he married?" Paul Gold said.

"I'm not a policeman," Greenspahn said.

"Jake's jealous because he's not getting any," Joe Fisher said.

"Loudmouth," Greenspahn said, "I'm a man in mourning."

The others at the table were silent. "Joe was kidding," Traub, the crier, said.

"Sure, Jake," Joe Fisher said.

"O.K.," Greenspahn said. "O.K."

For the rest of the lunch Greenspahn was conscious of Shirley and Howard. He hoped they would not see him, or if they did that they would make no sign to him. He stopped listening to the stories the men told. He chewed on his hamburger wordlessly. He heard someone mention George Stein and he looked up for a moment. Stein had a grocery in a neighborhood that was changing. He had said that he wanted to get out. He was looking for a setup like Greenspahn's. He could speak to him. Sure, he thought. Why not? What did he need the aggravation? What did he need it? He owned the building the store was in. He could live on the rents. Even Joe Fisher was a tenant of his. He could speak to Stein, he thought, feeling he had made up his mind about something. He waited until Howard and Shirley had finished their lunch and then he left. He went back to his store.

In the afternoon Greenspahn thought he might be able to move his bowels. He went into the toilet off the small room at the back of the store. He sat, looking up at the high ceiling. In the smoky darkness above his head he could just make out the small, square steel ceiling plates. They seemed pitted, soiled, like patches of war-ruined armor. Agh, he thought, the place is a pigpen. The sink bowl was stained darkly, the enamel chipped, long fissures radiating like lines on the map of some wasted country, some evacuated capital. The single faucet dripped steadily. Greenspahn thought sadly of his water bill. On the knob of the faucet he saw again a faded blue *S*. *S* he thought, what the hell does *S* stand for? *H* hot, *C* cold. What the hell kind of faucet is *S*? Old clothes hung on a hook on the back of the door. A man's blue wash pants hung inside out, the zipper split like a peeled banana, the crowded concourse of seams at the crotch like carelessly sewn patches.

He heard Howard in the store, his voice raised exaggeratedly. He strained to listen.

"FORTY-FIVE," he heard Howard say. "FORTY-FIVE, POP." He was talking to the old man. Deaf, he came in each afternoon for a piece of liver for his supper. "I CAN'T GIVE YOU TWO OUNCES. I TOLD YOU. I CAN'T BREAK THE SET." He heard a woman laugh. Shirley? Was Shirley back there with him? What the hell, he thought. It was one thing for them to screw around with each other at lunch. They didn't have to bring it into the store. "TAKE EIGHT OUNCES. INVITE SOMEONE OVER FOR DINNER. TAKE EIGHT OUNCES. YOU'LL HAVE FOR FOUR DAYS. YOU WON'T HAVE TO COME BACK." He was a wise guy, that Howard. What did he want to do, drive the old man crazy? What could you do? The old man liked a small slice of liver. He thought it kept him alive.

He heard footsteps coming toward the back room and voices raised in argument.

"I'm sorry," a woman said. "I don't know how it got there. Honest. Look, I'll pay. I'll pay you for it."

"You bet, lady," Frank's voice said.

"What do you want me to do?" the woman pleaded.

"I'm calling the cops," Frank said.

"For a lousy can of salmon?"

"It's the principle. You're a crook. You're a lousy thief, you know that? I'm calling the cops. We'll see what jail does for you."

"Please," the woman said. "Mister, please. This whole thing is crazy. I never did anything like this before. I haven't got any excuses, but please, please give me a chance." The woman was crying.

"No chances," Frank said. "I'm calling the cops. You ought to be ashamed, lady. A woman dressed nice like you are. What are you, sick or something? I'm calling the cops." He heard Frank lift the receiver.

"Please, please," the woman sobbed. "My husband will kill me. I have a little kid, for Christ's sake."

Frank replaced the phone.

"Ten bucks," he said quietly.

"What's that?"

"Ten bucks and you don't come in here no more."

"I haven't got it," she said.

"All right, lady. The hell with you. I'm calling the cops."

"You bastard," she said.

"Watch your mouth," he said. "Ten bucks."

"I'll write you a check."

"Cash," Frank said.

"O.K. O.K.," she said. "Here."

"Now get out of here, lady." Greenspahn heard the woman's footsteps going away. Frank would be fumbling now with his apron, trying to get the big wallet out of his front pocket. Greenspahn flushed the toilet and waited.

"Jake?" Frank asked, frightened.

"Who was she?"

"Jake, I never saw her before, honest. Just a tramp. She gave me ten bucks. She was just a tramp, Jake."

"I told you before. I don't want trouble," Greenspahn said angrily. He came out of the toilet. "What is this, a game with you?"

"Look, I caught her with the salmon. Would you want me to call the cops for a can of salmon? She's got a kid."

"Yeah, you got a big heart, Frank."

"I would have let you handle it if I'd seen you. I looked for you, Jake."

"You shook her down. I told you before about that."

"Jake, it's ten bucks for the store. I get so damned mad when somebody like that tries to get away with something."

"*Podler*," Greenspahn shouted. "You're through here."

"Jake," Frank said. "She was a tramp." He held the can of salmon in his hand and offered it to Greenspahn as though it were evidence.

Greenspahn pushed his hand aside. "Get out of my store. I don't need you. Get out. I don't want a crook in here."

"Who are you calling names, Jake?"

Greenspahn felt his rage, immense, final. It was on him at once, like an animal that had leaped upon him in the dark. His body shook with it. Frightened, he warned himself uselessly that he must be calm. A *podler* like that, he thought. He wanted to hit him in the face.

"Please, Frank. Get out of here," Greenspahn said.

"Sure," Frank screamed. "Sure, sure," he shouted. Greenspahn, startled, looked at him. He seemed angrier than even himself. Greenspahn thought of the customers. They would hear him. What kind of a place, he thought. What kind of a place? "Sure," Frank yelled, "fire me, go ahead. A regular holy man. A saint!

What are you, God? He smells everybody's rottenness but his own. Only when your own son — may he rest — when your own son slips five bucks out of the cash drawer, that you don't see."

Greenspahn could have killed him. "Who says tha'

Frank caught his breath.

"Who says that?" Greenspahn repeated.

"Nothing, Jake. It was nothing. He was going on a date probably. That's all. It didn't mean nothing."

"Who calls him a thief?"

"Nobody. I'm sorry."

"My dead son? You call my dead son a thief?"

"Nobody called anybody a thief. I didn't know what I was saying."

"In the ground. Twenty-three years old and in the ground. Not even a wife, not even a business. Nothing. He had nothing. He wouldn't take. Harold wouldn't take. Don't call him what you are. He should be alive today. You should be dead. You should be in the ground where he is. *Podler. Mumser*," he shouted. "I saw the lousy receipts, liar," Greenspahn screamed. In a minute Howard was beside him. He had his arm around Greenspahn.

"Calm down, Jake. Come on now, take it easy. What happened back here?" he asked Frank.

Frank shrugged.

"Get him away," Greenspahn pleaded. Howard signaled Frank to get out and led Greenspahn to a chair near the table he used as a desk.

"You all right now, Jake? You O.K. now?"

Greenspahn was sobbing heavily. In a few moments he looked up. "All right," he said. "The customers. Howard, please. The customers."

"O.K., Jake. Just stay back here and wait till you feel better."

Greenspahn nodded. When Howard left him he sat for a few minutes and then went back into the toilet to wash his face. He turned the tap and watched the dirty basin fill with water. It's not even cold, he thought sadly. He plunged his hands into the sink and scooped up warm water which he rubbed into his eyes. He took a handkerchief from his back pocket and unfolding it, patted his face carefully. He was conscious of laughter outside the door. It seemed old, brittle. For a moment he thought of the woman with the coffee. Then he remembered. The porter, he thought. He called his name. "Harold?" He heard footsteps coming up to the door.

"That's right, Mr. Greenspahn," the voice said, still laughing.

Greenspahn opened the door. His porter stood before him in torn clothes. His eyes, red, wet, looked as though they were bleeding. "You sure told that Frank," he said.

"You're late," Greenspahn said. "What do you mean coming in so late?"

"I been to Harold's grave," he said.

"What's that?"

"I been to Mr. Harold's grave," he repeated. "I didn't get to the funeral. I been to his grave cause of my dream."

"Put the stock away," Greenspahn said. "Some more came in this afternoon."

"I will," he said. "I surely will." He was an old man. He had no teeth and his gums lay smooth and very pink in his mouth. He was thin. His clothes hung on him, the sleeves of the jacket rounded, puffed from absent flesh. Through the rents in shirt and trouser Greenspahn could see the grayish skin, hairless, creased, the texture like the pit of a peach. Yet he had a strength Greenspahn could only wonder at and could still lift more stock than Howard or Frank or even Greenspahn himself.

"You'd better start now," Greenspahn said uncomfortably.

Greenspahn stepped to the screen door that opened on the alley.

"I tell you about my dream, Mr. Greenspahn?"

"No dreams. Don't tell me your dreams."

"It was about Mr. Harold. Yes, sir, about him. Your boy that's dead, Mr. Greenspahn."

"I don't want to hear. See if Howard needs anything up front."

"I dreamed it twice. That means it's true. You don't count on a dream less you dream it twice."

"Get away with your crazy stories. I don't pay you to dream."

"That time on Halsted I dreamed the fire. I dreamed that twice."

"Yeah," Greenspahn said, "the fire. Yeah."

"I dreamed that dream twice. Them police wanted to question me. Same names, Mr. Greenspahn, me and your boy we got the same names."

"Yeah. I named him after you."

"I tell you that dream, Mr. Greenspahn? It was a mistake. Frank was supposed to die. Just like you said. Just like I heard you say it just now. And he will. Mr. Harold told me in the dream. Frank, he's going to sicken and die his own self." The porter looked at Greenspahn, the red eyes filling with blood. "If you want it," he said. "That's what I dreamed, and I dreamed about the fire on Halsted the same way. Twice."

"You're crazy. Get away from me."

"That's a true dream. It happened just that very way."

"Get away. Get away," Greenspahn shouted.

"My name's Harold, too."

"You're crazy. Crazy."

The porter went off. He was laughing. What kind of a madhouse? Were they all doing it on purpose? Everything to aggravate him? For a moment he had the impression that that was what it was. A big joke, and everybody was in on it but himself. He was being *kibbitzed* to death. Everything. The cop. The receipts. His cheese man. Howard and Shirley. The men in the restaurant. Frank and the woman. The *shvartze*. Everything. He wouldn't let it happen. What was he, crazy or something? He reached into his pocket for his handkerchief but pulled out a piece of paper. It was the order Harold had taken down over the phone and left on the pad. Absently he unfolded it and read it again. Something occurred to him. As soon as he had the idea he knew it was true. The order had never been delivered. His son had forgotten about it. It couldn't be anything else. Otherwise would it have still been on the message pad? Sure, he thought, what else could it be? Even his son. What did he care? What the hell did he care about the business? Greenspahn was ashamed. It was a terrible thought to have about a dead boy. Oh God, he thought. Let him rest. He was a boy, he thought. Twenty-three years old and he was only a boy. No wife. No business. Nothing. Was the five dollars so important? In helpless disgust he could see Harold's sly wink to Frank as he slipped the money out of the register. Five dollars, Harold, *Five dollars,* he thought, as though he were admonishing him. "Why didn't you come to me, Harold?" he sobbed. "Why didn't you come to your father?"

He blew his nose. It's crazy, he thought. Nothing pleases me. Frank called him God. Some God, he thought. I sit weeping in the back of my store. The hell with it. The hell with everything. Clear the shelves, that's what he had to do. Sell the groceries. Get rid of the meats. Watch the money pile up. Sell, sell, he thought. That would be something. Sell everything. He thought of the items listed on the order his son had taken down. Were they delivered? He felt restless. He hoped they were delivered. If they weren't they would have to be sold again. He was very weary. Very tired. He went to the front of the store.

It was almost closing time. Another half hour. He couldn't stay to close up. He had to be in *shul* before sundown. He had to get to the *minion*. They would have to close up for him. For a year. If he couldn't sell the store, for a year he wouldn't be in his own store at sundown. He would have to trust them to close up for him. Trust who? he thought. My Romeo, Howard? Shirley? The crazy *shvartze*? Only Frank could do it. How could he have fired him? He looked for him in the store. He was talking to Shirley at the register. He would go up and talk to him. What difference did it make? He would have had to fire all of them. Eventually he would have to fire everybody who ever came to work for him. He would have to throw out his tenants, even the old ones, and finally whoever rented the store from him. He would have to keep on firing and throwing out as long as anybody was left. What difference would one more make?

"Frank," he said. "I want you to forget what we talked about before."

Frank looked at him suspiciously. "It's all right," Greenspahn reassured him. He led him by the elbow away from Shirley. "Listen," he said, "we were both excited before. I didn't mean it what I said."

Frank continued to look at him. "Sure, Jake," he said finally. "No hard feelings." He extended his hand.

Greenspahn took it reluctantly. "Yeah," he said.

"Frank," he said, "do me a favor and close up the place for me. I got to get to the *shul* for the *minion*."

"I got you, Jake," he said.

Greenspahn went to the back to change his clothes. He washed his face and hands and combed his hair. Carefully he removed his working clothes and put on the suit jacket, shirt and tie he had worn in the morning. He walked back into the store.

He was about to leave when he saw that Mrs. Frimkin had come into the store again. That's all right, he told himself, she can be a good customer. He needed some of the old customers now. They could drive you crazy but when they bought, they bought. He watched as she took a cart from the front and pushed it through the aisles. She put things in the cart as though she were in a hurry. She barely glanced at the prices. That was the way to shop, he thought. It was a pleasure to watch her. She reached into the frozen food locker and took out about a half-dozen packages. From the towers of canned goods on his shelves she seemed to take down only the largest cans. In minutes her shopping cart was overflowing. That's some order, Greenspahn thought. Then he watched as she went to the stacks of bread at the bread counter. She picked up a packaged white bread and first looking around to see if anyone were watching her, bent down quickly over the bread, cradling it to her chest as though it were a football. As she stood Greenspahn saw her brush crumbs from her dress. He saw her put the torn package into her cart with the rest of her purchases.

She came up to the counter where Greenspahn stood and unloaded the cart, pushing the groceries toward Shirley to be checked out. The last item she put on the counter was the wounded bread. Shirley punched the keys quickly. As she reached for the bread, Mrs. Frimkin put out her hand to stop her. "Look," she said, "what are you going to charge me for the bread? It's damaged. Can I have it for ten cents?"

Shirley turned to look at Greenspahn.

"Out," he said. "Get out you *podler*. I don't want you coming in here any more. You're a thief," he shouted. "A thief." Frank came rushing up.

"Jake, what is it? What is it?"

"Her. That one. A crook. She tore the bread. I seen her."

The woman looked at him defiantly. "I don't have to take that," she said. "I can make plenty of trouble for you. You're a crazy man. I'm not going to be insulted by somebody like you."

"Get out of here," Greenspahn shouted, "before I have you locked up."

The woman backed away from him and when he stepped forward she turned and fled.

"Jake," Frank said, putting his hand on Greenspahn's shoulder.

"That was a big order. So she tried to get away with a few pennies. What does it mean? You want me to find her and apologize?"

"Look," Greenspahn said, "she comes in again I want to know about it. I don't care what I'm doing. I want to know about it. She's going to pay me for that bread."

"Jake," Frank said.

"No," he said. "I mean it."

"Jake, it's ten cents."

"*My* ten cents. No more," he said. "I'm going to *shul.*"

He waved Frank away and went into the street. Already the sun was going down. He felt urgency. He had to get there before the sun went down.

That night Greenspahn had the dream for the first time.

He was in the synagogue waiting to say the prayers for his son. Around him were the old men, the *minion,* their faces brittle and pale. He recognized them from his youth. They had been old even then. One man stood by the window and watched the sun. At a signal from him the others would begin. There was always some place in the world where the prayers were being said, he thought, some place where the sun had just come up or just gone down, and he supposed there was always a *minion* to watch it and to mark its progress, the prayers following God's bright bird, going up in sunlight or in darkness, always, everywhere. He knew the men never left the *shul.* It was the way they kept from dying. They didn't even eat, but there was about the room the foul lemony smell of urine. Sure, Greenspahn thought in the dream, stay in the *shul.* That's right. Give the *podlers* a wide berth. All they have to worry about is God. Some worry, Greenspahn thought. The man at the window gave the signal and they all started to mourn for Greenspahn's son, their ancient voices betraying the queer melody of the prayers. The rabbi looked at Greenspahn and Greenspahn, imitating the old men, began to rock back and forth on his heels. He tried to sway faster than they did. I'm younger, he thought. When he was swaying so quickly that he thought he would be sick were he to go any faster, the rabbi smiled at him approvingly. The man at the window shouted that the sun was approaching the danger point in the sky and that Greenspahn had better begin as soon as he was ready.

He looked at the strange thick letters in the prayer book. "Go ahead," the rabbi said, "think of Harold and tell God."

He tried then to think of his son, but he could recall him only as he was when he was a baby standing in his crib. It was unreal, like a photograph. The others knew what he was thinking and frowned. "Go ahead," the rabbi said.

Then he saw him as a boy on a bicycle, as once he had seen him at dusk as he looked from his apartment onto the street, riding the gray sidewalks, slapping his buttocks as though he were on a horse. The others were not satisfied.

He tried to imagine him older but nothing came of it. The rabbi said, "Please, Greenspahn, the sun is almost down. You're wasting time. Faster. Faster."

All right, Greenspahn thought. All right. Only let me think. The others stopped their chanting.

Desperately he thought of the store. He thought of the woman with the coffee, incredibly old, older than the old men who prayed with him, her wig, fatuously red, the head beneath it shaking crazily as though even the weight and painted fire of the thick, bright hair were not enough to warm it.

The rabbi grinned.

He thought of the *shvartze,* imagining him on an old cot, on a damp and sheetless mattress, twisting in a fearful dream. He saw him bent under a huge side of red, raw meat he carried to Howard.

The others were still grinning but the rabbi was beginning to look a little bored. He thought of Howard, seeming to watch him through the *shvartze*'s own red, mad eyes, as Howard chopped at the fresh flesh with his butcher's axe.

He saw the men in the restaurant. The criers, ignorant of hope, the *kibbitzers,* ignorant of despair. Each with his pitiful piece broken from the whole of life, confidently extending only half of what there was to give.

He saw the cheats with their ten dollars, and their stolen nickels, and their luncheon lusts, and their torn breads.

All right, Greenspahn thought. He saw Shirley naked but for her brassière. It was evening and the store was closed. She lay with Howard on the butcher's block.

"The boy," the rabbi said impatiently, *"the boy."*

He concentrated for a long moment while all of them stood by silently. Gradually, with difficulty, he began to make something out. It was Harold's face in the coffin, his expression at the very moment of death itself, before the undertakers had had time to tamper with it. He saw it clearly. It was soft, puffy with grief; a sneer curled the lips. It was Harold, twenty-three years old, wifeless, jobless, sacrificing nothing even in the act of death, leaving the world with his life not started.

The rabbi smiled at Greenspahn and turned away as though he now had other business.

"No," Greenspahn called, "wait. Wait."

The rabbi turned and with the others looked at him.

He saw it now. They all saw it. The helpless face, the sly wink, the embarrassed, slow smug smile of guilt that must, volitionless as the palpitation of a nerve, have crossed his face when he had turned, his hand in the register, to see Frank watching him.

(From Redbook)

WHEAT CLOSED HIGHER, COTTON WAS MIXED

BY SEYMOUR EPSTEIN

*B*ERNIE HALPER met and married Sue several years after the war ended. They both were taking part in an amateur production of *The Sea Gull*. Bernie directed. Sue played the role of Masha. A newspaper theater critic was present at the performance, and he shed a few lines of grace over the efforts of the group. He wrote that some professionals heavy-laden with success might spend a profitable hour watching the enthusiasm and intelligence of these young people.

That same evening the whole cast — extras, helpers, all — met at someone's apartment and picked over those few words like augurs over the entrails of a chicken. Visions of triumph mingled with the cigarette smoke, and each one made out the shape of his own destiny.

"I still say the important word is 'intelligence,' " Bernie declared at one o'clock in the morning. "There are any number of dopes with the gift of talent, but an actor without brains is like a plant without water. He just won't grow."

Since all present were still too young to admit of any shortcoming, this remark was found to be acceptable as a parting shot. About fifteen people filed out of a room that would take two days to ventilate. In the street they deployed singly and in pairs toward the various subways that would take them home. It was no accident that Bernie fell in with Sue.

Throughout rehearsals he had managed to avoid so much as a single glance of partiality. This despite her gray eyes and cute nose

and hair as dark and ample as a moonless sea. There was an ampli-
tude in her figure as well, which filled every hollow of Bernie's desire. Nor was that desire made up of loneliness and inexperience.
Bernie had known women, being himself handsome in the way of
physical virility and generous features. He wasn't tall but he was
large: big head, heavy shoulders, large mouth, prominent nose. His
neck could have used another inch, and he had a way of hunching
forward when he walked. A football coach would have singled him
out in any group of freshmen.

Bernie and Sue walked toward the Seventh Avenue subway,
where the New Lots train would take Sue to her home in Brooklyn. Even Manhattan can be quiet along its side streets at one in
the morning, and their footsteps sounded brash and intrusive. A
young man to whom words came easily, Bernie found himself
stricken with silence. It was Sue who spoke.

"I'd like to ask you a question," she said. "Would you tell me the
truth?"

Bernie smiled. "If I know the truth," he replied.

"Do you think I have intelligence?"

This was as he had expected. The appeal to his honesty missed
its target, deflected by self-interest.

"Only people who have intelligence question it," he answered,
feeling that he did not so much lie as bedeck his love with silks and
spangles.

For Bernie Halper was in love, right there on Forty-eighth Street
between Fifth and Sixth avenues at one in the morning. He walked
on as if nothing had happened, but he felt as if he had been dealt
a blow that passed through his flesh, broke no bones, and landed
smack on the core of his being. He could have doubled over with
the pain of his joy.

"I wish you would tell me the truth," Sue repeated.

"You are intelligent," Bernie stated flatly. "And lovely," he
added.

"Sometimes I wonder if I can act at all," she said, exacting gentle
usury.

Bernie lifted his face to the neon-obscured sky. In his mind was
an image of Sue as she had stepped out of the wings in her long
dress and tiara of braided hair. She had held her hands as he had
shown her (precisely, a blueprint, no variation of her own) and

spoken her lines in the same way. If Truth was Beauty, then Sue was Truth. And can Truth be anything but intelligent? That she could not act was a matter of some regret and questionable significance. A deception for her sake was already coloring his love with poignance.

"You can act," Bernie said, ready to sign checks for any amount. "You can act beautifully. Why do you ask? I know. It's like being in love. You can't hear the words often enough. Are you in love, Sue?"

She turned and looked at him with her remarkable gray eyes. "Now, do you mean?"

"Ever."

"Yes."

"Are you in love with someone now?"

"No."

"Good. Will you see me tomorrow? Will you go with me to a movie? A play? Dinner? Anything?"

"All right," she said.

Two months later Bernie asked Sue to marry him. Sue said yes, but made it clear that she intended to go on with her acting career.

"What do you take me for?" Bernie cried. "I know a little something about ambition myself. Why should I deny it to you? . . . Listen, darling, will you do me a favor? I ask it only because I'll shrivel up and die if I don't hear you say it soon. Say you love me. I must have said it to you no less than six million times."

"Of course I love you," Sue said, taking his face between her hands. "Bernie . . ."

"Please don't say anything else," he pleaded.

"Tell me the truth. . . ."

Bernie swore that she had a rare, rich and beautiful talent and that the world would know it someday.

They married in August and almost perished from the heat in their wonderful room-and-a-half on East Twentieth. They took long walks in the city, since they could afford little else, and Bernie made every view and quaintness his personal gift to Sue. He gave her Greenwich Village, Chinatown, Riverside Drive, and all the magnificent bridges of New York.

About the Queensboro Bridge he said: "I was driving over it once before the war. It was just about twilight. Maybe a little later. Anyway, I was coming from the Queens side into the city, and I saw Manhattan lighted up like the Arabian Nights. I felt like climbing to the top of the bridge and taking a flying swan dive right into the city. I thought: What else do you want? If you can't make it here, you can't make it anywhere."

"Make what?" Sue asked.

"Anything! Golden apples! My private fairy tale! Turn thrice, Bernie Halper, Lord Mayor of Third Avenue!"

"Why not Fifth?"

"Fifth it is!"

"How much money *do* we have, Lord Mayor?" Sue asked.

Bernie took out a handkerchief and wiped his face. "There's a couple of hundred in the bank and about eight hundred in bonds. We're on Easy Street. Don't worry. I'm a provider."

It was Bernie who did the worrying. He had been promised a showcase production around the end of September, but there was no money in that. The immediate future was resplendent with moneyless doings. Sue was already cast in the Synge play Bernie planned to do. That too would contribute a big fat zero to their income. In addition, Sue was continuing her drama classes at the Academy. She miserably suggested that she quit and take a job.

Bernie burst into laughter at the look on her face. "Honeybunch, slash my wrists and see what you can get at the blood bank!" he said mockingly.

"I didn't say it that way at all," Sue protested.

"Please remember that expression," Bernie said. "It was great!"

But the question of money yipped at his heels like a Pekingese, too insignificant to be menacing yet embarrassing in its persistence. He had held a variety of jobs after finishing school on the GI Bill. He had worked in a department store as a salesman. His father had thrown some house-painting jobs his way. For a few months he crouched next to the driver and pointed out the splendors of New York in a plastic-domed bus. And just before taking on the production in which he had met Sue, Bernie had discovered a dormant ability. He became a worker in leather.

It happened that a friend of his with a real ability for the craft had set up shop in Greenwich Village as a custom maker of leather handbags and sandals. Very arty and bizarre stuff, but requiring innate skill if a lot of expensive leather was not to go to waste. The friend did quite well, in the marginal way of such businesses. Bernie dropped in often at the shop and began toying with the knife and awl. It became immediately apparent to both Bernie and his friend that he had the touch. He was able to pick up a few dollars helping out on occasional afternoons.

When Bernie cashed in the second hundred-dollar bond he paid a visit to his friend in the Village. The friend said yes, sure, he could use some help.

The Playboy of the Western World scourged Bernie. He gripped his skull between his hands as though he wanted to crush it. He asked himself in hoarse supplications why he had to pick such a play. To take innocent children from the Bronx, Brooklyn, New Jersey, God knows where, and make lilting Irishers out of them! Madness! He had counseled himself a thousand times never to make the sinful error of going on with a thing merely because he had begun, and here he was treading quicksand up to his neck. All right, the lead part was good. That boy would be an actor. But everyone else, including Sue . . . It was a goulash.

He had his first bad fight with Sue.

"Ear," he said to her, pulling on the lobe of his own. "You listen and then you reproduce the accent, the inflection. An actor who doesn't have an ear is a tone-deaf singer."

"I hate you!" Sue screamed.

The production rolled downhill like a vehicle without brakes. When certain death stared him in the face Bernie's nervous system reacted with a charge of adrenaline. He took the leading man aside and asked him if he could play it straight, no accent. The answer was yes. Then Bernie assembled the cast and informed them that they could stop torturing themselves. No brogues. He challenged them all to capture the spirit of the lines without the music. It would fail, he assured them, but it would fail interestingly rather than ludicrously. That was the best he could offer them at that late date.

The effect was somewhat like that on a baseball player who has swung three or four bats so that the one he wields at the plate will seem light. Just playing the roles without having to worry about the treachery of their tongues broke the tension and gave them an art and ease above their normal level.

The performance annoyed some, puzzled many and persuaded an all-important few. There is an attractive legend that great discoveries have been made through the inadvertence of somebody's maid leaving something where it shouldn't have been. Bernie's "experiment," as it was called, fell into such a category of fruitful accident. The same reviewer who had found *The Sea Gull* an enthusiastic and intelligent production found *Playboy* "a worthwhile experiment with a play that normally has to wait upon a miraculous pooling of accents and talents. It is to Mr. Halper's credit that he persevered in the face of what he must have known would seem high treason to lovers of the Irish theater. Certainly we missed the melodies of Synge, but we did enjoy a good play, well acted."

In their apartment afterward, Bernie improvised a wild Irish dance while whistling a jig through his teeth. Sue held on to his hands like the tail of a kite on a windy day. Then Bernie went down to the German delicatessen and bought two pounds of roast beef, a rye bread with caraway seeds, four bottles of beer and a container of Russian dressing. They made sandwiches, just the two of them, and ate and drank until their ears rang.

As a result of that one good review and several complimentary mentions, the production wound up having an unprecedented, if profitless, run of three months. More important, Bernie received an invitation from a producer to "read" a play. The producer wanted Bernie to submit his judgment on an original play, and if he found it good, to offer some suggestions about casting and direction. There were no promises and no contract — just a chance, if Bernie Halper wished to take it. Bernie Halper wished, in all modesty and trembling, to take the chance.

There followed days of perfect wholeness, into which hope and activity flowed in ideal proportion. Sue was acting, receiving a nightly potion of applause, which her thirsting heart drank greedily. She would come back to the apartment a stimulated drunk, a courtesan.

Bernie was spending his days at home. He read the play the producer had given him. It was not, to his mind, a good play, but he also knew that a producer doesn't go around asking people their opinions of what he considers a bad play. And it was not a bad play; it was just not a good one. With proper direction it could be made into something.

Bernie paced endless miles from the sink to the windows to the bathroom — an isosceles triangle at the apex of which he finally had his revelation. One character played as a self-perceiving opportunist instead of a Chekhovian failure not only made that character's lines wink with humor but added a wonderful ingredient of exasperation to all the other parts. It only remained to get his ideas on paper and see the producer.

There was no hurry about this. The producer had said he would like to see something in about a month, and Bernie had had the play in his possession for only a week. He checked his impulse to run with both hands full of bright ideas. There might have been some gain in doing this, but he succumbed to a more subtle pleasure.

It seemed now to Bernie that he had never doubted his eventual success. His personal contract with fate permitted much latitude, and at a guess Bernie would have put the date of delivery well beyond his twenty-ninth birthday. His twenty-ninth birthday was only four months away, and fate appeared to be frantically busy with gift wrapping and silver bows. Bernie wanted to pause. He wanted to savor. He wanted time to walk around like a long-barren woman confirmed in her first pregnancy, patronizing the world out of the overflow of her secret wealth.

Sue left their place at ten in the morning. She had her classes at the Academy, which were over by five. She then came home for an early dinner with Bernie before leaving for the theater. This left him the afternoons completely free.

He spent those afternoons roaming around the city. Even the thought that there was less than three hundred dollars between the Halpers and starvation couldn't put him off his tour of euphoria. The days were cloudy and cold, and this, for some reason, was in perfect keeping with his mood of ordainment. He strolled around the Village and looked into stores where he and Sue had mentally tagged items against their day of affluence. He walked into little coffee shops at off hours, delighting in the atmosphere of detachment generated by empty stools and apathetic counter girls. The city was busy, busy — but Bernie Halper would open a book, sit sideways and cross his legs (since there was no one on either side of him), and take a criminally long time over his Dutch apple pie and coffee.

His wanderings took him as far north as the Cloisters and as far south as the Battery. In all his life he had never enjoyed the city as much as he did in those few weeks. It spoke to him of creation and joy, of his name on billboards, of rights he could claim because he was a gifted young man beloved of the gods. Now was the time when he could have clambered up the Queensboro Bridge and taken his magnificent swan dive into all that awaited him.

At four o'clock, wherever he was, he would start back home. He would stop at a market on Third Avenue and buy things for their dinner.

"I won't have you cooking," Sue said.

"How are you going to stop me?" Bernie asked.

"But you *shouldn't!*" she protested. "You have your own work. How are you doing on the play?"

He had given her no inkling of the beautiful silk purse he had fashioned out of a sow's ear. He didn't know exactly when he would reveal it to her, but it would probably be about the time he had exhausted his little affair with Bernie Halper.

"It's a stinker," he told her, "but I've got ideas. . . . I don't know why it is, but my finest inspirations come to me over the stove. My boiling point is about the same as water's."

After Sue left, Bernie would clean up the dishes. He really didn't mind kitchen chores. He performed them with a background of music provided by the tinny little radio Sue had brought with her from Brooklyn. At that hour there was only the soppiest kind of music on the air — neither good jazz nor good swing nor good classical — tearoom tunes, the kind of stuff that could start a forest fire out of a spark of melancholy. But Bernie enjoyed it. It edged his thoughts with a pleasing blankness, like the margins of a printed page. It also created a time stasis for what followed.

Bernie always managed to finish the last of the dishes just as the seven o'clock news broadcast was concluding. He had regulated his tempo to synchronize. At the end of the news broadcast there was a summary of the market activity for the day. Bernie wasn't interested in stocks. He wouldn't have been interested if he'd had thousands of dollars lying around begging for safe investment. But during these days of solitary and delicious communion with his life

— present and future — he had discovered a phrase that was a per-fect distillation of all he felt. Perfect because it meant nothing and evoked everything: ". . . Wheat closed higher and cotton was mixed. . . ."

Wheat didn't always close higher, nor was cotton eternally mixed — whatever the devil either meant. There were variations to the formula, but for the sake of keeping his symbol pure Bernie trans-lated every market report into that precise phrase. And when it fell upon his ears Bernie Halper contracted his whole being into one transcendent discharge of love and hope. The million artifacts in the city that had assumed the shape of his dreams, his love for Sue, the long lifetime of good and happy work that lay before him — all these streamed into Bernie from every direction. These and the one ineffable thing no man can describe when he is young, stam-mers about in his middle years and replaces with sleep when he has grown old. Perhaps it is a secret suspicion of immortality — a nar-cissism so profound that it finds its reflection in every facet of life, including death.

Bernie didn't get to direct that original play. In fact, he never even had the satisfaction of having his ideas discussed. The producer simply vanished — or he might as well have. He left for California. This was the information Bernie received when he called the number the producer had given him.

"Any idea when he'll be back?" Bernie asked.

"Dunno," was the answer. "Couple of months. Maybe more."

"Is this his home?" Bernie asked.

"No. This is the Consolidated Syndicate."

"The *what?*"

"Con — It's a buying office."

Bernie ultimately met people who knew the producer. He talked to them. They told him that the man was known for his erratic be-havior. Yes, he had produced several plays on Broadway, but he was essentially a businessman. His muse was money, and he fol-lowed his muse wherever it yelled the loudest. Forget it, they told him.

Bernie naturally didn't forget it. He didn't mind his own loss of time and effort or the man's defection so much as he did the feeling of foolishness he was left with. The warm flow of felicity suddenly froze, and everything was caught in a posture of mockery.

"The city is full of nuts," Sue said by way of consolation.

But she failed to console. She said all the things a man might expect to hear from his wife under the circumstances, but she said them as one who understands rather than feels. The disappointment was not as much hers as his, and this crack of distinction marred the surface of his love.

"Don't take on so," Bernie said to her. "You'll get over it."

"What do you mean by that?" she asked.

"Nothing."

"Well, it's not the end of the world," Sue said, aware of her failure of feeling. "You said yourself it would be idiotic to pin any hopes on a thing like that."

"So I did. So it was. Amen."

"I don't know what you expect me to do."

"Shed one honest tear," Bernie snapped. "Just one of the many you would have shed if something of this sort had happened to you!"

Then Sue did cry, but her tears were not for the right thing.

Bernie went job hunting. He had no negotiable skill outside the theater, and the salaries offered him were ridiculous. He took a job selling a food-freezer plan to housewives and closed three deals the first day. That evening he figured out what the housewife was getting for her money and he didn't show up the next day. He went to see his friend in the Village.

"Look," said his friend, "I can use you, but I can't have you hopping in for a couple of hours a week. Can you give me three or four eight-hour days?"

"Sure," said Bernie.

Things settled down to what is normal for young people who hope to earn their bread in the arts. The bread was earned elsewhere and the arts glittered like stars. They may have been several million light-years away, but in the dark, clear night of longing it seemed as though you had only to reach out your hand to pluck one.

Sue continued with her drama classes during the day and found occasional work as an usher in a Broadway theater in the evening.

Bernie became more proficient in leathercraft and his friend allowed him to design some bags of his own, for which he received a percentage when they were sold. His and Sue's combined incomes, however, added up to the kind of financial uncertainty acceptable only to those whose eyes are fixed firmly on the heavens.

If they couldn't have heaven (the particular heaven they sought), they could at least gather together with other apprentice angels and imitate the noises of Paradise. Their friends were people like themselves: young, predatorily ambitious, and chronically separated from their rightful status by a hairbreadth of prejudice. They gathered at one another's cubicles in the city and drank wine or beer while flagellating this senile actress or that cretinous actor. If someone of their acquaintance made good in a Broadway show, they were loud in their acclamation — so loud as to stifle the cries of pain rasping in their throats.

And after these prayer meetings Bernie and Sue would return to their apartment so confirmed in their belief, so absolute in their hunger, that it seemed as if fate could not much longer withstand the pressure. It would succumb merely to get the Halpers off its neck.

On one such night Bernie and Sue lay unspeaking in their dark room, their thoughts privately prating in the silence.

Then Sue whispered, "Bernie . . ."

"Yeah?"

"I didn't know if you were asleep."

"Not even close. What did you want?"

"I'm not a good actress," she said.

"You are."

"I'm not. I know I'm not. I've always known it. What am I going to do? I thought maybe I'd get over it, but it gets worse all the time. There's nothing else I want. . . . Bernie, do you want very much to succeed as a director?"

"I can taste it."

"What would you do for it?"

"I don't get you."

"I mean," said Sue, "supposing you could make a pact with God. You could have success but at a sacrifice — like five years of your life, or someone who means very much to you. . . . You know, something important. Would you do it?"

"I wouldn't sacrifice you, if that's what you mean," Bernie said. "Would you me?"

"No."

"Meaning yes."

"I said no."

"I know you did," said Bernie, "but you were thinking something else. I'll tell you what you were thinking. You were thinking that sleeping with the right guy would be such a small thing compared to what you might get that you wonder how I could possibly make a fuss about it."

Her own unguardedness and Bernie's terrible accuracy left Sue bereft of words.

"Bernie . . ." she said after a moment.

Bernie moved his arm and touched her, not in a caress but adjuringly, as one might put his hand on a child to forestall its panic penitence. "There's a good likelihood neither one of us will amount to a damn in the theater," he said in a voice dry and lifeless enough to be prophetic. "Why ruin everything?"

When Sue became pregnant she was in rehearsals for her first Broadway production. It was a musical.

"You did it on purpose!" she raged and sobbed at Bernie. "You couldn't stand to see me get ahead!"

Bernie caught the fists she tried to use against him between his big hands and held them captive. "Think a minute!" he said beseechingly. "For God's sake, Sue, think a minute! It's no one's fault. And look, no one has to know. For months! There's no chance of your endangering yourself. It's just a walk-on part. . . ."

A walk-on part, and a miracle of percentages. A thousand-to-one shot. The director at that point had simply been looking at faces, and Sue's was one of the faces he chose. There were exactly three speaking lines — forty-two words — and these were to be spoken in chorus with six other girls.

"You can certainly be in rehearsals until the show opens," Bernie said soothingly. "And even if you have to quit afterward, you'll still have the show to your credit."

"And what happens after that?"

"Didn't you expect you'd ever have children?" Bernie asked her. She didn't answer. There was nothing to say. The question wasn't fair or honest — neither of them had thought of the possibility. There was no more room in their lives for a child than there was for a grand piano in their apartment.

Sue didn't allow herself to dwell on the future. Bernie did. He went to see his father.

The elder Halper scratched the bristles on his cheeks with nails as tough as bears' claws. Three decades of house painting had changed the composition of his flesh. It had the dry, grainy look of sun-baked wood.

"How much'll you need?" Mr. Halper asked.

"I figure I can set up shop for a thousand," Bernie said.

His father nodded. "A thousand I got," he said.

"This is a loan," Bernie said. "I want it made out in regular form. A note."

Mr. Halper nodded again without smiling. "Tomorrow I'll see a lawyer," he said.

With the thousand dollars Bernie went searching for a vacant store in the Village, as far away from his friend's shop as possible. When he found one he signed a year's lease and then set about purchasing the materials of his trade. He knew where to look. He had found out while working for his friend.

The show in which Sue appeared closed after one week. The reviews were awful and the backers pulled out. Sue cried half the night and lay silently awake the other half while Bernie slept. She woke Bernie at six in the morning to tell him they would have to go to the doctor.

Sue stayed in the hospital for several days after her miscarriage. Bernie went every day with a fresh bunch of flowers. He tried to console her for everything — for the show that closed, for the child she didn't want, for the child she didn't have. She listened to him, her remarkable gray eyes ringed with a tired bewilderment.

"Sue, I've started in business for myself," he finally told her. "A leather shop. I borrowed some money from my father."

"Why did you do that?"

"We were going to have a child!"

"What are you going to do with it now?"

"Keep it," said Bernie. "We've got to have something to fall back on."

*　　　*　　　*

The jobs Sue found were transient, as though those who employed her understood that she would be a transient too. She was a receptionist, a salesgirl, a poll taker and of course, intermittently, an usher.

There were amateur acting groups all over the city, and Sue was always among them. Sometimes she had a part. Sometimes she sat on a folding chair in a church basement or social hall and listened to other voices resound loudly in the emptiness.

Bernie's workday began at noon. He kept the shop open until ten in the evening on weekdays and eleven on Saturday. At times he wondered if he had given a single thought to the hours this business would entail.

Half the thousand was gone the first month in business, and Bernie saw that he wouldn't make it with the output of his own hands. So he rearranged the store, putting his workshop in the rear and taking in other merchandise he could turn over more quickly. He now sold ceramics and silver jewelry in addition to his leatherwork. It was just another store in the Village, but Bernie was saved from the worst implications by thinking of it as temporary.

At times rebellion seethed in his heart, and he would put out the lights and close the door of the shop. He would walk aimlessly around the streets for an hour, biting seeds of bitterness, telling himself it was impossible, absolutely impossible, to go back and face another desultory customer who fingered a dozen items and walked out with empty hands and a vague smile. But he would finally go back, because not to go back would commit him to something of which he had grown afraid.

"This is ridiculous," he said to Sue. "I must have some time to myself. I see no one. I'm a slave to that damn store."

"Get rid of it," Sue replied.

He looked at her. Her style as a woman had come to full flower. She had put on some flesh, just enough to bring to perfection her gray-eyed voluptuousness. . . . My Russian princess, Bernie thought to himself, limp with helplessness and dread.

"I'll close the store at seven two nights a week," he said. "The hell with it. Let's see some people."

So they began to invite people to their apartment again. Since they had more money now, they served liquor and elaborate spreads of food. The people who came were something like themselves,

but not exactly. They were a little younger, a great deal more certain of their future. But the excitement generated by these evenings was almost the same.

Bernie would watch Sue at these parties. He saw with a sick heart
the encroachment of mannerisms he knew too well. The extravagant gesture, the elocutionary speech, the whole synthetic bag of
tricks of the would-be actress who hadn't made it and never would.
He watched these things as a man might observe the symptoms of
a fatal disease, and he felt a searing pity for his pretty, afflicted darling.

When one such evening had come to an end, and they had
cleaned up the mess and mounted the fan on a window sill to ex-
haust the fumes, Bernie turned to see Sue standing in the center of
the room, her beautiful arms lifted as she slowly removed the pins
from her hair. Her eyes met his, and in that instant before she
spoke, Bernie made out his life.

He saw this room and all the rooms they would eventually oc-
cupy. He saw the store, every item in it, and the small segment of
sky vouchsafed from the window. He could hear the eternal seven
o'clock news broadcast telling of trouble and the fact that wheat
closed higher and cotton was mixed. But the words evoked nothing, because he had pinched off the nerve that fed illusion.

"Bernie . . ." Sue said.

"Yes."

"Tell me the truth. . . ."

Then Bernie went to her, kissed her, and carefully chose the
words he would have to go on saying.

(*From The Sewanee Review*)

THE OLD ARMY GAME

BY GEORGE GARRETT

*E*VERYBODY has got a story about the Bad Sergeant in Basic. Sit down some evening with your buddies, and you'll find that's one subject everybody can deal out like a hand of cards. And that's not a bad image for it, because those stories, told or written or even finally mounted in memory, acquire a bright, conventional, two-dimensional character. All the people in them are face cards. Which seems to me as good a way as any to introduce Sergeant First Class Elwood Quince.

Lean and hard-faced, a face all angles like a one-eyed jack. Perfectly turned out, everything tailored skintight, glossy, spit-shined and glowing. Field cap, white from wear and care, two fingers over the nose. Casts a flat gray semicircular shadow that way. Calls attention to the mouth. The thin tight lips. Open you'd expect to see even rows of fine white teeth; instead you'd see them yellow and no good and all awry and gaping like a worn-out picket fence. And when he did smile, it was all phony, "like a jackass chewing briars." Back to the field cap. Calls attention to the mouth and hides the eyes in shadow like a mask. The eyes — with the cap off and resting on a desk and his large restless hands patting his straw-blond hair, long and rich on top, but sidewalled so that with a cap or a helmet on he looks as shaved clean as a chicken ready for the oven — the eyes are peculiarly light and cloudy at the same time, like a clear spring that somebody has spit in or stirred the mud in the bottom of with a stick. Can you see him yet? But he's still. Let's breathe on him and let him walk because Quince's walk is important. He has two of them: (a) the official walk when he's marching troops, in formation, etc. and (b) when he's relaxed and just walking about the area. The former is conventional, ramrod, but natural. Well-trained soldier. The latter is quite special. Light-footed, easy, insinuative, cat- and woman-like. Creepy. He seemed like a ghost to us. You always look over your shoulder before you speak because the chances are he's right there behind you and every-where at once.

Talk? Oh my, yes, he can talk. Arkansas mountain accent. Part Southern and part Western and a little bit nasal and whiny and hard on the *r*'s. Picturesque. Rural similes abound. Some ex-tended to the epic proportion. For example, to Sachs, our fat boy from New York: "Sachs when I see you draggin' your lardass around the battery area, you put me in mind of a old woreout sow in a hog-pen with a measly little scrawny litter of piglets sniffin' and chasin' around behind her and that old sow is just so tired and fat and god-damn lazy she can't even roll over and let 'em suck." Also fre-quently scatalogical. Here is a dialogue. Sergeant Quince and Me. In open ranks. Inspection. He right in front of Me. I'm looking straight into the shadow his cap casts.

Quince: Do you know how low you are?

Me (learning to play by ear): Pretty low, Sergeant.

Quince: Pretty low? No, I mean just *how* low?

Me: I don't know, Sergeant.

Quince: Well then, since you're so ignorant, I'll tell you. You're lower than whale shit. And you know where that is, don't you?

Me: Yes, Sergeant.

Quince: On the bottom of the ocean.

(Quince passes on to the next victim.)

The tone of voice? Always soft. Never raises his voice except in giving commands. Otherwise speaks just above a whisper. You have to strain to hear him.

When we arrived at Camp Chaffee, Arkansas, the Army's man-sion pitched in the seat of excrement now that Camp Polk, La., and Camp Blanding, Fla., are closed up tight as a drum, left to hobos, rats, bugs, weeds, etc., we were assigned to take Basic Training in Sergeant Quince's outfit. I call it *his* outfit because the Battery Commander had a harelip and was as shy as a unicorn, stayed in his office all day. The First Sergeant had V-shaped wound stripes

from the First World War, I swear, and didn't care about anything but getting out a morning report without erasures and also
the little flower garden he had all around the Orderly Room shack,
that he tended and watered with a cute watering can just like Little
Bo Peep's. Nevertheless Sergeant Cobb started out as a *presence*.
Austere and lonely and unapproachable, but thought of as an ultimate tribunal where possibly wrongs might be righted, a kind of
tired old god we might turn to one day in despair of salvation from
Quince, come to him as broken children, and he'd sigh and forgive us. Until there came a test one day. Sergeant Quince marched
the whole battery, one hundred and sixty-odd men in four heavy-
booted platoons, right across one side of Cobb's garden. By the
time the First Platoon had passed by, Cobb was out of the office, hat-
less, necktie askew and loose like a long tongue, eyes burning.
(Ah ha! thought we of Sergeant Quince, the original "young man
so spic and span," something unpleasant will hit the fan now.) But
it didn't. Cobb stood there looking and wilted. Tears brimmed in
his eyes and spilled down his cheeks. He watched his tended stalks
and blossoms go down under the irresistible marching feet of Progress, of Mutability, of Change and Decay. And he never said a
word. He slumped and shook his fist, a helpless old man. Meanwhile Quince ignored him, counted a crisp cadence for the marching troops and grinned *just* like a jackass chewing briars. And our
hearts sank like stones to see the mighty fallen.

So, though he was merely the Field First, it was Quince's outfit
to make or break. His little brotherhood of lesser cadre revolved
like eager breathless planets around his indubitable magnificence.
From our first formation, we in rumpled new ill-fitting fatigues and
rough new boots, he sartorial with, glinting in the sun, the polished
brass of the whistle he loved so well.

"Gentlemens," he said. "You all are about to begin the life of a
soldier. My name is Sergeant Quince. Your name is Shit."

War going on in Korea, etc. We would learn how to soldier and
not get our private parts shot off by the gooks whether we liked it
or not. We would "rue the day" (his word) we ever saw his face or
this godforsaken battery area. We would learn to hate him. We
wouldn't have dreamed we were *able* to hate anybody as much as
we were going to hate him. Etc., etc., etc.

"Let's be clear about one thing," he said, looking down from the barracks steps into our upraised, motley, melting-pot faces, "I hate niggers. They're black bastards to me, but I'll just call them niggers for short around here, during duty hours." (A Negro standing next to me winced as if he'd been kicked in the stomach.) "If anybody don't like it, let him go and see the I.G. I also hate Jews, wops, spics, micks, cotton pickers, Georgia crackers, Catholics and Protestants. I hate all of you, damn your eyes."

I really believe he meant it.

At this point, according to the conventions of the Tale of the Bad Sergeant, written or told, the story usually takes a turn, a *peripeteia* of a modest sort. You're supposed to be given a hint of *his* problems before moving on. Let's do it. I have no objection. But I reserve the right to call it giving the devil his due.

We were a crazy mixed-up bunch. Farm boys, black and white, from the Deep South. Street boys from the jungle of fists in the big cities. College boys. Accidents: a thirty-five-year-old lawyer who got drafted by mistake, a cripple who was used for some weeks to fire up the boilers and keep the boiler rooms clean before his medical discharge finally came through. Two fat sullen American Indians . . . Mexican wetbacks. I remember one of these had a fine handlebar mustache. Quince walked up to him and plucked it. "Only two kinds of people can wear a mustache and get away with it," he said, "movie stars and queers." (He used another more vividly descriptive term, but I've never seen that particular one in print except in the Henry Miller books that you have to smuggle in, and since I'm not standing on Innovation, I'll let it pass.) "I don't recall seeing your ugly face in the picture show. Shave it off!" So there we were. I'll give Quince this much credit. He wasn't the least bit interested in "molding us into a fighting team." He wasn't crazy that way. His reach didn't exceed his grasp *that much*. He was merely involved in getting us through a cycle of Basic Training. We hated each other, fought each other singly and in groups in the barracks and the privacy of the boiler rooms (with that poor cripple who was responsible for the care and maintenance thereof cowering in a corner behind the boiler, but armed with a poker lest he too became involved). We stole from each other, ratted on each other, goofed off on each other ("soldiering on the job" this is sometimes called in Real Life with good reason) and thus made every bit of work about twice as hard and twice as long as it had to be.

And, if anything, this situation pleased Quince. He perched on his mobile (on roller skates) Olympus and chewed briars while we played roothog and grabass in the dust and mud below.

Strict? My Lord yes. I would say so. No passes at all during the whole cycle. G.I. Parties every night until our fatigues fell to shreds from splashed Clorox and the rough wood floors were as smooth and white as a stone by the shore. Polished the nailheads nightly too with matchsticks wrapped in cotton, dipped in Brasso. Long night hikes with full field pack. G.I. haircuts (marched to the so-called barber) once a week. Bald as convicts we were. Police Call was always an agony of duck-waddling "assholes and elbows" on our hands and knees like penitents. How he loved Police Call! How he loved Mail Call! Gave out all the letters himself. That is, threw them into the packed hopeful faces and let them fight and scramble for them in the dark. Opened mail and packages when he pleased. Withheld mail for days at a time as a whim. Didn't make soldiers out of us, but tractable brutes. Brutalized, cowed, we marched to and fro like the zombies in mental hospitals that they haven't got time to bother with, so they pump them full of great jolts of tranquilizers. And when we passed by, eyes front, in step, he was complimented by any high-ranking officers that witnessed.

Let me say this for Quince. I know another sergeant who tried exactly the same thing and failed. He was of the same mold as Quince, but somehow subtly defective. In the end he had to fall his troops out of the barracks with a drawn forty-five. Not Quince. His lips touched to the brass whistle, even before he breathed into it, was quite enough to make us shiver.

A sadist too. Individually. Poor white, soft, round, hairy, Jewish Sachs suffered indignities he couldn't have dreamed of in his worst nightmares. Once or twice was nearly drowned in a dirty toilet bowl. Sachs with the other fat and soft boys, Quince's "Fat Man's Squad," had regularly to participate in "weenie races." What's a weenie race? I think Quince invented it. The fat boys kneel down at the starting line, pants and drawers down. Quince produces a package of frankfurters, wrapped in cellophane. One each frankfurter is firmly inserted into each rectum. All in place? Everybody ready? Quince blows the whistle and away they crawl, sometimes a hundred yards going and coming. Last man back has to eat all the frankfurters on the spot. Tears and pleading move Quince not a whit. Nor puking nor anything else.

One time Quince lost his head about one barracks which had someway failed to live up to his expectations. He and his attendant cadre went raging through that barracks, tearing up beds, knocking over wall lockers, and destroying everything "personal" they could get their hands on: cameras, portable radios, fountain pens, books, letters, photographs, etc.

How did these various things happen? You're bound to ask. Didn't anybody go to the Inspector General, the Chaplain, write a Congressman or Mother? Not to my knowledge. Anyone could have, it's true, but all were very young and in mortal fear of the man. Who would be the first to go? No one went. And — *mirabilis!* — nobody cracked up. If anything we got tougher and tougher every day. Gave our souls to God.

Or maybe — entirely justified in your contempt, "Don't give me no sad tales of woe" — you'll just say: "So what: what do you want me to do, punch your TS Card?" That would be to misunderstand. Agreed that in a century like ours these things are small doings, negligible discomforts. It would be sheer sentimentality to claim otherwise. And I'm not cockeyed enough to think that such events could arouse your Pity and Terror. Nothing of Great Men Falling from High Place in our time. A battle in the anthill maybe. No, the simple facts, arranged and related, my hand of cards, will never do that. But they are nevertheless not insignificant. "Why?" you say. "Why bother?" Excuse me, but Maxim Gorky said it once and better than I can, so I quote:

> Why do I relate these abominations? So that you may know, kind sirs, that all is not past and done with! You have a liking for grim fantasies; you are delighted by horrible stories well told; the grotesquely terrible excites you pleasantly. But I know of genuine horrors, everyday terrors, and I have the undeniable right to excite you unpleasantly by telling you about them, in order that you may remember how we live, and under what cir-cumstances. A low and unclean life it is, ours, and that is the truth.
>
> I am a lover of humanity and I have no desire to make anyone miserable, but one must not be sentimental, nor hide the grim

truth with the motley words of beautiful lies. Let us face life as it is! All that is good and human in our hearts needs renewing.

Thus we survived, endured, lived through it, and the cycle came to an end, a screeching halt. Last day on the Range (rocket launchers) we fired $25,000 worth of ammunition into the side of a hill as fast as we could, so that the Range Officer could get back to camp early. If he didn't use the ammo all up, he'd be issued proportionately less for the following day. We were glad to assist him in his dilemma. We fired it away with joy and abandon. What explosions! What flashes of flame and clouds of smoke! It's a wonder we didn't kill each other.

That night we sat in the barracks packing our duffel bags. A fine cold rain was falling outside. And we were quiet inside, lonesome survivors, because somehow you never quite imagined something like that coming to an end. It was a calm, respectable, barracks-room scene. You could have photographed it and mailed the picture home.

Up the steps, weary-footed, his cap soaking wet and his rain-coat beaded with raindrops and dripping, came the old First Sergeant, Cobb. He asked us to gather around, and he talked to us quietly. There had been a personal tragedy in the family of Sergeant Quince. (That bastard had a family?) His wife had been in a terrible automobile accident and was dying. (A *wife* yet?) He wanted to go home before she died. He had to arrange for somebody to look after the children. (*Children?*) The trouble was that this time of the month Sergeant Quince didn't have the money, even for train fare one way. He was broke.

"Why don't he go to the Red Cross?" somebody said.

Sergeant Cobb shrugged. "He ain't got time, I guess," he said. "I know he ain't a kindhearted man, boys. And you don't *have* to do this. It's strictly voluntary. But give a little something. He's human and he needs your help. Give from your heart."

He took a helmet liner off of the top of somebody's wall locker and held it in his hand like a collection plate in church. Somebody hawked and spat on the floor. I didn't think anybody would give anything. We just stood there and stared at Sergeant Cobb until Sachs pushed through to the front.

"Here's my contribution," he said. And he dropped a dime into the helmet liner.

Everybody started to laugh, and even the thick-headed ones caught on. Each of us put a dime in the pot. Ten cents for Sergeant Quince in his hour of need. Sergeant Cobb emptied the liner, put the dimes in his raincoat pocket, placed the liner back on top of the wall locker and started to leave. At the front door he turned around, shook his head and giggled.

"Don't that beat all?" he said. "They done exactly the same thing in all the other barracks too."

Half an hour later we had the exquisite pleasure of looking out of the windows and seeing Sergeant Quince in his Class-A uniform with his double row of World War II ribbons stand in the rain in the middle of the battery area and get soaking wet. He cussed and cussed us and threw those dimes high, wide and handsome and away. He wished us all damnation, death and hell.

This is where it ought to end. It would be a swell place to end, with the picture of Quince *furioso* throwing fountains of dimes in the air. Enraged and possessed and frustrated, like that man wildly digging for nonexistent gold at the end of William Faulkner's *The Hamlet*. Yes, Quince in insane rage, hurling our proffered dimes in the air, wild and black-faced with frustration and tribulation, would be a fine fade-out in the modern manner. But not so. Not so soon did he fade out of my life. Nor, I guess, did I expect him to.

II

Sachs and I went to Leadership School. What happened to the rest of them I wouldn't know and couldn't care less. But Sachs and myself took our duffel bags and waited in front of the orderly room. The harelipped Captain came out and painfully wished us well. We climbed over the tailgate of a deuce and a half and rode to the other side of camp where they try and make you into an NCO in three months flat or turn you into jelly.

"Why are you going?" Sachs asked me. As if I understood at the outset why *he* was doing it. I had hardly spoken to Sachs before that.

"Because that sonofabitch Quince is trash," I said. "I don't like to be pushed around by trash."

Sachs grinned. "You Southerners," he said. "You Southerners and your pride and your squabbles!"

I won't bore you with the sordid details of that place except to say that they made us and we made it. It worked. Sachs shed thirty pounds, went at every bit of it with fury and determination and emerged the top man in the class. Believe it or not. Many a husky specimen fell among the thorns and withered out of school, but Sachs thrived, grew, bloomed. I was in the top ten myself, and both of us made Sergeant out of it. We soldiered night and day like madmen. We learned all the tricks of the trade. When we were finished we were sharp. Bandbox soldiers. The metamorphosis was complete. Still, it's only fair to point out that we kept laughing about it. Sachs called it "being in disguise" and referred to his uniform as a costume. He called us both "the masqueraders." I called myself "the invisible white man."

One anecdote only of that time I'll insert. The Anecdote of the Word. It helps to explain the game we were playing. One week early in the course I was doing badly and it looked like I would wash out. I'd get good marks and only a few gigs one day, poor marks and many the next. The TAC/NCO wrote on my weekly report that he thought I was "a good man," but that I had been "vacillating." He was a college boy himself and used that word. Well, shortly thereafter the Company Commander called us both into his inner sanctum. We got shaped up in a big hurry and reported. His office was a room as bare as a monk's cell except for one huge sign on the wall that read "THIS TOO SHALL PASS." He, the Captain, was a huge hulk of a man, a former All-American tackle from some place or other, a bull neck, a bulging chest behind the desk, and all jaw, lantern and/or granite with the Mussolini thrust to it. He was dead serious. We were quivering arrows at attention in front of him.

"I have this here report before me," he said. "You say here that this soldier has been *vacillating*. What do you mean?"

The TAC gulped and patiently tried to explain what he had meant by means of the image of the pendulum of a grandfather's clock swinging back and forth. The Captain heard him out, nodded.

"Clerk!" he roared.

The Company Clerk came tearing into the room like somebody trying to steal second. Saluted. Quivered too!

"Get me a dictionary."

We waited in breathless anticipation. The clerk soon returned with the dictionary. Captain opened it to the *v*'s and followed his index finger, thick and blunt-ended as a chisel, down the line of words. Looked at the word a while and the definition. It was a pocket dictionary and defined as follows:

VAC-IL-LATE, v.i.,-LATED,-LATING. 1. Waver; stagger 2. fluctuate 3. be irresolute or hesitant.

"Nothing about pendulums," he noted. "Damn good word, though. Good word."

He wrote it down on a pad in capitals and underlined it several times. That was that. We were dismissed.

Now from that Orderly Room issued forth each week reams of mimeographed material for the benefit of all students. Ever after that incident the Captain cautioned that those who wished to complete the course successfully *must not vacillate!* This got to be a standing joke in that mirthless place.

"If I catch any of you guys *vacillating* in the company area," the TAC used to tell us, "you've had it."

Sachs and I made it, were transformed from anarchists to impeccable sergeanthood. We didn't end up going to Korea to be shot at, but instead were sent to Europe to join a very sharp outfit where we would be able to maintain the high standards we had so recently acquired. Which we did for the rest of our service time. Sachs was so good he even made Sergeant First Class without time in grade.

More than a year later we were in Germany for maneuvers. It was the middle of summer and we were living in tents. In the evenings we used to go to a huge circus tent of a beer hall and get drunk. It was there one hot night that we met Quince again. He was sitting all alone at a table with a big crowd of empty 3.2 beer cans around him. He was a corporal now, two stripes down, and by the patch on his shoulder we knew he was in a mucked-up outfit, a whole division of stumblebums with a well-known cretin commanding. He looked it, too. His uniform was dirty. His shirt was open all the way down the front, revealing a filthy, sweat-soaked T-shirt. Of course it's hard to look sharp if you're living in the field in the middle of the summer. But Sachs and I took pride in our ability to look as sharp in the field as in garrison. It took some doing, but we could do it.

"Let's buy the bastard a beer," Sachs said.

He seemed glad to see us as if we were dear, old, long-lost friends. Once we had introduced ourselves, that is. He didn't recognize us at first. He marveled at our transformation and good luck. We couldn't help marveling at *his* transformation too. ("This is the worst outfit I was ever with," he admitted. "The Battery Commander has got it in for me.") He bought us a round and we bought more.

Late, just before they shut the place down and threw everybody out, Quince went maudlin. A crying drunk.

"I can't explain it, but it makes me feel bad to see you guys like this," he said. "I hated you guys, I'll admit that. Long before the dimes. But I didn't know you hated me so much."

"What do you mean by that?"

"To hunt me down after all this time and shame me. Soldiering is my life. It's just a couple of years for you guys. And here you are with all this rank looking like old soldiers. Sergeants! Goddamn, it isn't fair."

"Do you know what the Army is, Quince?"

"What? What's that?"

"I'll tell you what the Army is to me," Sachs said. "It's just a game, a stupid, brutal, pointless, simple-minded game. And you know what, Corporal Quince? I beat that game. I won. I'm a better soldier now than you ever were or ever will be and it doesn't mean a thing to me."

Quince turned his head away from us so we wouldn't see him crying.

"You hadn't ought to have said that," he said. "You can't take everything away from a guy. You got to leave a guy something."

We left him to cry in his beer until they tossed him out, and walked back under the stars to our tents, singing the whole way. We sat in our sleeping bags and had a smoke before we flaked out.

"You were great," I told Sachs. "That was worth waiting for."

But Sachs was a moody kind of a guy. He didn't see it that way. He was angry, in fact.

"You can't beat them down," he said. "No matter what you do. They always win out in the end. Sure I got in my licks. But he won anyway. *He made me do it.* That was the Quince in me kicking him while he's down. So in the end he still beat me."

"You worry about yourself too much."

"That's just the way I am," he said bitterly.

"You don't feel *sorry* for him, do you?"

That was a dumb question. Sachs was no Herman Wouk.

"Hell no," he said. "You don't get it. The trouble is I still hate him. I hate him worse than ever."

And he stubbed out his cigarette and turned over and went to sleep without another word, leaving me to ponder on that for a while.

THE PEDERSEN KID

BY W. H. GASS

Part One

1

*B*IG HANS yelled, so I came out. The barn was dark but the sun burned on the snow. Hans was carrying something from the crib. I yelled but Big Hans didn't hear. He was in the house with what he had before I reached the steps.

It was the Pedersen kid. Hans had put the kid on the kitchen table like you would a ham and started the kettle. He wasn't saying anything. I guess he figured one yell from the crib was enough noise. Ma was fumbling with the kid's clothes which were stiff with ice. She made a sound like "whew" from every outgoing breath. The kettle filled and Hans said,

"Get some snow and call your pa."

"Why?"

"Get some snow."

I took the big pail from under the sink and the shovel by the stove. I didn't hurry and nobody said anything. There was a drift over the edge of the porch and I spaded some out of that. When I brought the pail in, Hans said,

"There's coal dust in that. Get more."

"A little coal won't hurt."

"Get more."

"Coal's warming."

"It's not enough. Shut your mouth and get your pa."

Ma had rolled out some dough on the table where Hans had

dropped the Pedersen kid like a filling. Most of the kid's clothes lay on the floor where they were going to make a puddle. Hans began rubbing snow on the kid's face. Ma stopped undressing him for a moment and simply stood by the table with her hands held away from her as if they were wet, staring first at Big Hans and then at the kid.

"Get."

"Why?"

"I told you."

"It's Pa I mean — "

"I know what you mean. Get."

I found a cardboard box that condensed milk had come in and shoveled it full of snow. It was too small. I figured it would be. I found another with rags and an old sponge I threw out. Campbell's soup. I filled it too, using the rest of the drift. Snow would melt through the bottom of the boxes but that was all right with me. By now the kid was naked. I was satisfied mine was bigger.

"Looks like a sick shoat, don't he?"

"Shut up and get your pa."

"He's alseep."

"Yeah."

"He don't like to get waked."

"I know that. Don't I know that as good as you? Get him."

"What good'll he be?"

"We're going to need his whisky."

"He can fix that all right. He's good for fixing the crack in his face. If it ain't all gone."

The kettle was whistling.

"What are we going to do with these?" Ma said.

"Wait, Hed. Now I want you to get. I'm tired of talking. Get, you hear?"

"What are we going to do with them? They're all wet," she said.

I went to wake the old man. He didn't like being roused. It was too hard and far to come, the sleep he was in. He didn't give a damn about the Pedersen kid, any more than I did. Pedersen's kid was just a kid. He didn't carry any weight. Not like I did. And the old man would be mad, unable to see, coming that way from where he was asleep. I decided I hated Big Hans, though this was hardly something new for me. I hated Big Hans just then because I was thinking of how Pa's eyes would blink at me — as if I were the sun off the snow and burning to blind him. His eyes were old and they never saw well, but heated with whisky they'd glare at my noise, growing red and raising up his rage. I decided I hated the Pedersen kid too, dying in our kitchen while I was away where I couldn't watch, dying just to entertain Hans and making me go up snapping steps and down a drafty hall, Pa lumped under the covers at the end like dung covered with snow, snoring and whistling. Oh he'd not care about the Pedersen kid. He'd not care about getting waked so he could give up some of his whisky to a slit of a kid and maybe lose one of his hiding places in the bargain. That would make him mad enough if he was sober. I didn't hurry though it was cold and the Pedersen kid was in the kitchen.

He was all shoveled up like I thought he'd be. I pushed at his shoulder, calling his name. I think his name stopped the snoring but he didn't move except to roll a little when I shoved him. The covers slid down his skinny neck so I saw his head, fuzzed like a dandelion gone to seed, but his face was turned to the wall — there was the pale shadow of his nose on the plaster — and I thought, Well you don't look much like a pig-drunk bully now. I couldn't be sure he was still asleep. He was a cagey sonofabitch. I shook him a little harder and made some noise. "Pap-pap-pap-hey," I said.

I was leaning too far over. I knew better. He always slept close to the wall so you had to lean to reach him. Oh he was smart. It put you off. I knew better but I was thinking of the Pedersen kid mother-naked in all that dough. When his arm came up I ducked away but it caught me on the side of the neck, watering my eyes, and I backed off to cough. Pa was on his side, looking at me, his eyes winking, the hand that had hit me a fist in the pillow.

"Get the hell out of here."

I didn't say anything, trying to get my throat clear, but I watched him. He was like a mean horse to come at from the rear. It was better, though, he'd hit me. He was bitter when he missed.

"Get the hell out of here."

"Big Hans sent me. He told me to wake you."

"A fat hell on Big Hans. Get out of here."

"He found the Pedersen kid by the crib."

"Get the hell out."

Pa pulled at the covers. He was tasting his mouth.

"The kid's froze good. Hans is rubbing him with snow. He's got him in the kitchen."

"Pedersen?"

"No, Pa. It's the Pedersen kid. The kid."

"Nothing to steal from the crib."

"Not stealing, Pa. He was just lying there. Hans found him froze. That's where he was when Hans found him."

Pa laughed.

"I ain't hid nothing in the crib."

"You don't understand, Pa. The Pedersen kid. The kid — "

"I god damn well understand."

Pa had his head up, glaring, his teeth gnawing at the place where he'd grown a mustache once.

"I god damn well understand. You know I don't want to see Pedersen. That cock. Why should I? What did he come for, hey? God dammit, get. And don't come back. Find out something. You're a fool. Both you and Hans. Pedersen. That cock. Don't come back. Out. Out."

He was shouting and breathing hard and closing his fist on the pillow. He had long black hairs on his wrist. They curled around the cuff of his nightshirt.

"Big Hans made me come. Big Hans said — "

"A fat hell on Big Hans. He's an even bigger fool than you are. Fat, hey? I taught him, dammit, and I'll teach you. Out. You want me to drop my pot?"

He was about to get up so I got out, slamming the door. He was beginning to see he was too mad to sleep. Then he threw things. Once he went after Hans and dumped his pot over the banister. Pa'd been shit-sick in that pot. Hans got an axe. He didn't even bother to wipe himself off and he chopped part of Pa's door down before he stopped. He might not have gone that far if Pa hadn't been locked in laughing fit to shake the house. That pot put Pa in an awful good humor whenever he thought of it. I always felt the memory was present in both of them, stirring in their chests like a laugh or a growl, as eager as an animal to be out. I heard Pa cursing all the way downstairs.

Hans had laid steaming towels over the kid's chest and stomach. He was rubbing snow on the kid's legs and feet. Water from the snow and water from the towels had run off the kid to the table where the dough was, and the dough was turning pasty, sticking to the kid's back and behind.

"Ain't he going to wake up?"

"What about your pa?"

"He was awake when I left."

"What'd he say? Did you get the whisky?"

"He said a fat hell on Big Hans."

"Don't be smart. Did you ask him about the whisky?"

"Yeah."

"Well?"

"He said a fat hell on Big Hans."

"Don't be smart. What's he going to do?"

"Go back to sleep most likely."

"You'd best get that whisky."

"You go. Take the axe. Pa's scared to hell of axes."

"Listen to me, Jorge, I've had enough to your sassing. This kid's froze bad. If I don't get some whisky down him he might die. You want the kid to die? Do you? Well, get your pa and get that whisky."

"Pa don't care about the kid."

"Jorge."

"Well he don't. He don't care at all, and I don't care to get my head busted neither. He don't care, and I don't care to have his shit flung on me. He don't care about anybody. All he cares about is his whisky and that dry crack in his face. Get pig-drunk — that's what he wants. He don't care about nothing else at all. Nothing. Not Pedersen's kid neither. That cock. Not the kid neither."

"I'll get the spirits," Ma said.

I'd wound Big Hans up tight. I was ready to jump but when Ma said she'd get the whisky it surprised him like it surprised me, and he ran down. Ma never went near the old man when he was sleeping it off. Not any more. Not for years. The first thing every morning when she washed her face she could see the scar on her chin where he'd cut her with a boot cleat, and maybe she saw him heaving it again, the dirty sock popping out as it flew. It should have been nearly as easy for her to remember that as it was for Big Hans to remember going after the axe while he was still spattered with Pa's yellow sick insides.

"No you won't," Big Hans said.

"Yes, Hans, if they're needed," Ma said.

Hans shook his head but neither of us tried to stop her. If we had, then one of us would have had to go instead. Hans rubbed the kid with more snow . . . rubbed . . . rubbed.

"I'll get more snow," I said. I took the pail and shovel and went out on the porch. I don't know where Ma went. I thought she'd gone upstairs and expected to hear she had. She had surprised Hans like she had surprised me when she said she'd go, and then she surprised him again when she came back so quick like she must have, because when I came in with the snow she was there with a bottle with three white feathers on its label and Hans was holding it angrily by the throat.

Oh, he was being queer and careful, pawing about in the drawer and holding the bottle like a snake at the length of his arm. He was awful angry because he'd thought Ma was going to do something big, something heroic even, especially for her . . . I know him . . . I know him . . . we felt the same sometimes . . . while Ma wasn't thinking about that at all, not anything like that. There was no way of getting even. It wasn't like getting cheated at the fair. They were always trying so you got to expect it. Now Hans had given Ma something of his — we both had when we thought she was going straight to Pa — something valuable; but since she didn't know we'd given it to her, there was no easy way of getting it back.

Hans cut the foil off finally and unscrewed the cap. He was put out too because there was only one way of understanding what she'd done. Ma had found one of Pa's hiding places. She'd found one and she hadn't said a word while Big Hans and I had hunted and hunted as we always did all winter, every winter since the spring that Hans had come and I had looked in the privy and found the first one. Pa had a knack for hiding. He knew we were looking and he enjoyed it. But now Ma. She'd found it by luck most likely but she hadn't said anything and we didn't know how long ago it'd been or how many other ones she'd found, saying nothing. Pa was sure to find out. Sometimes he didn't seem to because he hid them so well he couldn't find them himself or because he looked and didn't find anything and figured he hadn't hid one after all or had drunk it up. But he'd find out about this one because we were

using it. A fool could see what was going on. If he found out Ma
found it — that'd be bad. He took pride in his hiding. It was all
the pride he had. I guess fooling Hans and me took doing. But he
didn't figure Ma for much. He didn't figure her at all, and if he
found out . . . a woman . . . it'd be bad.

Hans poured some in a tumbler.

"You going to put more towels on him?"

"No."

"Why not? That's what he needs, something warm to his skin,
don't he?"

"Not where he's froze good. Heat's bad for frostbite. That's
why I only put towels on his chest and belly. He's got to thaw slow.
You ought to know that."

Colors on the towels had run.

Ma poked her toe in the kid's clothes.

"What are we going to do with these?"

Big Hans began pouring whisky in the kid's mouth but his mouth
filled without any getting down his throat and in a second it was
dripping from his chin.

"Here, help me prop him up. I got to hold his mouth open."

I didn't want to touch him and I hoped Ma would do it but she
kept looking at the kid's clothes piled on the floor and the pool of
water by them and didn't make any move to.

"Come on, Jorge."

"All right."

"Lift, don't shove . . . lift."

"O.K., I'm lifting."

I took him by the shoulders. His head flopped back. His mouth
fell open. The skin on his neck was tight. He was cold all right.

"Hold his head up. He'll choke."

"His mouth is open."

"His throat's shut. He'll choke."

"He'll choke anyway."

"Hold his head up."

"I can't."

"Don't hold him like that. Put your arms around him."

"Well Jesus."

He was cold all right. I put my arm carefully around him. Hans
had his fingers in the kid's mouth.

"Now he'll choke for sure."

"Shut up. Just hold him like I told you."

He was cold all right, and wet. I had my arm behind his back. He sure felt dead.

"Tilt his head back a bit . . . not too much."

He felt cold and slimy. He sure was dead. We had a dead body in our kitchen. All this time he'd been dead. When Hans had brought him in, he'd been dead. I couldn't see him breathing. He was awful skinny, sunk between the ribs. We were getting him ready to bake. Hans was basting him. I had my arm around him, holding him up. He was dead and I had hold of him. I could feel my muscles jumping.

"Well Jesus Christ."

"He's dead, Hans. He's dead."

"You dropped him."

"Dead?" Ma said.

"He's dead. I could feel. He's dead."

"Dead?"

"Ain't you got any sense? You let his head hit the table."

"Is he dead? Is he dead?" Ma said.

"Well Christ no, not yet, not yet he's not dead. Look what you done, Jorge, there's whisky all over."

"He *is* dead. He *is*."

"Now he ain't. Not yet he ain't. Now stop yelling and hold him up."

"He ain't breathing."

"Yes he is, he *is* breathing. Hold him up."

"I ain't. I ain't holding any dead body. You can hold it if you want. You dribble whisky on it all you want. You can do anything you want to. I ain't. I ain't holding any dead body."

"If he's dead," Ma said, "what are we going to do with these?"

"Jorge, god damn you, come back here."

I went down to the crib where Big Hans had found him. There was still a hollow in the snow and some prints the wind hadn't sifted snow over. The kid must have been out on his feet, they wobbled so. I could see where he had walked smack into a drift and then backed off and lurched up beside the crib, maybe bumping into it before he fell, then lying quiet so the snow had time to curl around him, piling up until in no time it would have covered him completely. Who knows, I thought, the way it's been snowing, we mightn't have found him till spring. Even if he was dead in our kitchen, I was glad Big Hans had found him. I could see myself coming out of the house some morning with the sun high up and strong and the eaves dripping, the snow speckled with drops and the ice on the creek slushing up; coming out and walking down by the crib on the crusts of the drift . . . coming out to play my game with the drifts . . . and I could see myself losing, breaking through the big drift that was always sleeping up against the crib and running a foot right into him, right into the Pedersen kid curled up, getting soft.

That would have been worse than holding his body in the kitchen. The feeling would have come on quicker, and it would have been worse, happening in the middle of a game. There wouldn't have been any warning, any way of getting ready for it to happen, to know what I'd struck before I bent down, even though Old Man Pedersen would have come over between snows looking for the kid most likely and everybody would have figured that the kid was lying buried somewhere under the snow; that maybe after a high wind someday somebody would find him lying like a black stone uncovered in a field; but probably in the spring somebody would find him in some back pasture thawing out with the mud and have to bring him in and take him over to the Pedersen place and present him to Missus Pedersen. Even so: even with everyone knowing that, and hoping one of the Pedersens would find him first so they wouldn't have to pry him up out of the mud to fetch him out from a thicket and bring him in and give him to Missus Pedersen in soggy season-old clothes; even then, who would expect to stick a foot all of a sudden through the crust losing at the drift game and step on Pedersen's kid lying all crouched together right beside your own crib? It was a good thing Hans had come down this morning and found him, even if he was dead in our kitchen and I had held him up.

When Pedersen came over asking for his kid, maybe hoping that the kid had got to our place all right and stayed, waiting for the blizzard to quit before going home. Pa would meet him and bring him for a drink and tell him it was his fault for putting up all those snow fences. If I knew Pa, he'd tell Pedersen to look under the drifts his snow fences had made, and Pedersen would get so mad he'd go for Pa and stomp out calling for the vengeance of God like he was fond of doing. Now though, since Big Hans had found him, and he was dead in our kitchen, Pa might not say much when Pedersen came. He might just offer Pedersen a drink and keep his mouth shut about those snow fences. Pedersen might come yet this morning. That would be best because Pa would be still asleep. If Pa was asleep when Pedersen came he wouldn't have a chance to talk about those snow fences, or offer Pedersen a drink. Pedersen wouldn't have to refuse the drink then and could take his kid and go home. I hoped Pedersen would certainly come soon. I hoped he would come and take that cold damp body out of our kitchen. The way I felt I didn't think that today I'd be able to eat. I knew every time I'd see the Pedersen kid in the kitchen being fixed for the table.

The wind had dropped. The sun lay burning on the snow. I got cold just the same. I didn't want to go in but I could feel the cold crawling over me like it must have crawled over him while he was coming. It had slipped over him like a sheet, icy at first, especially around the feet, and he'd likely wiggled his toes in his boots and wanted to wrap his legs around each other like you do when you first come to bed. But then things would begin to warm up some, the sheet feeling warmer all the time until it felt real cozy and you went to sleep. Only when the kid went to sleep by our crib it wasn't like going to sleep in bed because the sheet never really got warm and he never really got warm either. Now he was just as cold in our kitchen with the kettle whistling and Ma getting ready to bake as I was out by the crib jigging my feet in our snow. I had to go in. I looked but I couldn't see anyone trying to come down where the road was. All I could see was a set of half-filled prints jiggling crazily away into the snow until they sank under a drift. There wasn't anything around. There wasn't anything: a tree or a stick or a rock whipped bare or a bush hugged by snow sticking up to mark the place where those prints came up out of the drift like somebody had come up from underground.

I decided to go around by the front though I wasn't allowed to track through the front room. I went back, thinking of where the kid lay on the kitchen table in all that dough, pasty with whisky and water, like spring had come all at once to our kitchen, and our all the time not knowing he was there, had thawed the top of his grave

off and left him for us to find, stretched out cold and stiff and bare;
and who was it that was going to have to take him to the Pedersen
place and give him to Missus Pederson, naked, and flour on his bare
behind?

2

"Just his back. The green mackinaw. The black stocking cap.
The yellow gloves. The gun."

Big Hans kept repeating it. He was letting the meaning have a
chance to change. He'd look at me and shake his head and say it
over.

"He put them down the cellar so I ran."

Hans filled the tumbler. It was spotted with whisky and flecks
of flour.

"He didn't say nothing the whole time," Hans said.

He put the bottle on the table and the bottom sank unevenly in
the paste, tilting heavily and queerly to one side — acting crazy,
like everything else.

"That's all he says he saw," Hans said, staring at the mark of the
kid's behind in the dough. "Just his back. The green mackinaw.
The black stocking cap. The yellow gloves. The gun."

"That's all?"

He waited and waited.

"That's all."

He tossed the whisky off and peered at the bottom of the glass.

"Now why should he remember all them colors?"

He leaned over, his legs apart, his elbows on his knees, and held
the glass between them with both hands, tilting it to watch the
liquor that was left roll back and forth across the bottom.

"How does he know? I mean, for sure."

"He thinks he knows," Hans said in a tired voice. "He thinks he
knows."

He picked up the bottle and a hunk of dough was stuck to it.

"Christ. That's all. It's how he feels. It's enough, ain't it?"
Hans said.

"What a mess," Ma said.

"He was raving," Hans said. "He couldn't think of anything else.
He had to talk. He had to get it out. You should have heard him
grunt."

"Poor poor Stevie," Ma said.

"He was raving?"

"All right, is it something you dream?" Hans said.

"He must have been dreaming. Look — how could he have got there. Where'd he come from? Fall from the sky?"

"He came through the storm."

"That's just it, Hans, he'd have had to. It was blizzarding all day. It didn't let up, did it? till late afternoon. He'd have had to. Now what chance is there of that? What?"

"Enough a chance it happened," Hans said.

"But listen. Jesus. He's a stranger. If he's a stranger he's come a ways. He'd never make it in a blizzard, not even knowing the country."

"He came through the storm. He came out of the ground like a grub. He came."

Hans poured himself a drink, not me.

"He came through the storm," he said. "He came through just like the kid came through. The kid had no chance neither, but he came. He's here, ain't he? He's right upstairs, right now. You got to believe that."

"It wasn't blizzarding when the kid came."

"It was starting."

"That ain't the same."

"All right. The kid had forty-five minutes, maybe an hour before it started to come on good. That isn't enough. You need the whole time, not a start. In a blizzard you got to be where you're going if you're going to get there."

"That's what I mean. See, Hans? See? The kid had a chance. He knew the way. He had a head start. Besides, he was scared. He ain't going to be lazying. And he's lucky. He had a chance to be lucky. Now yellow gloves ain't got that chance. He has to come farther. He has to come through the storm all the way. But he don't know the way, and he ain't scared proper, except maybe by the storm. He hasn't got a chance to be lucky."

"The kid was scared, you said. Right. Now why? You tell me that."

Hans kept his eyes on the whisky that was shining in his glass. He didn't want to give in. He was holding on hard.

"And yellow gloves — he ain't scared?" he said. "How do you

know he ain't scared, by something else besides wind and snow and cold and howling, I mean?"

"All right, I don't know, but it's likely ain't it? Anyway, the kid, well, maybe he ain't scared at all, starting out. Maybe his pa was just looking to tan him and he lit out. Then first thing he knows it's blizzarding again and he's lost, and when he gets to our crib he don't know where he is."

Hans slowly shook his head.

"Yes yes, hell Hans, the kid's scared of having run away. He don't want to say he done a fool stunt like that. So he makes the whole thing up. He's just a little kid. He made the whole thing up."

Hans didn't like that. He didn't want to believe the kid any more than I did, but if he didn't then the kid had fooled him sure. He didn't want to believe that either.

"No," he said. "Is it something you make up? It is something you come to, raving with frostbite and fever and not knowing who's there or where you are or anything, and make up?"

"Yeah."

"No it ain't. You don't make up them colors neither. You don't make up putting your folks down cellar where they'll freeze. You don't make up his not saying anything the whole time or only seeing his back or exactly what he was wearing. It's like something you see once and it hits you so hard you never forget it even if you want to; like something that sticks to you like burs you try and brush off while you're doing something else, but they never brush off, just roll a little, and first thing you know you ain't doing what you set out to, you're just trying to get them burs off. I know. I got things stuck to me like that. Everybody has. Pretty soon you get tired trying to pick them off. If they was just burs, it wouldn't matter, but they ain't. They never is. The kid saw something that hit him hard like that; hit him so hard that probably all the time he was running over here he didn't see anything else but what hit him. Not really. It hit him so hard he couldn't do anything but spit it out raving when he come to. You don't make things like that up, Jorge. No. He came through the storm, just like the kid. He had no business coming, but he came. I don't know how or why or when exactly, except it must have been during the blizzard yesterday. He got to the Pedersen place just before or just after it stopped snowing. He got there and he shoved them all in the fruit cellar to freeze and I'll bet he had his reasons."

"You got dough stuck to the bottom of your bottle."

I couldn't think of anything else to say. It sounded right. It sounded right but it couldn't be right. It just couldn't be. Whatever was right, the Pedersen kid had run off from his pa's place probably late yesterday afternoon when the storm let up, and had turned up at our crib this morning. I knew he was here. I knew that much. I'd held him. I'd felt him dead in my hands, only I guess he wasn't dead now. Hans had put him to bed upstairs but I could still see him in the kitchen, so skinny naked, two towels steaming on him, whisky drooling from the corners of his mouth, lines of dirt between his toes, squeezing Ma's dough in the shape of his behind.

I reached for the bottle. Hans held it away.

"He didn't see him do it though," I said.

Hans shrugged.

"Then he ain't sure."

"He's sure, I told you. Do you run out in a blizzard unless you're sure?"

"It wasn't blizzarding."

"It was starting."

"I don't run out in blizzards."

"Crap."

Hans pointed the doughy end of the bottle at me.

"Crap."

He shook it.

"You come in from the barn — like this morning. As far as you know there ain't a gun in yellow gloves in a thousand miles. You come in from the barn not thinking anything special. You just get inside when you see a guy you never saw before, the guy that wasn't in a thousand miles, that wasn't in your mind even, he was so far away, and he's wearing them yellow gloves and that green mackinaw, and he's got me and your ma and pa lined up with our hands back of our necks like this — "

Hans hung the bottle and the glass behind his head.

" — he's got a rifle in between them yellow gloves and he's waving the point of it up and down in front of your ma's face real slow and quiet."

Hans got up and waved the bottle violently in Ma's face. She shivered and shooed it away. Hans stopped to come to me. He stood over me, his black eyes buttons on his big face, and I tried to look like I wasn't hunching down any in my chair.

"What do you do?" Hans roared. "You drop a little kid's head on the table."

"Like hell — "

Hans had the bottle in front of him again, smack in my face.

"Hans Esbyorn," Ma said, "don't pester the boy."

"Like hell — "

"Jorge."

"I wouldn't run, Ma."

Ma sighed. "I don't know. But don't yell."

"Well Christ almighty, Ma."

"Don't swear neither. Please. You been swearing too much — you and Hans both."

"But I wouldn't run."

"Yes, Jorgie, yes. I'm sure you wouldn't run," she said.

Hans went back and sat down and finished his drink and poured another. He could relax now he'd got me all strung up. He was a fancy bastard.

"You'd run all right," he said, running his tongue across his lips. "Maybe you'd be right to run. Maybe anybody would. With no gun, with nothing to stop him."

"Poor child. Whewee. And what are we going to do with these?"

"Hang them up, Hed, for Christ's sake."

"Where?"

"Well, where do you mostly?"

"Oh no," she said, "I wouldn't feel right doing that."

"Then Jesus, Hed, I don't know. Jesus."

"Please Hans, please. Those words are hard for me to bear."

She stared at the ceiling.

"Dear. The kitchen's such a mess. I can't bear to see it. And the baking's not done."

That's all she could think of. That's all she had to say. She didn't care about me. I didn't count. Not like her kitchen. I wouldn't have run.

"Stick the baking," I said.

"Shut your face."

He could look as mean as he liked, I didn't care. What was his meanness to me? A blister on my heel, another discomfort, a cold bed. Yet when he took his eyes off me to drink, I felt better. I was going to twist his balls.

"All right," I said. "All right. All right."

He was lost in his glass, thinking it out.

"They're awful cold in that cellar," I said.

There was a little liquor burning in the bottom. I was going to twist his balls like the neck of a sack.

"What are you going to do about it?"

He was putting his mean look back but it lacked enthusiasm. He was seeing things in his glass.

"I saved the kid, didn't I?" he finally said.

"Maybe you did."

"You didn't."

"No. I didn't."

"It's time you did something then, ain't it?"

"Why should I? I don't think they're freezing. You're the one who thinks that. You're the one who thinks he ran for help. You're the one. You saved him. All right. You didn't let his head hit the table. I did that. You didn't. No. It was you who rubbed him. All right. You saved him. That wasn't the kid's idea though. He came for help. According to you, that is. He didn't come to be saved. You saved him, but what are you going to do now to help him? You've been feeling mighty, ain't you? thinking how you did it. Still feel like a savior, Hans? How's it feel?"

"You little bastard."

"All right. Little or big. Never mind. You did it all. You found him. You raised the rumpus, ordering everybody around. He was as good as dead. I held him and I felt him. Maybe in your way he was alive, but it was a way that don't count. No, but you couldn't leave him alone. Rubbing. Well, I felt him . . . cold . . . God! Ain't you proud? He was dead, right here, dead. And there weren't no yellow gloves. Now, though, there is. That's what comes of rubbing. Rubbing . . . ain't you proud? You can't believe the kid was lying good enough to fool you. So he was dead. But now he ain't. Not for you. He ain't for you."

"He's alive for you too. You're crazy. He's alive for everybody."

"No he ain't. He ain't alive for me. He never was. I never seen him except he was dead. Cold . . . I felt him . . . God! He's in your bed. All right. You took him up there. It's your bed he's in, Hans. It was you he babbled to. You believe him too, so he's alive for you, then. Not for me. Not for me he ain't."

"You can't say that."

"I am saying it though. Rubbing . . . You didn't know what you was bringing to, did you? Something besides the kid came through the storm, Hans. I ain't saying yellow gloves did neither. He didn't. He couldn't. But something else did. While you was rubbing you didn't think of that."

"You little bastard."

"Hans, Hans, please," Ma said.

"Never mind that. Little or big, like I said. I'm asking what you're going to do. You believe it. You made it. What are you going to do about it? It'd be funny if right now while we're sitting here the kid's dying upstairs."

"Jorge," Ma said, "what an awful thing — in Hans's bed."

"All right. But suppose. Suppose you didn't rub enough — not long and hard enough, Hans. And suppose he dies up there in your bed. He might. He was cold, I know. That'd be funny because that yellow gloves — he won't die. It ain't going to be so easy, killing him."

Hans didn't move or say anything.

"I ain't no judge. I ain't no hand at saving, like you said. It don't make no difference to me. But why'd you start rubbing if you was going to stop? Seems like it'd be terrible if the Pedersen kid was to have come all that way through the storm, scared and freezing, and you was to have done all that rubbing and saving so he could come to and tell you his fancy tale and have you believe it, if you ain't going to do nothing now but sit and hold hands with that bottle. That ain't a bur so easy picked off."

Still he didn't say anything.

"Fruit cellars get mighty cold. Of course they ain't supposed to freeze."

I leaned back easy in my chair. Hans just sat.

The top of the kitchen table looked muddy where it showed. Patches of dough and pools of water were scattered all over it. There were rusty streaks through the paste and the towels had run. Everywhere there were little sandy puddles of whisky and

water. Something, it looked like whisky, dripped slowly to the floor
and with the water trickled to the puddle by the pile of clothes.
The boxes sagged. There were thick black tracks around the table and the stove. I thought it was funny the boxes had gone so
fast. The bottle and the glass were posts around which Big Hans
had his hands.

Ma began picking up the kid's clothes. She picked them up one
at a time, delicately, by their ends and corners, lifting a sleeve like
you would the flat, burned, crooked leg of a frog dead of summer
to toss it from the road. They didn't seem human things, the way
her hands pinched together on them, but animal — dead and rotting things out of the ground. She took them away and when she
came back I wanted to tell her to bury them — to hide them somehow quick under the snow — but she scared me, the way she came
with her arms out, trembling, fingers coming open and closed,
moving like a combine between rows.

I heard the dripping clearly, and Hans swallow. I heard the
water and the whisky fall. I heard the frost on the window melt to
the sill and drop into the sink. Hans poured whisky in his glass. I
looked past Hans and Pa was watching from the doorway. His nose
and eyes were red, his feet in red slippers.

"What's this about the Pedersen kid?" he said.

Ma stood behind him with a mop.

3

"Ever think of a horse?" Pa said.

"A horse? Where'd he get a horse?"

"Anywhere — on the way — anyplace."

"Could he make it on a horse?"

"He made it on something."

"Not on a horse, though."

"Not on his feet."

"I ain't saying he made it on anything."

"Horses can't get lost."

"Yes they can."

"They got a sense."

"That's a lot of manure about horses."

"In a blizzard a horse'll go home."

"That's so."

"You let them go and they go home."

"That's so."

"If you steal a horse, and let him go, he'll take you to the barn you stole him from."

"Couldn't give him his head then."

"Must have really rode him then."

"If he had a horse."

"Yeah, if he had a horse."

"If he hooked a horse before the storm and rode it a ways, then when the snow came, the horse would be too far off and wouldn't know how to head for home."

"They got an awful good sense."

"Manure."

"What difference does it make? He made it. What difference does it make how?" Hans said.

"I'm considering if he could have," Pa said.

"And I'm telling you he did," Hans said.

"And I've been telling you he didn't. The kid made the whole thing up," I said.

"The horse'd stop. He'd put his head into the wind and stop."

"I've seen them put their rears in."

"They always put their heads in."

"He could jockey him."

"If he was gentle and not too scared."

"A plower is gentle."

"Some are."

"Some don't like to be rid."

"Some don't like strangers neither."

"What the hell," Hans said.

Pa laughed. "I'm just considering," he said. "Just considering, Hans, that's all."

Pa'd seen the bottle right away. He'd been blinking but he hadn't missed that. He'd seen it and the glass in Hans's hand. I'd expected him to say something. So had Hans. He'd held on to the glass long enough so no one would get the idea he was afraid to, then he'd set it down casual, like he hadn't any reason to hold it or any reason to put it down, but was putting it down anyway, without thinking. I'd grinned but he hadn't seen me, or else he made out he hadn't. Pa'd kept his mouth shut about the bottle. I guess we had the Pedersen kid to thank for that, though we had him to thank for the bottle too.

"It's his own fault for putting out all them snow fences," Pa said. "You think, being here the time he has, he'd know the forces better."

"Pedersen just likes to be ready, Pa, that's all."

"Hell he does. He likes to *get* ready, that cock. Get, get, get, get. He's always getting ready, but he ain't never got ready. Not yet, he ain't. Last summer, instead of minding his crops, he got ready for hoppers. Christ. Who wants hoppers? Well, that's the way to get hoppers — that's the sure way — get ready for hoppers."

"Bull."

"Bull? You say bull, Hans, hey?"

"I say bull, yeah."

"You're one to get ready, ain't you? Like Pedersen, ain't you? Oh what a wrinkled scrotum you got, with all that thinking. You'd put out poison for a million, hey? You know what you'd get? Two million. Wise, oh the wise men, yeah. Pedersen asked for hoppers. He begged for hoppers. He went on his knees for hoppers. And he got hoppers. That just exactly how you get hoppers. So me? I got hoppers too. Now he's gone and asked for snow, gone on his knees for snow, wrung his fingers for snow. Is he ready, tell me? Hey? Snow? For real snow? Anybody ever ready for real snow? Oh Jesus, that fool. He should have kept his kid behind them fences. What business . . . what . . . what business . . . to send him here. Look — " Pa pointed out the window. "See . . . see . . . what did I tell you . . . snowing . . . always snowing . . ."

"You seen a winter it didn't snow?"

"You were ready, I guess."

"It always snows."

"You were ready for the Pedersen kid, too, I guess. You was just out there waiting for him, cooling your cod."

Pa laughed and Hans got red.

"Pedersen's a fool. Wise men can't be taught. Oh no, not old holy Pete. He never learned all the things that can fall out the sky and happen to wheat. His neck's bent all the time too, studying clouds, hah — that shit. He don't even keep an eye on his kid in a blizzard. But you'll keep an eye out for him, hey Hans? You're a bigger fool because you're fatter."

Hans's face was red and swollen like the skin around a splinter. He reached out and picked up the glass. Pa was sitting on a corner of the kitchen table, swinging a leg. The glass was near his knee. Hans reached by Pa and took it. Pa watched and swung his leg, laughing. The bottle was on the counter and Pa watched closely while Hans took it.

"Ah, you plan to drink some of my whisky, Hans?"

"Yeah."

"It'd be polite to ask."

"I ain't asking," Hans said, tilting the bottle.

"I suppose I'd better make some biscuits," Ma said.

Hans looked up at her, keeping the bottle tilted. He didn't pour.

"Biscuits, Ma?" I said.

"I ought to have something for Mr. Pedersen and I haven't a thing."

Hans straightened the bottle.

"There's a thing to consider," he said, beginning to smile. "Why ain't Pedersen here looking for his kid?"

"Why should he be?"

Hans winked at me through his glass.

"Why not? We're nearest. If the kid ain't here he can ask us to help him hunt."

"Fat chance."

"He ain't come though. How do you consider that?"

"I ain't considering it," Pa said.

"Why ain't you? Seems to me like something worth real fancy considering."

"No it ain't."

"Ain't it?"

"Pedersen's a fool."

"So you like to say. I've heard you often enough. All right, maybe he is. How long do you expect he'll wander around looking before he comes over this way?"

"A long time. A long time maybe."

"The kid's been gone a long time."

Pa arranged his nightshirt over his knee. He had on the striped one.

"Oh Pedersen'll be here before too long now," he said.

"And if he don't?"

"What do you mean, if he don't? Then he don't. It ain't no skin off my ass. I don't care what he does."

"Yeah," Big Hans said. "Yeah."

Pa folded his arms, looking like a judge. He swung his leg.

"Where'd you find the bottle?"

Hans jiggled it.

"You're pretty good at hiding, ain't you?"

"I'm asking the questions. Where'd you find it?"

Hans was enjoying himself too much.

"I didn't."

"Jorge, hey." Pa chewed his lip. "So you're the nosy bastard."

He didn't look at me and it didn't seem like he was talking to me at all. He said it like I wasn't there and he was thinking out loud.

"It wasn't me, Pa," I said.

I didn't want him to think I'd found it — not then anyway — but I didn't want him to know Ma had either. I tried to get Hans's attention so he'd shut up but he was enjoying himself.

"Little Hans ain't no fool," Big Hans said.

"No." Pa wasn't paying attention. "He ain't no kin to you."

"Why ain't he here then? He'd be looking too. Why ain't he here?"

"Gracious, I'd forgot all about Little Hans," Ma said, quickly taking a bowl from the cupboard.

"Hed, what are you up to?" Pa said.

"Oh, biscuits."

"Biscuits? What in hell for? Biscuits. I don't want any biscuits. Make some coffee. All this time you been just standing around."

"For Pedersen and Little Hans. They'll be coming and they'll want some biscuits and coffee, and I'll put out some elderberry jelly. The coffee needed reminding, Magnus, thank you."

"Who found the bottle?"

She scooped some flour from the bin.

Pa'd been sitting, swinging. Now he stopped and stood up.

"Who found it? Who found it? God dammit, who found it? Which one of them was it?"

Ma was trying to measure the flour but her hands shook. The

flour ran off the scoop and fell across the rim of the cup, and I thought, Yeah, you'd have run, yeah, your hands shake.

"Why don't you ask Jorge?" Big Hans said.

How I hated him, putting it on me, the coward. And he had thick arms.

"That snivel," Pa said.

Hans laughed heartily.

"He couldn't find nothing I hid."

"You're right there," Hans said.

"I could," I said. "I have."

"A liar, Hans, hey? You found it."

Pa was somehow pleased and sat on the corner of the table again. Was it Hans he hated most, or me?

"I never said Jorge found it."

"I've got a liar working for me. A thief and a liar. Why should I keep a liar? I'm just soft on him, I guess, and he's got such a sweet face. But why should I keep a thief . . . little movey eyes like traveling specks . . . why?"

"I ain't like you. I don't spend every day drinking just to sleep the night and then sleeping half the day too, fouling your bed and your room and half the house."

"You been doing your share of lying down. Little Hans is half your size and worth twice."

Pa's words didn't come out clear.

"How about Little Hans? Little Hans ain't showed up. Folks must be getting pretty worried at the Pedersens'. They'd like some news maybe. But Pedersen don't come. Little Hans don't come. There's a thousand drifts out there. The kid might be under any one. If anybody's seen him, we have, and if we haven't, nobody's going to till spring, or maybe if the wind shifts, which ain't likely. But nobody comes to ask. That's pretty funny, I'd say."

"You're an awful full-up bastard," Pa said.

"I'm just considering, that's all."

"Where'd you find it?"

"I forgot. I was going to have a drink."

"Where?"

"You're pretty good at hiding," Hans said.

"I'm asking. Where?"

"I didn't, I told you, I didn't find it. Jorge didn't find it neither."

"You bastard, Hans," I said.

"It hatched," Hans said. "Like the fellow, you know, who blew in. He hatched. Or maybe the kid found it — had it hid under his coat."

"Who?" Pa roared, standing up quick.

"Oh Hed found it. You don't hide worth a damn and Hed found it easy. She knew right away where to look."

"Shut up, Hans," I said.

Hans tilted the bottle.

"She must have known where it was a long time now. Maybe she knows where they're all hid. You ain't very smart. Or maybe she's took it up herself, eh? And it ain't yours at all, maybe that."

Big Hans poured himself a drink. Then Pa kicked the glass out of Hans's hand. Pa's slipper flew off and sailed by Hans's head and bounced off the wall. The glass didn't break. It fell by the sink and rolled slow by Ma's feet, leaving a thin line. The scoop flew a light white cloud. There was whisky on Hans's shirt and on the wall and cupboards, and a splash on the floor where the glass had hit.

Ma had her arms wrapped around her chest. She looked faint and she was whewing and moaning.

"OK," Pa said, "we'll go. We'll go right now, Hans. I hope to God you get a bullet in your belly. Jorge, go upstairs and see if the little sonofabitch is still alive."

Hans was rubbing the spots on his shirt and licking his lips when I hunched past Pa and went out.

Part Two

1

There wasn't any wind. The harness creaked, the wood creaked, the runners made a sound like a saw working easy, and everything was white about Horse Simon's feet. Pa had the reins between his knees and he and Hans and I kept ourselves close together. We bent our heads and clenched our feet and wished we could huddle both hands in one pocket. Only Hans was breathing through his nose. We didn't speak. I wished my lips could warm my teeth.

The blanket we had wasn't worth a damn. It was just as cold underneath and Pa drank from a bottle by him on the seat.

I tried to keep the feeling I'd had starting out, when we'd hitched up Horse Simon when I was warm and decided to risk the north corn road to the Pedersen place. It cut across and came up near the grove behind his barn. We figured we could look at things from there. I tried to keep the feeling but it was a warm feeling, like I was setting out to do something special and big, worth remembering. I thought about coming in from the barn and finding his back to me in the kitchen and wrestling with him and pulling him down and beating the stocking cap off his head with the barrel of the gun. I thought about coming in from the barn still blinking with the light and seeing him there and picking the shovel up and taking him on. That had been at the beginning, when I was warm and felt like doing something big, something special and heroic even. I couldn't put the feeling down in Pedersen's back yard or Pedersen's porch or barn. I couldn't see myself, or him, there. I could only see him back where I wasn't any more — standing quiet in our kitchen with his gun going slowly up and down in Ma's face and Ma shooing it away and at the same time trying not to move an inch for getting shot.

When I got good and cold the feeling slipped away. I couldn't imagine him with his gun or yellow gloves. I couldn't imagine me coming on to him. We weren't anyplace and I didn't care. Pa drove by staring down the sloping white road and drank from his bottle. Hans rattled his heels on the back of the seat. I just tried to keep my mouth shut and breathe and not think why in the name of the good Jesus Christ I had to.

It wasn't like a sleigh ride on an early winter evening when the air is still, the earth is warm, and the stars are flakes being born that will not fall. The air was still all right, the sun straight up and cold. Behind us on the trough that marked the road I saw our runners and the holes that Simon tore. Ahead of us it melted into drifts. Pa squinted like he saw where he knew it really went. Horse Simon steamed. Ice hung from his harness. Snow caked his belly. I was afraid the crust might cut his knees. I wanted a drink out of Pa's bottle. Big Hans seemed asleep and shivered in his dreams. My rear was God almighty sore.

We reached a drift across the road and Pa eased Simon round

her where he knew there wasn't any fence. Pa figured to go back to the road but after we got round the bank I could see there wasn't any point in that. There were rows of high drifts across it.

"They ain't got no reason to do that," Pa said.

It was the first thing Pa'd said since he told me to go upstairs and see if the Pedersen kid was still alive. He hadn't looked alive to me but I'd said I guessed he was. Pa'd gone and got his gun first, without dressing, one foot still bare so he favored it, and took the gun upstairs cradled in his arm, broke, and pointing down. He had a dark speckled spot on the rump of his nightshirt where he'd sat on the table. Hans had his shotgun and the forty-five he'd stolen from the Navy. He made me load it and when I'd stuck it in my belt he'd said it'd likely go off and keep me from ever getting out to stud. The gun felt like a chunk of ice against my belly and the barrel dug.

Ma'd put some sandwiches and a thermos of coffee in a sack. The coffee'd be cold. My hands would be cold when I ate mine even if I kept my gloves on. Chewing would be painful. The lip of the thermos would be cold if I drank out of that, and I'd spill some on my chin to dry to ice; or if I used the cup, the tin would stick to my lip like rotten liquor you didn't want to taste by licking off, and it would burn and then tear my skin coming away.

Simon went into a hole. He couldn't pull out so he panicked and the sleigh skidded. We'd had crust but now the front right runner broke through and we braked in the soft snow underneath. Pa made quiet impatient noises and calmed Simon down.

"That was damn fool," Hans said.

"He lost his footing. Jesus, I ain't the horse."

"I don't know. Simon's a turd binder," Hans said.

Pa took a careful drink.

"Go round and lead him out," he said.

"Jorge is on the outside."

"Go round and lead him out."

"You. You go round. You led him in."

"Go round and lead him out."

Sometimes the snow seemed as blue as the sky. I don't know which seemed colder.

"Oh God, I'll go," I said. "I'm on the outside."

"You practicing to be a bird?" Hans said.

"Your old man's on the outside," Hans said.

"I guess I know where I am," Pa said. "I guess I know where I'm staying."

"Can't you let up, for Christ's sake? I'm going," I said.

I threw off the blanket and stood up but I was awful stiff. The snow dazzle struck me and the pain of the space around us. Getting out I rammed my ankle against the sideboard's iron brace. The pain shot up my leg and shook me like an axe handle will when you strike wrong. I cursed, taking my time jumping off. The snow looked as stiff and hard as cement and I could only think of the jar.

"You've known where that brace was for ten years," Pa said.

The snow went to my crotch. The gun bit. I waded round the hole trying to keep on tiptoe and the snow away from my crotch but it wasn't any use.

I got hold of Horse Simon and tried to coax him out. Pa swore at me from his seat. Simon kicked and thrashed and lunged ahead. The front right runner dug in. The sleigh swung around on it and the left side hit Simon's back legs hard behind the knees. Simon reared and kicked a piece out of the side of the sleigh and then pulled straight ahead tangling the reins. The sleigh swung back again and the right runner pulled loose with a jerk. Pa's bottle rolled. From where I sat in the snow I saw him grab for it. Simon went on ahead. The sleigh slid sideways into Simon's hole and the left runner went clear of the snow. Simon pulled up short though Pa had lost the reins and was holding on and yelling about his bottle. I had snow in my eyes and down my neck.

"Simon didn't have no call to do that," Hans said, mimicking Pa.

"Where's my bottle?" Pa said, looking over the side of the sleigh at the torn snow. "Jorge, go find my bottle. It fell in the snow here somewheres."

I tried to brush the snow off without getting more in my pockets and up my sleeves and down my neck.

"You get out and find it. It's your bottle."

Pa leaned way over.

"If you hadn't been so god damn dumb it wouldn't have fell out. Where'd you learn to lead a horse? You never learned that dumb trick from me. Of all the god damn dumb tricks I never seen any dumber."

Pa waved his arm in a circle.

"That bottle fell out about here. It couldn't have got far. It was corked, thank God. I won't lose none."

Snow was slipping down the hollow of my back. The forty-five had slipped through my belt. I was afraid it would go off like Big Hans said. I kept my right forearm pressed against it. I didn't want it slipping off down my pants. Pa shouted directions.

"You hid it," I said. "You're such a hand at hiding. You find it then. I ain't good at finding. You said so yourself."

"Jorge, you know I got to have that bottle."

"Then get off your ass and find it."

"You know I got to have it."

"Then get off."

"If I get down off here, it ain't the bottle I'm coming after. I'll hold you under till you drown, you little smart-talking snot."

I started kicking around in the snow.

Hans giggled.

"There's a trace broke," he said.

"What's so damn funny?"

"I told you that trace was worn."

I kicked about. Pa followed my feet.

"Hell. Not that way." He pointed. "You know about everything there is, Hans, I guess," he said, still watching me. "First little thing you figure out you tell somebody about. Then somebody else knows. So then they can do what needs to be done and you don't have to . . . Jesus, not there, there . . . don't it, Hans? Don't it always let you out? You ain't going deep enough. I never figured that out. How come somebody else's knowing always lets you out? You're just a pimp for jobs, I guess. You ain't going deep enough, I said."

"It ain't my job to fix traces."

"Hey, get your hands in it. It's clean. You always was that way about manure. Why ain't it your job? Too busy screwing sheep? Try over there. You ought to have hit it. No, there, not there."

"I never fixed traces."

"Christ, they never needed fixing while you been here hardly.

Jorge, will you stop nursing that fool gun with your cock and use both hands."

"I'm cold Pa."

"So'm I. That's why you got to find that bottle."

"If I find it do I get a drink?"

"Ain't you growed up . . . a man . . . since yesterday."

"I've had a few, Pa."

"Ha. Of what, hey? Hear that Hans? He's had a few. For medicine maybe, like your ma says. The spirits, the spirits, Jorgen Segren, ha."

"I'm cold."

"Maybe. Only look, for God's sake, don't just thrash about like a fool chicken."

"Well, we're finished anyway," Hans said.

"We're finished if we don't find that bottle."

"You're finished, maybe. You're the only one who needs that bottle. Jorge and I don't need it, but there you are, old man, eh? Lost in the snow."

My gloves were wet. Snow had jammed under my sleeves. It was working down into my boots. I stopped to pick some out with a finger if I could.

"Maybe some of Ma's coffee is still hot," I said.

"Say. Yeah. Maybe. But that's my coffee, boy. I never got none. I ain't even had breakfast. What are you stopping for? Come on. Hell Jorge, it's cold."

"I know that better than you. You're sitting there all nice and dry, bossing; but I'm doing all the work and getting the snow inside me."

Pa leaned back and grinned. He clutched the blanket to him and Hans pulled it back.

"It's easier to keep warm moving around, anybody knows that. Ain't that right, Hans? It's easier to keep warm moving, ain't it?"

"Yeah," Hans said. "If you ain't got a blanket."

"See there, Jorge, hey? You just keep good and warm . . . stirring. It'd be a pity if your pee should freeze. And moving around good prevents calluses on the bottom. Don't it Hans?"

"Yeah."

"Hans here knows. He's nothing but calluses."

"You'll wear out your mouth."

"I can't find it, Pa. Maybe some of Ma's coffee is still warm."

"You damn snivel — you ain't looking. Get tramping proper like I told you, and find it. Find it fast, you hear. You ain't getting back up on this sleigh until you do."

I started jumping up and down, not too fast, and Pa blew his nose with his fingers.

"Cold makes the snot run," he says, real wise.

If I found the bottle I'd kick it deep under the snow. I'd kick it and keep kicking it until it sank under a drift. Pa wouldn't know where it was. I wouldn't come back to the sleigh either. They weren't going anywhere anyway. I'd go home though it was a long walk. Looking back I could see our tracks in the trough of the road. They came together before I lost them. It would be warm at home and worth the walk. It was frightening — the great bright space. I'd never wanted to go to Pedersen's. That was Hans's fight, and Pa's. I was just cold . . . cold . . . and burned by the light and sick of snow. That's what I'd do if I found it — kick it under a drift. Then later, a lot later in the spring one day I'd come out here and find the old bottle sticking out of the rotting snow and the mud and hide it back of the barn and have a drink whenever I wanted. I'd get some real cigarettes, maybe a carton, and hide them too. Then someday I'd come in and Pa'd smell whisky on me and think I'd found one of his hiding places. He'd be mad as hell and not know what to say. It'd be spring and he'd think he'd taken them all in like he always did, harvesting the crop like he said.

I looked to see if there was something to mark the place by but it was all gone under snow. There was only the drifts and the deep holes of snow and the long runnered trough of the road. It might be a mudhole we was stuck in. In the spring cattails might grow up in it and the blackbirds come. Or it might be low and slimy at first and then caked dry and cracked. Pa'd never find out how I came by the bottle. Someday he'd act too big and I'd stick his head under the pump or slap his skinny rump with the backside of a fork full of manure. Hans would act smart and then some-day . . .

"Jee-suss, will you move?"

"I'm cold, Pa."

"You're going to be a pig's size colder."

"Well, we're finished anyway," Hans said. "We ain't going nowhere. The trace is broke."

Pa stopped watching me thrash the snow. He frowned at Horse Simon. Simon was standing quiet with his head down.

"Simon's shivering," he said. "I should have remembered he'd be heated up. It's so cold I forgot."

Pa yanked the blanket off of Hans like Hans was a bed he was stripping and jumped down. Hans yelled but Pa didn't pay attention. He threw the blanket over Simon.

"We got to get Simon moving. He'll stiffen up."

Pa ran his hand tenderly down Simon's legs.

"The sleigh don't seem to have hurt him none."

"The trace is broke."

Then Hans stood up. He beat his arms against his body and jigged.

"We'll have to walk him home," he said.

"Home, hey," Pa said, giving Hans a funny sidewise look. "It's a long walk."

"You can ride him then," Hans said.

Pa looked real surprised and even funnier. It wasn't like Hans to say that. It was too cold. It made Hans generous. There was some good in cold.

"Why?"

Pa waded, patting Simon, but he kept his eye on Hans like it was Hans might kick.

Hans let out a long impatient streamer.

"Jesus — the trace."

Hans was being real cautious. Hans was awful cold. His nose was red. Pa's was white but it didn't look froze. It just looked white like it usually did — like it was part of him had died long ago. I wondered what color my nose was. Mine was bigger and sharper at the end. It was Ma's nose, Ma said. I was bigger all over than Pa. I was taller than Hans too. I pinched my nose but my gloves were wet so I couldn't feel anything except how my nose hurt when I pinched it. It couldn't be too cold. Hans was pointing at the ends of the trace which were trailing in the snow.

"Tie a knot in it," Pa was saying.

"It won't hold," Hans said, shaking his head.

"Tie a good one, it will."

"It's too cold to get a good knot. Leather's too stiff."

"Hell no, it ain't too stiff."

"Well, it's too thick. Can't knot something like that."

"You can do it."

"She'll pull crooked."

"Let her pull crooked."

"Simon won't work well pulling her crooked."

"He'll have to do the best he can. I ain't going to leave this sleigh out here. Hell, it might snow again before I got back with a new trace. When I get home I'm going to stay there and eat my breakfast if it's suppertime. I ain't coming back out here trying to beat another blizzard and wind up like the Pedersen kid."

"Yeah," Hans said, nodding. "Let's get this damn thing out of here and get Simon home before he stiffens. I'll tie the trace."

Hans got down and I stopped kicking. Pa watched Hans real careful from his side of Horse Simon and I could see him smiling like he'd thought of something dirty. I started to get on the sleigh but Pa shouted and made me hunt some more.

"Maybe we'll find it when we move the sleigh," I said.

Pa laughed but not at what I said. He opened his mouth wide, looking at Hans, and laughed hard, though his laugh was quiet.

"Yeah, maybe we will," he said, and gave Simon an extra hard pat. "Maybe we will, hey, at that."

I didn't find the bottle and Big Hans tied the trace. He had to take his gloves off to do it but he did it quick and I had to admire him for it. Pa coaxed Simon while Hans boosted. She got clear and then was going and skidded out. I heard a noise like a light bulb busting. A brown stain spread over the sleigh track. Pa peered over his shoulder at the stain, his hands on the halter, his legs wide in the snow.

"Oh no," was all he said, "oh no."

But Big Hans broke up. He lifted a leg clear of the snow. He hit himself. He shook. He hugged his belly. He rocked back and forth. "Oh . . . oh . . . oh," he screamed, and he held his sides. Tears streamed down his cheeks. "You . . . you . . . you," he howled. Hans's cheeks, his nose, his head was red. "Found . . . found . . . found," he choked.

Everything about Pa was frozen. The white hair that stuck out from his hat looked hard and sharp and seemed to shine like snow.

Big Hans went on laughing. I never saw him so humored. He staggered, weakening — Pa as still as a stake. Hans began to heave and gasp, running down. In a minute he'd be cold again, worn out, and then he'd wish he could drink out of that bottle. The stain had stopped spreading and was fading, the snow bubbling and sagging. All that whisky was gone. We could melt and drink the snow, I thought. I wanted that bottle back bad. I hated Hans. I'd hate Hans forever, as long as there was snow.

Hans was puffing quietly when Pa told me to get in the sleigh. Then Hans climbed awkwardly on. Pa took the blanket off Horse Simon and threw it in the sleigh. Then he got Simon started. I pulled the blanket over me and tried to stop shivering. Our stove, I thought, was black . . . God . . . lovely black . . . and glowed rich cherry through its holes. I thought of the kettle steaming on it, the steam alive, hissing white and warm, not like my breath coming slow and cloudy and hanging heavy and dead in the still air.

Hans jumped.

"Where we going?" he said. "Where we going?"

Pa didn't say nothing.

"This ain't the way," Hans said. "Where we going?"

The gun was an ache in my stomach. Pa squinted at the snow.

"For Christ's sake," Hans said. "I'm sorry about the bottle."

But Pa drove.

2

Barberry had got in the grove and lay about the bottom of the trees and hid in snow. The mossycups went high, their branches put straight out, the trunk-bark black and wrinkled. There were spots where I could see the frosted curls of dead grass frozen to the ground and high hard-driven piles of snow the barberry stuck its black barbs from. The wind had thrown some branches in the drifts. The sun made shadows of more branches on their sides and bent them over ridges. The ground rose up behind the grove. The snow rose. Pa and Hans had their shotguns. We followed along the drifts and kept down low. I could hear us breathing and the snow, earth, and our boots squeaking. We went slow and all of us was cold.

Above the snow, through the branches, I could see the peak of Pedersen's house, and nearer by, the roof of Pedersen's barn. We were making for the barn. Once in a while Pa would stop and watch for smoke but there was nothing in the sky. Big Hans bumped into a bush and got his hand barbed through his woolen glove. Pa gestured for Hans to shut up. I could feel my gun through my glove — heavy and cold. Where we went the ground was driven nearly bare. Mostly I kept my eyes on Big Hans's heels because it hurt my neck so to look up. When I did, for smoke, the faint breeze caught my cheek and drew the skin across the bone. I didn't think of much except how to follow Hans's heels and how, even underneath my cap, my ears burned, and how my lips hurt and how just moving made me ache. Pa followed where a crazy wind had got in among the oaks and blown the snow bare from the ground in flat patches against their trunks. Sometimes we had to break through a small drift or we'd gone in circles. The roof of Pedersen's house grew above the banks as we went until finally we passed across one corner of it and I saw the chimney very black in the sun stick up from the steep bright pitch like a dead cigar rough-ashed with snow.

I thought: The fire's dead, they must be froze.

Pa stopped and nodded at the chimney.

"You see," Hans said unhappily.

Just then I saw a cloud of snow float from the crest of a drift and felt my eyes smart. Pa looked quick at the sky but it was clear. Hans stomped his feet, hung his head, swore in a whisper.

"Well," Pa said, "it looks like we made this trip for nothing. Nobody's to home."

"The Pedersens are all dead," Hans said, still looking down.

"Shut up." I saw Pa's lips were chapped . . . a dry hole now. A muscle jumped along his jaw. "Shut up," he said again after a pause.

A faint ribbon of snow suddenly shot from the top of the chimney and disappeared. I stood as still as I could in the tubes of my clothes, the snow shifting strangely in my eyes, alone, frightened by the space that was bowling up inside me, a blank white glittering waste like the waste outside, coldly burning, roughed with waves, and I wanted to curl up, face to my thighs, but I knew my tears would freeze my lashes together. My stomach began to growl.

"What's the matter with you, Jorge?" Pa said.

"Nothing." I giggled. "I'm cold, Pa, I guess," I said. Then I belched.

"Jesus," Hans said loudly.

"Shut up."

I poked at the snow with the toe of my boot. I wanted to sit down and if there'd been anything to sit on I would have. All I wanted was to go home or sit down. Hans had stopped stomping and was staring back through the trees toward the way we'd come.

"Anybody in that house," Pa said, "would have a fire."

He sniffed and rubbed his sleeve across his nose.

"Anybody — see?" He began raising his voice. "Anybody who was in that house now would have a fire. The Pedersens is all most likely out hunting that fool kid. They probably tore ass off without minding the furnace. Now it's out." His voice got braver. "Anybody who might have come along while they was gone, and gone in, would have started a fire someplace first thing, and we'd see the smoke. It's too damn cold not to."

Pa took the shotgun he'd carried broken over his left arm and turned the barrel over, slow and deliberate. Two shells fell out and he stuffed them in his coat pocket.

"That means there ain't anybody to home. There ain't no smoke," he said with emphasis, "and that means there ain't *no*-body."

Big Hans sighed. "O.K.," he muttered remotely. "Let's go home."

I wanted to sit down. Here was the sofa, here the bed, mine, white and billowy. And the stairs, cold and snapping. And I had the dry cold toothaching mouth I always had at home, and the cold storm in my belly, and my pinched eyes. There was the print of the kid's rear in the dough. I wanted to sit down. I wanted to go back where we'd tied up Horse Simon and sit numb in the sleigh.

"Yes yes yes, let's," I said.

Pa smiled, oh the bastard, and he didn't know half what I knew now, numb in the heart the way I felt, and with my burned-off ears.

"We could at least leave a note saying Big Hans saved their kid.

Seems to me like the only neighborly thing to do. And after all the way we come. Don't it you?"

"What the hell do you know about what's neighborly?" Hans shouted.

With a jerk he dumped his shotgun shells into the snow and kicked at them hard until one skidded into a drift and only the brass showed. The other sank in the snow before it broke. Black powder spilled out under his feet.

Pa laughed.

"Come on, Pa, I'm cold," I said. "Look, I ain't brave. I ain't. I don't care. All I am is cold."

"Quit whimpering, we're all cold. Big Hans here is awful cold."

"Sure, ain't you?"

Hans was grinding the black stain under.

"Yeah," Pa said, grinning. "Some. I'm some." He turned around. "Think you can find your way back, Jorge?"

I got going and he laughed again, loud and ugly, damn his soul. I hated him. Jesus, how I did. But no more like a father. Like the burning space.

"I never did like that bastard Pedersen anyway," he said as we started. "Pedersen's one of them that's always asking for trouble. On his knees for it all the time. Let him find out about his kid himself. He knows where we live. It ain't neighborly but I never said I wanted him for a neighbor."

"Yeah," Hans said. "Let the old bastard find out himself."

"He should have kept his kid behind them fences. What business did he have, sending his kid to us to take care of? He went and asked for snow. He went on his knees for snow. Was he ready? Hey? Was he? For real snow? Nobody's ever ready for real snow."

"The old bastard wouldn't have come to tell you if it'd been me who'd been lost," I said, but I wasn't minding my words at all, I was just talking. I was thinking of the feel of the sleigh moving under me.

"Can't tell holy Pete," Hans said.

I was going fast. I didn't care about keeping low. I had my eyes on the spaces between trees. I was looking for the place where we'd left Simon and the sleigh. I thought I'd see Simon first, maybe his breath above a bank or beside the trunk of a tree. I slipped on a little snow the wind hadn't blown from the path we'd took. I still had the gun in my right hand and I lost my balance. When I put out my left hand for support, it went into a drift to my elbow and into the barberry thorns. I jerked back and fell hard. Hans and Pa found it funny. But the legs that lay in front of me weren't mine. I'd gone out in the blazing air. It was queer. Out of the snow I'd kicked away with my foot stuck a horse's hoof and I didn't feel the least terror or surprise.

"Looks like a hoof," I said.

Hans and Pa were silent. I looked up at them. Nothing. Three men in the snow. A red scarf and some mittens . . . somebody's ice and coal . . . the picture for January. But behind them on the blank hills? Then it rushed over me and I thought: This is as far as he rid him. I looked at the hoof and the shoe which didn't belong in the picture. No dead horses for January. And on the snowhills there would be wild sled tracks and green trees and falling toboggans. This is as far. Or a glazed lake and rowdy skaters. Three men. On his ass: one. Dead horse and gun. And the question came to me very clearly, as if out of the calendar a girl had shouted: Are you going to get up and walk on? Maybe it was the Christmas picture. The big log and the warm orange wood I was sprawled on in my flannel pajamas. I'd just been given a pistol that shot BB's. And the question was: Was I going to get up and walk on? Hans's shoes, and Pa's, were as steady as the horse's. Were they hammered on? Their bodies stolen? Who'd left them standing here? And Christmas cookies cut in the shape of the kid's dead wet behind . . . with maybe a cherry to liven the pale dough . . . a coal from the stove. But I couldn't just say that looks like a hoof or that looks like a shoe and go right on because Hans and Pa were waiting behind me in their wool hats and pounding mittens . . . like a picture for January. Smiling. I was learning to skate.

"Looks like this is as far as he rid him."

Finally Pa said in a flat voice: "What are you talking about?"

"You said he had a horse, Pa."

"What are you talking about?"

"This here horse."

"Ain't you never seen a shoe before?"

"It's just a horse's hoof," Hans said. "Let's get on."

"What are you talking about?" Pa said again.

"The man who scared the Pedersen kid. The man he saw."

"Manure," Pa said. "It's one of Pedersen's horses. I recognize the shoe."

"That's right," Big Hans said.

"Pedersen only has one horse."

"This here's it," Big Hans said.

"This horse's brown, ain't it?"

"Pedersen's horse has got two brown hind feet. I remember," Big Hans said.

"His is black."

"It's got two brown hind feet."

I started to brush away some snow. I knew Pedersen's horse was black.

"What the hell," Hans said. "Come on. It's too cold to stand here and argue about the color of Pedersen's god damn horse."

"Pedersen's horse is black," Pa said. "He don't have any brown on him at all."

Big Hans turned angrily on Pa. "You said you recognized his shoe."

"I thought I did. It ain't."

I kept scraping snow away. Hans leaned down and pushed me. The horse was white where frozen snow clung to his hide.

"He's brown, Hans. Pedersen's horse is black. This one's brown."

Hans kept pushing at me. "God damn you," he was saying over and over in a funny high voice.

"You knew all along it wasn't Pedersen's horse."

It was like singing the way it went on. I got up carefully, taking the safety off. Later in the winter maybe somebody would stumble on his shoes sticking out of the snow. Shooting Hans seemed like something I'd done already. I knew where he kept his gun — under those magazines in his drawer — and while I'd really never thought of it before, the whole thing moved before me now so naturally it must have happened that way. Of course I shot them all — Pa in his bed, Ma in her kitchen, Hans when he came in from his rounds. They wouldn't look much different dead than alive only they wouldn't be so loud.

"Jorge, now . . . look out with that thing Jorge. Jorge . . ."

His shotgun had fallen in the snow. He was holding both hands in front of him. Afterwards I stood alone in every room.

"You're yellow, Hans."

He was backing slowly, fending me off . . . fending . . . fending . . .

"Jorge . . . Jorge . . . hey now . . . Jorge . . ." like singing.

Afterwards I looked through his magazines, my hand on my pecker, hot from head to foot.

"I've shot you, yellow Hans. You can't shout or push no more or goose me in the barn."

"Hey now wait, Jorge . . . listen . . . what? Jorge . . . wait . . ." like singing.

Afterwards only the wind and the warm stove. Shivering I rose on my toes. Pa came up and I moved the gun to take him in. I kept it moving back and forth . . . Hans and Pa . . . Pa and Hans. Gone. Snow piling in the window corners. In the spring I'd shit with the door open, watching the blackbirds.

"Don't be a damn fool, Jorge," Pa said. "I know you're cold. We'll be going home."

". . . yellow yellow yellow yellow . . ."

"Now Jorge, I ain't yellow," Pa said, smiling pleasantly.

"I've shot you both with bullets."

"Don't be a fool."

"The whole house with bullets. You too."

"Funny I don't feel it."

"They never does, do they? Do rabbits?"

"He's crazy, Jesus, Mag, he's crazy . . ."

"I never did want to. I never hid it like you did. I never believed him. I ain't the yellow one but you made me come but you're the yellow ones, you were all along the yellow ones."

That's what the kid had done, I thought. Of course he'd seen his chance and shot them all — his Ma, his Pa, and little Hans. Of course that's what he'd done.

Then Pa took the gun away, putting it in his pocket. He had his shotgun hanging easy over his left arm but he slapped me and I bit my tongue. Pa was spitting. I turned and ran down the path we'd come, putting one arm over my face to ease the stinging.

"You little shit," Big Hans called after me.

3

Pa came back to the sleigh where I was sitting hunched up under the blanket and got a shovel out of the back.

"Feeling better?"

"Some."

"Why don't you drink some of that coffee?"

"It's cold by now. I don't want to anyhow."

"How about them sandwiches?"

"I ain't hungry. I don't want anything."

Pa started back with the shovel.

"What are you going to do with that?" I said.

"Dig a tunnel," he said, and he went around a drift out of sight, the sun flashing from the blade.

I almost called him back but I remembered the grin in his face so I didn't. Simon stamped. I pulled the blanket closer. I didn't believe him. Just for a second, when he said it, I had. It was a joke. Well, I was too cold for jokes. What did he want a shovel for? There'd be no point in digging for the horse. They could see it wasn't Pedersen's.

Poor Simon. He was better than they were. They'd left us in the cold.

Pa'd forgot about the shovel in the sleigh. I could have used it hunting for his bottle. That had been a joke too. Pa'd sat there thinking how funny Jorge is out there beating away at the snow, I'll just wait and see if he remembers about that shovel. It'd be funny if Jorge forgot, he'd thought, sitting there in the blanket and bobbing his head here and there like a chicken. I'd hear about it when we got home till I was sick. I put my head down and closed my eyes. All right. I didn't care. I'd put up with it to be warm. But that couldn't be right. Pa must have forgot the same as me. He wanted that bottle too bad. Now it was all gone. It was colder with my eyes closed. I tried to think about all that underwear and the girls in the pictures. I had a crick in my neck.

Whose horse was it, then?

I decided to keep my eyes closed a while longer, to see if I could do it. Then I decided not to. There was a stream of light in my eyes. It was brighter than snow, and as white. I opened them and straightened up. Keeping my head down made me dizzy. Everything was blurry. There were a lot of blue lines that moved.

Did they know the horse even so? Maybe it was Carlson's horse, or even Schmidt's. Maybe he was Carlson in yellow gloves, or Schmidt, and the kid, because he came in sudden from the barn and didn't know Carlson had come, saw him in the kitchen holding a gun like he might of if it'd been Schmidt, and the kid got scared and run, because he didn't understand and it'd been snowing lots, and how did Schmidt get there, or Carlson get there, if it was one of them, so the kid got scared and run and came to our crib when the snow grew around him and then in the morning Hans found him.

And we'd been god damn fools. Especially Hans. I shivered. The cold had settled in my belly. The sun had bent around to the west. Near it the sky was hazy. The troughs of some of the drifts were turning blue.

He wouldn't have been that scared. Why'd Carlson or Schmidt be out in a storm like that? If somebody was sick, they were closer to town than either the Pedersens or us. It was a long way for them in this weather. They wouldn't get caught out. But if the horse was stole, who was there but Carlson and Schmidt or maybe Hansen to steal it from?

He goes to the barn before the snow, most likely in the night, and knows horses. Oats or hay lead it out. He's running away. The blizzard sets down. He drives himself and the horse hard, bending in the wind, leaning over far to see fences, any marks, a road. He makes the grove. He might not know it. The horse runs into the barberry, rears, goes to its knees; or a low branch of a mossycup he doesn't see knocks him into a drift; or he slides off when the horse rears as the barbs go in. The horse wanders a little way, not far. Then it stops — finished. And he — he's stunned. He's frozen and tired. The wind's howling. He's blind. He's hungry and scared. The snow is stinging his face. Standing still, alone. Then the snow hides him. The wind blows a crust over him. Only a shovel poking in the drifts or a warm rain will find him lying by the horse.

I threw off the blanket and jumped down and ran up the path

we'd made between the drifts and trees, slipping, cutting sharply
back and forth, working against my stiffness, but all the time keeping my head up, looking out carefully ahead.

They weren't by the horse. A hoof and part of the leg I'd uncovered lay by the path like nothing more went with them. Seeing
them like that, like they might have blown down from one of the
trees in a good wind, gave me a fright. Now there was a slight
breeze and I discovered my tongue was sore. Hans's and Pa's
tracks went farther on — toward Pedersen's barn. I wasn't excited
any more. I remembered I'd left the blanket on the seat instead of
putting it on Simon. I thought about going back. Pa'd said a tunnel. That had to be a joke. But what were they doing with the
shovel? Maybe they'd found him by the barn. What if it really
was Schmidt or Carlson? I thought about which I wanted it to be.
I went more slowly in Pa's tracks. Now I kept down. The roof of
Pedersen's barn got bigger; the sky was hazier; here and there little
clouds of snow leapt up from the top of a drift like they'd been
pinched off, and sailed swiftly away.

They *were* digging a tunnel. They didn't hear me come up.
They were really digging a tunnel.

Hans was digging in the great drift. It ran from the grove in a
high curve against the barn. It met the roof where it went lowest
and flowed onto it like there wasn't a barn underneath. It seemed
like the whole snow of winter was gathered there. If the drift
hadn't ended in the grove it would have been swell for sledding.
You could put a ladder on the edge of the roof and go off from
there. The crust looked hard enough.

Hans and Pa had put about a ten-foot hole in the bank. Hans
dug and Pa put what Hans dug in small piles behind him. I figured it was near a hundred feet to the barn. If we'd been home
and not so cold, it would have been fun. But it would take all day.
They were great damn fools.

"I been thinking," I started out, and Hans stopped in the tunnel with a shovel of snow in the air.

Pa didn't turn around or stop.

"You can help dig," he said.

"I been thinking," I said, and Hans dropped the shovel, spilling
the snow, and came out, "that you're digging in the wrong place."

Hans pointed to the shovel. "Get digging."

"We need something to carry snow with," Pa said. "It's getting too damn far."

Pa kicked at the snow and flailed with his arms. He was sweating and so was Hans. It was terrible foolish.

"I said you was digging in the wrong place."

"Tell Hans. It's his idea. He's the hot digger."

"You thought it was a good idea," Hans said.

"I never did."

"Well," I said, "it ain't likely you'll find him clear in there."

Pa chuckled. "He ain't going to find us neither."

"He ain't going to find anybody if he's where I think."

"Oh yeah, think." Hans moved nearer. "Where?"

"As far as he got." It really didn't make much difference to me what Hans did. He could come as close as he liked. "In the snow near that horse."

Hans started but Pa chewed on his lip and shook his head.

"Probably Schmidt or Carlson," I said.

"Probably Schmidt or Carlson, shit," Pa said.

"Of course," Hans shouted.

Hans scooped up the shovel, furious, and carried it by me like an axe.

"Hans has been working like a thrasher," Pa said.

"You'll never finish it."

"No."

"It's higher than it needs to be."

"Sure."

"Why are you digging it then?"

"Hans. Hans wants to."

"Why, for Christ's sake?"

"So we can get to the barn without being seen."

"Why not cross behind the drift?"

"Hans. Hans says no. Hans says that from an upstairs window he could see over the bank."

"What the hell."

"He's got a rifle."

"But who knows he's upstairs?"

"Nobody. We don't know he's even there. But that horse is."

"He's back where I said."

"No he ain't. You only wish he was. So does Hans, hey? But he ain't. What did the kid see if he is — his ghost?"

I walked into the tunnel to the end. Everything seemed blue. The air was dead and wet. It could have been fun, snow over me, hard and grainy, the excitement of a tunnel, the games. The face of a mine, everything muffled, the marks of the blade in the snow. Well I knew how Hans felt. It would have been wonderful to burrow down, disappear under the snow, sleep out of the wind in soft sheets, safe. I backed out. We went to get Hans and go home. Pa gave me the gun with a smile.

We heard the shovel cutting the crust and Hans puffing. He was using the shovel like a fork. He'd cut up the snow in clods around the horse. He grunted when he drove the shovel in. Next he began to beat the shovel against the snow, packing it down, then ripping the crust with the side of the blade.

"Hans. It ain't no use," Pa said.

But Hans went right on pounding with the shovel, spearing and pounding, striking out here and there like he was trying to kill a snake.

"You're just wasting your time. It ain't no use, Hans. Jorge was wrong. He ain't by the horse."

But Hans went right on, faster and faster.

"Hans." Pa had made his voice hard and loud.

The shovel speared through the snow. It struck a stone and rang. Hans went to his knees and pawed at the snow with his hands. When he saw the stone he stopped. On his knees in the snow he simply stared at it.

"Hans."

"The bastard. I'd have killed him."

"He ain't here, Hans. How could he be here? The kid didn't see him here, he saw him in the kitchen."

Hans didn't seem to be listening.

"Jorge was wrong. He ain't here at all. He sure ain't here."

Hans grabbed up the shovel like he was going to swing it and jumped up. He looked at me so awful I forgot how indifferent I was.

"We got to think of what to do," Pa said. "The tunnel won't work."

Hans didn't look at Pa. He would only look at me.

"We can go home," Pa said. "We can go home or we can chance crossing behind the bank."

Hans slowly put the shovel down. He started dragging up the narrow track to the barn.

"Let's go home, Hans," I said. "Come on, let's go home."

"I can't go home," he said in a low flat voice as he passed us.

Pa sighed and I felt like I was dead.

Part Three

1

Pedersen's horse was in the barn. Pa kept her quiet. He rubbed his hand along her flank. He laid his head upon her neck and whispered in her ear. She shook herself and nickered. Big Hans opened the door a crack and peeked out. He motioned to Pa to hush the horse but Pa was in the stall. I asked Hans if he saw anything and Hans shook his head. I warned Pa about the bucket. He had the horse settled down. There was something that looked like sponges in the bucket. If they were sponges, they were hard. Hans turned from the door to rub his eyes. He leaned back against the wall.

Then Pa came and looked out the crack.

"Don't look like anybody's to home."

Big Hans had the hiccups. Under his breath he swore and hiccuped.

Pa grunted.

Now the horse was quiet and we were breathing careful and if the wind had picked up we couldn't hear it or any snow it drove. It was warmer in the barn and the little light there was was soft on hay and wood. We were safe from the sun and it felt good to use the eyes on quiet tools and leather. I leaned like Hans against the wall and put my gun in my belt. It felt good to have that hand empty. My face burned and I was drowsy. I could dig a hole in the hay. Even if there were rats, I would burrow with them in it. I could curl up tight and warm my ears in my arms. Even if there were rats, I would sleep with them in it. Everything was still in the barn. Tools and harness hung from the walls, and pails and bags and burlap rested on the floor. Nothing shifted in the straw or moved in hay. The horse stood easy. And Hans and I rested up against the wall, Hans sucking in his breath and holding it, and we waited for Pa, who didn't make a sound. Only the line of sun that snuck under him and lay along the floor and came up white and dangerous to the pail seemed a living thing.

"Don't look like it," Pa said finally. "Never can tell."

Now who will go, I thought. It isn't far. Then it'll be over. It's just across the yard. It isn't any farther than the walk behind the drift. There's only windows watching. If he's been, he's gone, and nothing's there to hurt.

"He's gone."

"Maybe, Jorge. But if he came on that brown horse you stumbled on, why didn't he take this mare of Pedersen's when he left?"

"Jesus," Hans whispered. "He's here."

"Could be in the barn, we'd never see him."

Hans hiccuped. Pa laughed softly.

"Damn you," said Big Hans.

"Thought I'd rid you of them hics."

"Let me look," I said.

He must be gone, I thought. It's such a little way. He must be gone. He never came. It isn't far but who will go across? I saw the house by squinting hard. The nearer part, the dining room, came toward us. The porch was on the left and farther off. You could cross to the nearer wall and under the windows edge around. He might see you from the porch window. But he'd gone. Yet I didn't want to go across that little winded space of snow to find it out.

I wished Big Hans would stop. I was counting the spaces. It was comfortable behind my back except for that. There was a long silence while he held his breath and afterwards we waited.

The wind was rising by the snowman. There were long blue shadows by the snowman now. The eastern sky was clear. Snow sifted slowly to the porch past the snowman. An icicle hung from the nose of the pump. There were no tracks anywhere. I asked did they see the snowman and I heard Pa grunt. Snow went waist-high to the snowman. The wind had blown from his face his eyes. A silent chimney was an empty house.

"There ain't nobody there," I said.

Hans had hiccups again so I ran out.

I ran to the dining room wall and put my back flat against it, pushing hard. Now I saw clouds in the western sky. The wind was rising. It was O.K. for Hans and Pa to come. I would walk around the corner. I would walk around the wall. The porch was there. The snowman was alone beside it.

"All clear," I shouted, walking easily away.

Pa came carefully from the barn with his arms around his gun. He walked slow to be brave but I was standing in the open and I smiled.

Pa sat hugging his knees as I heard the gun, and Hans screamed. Pa's gun stood up. I backed against the house. My God, I thought, he's real.

"I want a drink."

I held the house. The snow'd been driven up against it.

"I want a drink." He motioned with his hand to me.

"Shut up. Shut up." I shook my head. "Shut up." Shut up and die, I thought.

"I want a drink, I'm dry," Pa said.

Pa bumped when I heard the gun again. He seemed to point his hand at me. My fingers slipped along the boards. I tried to dig them in but my back slipped down. Hopelessly I closed my eyes. I knew I'd hear the gun again though rabbits don't. Silently he'd come. My back slipped. Rabbits, though, are hard to hit the way they jump around. But prairie dogs, like Pa, they sit. I felt snowflakes against my face, crumbling as they struck. He'd shoot me, by God. Was Pa's head tipped? Don't look. I felt snowflakes falling softly against my face, breaking. The glare was painful, closing the slit in my eyes. That crack in Pa's face must be awful dry. Don't look. Yes . . . the wind was rising . . . faster flakes.

2

When I was so cold I didn't care I crawled to the south side of the house and broke a casement window with the gun I had forgot I had and climbed down into the basement ripping my jacket on the glass. My ankles hurt so I huddled there in the dark corner places and in the cold moldy places by boxes. Immediately I went to sleep.

I thought it was right away I woke though the light through the window was red. He put them down the cellar, I remembered. But

I stayed where I was, so cold I seemed apart from myself, and wondered if everything had been working to get me in this cellar as a trade for the kid he'd missed. Well, he was sudden. The Pedersen kid — maybe he'd been a message of some sort. No, I liked better the idea that we'd been prisoners exchanged. I was back in my own country. No, it was more like I'd been given a country. A new blank land. More and more, while we'd been coming, I'd been slipping out of myself, pushed out by the cold maybe. Anyway I had a queer head, sear-eyed and bleary, everywhere ribboned. Well, he was quick and quiet. The rabbit simply stumbled. Tomatoes were unfeeling when they froze. I thought of the softness of the tunnel, the mark of the blade in the snow. Suppose the snow was a hundred feet deep. Down and down. A blue-white cave, the blue darkening. Then tunnels off of it like the branches of trees. And fine rooms. Was it February by now? I remembered a movie where the months had blown from the calendar like leaves. Girls in red peek-a-boo BVD's were skiing out of sight. Silence of the tunnel. In and in. Stairs. Wide tall stairs. And balconies. Windows of ice and sweet green light. Ah. There would still be snow in February. Here I go off of the barn, the runners hissing. I am tilting dangerously but I coast on anyway. Now to the trough, the swift snow-trough, and the Pedersen kid floating chest down. They were all drowned in the snow now, weren't they? Well more or less, weren't they? The kid for killing his family. But what about me? Must freeze. But I would leave ahead of that, that was the nice thing, I was already going. Yes. Funny. I was something to run my hands over, feeling for its hurts, like there were worn places in leather, rust and rot in screws and boards I had to find, and the places were hard to reach and the fingers in my gloves were stiff and their ends were sore. My nose was running. Mostly interesting. There was a cramp in my leg that must have made me wake. Distantly I felt the soft points of my shoulders in my jacket, the heavy line of my cap around my forehead, and on the hard floor my harder feet, and to my chest my hugged tight knees. I felt them but I felt them differently . . . like the pressure of a bolt through steel or the cinch of leather harness or the squeeze of wood by wood in floors . . . like the twist and pinch, the painful yield of tender tight together wheels, and swollen bars, and in deep winter springs.

I couldn't see the furnace but it was dead. Its coals were cold, I

knew. The broken window held a rainbow and put a colored pattern on the floor. Once the wind ran through it and a snowflake
turned. The stairs went into darkness. If a crack of light came
down the steps, I guessed I had to shoot. I fumbled for my gun.
Then I noticed the fruit cellar and the closed door where the Pedersens were.

Would they be dead already? Sure they'd be. Everybody was
but me. More or less. Big Hans, of course, wasn't really, unless the
fellow had caught up with him, howling and running. But Big
Hans had gone away a coward. I knew that. It was almost better
he was alive and the snow had him. I didn't have his magazines
but I remembered how they looked, puffed in their brassières.

The door was wood with a wooden bar. I slipped the bar off
easily but the door itself was stuck. It shouldn't have stuck but it
was stuck at the top. I tried to see the top by standing on tiptoe,
but I couldn't bend my toes well and kept toppling to the side. Got
no business sticking, I thought. There's no reason for that. I pulled
again, very hard, and a chip fell as it shuddered open. Wedged some
way. Why? It had a bar. It was even darker in the fruit cellar and
the air had a musty earthen smell.

Maybe they were curled up like the kid was when he dropped.
Maybe they had frost on their clothes, and stiff hair. What color
would their noses be? Would I dare to tweak them? Say. If the
old lady was dead I'd peek at her crotch. I wasn't any Hans to rub
them. Big Hans had run. The snow had him. There wasn't any
kettle, any stove, down here. Before you did a thing like that, you'd
want to be sure. I thought of how the sponges in the bucket had got
hard.

I went back behind the boxes and hid and watched the stairs.
The chip was orange in the pattern of light. He'd heard me when
I broke the glass or when the door shook free or when the wedge
fell down. He was waiting behind the door at the top of the stairs.
All I had to do was come up. He was waiting. All this time. He
waited while we stood in the barn. He waited for Pa with his arms
full of gun to come out. He took no chances and he waited.

I knew I couldn't wait. I knew I'd have to try to get back out.
There he'd be waiting too. I'd sit slowly in the snow like Pa.
That'd be a shame, a special shame after all I'd gone through, be-
cause I was on the edge of something wonderful, I felt it trembling

in me strangely, in the part of me that flew high and calmly looked down on my stiff heap of clothing. Oh Pa'd forgot. We could have used the shovel. I'd have found the bottle with it. With it we'd gone on home. By the stove I'd come to myself again. By it I'd be warm again. But as I thought about it, it didn't appeal to me any more. I didn't want to come to myself that way again. No. I was glad he'd forgot the shovel. But he was . . . he was waiting. Pa always said that he could wait; that Pedersen never could. But Pa and me, we couldn't — only Hans stayed back while we came out, while all the time the real waiter waited. He knew I couldn't wait. He knew I'd freeze.

Maybe the Pedersens were just asleep. Have to be sure the old man wasn't watching. What a thing. She wasn't much. Fat. Gray. But a crotch is a crotch. The light in the window paled. The sky I could see was smoky. The bits of broken glass had glimmered out. I heard the wind. Snow by the window rose. From a beam a cobweb swung stiffly like a net of wire. Flakes followed one another in and disappeared. I counted desperately three, eleven, twenty. One lit beside me. Maybe the Pedersens *were* just asleep. I went to the door again and looked in. New little rows of lights lay on the glasses and the jars. I felt the floor with my foot. I thought suddenly of snakes. I pushed my feet along. I got to every corner but the floor was empty. Really it was a relief. I went back and hid behind the boxes. The wind was coming now, with snow, the glass glinting in unexpected places. The dead tops of roofing nails in an open keg glowed white. Oh for the love of God. Above me in the house I heard a door slam sharply. He was finished with waiting.

The kid for killing his family must freeze.

The stair was railless and steep. It seemed to stagger in the air. Thank God the treads were tight and didn't creak. Darkness swept under me. Terror of height. But I was only climbing with my sled under my arm. In a minute I'd shoot from the roof edge and rush down the steep drift, snow-smoke behind me. I clung to the stair, stretched out. Fallen into space I'd float around a dark star. Not the calendar for March. Maybe they would find me in the spring, hanging from this stairway like a wintering cocoon.

I crawled up slowly and pushed the door open. The kitchen wallpaper had flower pots on it, green and very big. Out of every one a great red flower grew. I began laughing. I liked the wall-

paper. I loved it; it was mine; I felt the green pots and traced the
huge flower that stuck out of it, laughing. To the left of the door at
the head of the stair was a window that looked out on the back
porch. I saw the wind hurrying snow off toward the snowman.
Down the length of it the sky and all its light was lead and all the
snow was ashy. Across the porch were footprints, deep and precise.

I was on the edge of celebration but I remembered in time and
scooted in a closet, hunkering down between brooms, throwing my
arms across my eyes. Down a long green hill there was a line of
sheep. It had been my favorite picture in a book I'd had when I
was eight. There were no people in it.

I'd been mad and Pa had laughed. I'd had it since my birthday
in the spring. Then he'd hid it. It was when we had the privy in
the back. God, it was cold in there, dark beneath. I found it in the
privy torn apart and on the freezing soggy floor in leaves. And
down the hole I'd seen the curly sheep floating. There was even
ice. I'd been mad, rolling and kicking. Pa had struck himself and
laughed. I only saved a red-cheeked fat-faced boy in blue I didn't
like. The cow was torn. Ma'd said I'd get another one someday.
For a while, every day, even though the snow was piled and the sky
dead and the winter wind was blowing, I watched for my aunt to
come again and bring me a book like my Ma'd said she would. She
never came.

And I almost had Hans's magazines.

But he might come again. Yet he'd not chase me home, not now,
no. By God, the calendar was clean, the lines sharp and clear, the
colors bright and gay, and there were eights on the ice and red
mouths singing and the snow belonged to me and the high sky too,
burningly handsome, fiercely blue. But he might. He was quick.

If it was warmer I couldn't tell but it wasn't as damp as by the
boxes and I could smell soap. There was light in the kitchen. It
came through the crack I'd left in the closet door to comfort me.
But the light was fading. Through the crack I could see the sink,
now milky. Flakes began to slide out of the sky and rub their corners off on the pane before they were caught by the wind again and
blown away. In the gray I couldn't see them. Then they would
come, suddenly, from it, like chaff from grain, and brush the window while the wind eddied. Something black was bobbing. It was

deep in the gray where the snow was. It bounced queerly and then
it went. The black stocking cap, I thought.

I kicked a pail coming out and when I ran to the window my left
leg gave way, banging me against the sink. The light was going.
The snow was coming. It was coming almost even with the
ground, my snow. Puffs were rising. Then, in a lull when the snow
sank and it was light enough to see the snowbank shadows growing,
I saw his back upon a horse. I saw the tail flick. And the snow came
back. Great sheets flapped. He was gone.

3

Once, when dust rolled up from the road and the fields were high
with heavy-handled wheat and the leaves of every tree were gray
and curled up and hung head down, I went in the meadow with an
old broom like a gun, where the dandelions had begun to seed and
the low ground was cracked, and I flushed grasshoppers from the
goldenrod in whirring clouds like quail and shot them down. I
smelled wheat in the warm wind and every weed. I tasted dust in
my mouth, and the house and barn and all the pails burned my
eyes to look at. I rode the broom over the brown rocks. I hunted
Horse Simon in the shade of a tree. I rode the broom over the
brown meadow grass and with a fist like pistol butt and trigger shot
the Indian on Horse Simon down. I rode across the dry plain. I
rode into the dry creek. Dust rose up behind me. I went fast and
shouted. The tractor was bright orange. It shimmered. Dust rolled
behind it. I hid in the creek and followed as it came. I waited as
its path curved toward me. I watched and waited. My eyes were
tiny. I sprang out with a whoop and rode across the dry plain. My
horse had a golden tail. Dust rolled up behind me. Pa was on the
tractor in a broad-brimmed hat. With a fist like pistol butt and
trigger, going fast, I shot him down.

Pa would stop the tractor and get off and we'd walk across the
creek to the little tree Simon stood his bowed head under. We'd
sit by the tree and Pa would pull a water bottle out from between
its roots and drink. He'd swish it around in his mouth good before
he swallowed. He'd wipe off the top and offer it to me. I'd take a
pull like it was fiery and hand it back. Pa'd take another drink and
sigh and get on up. Then he'd say, "You feed the chickens like I

told you?" and I'd say I had, and then he'd say, "How's the hunting?" and I'd say pretty good. He'd nod like he agreed and clap
Simon on the behind and go on off, but he'd always say I'd best not
stay in the sun too long. I'd watch him go over the creek, waving
his hat before his face before he put it on. Then I'd take a secret
drink out of the bottle and wipe my lips and the top. After that I'd
go and let the ragweed brush against my knees and then,
sometimes, go home.

The fire had begun to feel warm. I rubbed my hands. Then I
ate a stale biscuit.

Pa had taken the wagon to town. The sun was shining. Pa had
gone to meet Big Hans at the station. There was snow around but
mud was flowing and the fields had green in them again. Mud
rode up on the wagon wheels. There was sweet air sometimes and
the creek had water with the winter going. Through a crack in the
privy door I saw him take the wagon to the train. I'd a habit, when
I was twelve, of looking down. Something sparkled on the water.
It was then I found the first one. The sun was shining. Mud was
climbing the wagon wheels and Pa was going to the train and
down the tight creek snow was flowing. He had a ledge beneath
the seat. You could reach right down. Already he had a knack for
hiding. So I found it and poured it out in the hole. That was the
last year we had the privy because when Big Hans came we tore it
down.

I ate an apple I'd found. The skin was shriveled but the meat
was sweet.

Big Hans was stronger than Simon, I thought. He let me help
him with his chores, and we talked, and later he showed me some
of the pictures in his magazines. "See anything like that around
here?" he'd say, shaking his head. "Only teats like that round here
is on a cow." And he would tease, laughing while he spun the
pages, giving me only a glimpse. Or he would come up and spank
me on the rump. We tore the privy down together. Big Hans
hated it. He said it was a dirty job fit only for soldiers. But
I helped him a lot, he said. He told me that Jap girls had their slice
on sideways and no hair. He promised to show me a picture of one
of them and though I badgered him, he never did. We burned the
boards in a big pile back of the barn and the flames were a deep
orange like the sun going down and the smoke rolled. "It's piss

wet," Hans said. We stood by the fire and talked until it sank down and the stars were out and the coals glowed and he told me about the war in whispers and the firing of big guns.

Pa liked the summer. He wished it was summer all year long. He said once whisky made it summer for him. But Hans liked the spring like me, though I liked summer too. Hans talked and showed me this and that. He measured his pecker once when he had a hard on. We watched how the larks ran across the weeds and winked with their tails taking off. We watched the brown spring water foam by the rocks in the creek, and heard Horse Simon blow and the pump squeak.

Then Pa took a dislike to Hans and said I shouldn't go with Hans so much. And then in the winter Hans took a dislike to Pa as he almost had to, and Hans said fierce things to Ma about Pa's drinking, and one day Pa heard him. Pa was furious and terrible to Ma all day. It was a night like this one. The wind was blowing hard and the snow was coming hard and I'd built a fire and was sitting by it, dreaming. Ma came and sat near me, and then Pa came, burning inside himself, while Hans stayed in the kitchen. All I heard was the fire, and in the fire I saw Ma's sad quiet face the whole evening without turning, and I heard Pa drinking, and nobody not even me said anything the whole long long evening. The next morning Hans went to wake Pa and Pa threw the pot and Hans got the axe and Pa laughed fit to shake the house. It wasn't long before Hans and I took to hating one another and hunting Pa's bottles alone.

The fire was burning down. There was some blue but mostly it was orange. For all Pedersen's preparing like Pa said he always did, he hadn't got much wood in the house. It was good to be warm but I didn't feel so set against the weather as I had been. I thought I'd like winter pretty well from now on. I sat as close as I could and stretched and yawned. Even if his cock was thicker than mine . . . I was here and he was in the snow. I was satisfied.

He was in the wind now and in the cold now and sleepy now like me. His head was bent down low like the horse's head must be and he was rocking in the saddle very tired of holding on and only rocking sleepy with his eyes shut and with snow on his heavy lids and on his lashes and snow in his hair and up his sleeves and down inside his collar and his boots. It was good I was glad he was there it wasn't me was there sticking up bare in the wind on a horse like a stick with the horse most likely stopped by this time with his bowed head bent into the storm, and I wouldn't like lying all by myself out there in the cold white dark, dying all alone out there, being buried out there while I was still trying to breathe, knowing I'd only come slowly to the surface in the spring and would soon be soft in the new sun and worried by curious dogs.

The horse must have stopped though he made the other one go on. Maybe he'd manage to drive this one too until it dropped, or he fell off, or something broke. He might make the next place. He just might. Carlson's or Schmidt's. He had once before though he never had a right or any chance to. Still he had. He was in the thick snow now. More was coming. More was blowing down. He was in it now and he could go on and he could come through it because he had before. Maybe he belonged in the snow. Maybe he lived there, like a fish does in a lake. Spring didn't have anything like him. I surprised myself when I laughed the house was so empty and the wind so steady it didn't count for noise.

I saw him coming up beside our crib, the horse going down to its knees in the drift there. I saw him going to the kitchen and coming in unheard because of all the wind. I saw Hans sitting in the kitchen. He was drinking like Pa drank — lifting the bottle. Ma was there, her hands like a trap on the table. The Pedersen kid was there too, naked in the flour, towels lapping his middle, whisky and water steadily dripping. Hans was watching, watching the kid's dirty toes, watching him like he watched me with his pin black eyes and his tongue sliding in his mouth. Then he'd see the cap, the mackinaw, the gloves wrapped thick around the gun, and it would be the same as when Pa kicked the glass from Big Hans's hand, only the bottle this time would roll on the floor, squirting. Ma would worry about her kitchen getting tracked and get up and mix biscuits with a shaky spoon and put the coffee on.

They'd disappear like the Pedersens had. He'd put them away somewhere out of sight for at least as long as the winter. But he'd leave the kid, for we'd been exchanged, and we were both in our own new lands. Then why did he stand there so pale I could see through? "Shoot. Go on. Hurry up. Shoot."

The horse had circled round in it. He hadn't known the way. He hadn't known the horse had circled round. His hands were

loose upon the reins and so the horse had circled round. Everything was black and white and everything the same. There wasn't
any road to go. There wasn't any track. The horse had circled
round in it. He hadn't known the way. There was only snow to the
horse's thighs. There was only cold to the bone and driving snow
in his eyes. He hadn't known. How could he know the horse had
circled round in it? How could he really ride and urge the horse
with his heels when there wasn't any place to go and everything
was black and white and all the same? Of course the horse had
circled round, of course he'd come around in it. Horses have a
sense. That's all manure about horses. No it ain't, Pa, no it ain't.
They do. Hans said. They do. Hans knows. He's right. He was
right about the wheat that time. He said the rust was in it and it
was. He was right about the rats, they do eat shoes, they eat anything, so the horse has circled round in it. That was a long time
ago. Yes, Pa, but Hans was right even though that was a long
time ago, and how would you know anyway, you was always drinking . . . not in summer . . . no, Pa . . . not in spring or fall
either . . . no, Pa, but in the winter, and it's winter now and
you're in bed where you belong, don't speak to me, be quiet. The
bottle made it spring for me just like that fellow's made it warm
for you. Shut up. Shut up. I wanted a cat or a dog awful bad since
I was a little kid. You know those pictures of Hans's, the girls with
big brown nipples like bottle ends . . . shut up, shut up. I'm not
going to grieve. You're no man now. Your bottle's broken in the
snow. The sled rode over it, remember? I'm not going to grieve.
You were always after killing me, yourself, Pa, oh yes you were. I
was cold in your house always, Pa. Jorge, so was I. No. I was. I
was the one wrapped in the snow. Even in the summer I'd shiver
sometimes in the shade of a tree. And Pa — I didn't touch you, remember — there's no point in haunting me. He did. He's come
round maybe. Oh no Jesus please. Round. Wakes. Sees the horse
has stopped. He sits and rocks and thinks the horse is going on and
then he sees it's not. He tries his heels but the horse has finally
stopped. He gets off and leads him on smack into the barn, and
there it is, the barn, the barn he took the horse from. Then in the
barn he begins to see better and he makes out something solid in
the yard where he knows the house is and there are certain to be
little letups in the storm and through one of them he sees a flicker

of something almost orange, a flicker of the fire and a sign of me by it all stretched out my head on my arm and near asleep. If they'd given me a dog, I'd have called him Shep.

I jumped up and ran to the kitchen but then I stopped and ran back for the gun and then ran back to the closet for the pail which I dropped with a terrible clatter. The tap gasped. The dipper in the pail beneath the sink rattled. So I ran to the fire and began to poke at it, the logs tumbling, and then I beat the logs with the poker so that sparks flew in my hair.

I crouched down behind a big chair in a corner away from the fire. Then I remembered I'd left my gun in the kitchen. My feet were bare and sore. The room was full of orange light and blackened shadows, moving. The wind whooped and the house creaked like steps do. I began to wonder if the Pedersens had a dog, if the Pedersen kid had a dog or cat maybe and where it was if they did, and if I'd known its name, whether it'd come if I called. I tried to think of its name as if it was something I'd forgot. I knew I was all muddled up and scared and crazy and I tried to think god damn over and over or what the hell or Jesus Christ, instead, but it didn't work.

The wagon had a great big wheel. Papa had a paper sack. Mama held my hand. High horse waved his tail. Papa had a paper sack. We both ran to hide. Mama held my hand. The wagon had a great big wheel. High horse waved his tail. We both ran to hide. Papa had a paper sack. The wagon had a great big wheel. Mama held my hand. Papa had a paper sack. High horse waved his tail. The wagon had a great big wheel. We both ran to hide. High horse waved his tail. Mama held my hand. We both ran to hide. The wagon had a great big wheel. Papa had a paper sack. Mama held my hand. High horse waved his tail. Papa had a paper sack. We both ran to hide. Papa had a paper sack. We both ran to hide.

The wind was still. The snow was still. The sun burned on the snow. The fireplace was cold and all the logs were ashy. I lay stiffly on the floor, my legs drawn up, my arms around me. The fire had gone steadily into gray while I slept, and the night away, and I saw the dust float and glitter and settle down. The walls, the rug, the furniture, all that I could see from my elbow looked pale and tired and drawn up tight and cramped with cold. I felt I'd never seen these things before. I'd never seen a wasted morning, the sick drawn look of a winter dawn, or how things were in a room where things were stored away and no one ever came, and how the dust came gently down.

I put my socks on. I didn't remember at all coming from behind the chair, but I must have. I got some matches from the kitchen and some paper twists out of a box beside the fireplace and I put them down, raking the ashes aside. Then I put some light kindling on top. Pieces of orange crate I think they were. And then a log. I lit the paper and it flared up and flakes of the kindling curled and got red and black and dropped off and finally the kindling caught when I blew on it. It didn't warm my hands any though I kept them close, so I rubbed my arms and legs and jigged, but my feet hurt. Then the fire growled. Another log. I found I couldn't whistle. I warmed my back some. Outside snow. Steep. There were long hard shadows in the hollows of the drifts but the eastern crests were bright. After I'd warmed up a little I walked about the house in my stocking feet, and snagged my socks on the stairs. I looked under all the beds and in all the closets and behind most of the furniture. I remembered the pipes were froze. I got the pail from under the sink and opened the door to the back porch against a drift and scooped snow in the pail with a dipper. Snow had risen to the shoulders of the snowman. The pump was banked. There were no tracks anywhere.

I started the stove and put snow in a kettle. The stove was beautifully black. I went back to the fireplace and put more logs on. It was beginning to roar and the room was turning cheerful. I wriggled into my boots. Somehow I had a hunch I'd see a horse.

The front door was unlocked. All the doors were, likely. He could have walked right in. I'd forgot about that. But now I knew he wasn't meant to. I laughed to see how a laugh would sound. Again. Good.

The road was gone. Fences, bushes, old machinery: what there might be in any yard was all gone under snow. All I could see was the steep snow and the long shadow lines and the hard bright crest about to break but not quite breaking and the hazy sun rising, throwing down slats of orange like a snow fence had fallen down. He'd gone off this way yet there was nothing now to show he'd gone; nothing like a bump of black in a trough or an arm or leg sticking out of the side of a bank like a branch had blown down

or a horse's head uncovered like a rock; nowhere Pedersen's fences
had kept bare he might be lying huddled with the horse on its
haunches by him; nothing even in the shadows shrinking while I
watched to take for something hard and not of snow and once alive.

I saw the window I'd broke. The door of the barn hung open,
banked with snow. The house threw a narrow shadow clear to one
end of the barn where it ran into the high drift that Hans had tun-
neled in. Later I'd cut a path to it. Make the tunnel bigger maybe.
Like a hollow tree. There was time. I saw the oaks too, blown
clean, their twigs about their branches stiff as quills. The path I'd
taken from the barn to the house was filled and the sun was burning brightly on it. The wind had curled in and driven a bank of
snow against the house where I'd stood. As I turned my head the
sun flashed from the barrel of Pa's gun. The snow had risen
around him. Only the top of the barrel was clear to take the sun
and it flashed squarely in my eye when I turned my head just right.
There was nothing to do about that till spring. Another snowman,
he'd melt. I picked my way back to the front of the house, a dark
spot dancing in the snow ahead of me. Today there was a fine large
sky.

It was pleasant not to have to stamp the snow off my boots, and
the fire was speaking pleasantly and the kettle was sounding softly.
There was no need for me to grieve. I had been the brave one and
now I was free. The snow would keep me. I would bury Pa
and the Pedersens and Hans and even Ma. I hadn't wanted to come
but now I didn't mind. The kid and me, we'd done brave things
well worth remembering. The way that fellow had come so mysteriously through the snow and done us such a glorious turn — well
it made me think of church. The winter time had finally got them
all, and I really did hope that the kid was as warm as I was now,
warm inside and out, burning up, inside and out, with joy.

(From The Virginia Quarterly Review)

THE MODEL CHAPEL

BY SISTER MARY GILBERT

ALL THE NUNS seemed to think that the plastic pigs were a wonderful idea. Sister Jude, the bursar, came home from the bank one September morning with a paper bag full of them and set them out on the community room table in three rows — red, yellow, and green — with *Lincoln First Federal Savings & Loan* stamped on their fat sides.

"Now!" she said, picking up a red pig and setting it a little apart from the others, "maybe our novena will work faster." She giggled and looked around at the other Sisters, her eye coming to rest on Sister Constance with a calculated gleam. "Sister Constance can write a little poem to put on the banks, can't she, Sister Superior?" Sister Jude asked. "You know, something to let people know what they're for."

Sister Constance groaned. Even after twenty years she loathed these impromptu orders for verse. (They always called them poems, of course.) In the novitiate it had been different. Everybody wrote jingles there, as if rhyme were the only language audible in that rarefied atmosphere. But in a college, supposedly peopled by adults, it was like using a fountain pen to dig worms.

Sister Superior sent a mischievous look in the direction of Sister Constance, who instantly felt childish and ashamed. "Maybe you can do something in the Edgar Guest tradition," she suggested, and Sister Constance felt her amusement even as she warmed to her sympathy.

In the end Sister Constance had escaped writing the jingle. She had intended to, really, but the bursar was in a hurry and Sister Marian, head of the music department, comprehending the urgency of the situation, had responded. She had seemed eager to demonstrate that art was in no way inconsistent with the practical, even if certain people stubbornly took that view.

Sister Constance had learned, on the other hand, that nuns are people and that, among them, inconsistencies turned up in about the same proportions as elsewhere. If the inconsistencies showed more at times, well, that was because nuns lived so close together.

So now the pigs were being fattened for market. There was a red one on the table in the tiny reception room beside the front entrance of the administration building. Its yellow counterpart stood in the dim recesses of the room across the entry, just beneath the ornate gold-framed Fra Angelico angels. Each morning after breakfast, Sister Jude stopped in the parlor on her way to the novena and opened the venetian blinds enough to frame the pig in a pool of sunlight, but Sister Clare, whose charge it was to dust the parlors, always closed the blinds when Sister Jude was out of sight.

The other eight banks were distributed at strategic points throughout the house, in areas open to visitors and students: one in the bursar's office, one on the cafeteria counter, three in the music room (Sister Constance didn't know whether music students were three times as responsive or triply resistant), one in an obscure corner of the president's office, one in the library, and one, green and animal, at the very feet of the statue of Our Lady of Fatima in the main hall. On one side of each of them, Scotch-taped over the bank imprint, was a small typed message: "A fervent prayer/ An extra penny/ For our new chapel/ To sanctify many." Sister Constance still cringed at the sight of it.

She went to the novena, though, every morning except Tuesday, when it was her turn to do the breakfast dishes. Several of the nuns remained stubbornly away, preferring their private prayer to the choral recitation of one honoring the Infant Jesus of Prague. But Sister Constance, whose reservations about the devotion were equally strong, yielded her judgment and offered the sacrifice of seeming concurrence. She would enter the chapel, genuflect slowly, bow her head in silent adoration and recite the words mechanically. When her eye fell on the dressed-up doll with the crown of gilt and pearls, that took the place of a real statue of the Infant in their tiny chapel, she was sometimes moved to genuine prayer — but it was prayer of atonement and not of petition.

As a young nun, she might have felt obliged to muffle her distaste for cheap religious art. Now she knew that God does not demand suspension of the critical faculties; that obedience and intelligence, taste even, can be reconciled without compromise. Yet it was difficult to apply the principle in particular cases.

Her reaction bothered her sometimes, it seemed so pharisaical. After all, there was something beautiful about the faith and fervor of her Sisters: they were so positive that the Infant could not refuse a petition obviously in accord with the Divine Will. What could more evidently be for God's glory than a new chapel? Their present one was too small entirely and hardly a fitting House for the Divine Guest. When they had outgrown the original chapel, they had removed the sliding doors between it and the community room, moved the altar from the east wall to the south and turned the *prie-dieux* to face it. Gradually they had added more of the tiny kneelers until the whole recess about the Wurlitzer organ was filled with them, and the junior Sisters, turned sideways in the alcove that had once housed the altar, were scarcely three feet from the priest as he offered Mass.

There was no Communion railing either, and two Sisters had to leave the chapel, carrying their chairs, and wait in the hall if one of the nuns wanted to go to Confession before morning Mass.

Sister Constance's place was in the second row at the side, wedged between Sister Catherine and the small niche for the Blessed Mother's statue. Sometimes on feast days the sacristan moved the statue to a pedestal in front of the chapel, where it belonged really, and Sister Constance used the shelf for her hymn books and prayer books. That was why she liked the place, even though she sometimes jabbed her left arm on the base of the niche when someone moved the kneelers a fraction and disturbed their alignment. Yes, a new chapel would be a great convenience, and it was something to pray and suffer for, but not too eagerly, for Sister Constance had learned that so long as a thing matters too much, nothing comes of it.

So she continued to attend the novena, all through the fall, and by November she took one of the plastic pigs from the music room and perched it on a filing case in her classroom. She removed the verse, though, substituting a small notation which read, "How about a dime? I'm building a chapel."

It seemed more honest and more direct; for though she could muster little enthusiasm for Walt Disney cartoons and talking animals generally, the message did avoid the trap of confusing piety and fund-raising.

Sister Constance couldn't help noting, though, that the direct approach seemed less effective. While two or three coins rattled forlornly in her bank, Sister Marian's had already been downtown and back for a refill several times. Once or twice, there had even been a dollar bill among the nickels and pennies and quarters; and the bank balance, padded out with a couple of checks from Sister Marian's friends and the proceeds from the sale of some scrap metal, now stood at an impressive $323.89.

It would take at least fifty thousand before they could start, Sister Superior said. But even at the present rate, there could be a new chapel in about eighty years — hardly a long time in the light of eternity, as Sister Jude was at pains to point out. And that would be entirely apart from the novena, which might, at any instant, produce a miracle. Not that they were looking for something extraordinary, you understand, just the softening of an indifferent or hardened heart with purse strings conveniently attached. Didn't the Jesuits experience things like that almost every week? And weren't the Sisters entitled to some mark of Divine favor? After all, Our Lord had urged His followers to ask and they should receive.

Sister Constance wanted to remind Sister Jude that He had also chosen a stable as His birthplace and Nazareth for a home town, but she thought better of it and continued to attend the novena.

Early in December, Sister Jude brought another surprise to the community recreation. The Sisters were sitting around darning their stockings, crocheting or playing Scrabble when Sister Jude walked in with a large carton, which she deposited squarely in front of Sister Superior. There was a rustle of curiosity, and the voices trailed off as Sister Superior rapped with her ring on the table for attention. Sister Jude opened the carton slowly, pushing each flap out of the way and then looking round as if to ask, "Do they really deserve to see this exquisite thing that I have brought them?"

After the carton was undone, there was tissue paper. Sister Jude removed it carefully, piece by piece, smoothing each one out and folding it neatly in four before taking another.

Her timing is all off, Sister Constance thought, as Sister Clare and Sister Timothy went wordlessly back to their Scrabble. Even the sacristan, who might have guessed that it would have something to do with the chapel, stopped looking at Sister Jude and returned to her mending with that terrible concentration known only to those newly fitted with bifocals.

By that time even Sister Jude realized that the game was up, so she cleared her throat and said, "Mr. Henry A. Madison, of Madison, Madison & Caldwell, has prepared a scale model of our chapel for display purposes." She reached into the box, took it out, and held it aloft for the Sisters' admiration.

When everyone had exclaimed sufficiently and had examined it at close range, the whole community straggled to the parlor, where the model chapel was enshrined beside the piggy bank. The pig, Sister Constance noted, was not in scale. Its yellow bulk, fully two inches above the clerestory, interposed an earthy barrier between the beholder and the concave shaft from which rose a slim, modernistic cross. The architect had remembered everything: there was a small flashlight battery attached, and when you pushed a switch on the green cork lawn, light streamed through the tiny stained-glass windows in a blue and mystic haze. The Sisters never stopped marveling at the perfection of it, and ten days later the battery had gone dead, though the novena had been thoroughly recharged, and even Sister Clare, who had at first referred to the morning chapel goers as Holy Rollers, now stopped ducking into the parlor to close the venetian blinds and went, instead, to her place in the third row behind Sister Constance.

Seeing the model chapel was certain to draw questions from visitors, the Sisters agreed, and who could tell when the Little King might send a millionaire — one looking for just such an opportunity on which to lavish a fraction of his wealth?

But as day followed day and no benefactor appeared, the novena thinned out a little. Oh no! they had not lost faith nor relinquished hope; it was just that activities multiplied as the school year continued, and some found their early-morning duties too urgent to leave time for spiritual extras.

So the scale model began to disappear into the other indistinguishable features of the reception room until one day when a newspaper reporter spied it, as he was coming in on another assignment. The inevitable questions drew the inevitable answers, and when he asked to do a story and use a picture, Sister Superior reluctantly consented, after making it clear that plans were still tentative and that no date had been set for starting construction. "But," as she remarked, "you never know who might read the story. Remember the nuns in the Old Folks' Home in Kentucky? They had been praying to St. Joseph for a new furnace, and a single news item brought them more than enough donations to pay for the project."

So the story appeared — a fine, inspiring account with a modest, two-column headline and a dignified photograph of Sister Superior examining the architect's model. But days passed, and the only communication elicited by the newspaper story was a frosty reprimand from the provincial superior, who wrote that she had "read with interest of your building program in the public press."

A few days later, Sister Superior and Sister Jude put the model chapel away in the parlor cupboard. The pig now presided over a heavy glass ashtray, the single concession to outsiders in the stiff, airless room with nothing to look at but a plastic-covered pamphlet containing the encyclical on Christian education and a finger-marked copy of last season's college yearbook.

By springtime the nuns were convinced that the Little King was testing their perseverance. St. Monica had prayed twenty or thirty years for Augustine's conversion, and who were they to presume? Of course they must do their part — supplement prayer with whatever action seemed advisable, for Christ had also said, hadn't He, that they must be wise as serpents?

Sister Jude reminded the Sisters at supper one evening that Mrs. McKinstry, a graduate of the normal school and widow of their good friend, might be approached for help. "Why don't we offer our regular novena with special fervor for nine days," she asked, "and then invite her over and propose a memorial chapel?"

It seemed like a direct inspiration, and fervor flared again in the little chapel each morning after breakfast. On the ninth day, Sister Superior, Sister Jude, and Sister Constance came to the parlor with

Sister Timothy, who had been in Mrs. McKinstry's class in normal school. The model had been re-enthroned after meticulous dusting, and the plastic pig, stationed at a respectful distance, had been hollowed out to receive a check, for the Sisters believed in preparedness.

Sister Timothy led the conversation adroitly round to the subject which had brought them together. Sister Superior, who was really rather shy, confined her remarks to quiet affirmations of what had just been said. Sister Constance prayed soundlessly that Sister Jude would not disgrace them all.

Mrs. McKinstry was a wizened, white-haired arthritic, who blossomed profusely when cultivated. Since her husband's death, she had experienced a renewal of vigor and, from a complaining semi-invalid, had become a venturesome little grandmother, who drove the car and bought new clothes and went to all the club meetings she had skipped for the last fifteen years. She loved the Sisters, enjoyed reminiscing with them, and asked their prayers for whatever business matters or family problems absorbed her at the moment.

Midway in one of Sister Timothy's most dramatic sentences, Mrs. McKinstry's roving eye fastened on the pig, and she let out a little exclamation of curiosity and delight as she recognized one of the banks from her son's place of business. She would have gone for it immediately, except that Sister Jude anticipated the movement and placed it in her knotted, eager hands. She read the inscription while everyone waited. Everyone, except Sister Constance, who couldn't restrain the remark: "Poetry just seems to go with pigs, don't you think, Mrs. McKinstry?" She lowered her eyes to avoid Sister Jude's swift reproach.

Mrs. McKinstry chuckled and read the rhyme aloud in skittishly pious tones: "A fervent prayer/ An extra penny/ For our new chapel/ To sanctify many." She reached for her handbag. She rustled about among the lipstick and car keys and Sunday collection envelopes until she found a quarter and three pennies.

"There," she said, bringing them to the surface with a triumphant cluck, "*three* extra pennies and a quarter besides!" She dropped them, one at a time, with a hollow plastic thud, the quarter last, poising it above the slot with a lingering farewell look.

"We knew the Little King would help us," Sister Jude said, interrupting Sister Constance's reflections on the widow's mite.

"What a fine *beginning!*" She looked toward Sister Timothy encouragingly.

"Agnes," Sister Timothy said, "wouldn't it be beautiful to have a chapel named for Tom? St. Thomas Chapel . . . There's something so right about it."

Mrs. McKinstry shifted uneasily in her chair. "Of course I'd be thrilled to have you name the chapel for Tom," she said, her voice breaking a little. "Do you intend to build soon?"

"Everything depends upon the necessary funds, Mrs. McKinstry," Sister Jude answered. It was the tone she reserved for bank presidents and auditors from the Bureau of Internal Revenue.

"We were just saying before you came," Sister Timothy said, pressing her advantage, "whoever gives us a major donation — say, anything up to fifty thousand — should have the consolation and the joy of naming the chapel for a dear one."

"I shouldn't think there'd be many folks in Carlton who could give so much," Mrs. McKinstry said. "Where are the African violets you promised to show me?"

Less than two hours later, Sister Constance brought a message to Sister Superior. One of the Franciscan Sisters had called from the hospital to say that Mrs. McKinstry had driven her car into a telephone pole. She was not hurt seriously, just shaken, but in view of her age, the doctor was concerned about the circumstances leading up to the accident. Had they, perhaps, been aware of any emotional disturbance during her visit to the college?

The older members of the community contended that Mrs. McKinstry would come through. Time often worked wonders. Time and prayer. Her brush with death would make her think seriously. Sister Timothy announced that she was putting the whole matter in the hands of Agnes's Guardian Angel, and her evening vigils in the chapel lengthened visibly.

Father Morgan's years in the movie capital had given him a theatrical air. He had mastered the gestures: the flow of the hands, wrists leading like a ballet dancer, and the three-quarter profile with compelling eyes. But Sister Constance felt that the parish public address system and his own vibrato reduced Father Morgan's Hooper Rating when it came to delivery. The more emphatic portions of his Sunday sermons rattled the chandeliers in the high-ceilinged sanctuary, making her yearn for the dramatic pause and the whispered resonance that signalized his Master's voice.

His eloquence had been instrumental in building the new church, it was true, and he was in general favor among the parishioners, especially the women. But even the men appeared to derive vicarious enjoyment from his preaching, sitting with folded arms and eyes rolled upwards to the towering pulpit.

Today he was launching a drive for the parish hall. Some of the old-timers said that it wasn't really needed, but others accused them of obstructing progress. St. Clement's was a growing parish with an up-to-date school, a well-planned, well-built rectory (the old one had been converted to a convent for the Sisters who taught the parish school), and plans for an eighty-five-thousand-dollar hall, complete with stainless steel automatic kitchen, auditorium, meeting rooms, recreation area, nursery facilities, and baby sitters for children whose parents were attending church services.

While Father Morgan outlined the need, Sister Constance trimmed the budget by thirty thousand. That would be a good beginning for their chapel, she thought. Get that close to the goal, and everyone would tax his ingenuity to do more. But of course it was out of the question. As an institution owned and operated by the teaching Congregation to which she belonged (or more accurately, by the loan company which had financed the building), the college was not entitled to Church support.

Father Morgan had reached the part about needing the co-operation of "every man, woman, and child in this parish if we are to succeed in this gigantic undertaking for the glory of God." Sister Constance looked at him and wished that he would reserve his hypnotic powers for more willing victims.

After Mass Father Morgan took the children's envelopes to the convent so that the Sisters could count the money. On his way he passed by the college and stopped to ask the superior's help in reaching the college students of his parish.

Sister Constance greeted him at the door, led him into the reception room, and went in quest of Sister Superior. She returned and found Father Morgan thoughtfully examining the plastic pig.

Nobody knew exactly what happened, but soon afterwards, the piggy banks were gathered up again and stored away in the bursar's cupboard — all except one, which had slipped out of sight behind a row of books in Sister Superior's office. Sister Constance used to see it there when she dusted the furniture in the morning, and it gave her a gloomy satisfaction to know that the animal was at large. Much as she had hated the bald beggary and the doggerel, she hated pettiness more, and on good days she constructed fierce fantasies in which the wandering pig disgorged five-figure bank notes with "Sisters' Chapel" franked into the grain.

May was unusually warm that year, and Sister Constance found the hour and one-half required for morning prayer, meditation, and Mass longer than she cared to admit. The whir of the electric fan reminded her that it was cooler at the rear of the chapel, but twenty years separated her from the relative comfort in which the senior Sisters sat. Where would she be in twenty years? Still fighting off the drowsiness and the suffocation of this early-morning tryst?

Sister Catherine reached for her rosary, and Sister Constance gathered her skirts closer to keep her neighbor's hand out of a strange pocket. The beads rattled annoyingly, and from somewhere out in the hall, the distracting fragrance of coffee and frying bacon wrestled with her prayer.

She gathered her veil with a practiced twist and brought it forward over her shoulder, edging away from the back of the seat so that Sister Clare might rest her hands on the *prie-dieu*. Fifteen minutes more before Mass. She gathered her distractions into a brief lament and laid them before the tabernacle. Outside, the endless freight cars bumped and shook, invading the chapel with bleating cries and the strong, medicinal odor of sheep dip.

Sister Constance skipped the novena that morning, even though it wasn't Tuesday. She wanted to polish the floor in Sister Superior's office, and it was easier to get started before the Sisters began filing in to ask for bus tokens or advice in dealing with violations of dormitory regulations.

The janitor stuck his head in the doorway. "Do you want some more wax to keep the shine on?" He held the mop carefully away from his freshly laundered overalls.

He applied the wax with eager scrupulosity, for in his eighteen years at the college, Otto had contracted some of the Sisters' passion for perfection. He moved the chairs gently aside, sought out the corners, avoiding the baseboards, and gave the space beneath the radiator two coats.

"By golly," he said, frowning at the black marks around the desk, "we got to take all the wax off and clean it before summer school. You tell me when. Maybe Sister Superior go away." He picked up the plastic pig, shook it, and held it out to Sister Constance.

"This pig sounds empty," he said. He backed out gingerly, waiting for the wax to dry. "I put three dimes in the one in the hall before they take it away. You got enough?"

Sister Constance looked ruefully at the wet wax and stuffed the bank in her pocket. She gave him a quick lesson in elementary economics, carefully omitting Father Morgan's part in the total scheme. Otto is so good, she thought. We take vows of poverty and obedience, and he keeps them. She unwound the cord and plugged the polisher into the wall outlet.

"Say," Otto said excitedly, forgetting to tiptoe in his eagerness, "maybe we get the chapel anyway?" He reached into his pocket, pulled out his billfold, and extracted two small pieces of paper. "Sweepstakes tickets," he said. "Maybe we win fifty thousand *pounds*. You know how much a pound is? That be enough?"

"These tickets cost between three and four dollars," Sister Jude said evenly, as Sister Constance, following Sister Superior's orders, left them in the bursar's office. "And he's bought two of them. Why didn't he give the *money* to the chapel instead?"

"There's really only one ticket," Sister Constance said. "The other is a confirmation. Be sure to put them away carefully. Otto says you have to produce the ticket if you win. He almost lost a thousand dollars once because he forgot where he put the thing."

The community was split on the Sweepstakes Question, and for once the division was not chronological. Sister Timothy, the oldest in the house, was not one to condone gambling, but she was a firm believer in charity. Didn't the tickets say plainly that this was a hospital benefit? It was really another form of the corporal works of mercy, you know, and the Irish sense of compassion is much stronger than anything we find here in America.

Sister Timothy wanted to put the tickets beneath the Infant's statue in the chapel. Or maybe St. Joseph's because it was larger, but Sister Superior objected on the grounds that it savored of superstition and seemed like putting limits on God's power.

Sister Constance, tempted by the ironic possibilities of the situation, succumbed. The notion of building a chapel on sweepstakes winnings was so delightfully incongruous that it blurred her judgment for a time. The strangeness that others attribute to fate she identified with Divine Providence, and she told herself that it would be just like God to answer their prayers in this unexpected fashion.

But she knew she was dramatizing. In certain characters there is an intermittent romance between cynicism and naïveté, and Sister Constance was one of these. So it didn't surprise her when June 6 came and went without a telegram of victory. Sister Timothy took the silence harder, and padded about the house with pinched features, pulling the black shawl closer about her shoulders, and saying at intervals, "I don't understand it. God must have some magnificent treat in store for us."

The community bell rang at four-thirty the next afternoon, and since it was neither the day for Confessions nor for Holy Hour, the Sisters were all asking the reason for the summons. They stood about in the community room keeping a token silence, impatient to be about their work but too obedient to ignore the bell. Sister Superior and Sister Jude entered together, their faces serious, their eyes taking a quick census before the business began.

At Sister Superior's direction, the Sisters seated themselves after a brief offering and waited with folded arms, their hands concealed within the large outer sleeves.

"Sister Jude has something to tell us about the chapel," Sister Superior said, and the community searched her face for an answer to their prayers but found no clue.

Sister Jude glanced at Sister Superior. "We've really been very fortunate," she began.

"I knew it!" Sister Timothy said. "I knew something would come of all those prayers," but Sister Jude looked sharply at her, and Sister Superior nodded to Sister Jude to go on.

"As you know, the fire department has inspected our building," Sister Jude said, "and *they* feel that our chapel is . . . inadequate." The Sisters began talking all at once, and Sister Superior tapped her ring for silence. Sister Jude hurried toward the climax.

"We have to put in another exit," she said. "The aisles are so narrow — and an outside stairway." She took an envelope from her pocket. "This is the official notice."

"Providentially," Sister Jude said, "we have the money to do what is required." She looked with deference toward the head table and said, "Maybe Sister Superior would like to tell you about the changes in schedule before I present the financial part."

"For a while, at least," Sister Superior said, "we'll have to have two Masses. The younger Sisters up to and including Sister Constance will rise half an hour earlier — at five instead of five-thirty." She smiled to cushion the shock. "The workmen would like to start at eight each morning, so please try to get your private devotions in before that time or after five P.M. Our noon examination of conscience will be in the community room." She turned the meeting back to Sister Jude, now thoroughly in command of the situation, and ready for a detailed report in which the light of her business acumen gleamed from a bushel of extraneous data. The estimated cost of the remodeling was three hundred dollars. Two of the windows would have to be sealed off, but on good days they could have the fire door open. They couldn't afford to have the whole interior refinished, so it might not be beautiful to look at, but then the chapel was only temporary anyway.

Sister Timothy began asking the Sister nearest her to repeat what Sister Superior had said. "It's awful to get old," she complained. "It sounded to me as if Sister Superior said we'd get up at five."

Sister Constance turned unwillingly as Sister Jude spoke again. "One more thing, Sisters," she said. "Sister Superior and I have been talking this over, and we've agreed that it is a blessing in disguise. If we hadn't had the banks, of course, there would be no provision for meeting this added burden."

If we hadn't had the banks, Sister Constance thought, there would be no burden. But she merely meant that it would have been a different one.

"Perhaps you know," Sister Jude said, "our chapel fund was a little more than three hundred and sixty dollars, and Sister Superior has a wonderful idea for the other sixty dollars." Sister Superior blinked when the gentle rod of her authority coiled in Sister Jude's aggressive hand.

Sister Jude seemed not to notice. "We were down at Jamison's today," she said, her voice growing slightly nasal, "and we found a perfectly lovely statue of the Infant of Prague." She smiled expectantly and looked around.

Sister Constance averted her eyes. Already she realized that the odds favored 100 per cent attendance at tomorrow's novena. It didn't really matter when or how they got the chapel. What mattered was that they kept on wanting one. She smiled with what Sister Jude was sure to interpret as satisfaction over the new statue. Then she plunged a hand deep into her pocket and loosened the sticky rhyme that still clung to the plastic pig.

(From The New Yorker)

A DAY ON RAGGED

BY DONALD HALL

ONE DAY in late July, 1945, I woke at six, when my grand-mother brought my morning cup of black coffee into my bedroom. I sat on the edge of the bed and gulped the bitter coffee. It had been made in an old drip pot on the iron stove, where a kettle was always simmering, and it was nearly as thick as Turkish. The shades in my room were still down, and the morning light showed in a thousand pinpricks through the worn green cloth. I crossed the room and opened the shades and heard a rooster crow in the henyard across the road. A big automobile slurred past, making an early start for the White Mountains. I always looked out to see what kind of day it would be. Rain? A scorcher? It looked fine and sunny today. I walked back toward the bed, where my coffee cup sat on the table, between my typewriter and a vase of flowers that my grandmother had picked. I sat on the bright quilt and finished the coffee. Usually I would get another cup of coffee after I had dressed, and sit at my brown table and work at poems. But this morning was the start of a day we had planned since I had arrived from Connecticut in mid-June to spend the summer, as I always did, at my grandparents' farm in New Hamp-shire. In years past, before I was born, my grandfather had made an annual excursion to pick blueberries. I had heard about those days in many of the stories my grandfather told me. I was sixteen that summer, and able to help him with the haying and the daily chores more than in previous years. As we worked together, I some-times imagined that I was living in my grandfather's old stories, just as I was in fact living in the farmhouse where my grandmother had been born and where a gallery of ancient relatives stared down at me from photographs and daguerreotypes on the parlor wall. The blueberries my grandfather talked about were the low, wild kind, and they grew among the ledges of blue rock at the top of Ragged Mountain. They were a three-mile walk from the farmhouse, and the walk was mostly up. When my grandfather was younger, he and a hired man would pick for one long day, and my grandmother and her daughters, one of whom was my mother, would wash, sort, and can them for two days. A shelf of cold-packed quarts of blueberries would wait in the cellar for the piecrusts of winter. It was one of the many ways a farmer compensated for his lack of money — like the eggs from the laying season stored in waterglass, and like the salted meat from the slaughtering.

My grandfather had talked about the blueberry-picking so often that it seemed as much a part of his past as the two-hour sermons he had endured as a boy, and the lyceums at which he had recited set pieces and comic poems. But a few weeks earlier this past had strangely seemed present to us. A neighbor named Paul Whittier had been chasing a bear that had tramped down his peas, and had followed it all the way to the top of Ragged. (It was not only a lust for revenge that drove him; the bounty on bears was five dollars.) He had lost his bear among the rocks on the other side of the mountain, but among the blue ledges of the top he had found the blueberries thicker than ever. They were green then, he said, or he would have been up there eating them still.

No one, as far as my grandfather knew, had picked there for twenty years. The berries were higher up than the forests that had been cut of their softwood years before, or the lumberjacks would have stripped them. No one else in the neighborhood cared to make the climb. The thought of all those blueberry pies growing, maturing, and dropping every year, unappreciated except by the birds, troubled my grandfather's sense of propriety. We decided we would go blueberry-picking.

My grandmother fretted a little. It was a long trip; the rocks were hard to climb; the blueberries would be too heavy for us to carry; my grandfather was seventy-two years old. But the thought of her rows of canned blueberries, cold-packed in their quart jars, overcame her opposition. She made us promise to stop and rest when we were tired, and my grandfather fixed the time when he thought the blueberries would be ripe.

This morning, I took my second cup of coffee in the kitchen and ate breakfast in the old chair beside the window, under the caged canary named Christopher. I was impatient to be started. I heard a strange noise outside a high-pitched hoot from behind the sheep barn, where railroad tracks of the Boston & Maine cut through the soft dirt. It was the time for the morning Peanut, the train — actually named, as I recall, the Penult — that went up to White River Junction in the evening and came back in the morning. But the whistle of the Peanut was the long, throaty lament of the steam engine. I stared at the gap in the ensilage corn, through which I would be able to see the train flash. When it came, it looked like a trolley car, short and self-propelled, and again it hooted its ridiculous horn. "I suppose that's one of those funny new trains," my grandmother said. "Somebody said they'd seen one this summer."

When I had finished my eggs, I walked up to the tieup, where the cows stood, morning and evening, to be milked. The cows were moving out to pasture now, and behind them my grandfather was clapping his hands and shouting. In the spring, they would gallop out like young horses, but by this time of year they acted like cows again, and my grandfather was in a hurry to shut the gates behind them. I went into the tieup to start cleaning it. With the edge of a hoe, I lifted up the hinged floorboard over the manure pit and pushed the cow flops onto their cousins below.

My grandfather came in. "How did you like the new whistle?" he said.

"Not so much," I told him. "I like the old kind."

"I suppose there's a reason for it," he said. He picked up the other hoe and scraped along with me. "You should be resting for what's ahead of you," he said. He sang one of his tuneless songs and seemed as excited as I was.

When we walked into the kitchen, my grandmother was packing pie and sandwiches into an enormous paper bag. "You'll need your strength, Wesley," she said to my grandfather. "Now, you eat a good breakfast."

He ate his oatmeal and bread and coffee, sitting at one of the set tubs, which was covered with oilcloth. My grandmother finished packing the paper bag and disappeared into the shed. A moment later, I heard her pumping at the deep well in the back, and I followed her out to relieve her. I pumped, and we filled three milk bottles with cold well water, and she put cardboard tops on the bottles.

We left them inside the shed and brought the paper bag out with us when my grandfather had finished eating. Two huge pails, shaped wider at the bottom than at the top, lay waiting for us. We put the food in one and the water in the other. Then my grandfather found a wooden yoke, which he placed over the back of his neck and from which he hung the two great pails. It was the apparatus he used when he made maple sugar in the winter, pouring the sap from the little buckets at each sugar maple into the big pails. I carried two sap buckets, into which we would pick the berries, and we started off.

It was seven o'clock. The air was cool and the grass was soaking wet under our feet. Low light from the east came through the trees, which were full and dark green. My grandmother called after us from the end of the porch, warning us to be careful. We turned into New Canada Road and started to climb. "It'll be harder coming back," said my grandfather, "but at least it will be downhill." He paused, the pails swinging easily from the ends of the yoke. Then he laughed. "The only man I ever knew who could walk all day and not be tired," he said, "was your Great-Grampa Keneston. He must have touched every inch of this mountain. Days when he couldn't do much else, he would walk around his pasture looking at the fencing. My, he was sprightly! You heard your mother tell about how, the day before he died, he walked clear down to West Andover to buy some Canada Mints. He was eighty-seven then. When he had his seventieth birthday, he stood up on the horse's back and galloped up the hill to the barn. Bethuel Peasley told how when he was seventy-five or so he set off on a walk with a two-year-old dog following him and he came back four hours later with the dog slung along the back of his neck like a lamb. All tired out."

In the shade of the gray birches and of the maples that met over New Canada Road, it was almost cold that morning, but I was already sweating because of the climb. I took off the sweater that my grandmother had asked me to wear and tied it around my waist. "That's the last you'll use your sweater today," my grandfather said.

After a mile of New Canada Road, we climbed over some bars into a pasture. I thought I felt ruts underneath the old leaves where we were walking. "Is this a lumber road?" I asked.

"Yes," said my grandfather. "It's Paul Whittier's pasture, though he only keeps a few head now. He took the lumber off about ten years ago."

The only old trees were twisted ones that the lumberers had scorned. Young fir was growing thickly everywhere but in the road, which the spring waters had eroded into cliffs and islands of rock. I stumbled once and scraped my knee. We climbed most of the time, but the road avoided the steepest parts. Sometimes we passed through a clearing, full of squashed bushes and flatter than the rest of the land, which the cows patronized.

A little after eight, we paused in one of the clearings and sat on rocks to catch our breath. My grandfather's shirt was wet through. I already felt as tired as if I had hayed for a whole afternoon. We said nothing for a while. Then I said, "I'm thirsty."

My grandfather shook his head. "You'll be thirstier," he said. "It's thirsty work. You'll do better to wait."

In a moment, we set out again. The road failed us and we climbed a stone wall out of Paul Whittier's pasture. "I reckon this is part of our land you've never seen," said my grandfather. "Took the timber off nearly twenty years ago." Pine grew tall around us. "It won't be long before we take it off again."

We walked parallel to the stone wall until we came to a dry creek bed, and we used it as our road up the mountain. It was very rocky. I fitted one bucket inside the other and used my free hand to climb with. "How will we get down when we're carrying blueberries?" I asked.

"There's another way," said my grandfather. We stood still for a moment in order to talk. "Or there used to be. It's steeper than most of this, but it's steadier. Not that this creek used to be so dug out. I suppose you can't know what you will find." We both wiped our faces with our handkerchiefs. I looked at my watch; it was only eight-thirty. "We'd better move on," my grandfather said.

After fifteen minutes of climbing, we left the creek and came to more level land. A surprising plain of heavy grass made easy walking for a moment. "Too bad we can't get the hayrack up here," I said. My grandfather nodded and smiled. He was looking ahead at the fringe of trees on the edge of the clearing. When we came up to them, he motioned to me to go first. I stepped through and stopped still. The land in front of me sloped slightly, and I saw that it rose again two hundred yards ahead, making a little saucer of a valley high up on the mountain. In the bowl, flat down and rust red, lay a forest of dead trees, all pointing in the same direction. It could not have been larger than five acres, but it seemed vast as I looked at it, like a crater of the dead. Desolation made it look immense. There seemed to be no growth under the dead branches of the huge trees. The soil had fallen away from the exposed roots, and the roots looked like bunches of dead nerves. We were so high, beyond paths and people, that it seemed as if we were the first to know. I felt as if I had been walking on the shore and found a drowned submarine rolled up by the tide.

My grandfather was looking over my shoulder. "The hurricane?" I asked. I meant the storm of September, 1938.

"Yes," said my grandfather. "Do you know what kind of trees they were?"

I shook my head.

"This was the stand of rock maple," he said. "It must have taken them a hundred and fifty years to grow so big. They would have been worth hauling from here, being rock maple." The chopping block in the woodshed was rock maple, I knew. It was about the hardest wood that grew in New England. "We were planning to sell them in 1940, but after everything blew down, nobody would come up here for them. They were too busy with the trees low down."

I had nothing to say. I just stared. It was so huge and so wasted.

"Dead but not buried," my grandfather went on. "I haven't seen it since the time I climbed up here after the hurricane. Pine a few rods away wasn't touched. The roots aren't deep enough here, for there's ledge down a few feet under the soil. That's why I feared and climbed up. It looked different then. You couldn't see the trunks for all the leaves, and of course you couldn't walk through it. I could see that everything was pointing the same way. A lumberman from the government told me one gust probably did it."

A moment later, my grandfather stepped past me and we began to pick our way through the dead trees. The branches made a continual dry hedge that snapped at our touch and scratched our faces and arms. My watch was nearly torn from my wrist. I put it in my pocket. We climbed over and under the great trunks and weaved back and forth as if we were lost in a maze. Finally, we rose at the other side of the lot and looked back again. "We won't be coming through here on the way back," said my grandfather. "Lucky thing." He took one last look at the trees and then turned up the hill.

We were beginning to climb the blue ledges that made the top of Ragged. It was only four hundred yards to the blueberries, but they were hard going. "I can see the bushes," said my grandfather. My feet felt lighter and I climbed more rapidly. Only my throat remained tight and dry, and I looked forward to water as much as to sitting down. Soon the dome of Ragged flattened out, and the rocks, which had seemed to lie close together, turned into islands in a sea of blueberries. The bushes were as low as grass, hardly taller than the flat rock they surrounded. The blue of the berries seemed more prominent than the green of the leaves, so that the earth looked blue everywhere, from blue stone to blue fruit. Only the texture varied. The berries were ripe and full. Some of them had burst and oozed a blue liquid. Most of them were small and as sweet as I had ever tasted.

We squatted on a rock. My grandfather delved into his pails. "Now's when the work starts," he said, "so I reckon you'll want some strength." He opened the paper bag and handed me a sandwich. I looked at my watch and saw it was nine o'clock. "Have yourself some water," he said.

The milk bottle of well water was already warm. I pried the top off and tilted my head back and swallowed luxuriously. When I took it away, I had drunk nearly half the bottle. My grandfather looked over. "Careful," he said. "It's a hot day and a long way to water."

I nodded, but I didn't really care. I took another sip before I put the bottle back. Then I ate my egg sandwich while the sun rose higher and warmed the back of my neck. There was no wind this morning, or we would have been open to it. I realized that we had left trees behind at the level of the dead forest. I looked down at it now, a red-brown patch among the green. Elsewhere, as far as I could see, there was only the green of the trees and the blue silver of small lakes. Here and there in the distance I saw the white of a farmhouse. Suddenly something occurred to me. "I should think that rock maple might catch on fire," I said.

My grandfather nodded. "Lightning might do it," he said. "Of course, nobody walks up here to throw a cigarette away. I've thought of it. It would blaze down the whole mountain if it started, and we're on the mountain."

I stood up and walked a little way toward the other side of Ragged. I felt as solitary as an explorer. Low clouds cut off the tops of other peaks a mile or two off, and in between I saw the same green and the same white specks of the farms.

I heard my grandfather call "Want any more to eat now?" He was packing up the lunch.

"I guess not," I said, and walked back to him.

He put the bag and the bottles in a crack in the rock and stood up. "All set?" he said. He picked up one of the sap buckets. The two big pails were standing on a flat piece of rock. "These berries are mighty low," he said. "You may prefer to sit on the rock and pick them. A sore back is a sore back."

We took our buckets and set out in different directions. I had never picked low-bush berries before, and there were tricks I didn't know. When I tried to scoop off a whole handful, I crushed some of the berries and pulled a leaf or a bit of stem along with them. My bucket was soon full of foreign matter, which would make for a lot of picking over back at the farm. Yet when I tried to be careful I went so slowly that it would have taken all morning to pick one bucketful. The trouble with sitting was that I had to slide myself over the bumpy rock, and I began to feel paralyzed where I sat. The heaviest stems of berries were always slightly out of reach. I tried kneeling, but my knees gave out. I tried standing, and it felt all right until I unbent, when I thought I would crack apart. Finally, I sat again, as the least evil.

My grandfather stood and bent. Whenever he straightened up, he grimaced. "Why don't *you* sit down?" I asked.

"I'd never stand up again!" he said. He pointed to the calves of his legs without breaking the rhythm of his fast picking. "Cramps," he said. "From climbing up here."

I picked and picked. I switched from the right hand to the left and back again, and picked two-handed, and still my bucket was only a quarter full. I realized that even when I had filled it, the berries would barely cover the bottom of one of the big pails. I thought we would never fill even one of them. Then I heard my grandfather grunt as he straightened up, and saw him empty his full bucket into one of the big pails. "There's one," he said.

"Look at all I've done," I said, lifting my bucket to show it to him.

"You don't know how to pick them yet." He walked over to me and leaned down. He took hold of a stem heavy with blueberries and stripped it clean between his index and middle fingers without crushing a berry or tearing off a leaf. "Do you see?" he said. "You have to be gentle and let your hand feel them coming. You'll learn it."

In the whole morning I only filled my bucket twice, while his bucket emptied itself five times into our storage bins on the flat rock. My hands felt twisted out of shape and nervous with their continual darting. My back felt welded in a leaning curve. Worst of all, my throat parched with thirst, and parched more and more as the sun rose in the sky and the sweat dried on my body. A hundred times I almost complained, or almost rose to have a drink of the water without saying anything, but each time the sight of my grandfather, picking steadily and humming to himself, and seventy-two years old, shamed me into silence. He worked with utter delight in the growing pile of berries. He talked of the number of blueberry pies we had already gathered, and all I could think of was the dampness of them. When I ate a handful of blueberries, my mouth felt better for a moment but then felt unutterably worse — so thick that my cheeks clung to my teeth and my tongue stuck to the roof of my mouth. I knew that we would break for lunch, but I had put my watch in my pocket. I kept squinting up at the sun to guess the time. Finally, when I didn't even know I was going to say it, I heard my dry voice squeaking, "I think I'll have a drink."

My grandfather pulled his gold watch from the pocket of his trousers. "My, my," he said. "It's past lunchtime. Twelve-fifteen." He put his watch away and stretched carefully. "I guess we'd better do some eating."

I rose gratefully and walked toward our cache of food and water. I lifted the bottle I had started before and, though I knew I was foolish, drained it dry. A minute after I had set it back on the rock, my thirst returned. I reached for a second quart, which stood propped in the crack of rock, and when I lifted it out my stiff fingers slipped and the bottle fell and rolled from me, and the water poured out over the blue rocks and drained among the blueberry plants.

"Look!" I said. I was exhausted and angry to the point of tears. I could say nothing more.

My grandfather shook his head and smiled at me. "I suspect you'll wish you had that quart of water," he said.

I dipped my finger in a small puddle in the rock and sucked it. The third quart had to do for both of us now, and my grandfather hadn't drunk anything yet. "You handle the other quart," I said.

"We'll be careful with that one," my grandfather said.

As I ate, I felt a little better. The custard pie, the pickles, and the butter in the chicken sandwiches were all damp. I ate as slowly as I could, pushing away the moment when the picking would begin again. When we had finished the whole bag, my grandfather tucked it tidily — waxed paper and hard-boiled-egg shells inside — into a crevice of the stone.

"Now let's have a bit of that water," said my grandfather. He lifted the remaining bottle and took a mouthful, keeping it in his mouth a long time and letting it go down in slow sips, scrupulously. "That's good," he said, and handed it to me.

I tried to do the same trick, and choked.

He stood up and stretched again. "I could relish a few minutes on the sofa just now," he said. "Don't see any sofas hereabouts." He walked to where he had left his bucket and began to pick again.

I looked at my watch. It was nearly one. On the way to my bucket, I looked in the big pails. One was nearly full, and the other was barely covered with berries on the bottom. When I sat down on the hard rock again, my old bruises of the morning felt worse than before.

During the afternoon, I filled my bucket more rapidly, and every time I emptied it I took a sip of water. It was my reward for being quick. I saw my grandfather wet his lips once and stand staring across the valley below us at the hills on the other side. I stood up

and watched with him, and for a moment forgot blueberries and
sore backs, fatigue and thirst. But in a moment my throat contracted with its drought again, and I raced to fill up another bucket.

My grandfather seemed to pick more slowly than he had picked
in the morning, and when he stood up now to carry the bucket to
the big pail, he usually paused for a minute before walking. In
the middle of the afternoon, I calculated that two more bucketfuls
would fill the last big pail, and I raced to fill my bucket and be
done. My grandfather and I met at the big pails at the same time
and poured our blueberries to the very top. I took another sip of
water, unable to speak for the dryness of my throat. About an inch
was left in the bottom of the bottle. I was already thinking of the
well water at home, after our walk down the mountain. But then
I saw my grandfather walk back to the berries.

"What are you doing?" I said. "We filled the pails."

"Not these," he said, waving his sap bucket. "Are you tired?"
He set the bucket down and walked back to where I was standing.
"I didn't think of that."

"No," I said.

"We could go home," he said. "We have plenty of berries."

"No, no," I said. "I don't want to."

I would have been ecstatic if he had overruled me, but he didn't.
He said, "You really sure?" and when I nodded, he walked back to
his berries. When he turned away, I was filled with anger and frustration, and I lifted the milk bottle and drained the last of the water.

We filled our buckets. My grandfather was finished a moment
before me, and he gathered a few handfuls to top off mine. We
carried the sap buckets to the high rock where the two big pails
stood. We looked all around us once more. It was only three-thirty,
but a wind was rising and I began to feel a little cool. My grandfather put the milk bottles in the pockets of his overalls. He fastened the ends of the wooden yoke to the two big pails and lifted
them. His face looked red, and veins stood out on his temples.

"It must be very heavy," I said. I lifted the sap buckets and they
were heavy enough to suit me.

"They're tolerably heavy," he said, and started along the stones.

"Let me carry them," I said rather feebly. I didn't even hear his
answer, and he kept walking straight on.

As I walked, my thirst seemed to grow and grow, until I found it utterly intolerable. We were going down a steep grassy slope. If there had been a cliff handy, I would have been tempted to jump from it. I felt as if my throat were being stung by red ants. My lips felt as if they were cracking open, and my tongue felt swollen and as dry as old newspaper. "Is there any water on the way?" I asked when I came abreast of my grandfather.

We had been walking for ten minutes. When my grandfather turned to me, his face was dead white. I was shocked. He knelt until the pails touched the ground, and then shrugged from under the yoke. He sat on the ground, and I thought he was going to be sick. "Might be," he said.

"Are you all right?" I asked.

"Don't worry," he said. "Don't worry." His face gradually relaxed and color returned to his cheeks.

"It's my turn to carry the yoke," I said. "My hands hurt from carrying the wire handles of these buckets, and, anyway, I want to learn how to carry the yoke."

He looked at me. "It's a longer walk if we go by water. Are you that thirsty?"

"I am thirsty, but I want to carry."

"All right," he said, "you young bull." I didn't feel much like a bull. "I guess I shouldn't be surprised. See how you like it."

For a while, the novelty of the yoke took my mind off my thirst. When I crouched under it and stood up, I nearly lost my balance. I swayed, with the pails dangling clumsily at my sides. Then I hunched forward and they settled. My grandfather picked up the sap buckets and looked at me. "All right?" he said.

"I guess so," I said. "Go slowly."

We doubled back a few yards and then started to walk north on the same level, moving at first in a direction away from home. At first, I had to walk very cautiously, because the rhythm of the swinging pails threatened my balance, but soon I learned to use the swing of the weight to help me keep moving, and I shrugged until the yoke felt comfortable on the back of my neck. When I felt secure in the walking, the thirst came back upon me.

After a few minutes, my grandfather felt able to talk again. I realized that today had been the most silent day we had ever spent together, and I decided that he must have been more tired all along than I had suspected. "I had that pain in my side which comes when I run sometimes," he said. "I'd rather you didn't say much about it back home."

I said I wouldn't.

"I'm glad to show you the pool where we'll find the water, if it's still there," he said. "It was there six years ago. No, eight years. It was there about eighty years ago, for that matter. But on the way I'm going to show you something else. I don't know if I ever told you about it."

"What is it?"

"You wait," he said. "Seeing will be good enough for you." Then he snorted and remembered an anecdote about a man from Concord who was curious about how Lucas Blount had lost his leg, and how Lucas Blount left him more curious than ever. He seemed himself again.

We had passed the forest of dead rock maples, going slightly below it, and then we had followed a steep path downhill for several hundred yards. Now we came onto a part of Ragged that was entirely new to me. It seemed to be a high plain, quite level and thick with fir trees. Then we descended a few feet into what looked like a narrow, flat road. I saw that banks rose on either side of it, perhaps twelve feet apart. It was too level for one of the makeshift lumber roads. Branches leaned together over it, but only goldenrod and small bushes were growing in its narrow path. "What's this?" I asked.

"Look," said my grandfather and pointed to the ground. First, I was aware that the path seemed made of ridges going from side to side, like a corduroy road, except that the ridges were a foot apart. Then I saw what looked like long streaks of orange, running parallel along the outer ends of the ridges.

"It's a railroad!" I said.

"It used to be," he said. "I remember when they closed it down. It's narrow-gauge, see? One of your Foster cousins was a brakeman here. It was just a little branch line, built for hauling timber to the freight depots. They took the mail, and some passengers, too, when there were any, when there were more people here."

We walked on the rotted ties. Except for the fact that we had to duck overhanging branches, it was the easiest walking of the day. Here and there, one of the banks had caved in and dirt had fallen onto the old track, but most of it seemed nearly intact. It was like Pompeii, and the close foliage of the heavy trees around us closed us in, as if we were sealed off in an alley separate from the world of strange modern trains.

"Where did it go?" I asked.

"It stopped just back there, at no place. They called it Ragged Station. Nothing's there now, but I'll show you where it was sometime. Washington Woodward used the wood from the old station when he built his lean-to. Up here is where your Great-Grampa Keneston came from, you know."

I had the pails working well now and took giant steps, two ties at a time. We walked in silence for a way. I was watching the ties as I walked, and seldom looked up. To slip and fall would have meant blueberry-picking all over again, and the very thought of it made the fire in my throat hotter. Then I heard my grandfather say "Hold on there, boy. Look ahead."

He stood out of my way. Ahead was something dark and covered with vines. It obstructed the track bed we walked on. I set down the blueberries and the yoke and walked past my grandfather. It was a coal car. Under its wooden hulk, red wheels fitted the red tracks. I could see fungi growing on the rotten sides, where the vines were thinnest. Then I looked beyond the coal car to the red pitted hulk of a locomotive. As I started to edge my way toward it, I looked back and saw my grandfather follow, grinning in his delight at my excitement.

Branches leaned into the cab, where the throttle, corroded with rust, stood out from the rusted instruments. A coal shovel lay in the bottom of the cab, and though leaves had drifted everywhere, I could see that there was still a heap of coal in the coal car. I walked around the engine. It was intact, down to the chain that led to the bell dangling in front. The smokestack was tall, and the unbroken glass of the headlight covered an oil lamp. The apparatus of wheels and pistons was fixed in a red trance, yet it looked as if it had just moved to a stop. Nothing had come loose or fallen. I had a momentary vision that my grandfather and I would clean the boiler, carry water, light a fire, heap on coal, blow the whistle, and gradually pull the throttle toward us; I saw the old pistons groan and start to move, flecks of rust fall like red snow from the whole machine, and the wheels turn on the red tracks as we plunged ahead on the dead railway, going nowhere on an errand among the farms of the past.

"Why did they leave it here?" I said.

"Nobody ever said. I suppose because of the gauge. It would be hard work moving it anywhere anybody could use it, even for scrap." He was grinning at me. "Now I bet you feel like an explorer," he said.

I didn't want to tell him what I had been thinking. I came back to the cab with the idea of getting up into it, but when I set my foot on the rung outside, it broke off.

"I wonder how long it will stay here," I said.

"Shouldn't wonder if it kept up a hundred years," he said. "It's been here for fifty now."

We walked back along the coal car. I knocked off some of the fungi and saw the black paint blistered underneath. My grandfather walked ahead of me and lifted the yoke and straightened his shoulders under it. "You ready?" he said. "You've got more to see before you're home again."

"You let me do that," I said.

"I'll carry it to the water," he said. "You fetch the buckets." He started off. I walked after him, edging past the locomotive, and my neck began to straighten itself from the posture it had learned under the yoke. But as soon as we were well past the engine, my thirst returned.

We continued on the track for only two hundred yards. Then my grandfather turned and squatted so that the big pails rested on the ground and relieved him of their weight. "Here's where we go off," he said. "First, you walk up ahead fifty yards and take a look. Leave your buckets. Be careful when you get up there."

My thirst had returned so strongly that any delay was agony, but I did what he said. The foliage leaned over the track thickly, and I couldn't see far ahead. Then suddenly the foliage thinned and I saw the track go on ahead of me in midair. Below was a ravine, cut by a tiny stream I could see at the bottom. It was crossed by a rotting trestle, which had mostly fallen away but across which the red rails still made a tottery passage. I took one long look. This was where my grandfather and I would have driven the train. Then I turned and trotted back to my grandfather.

When he saw me coming, he rose up under the yoke again. I saw the veins swell out at his temples. I picked up my buckets. "Is it standing?" he said.

I told him it was.

"When they built it," he said, "they said it would last. Wash helped to keep it up, when he was a young man."

We turned from the track into the forest and immediately started to go downhill. The growth was thick, and my grandfather moved slowly with the yoke.

"Are you all right, carrying that?" I asked.

"We're pretty close," he said.

Soon we came into a pine forest. The trees were tall and as straight as the masts of ships. It was like walking underwater, the way the light came through the needles way above us. Only a few low branches bothered our walking, and they snapped off when we brushed at them. The needles felt as soft as air underneath my hot feet. I would have enjoyed it if the thirst had not throbbed in my mouth and throat. I wanted to talk just to forget the pain. "Is this virgin pine?" I asked. The moment I asked it, I knew it was a stupid question.

My grandfather laughed. He started to say something, but he was out of breath. "I'll tell you later," he said in gasps.

In a few minutes, we left the pine and entered a clearing where I could see only a few ancient maples and some bushes. He set the pails on the ground and ducked out of the yoke. I could see by his face that he had the pain again. I set my buckets beside the pails. "It's my turn now," I said.

He gestured down a slope at one side of the clearing. "Water down there," he said.

I jogged down the slope and found a pool at the bottom. I dropped to my knees and cupped the water in my hands and splashed it into my mouth. The first water seemed painful, because there was so little of it. I brought more and more up to my mouth and covered my shirt with the drips from my fingers. Finally I sat back, panting, to wait for a second wind. Then my grandfather came walking down the slope to where I was and took a quart bottle from his pocket and filled it and drank from it.

I borrowed it for my second round of drinking, and in a few minutes stood up, my stomach cramped full of water. My grandfather filled the bottle again and put the cardboard stopper on it. "For the trip home," he said. He looked better now.

I looked at the pool for the first time. It was small and perfectly round. It looked utterly still, yet the water was clear and cool, with no scum on top and only a few lily pads to vary the surface.

My grandfather saw me looking at it. "God's Pool," he said. "Uncle Luther used to walk here from Sabine, summers when he took a vacation from Connecticut, back when he was young enough, back before he retired. I believe he used to read books here, or write sermons maybe. I was afraid it might not be here any more. You never can be sure. A stream can shift underground. It comes from that stream which you saw under the trestle, and it goes out beneath that tree. I suppose it's one of the streams which fills up our lake down below."

"It's good water," I said. "I remember Uncle Luther telling me about God's Pool."

"In the old days, before they had a well, lots of your ancestors drew all their water here. Come back up and I'll show you something."

"How do you feel?" I asked.

"Better," he said. "Come along."

I followed him back to the clearing with the maples. He pointed with his foot to a flat stone. "Many people of your blood stepped on that stone," he said. "That's the doorstep, and there's the cellar hole."

I looked behind the stone and saw the depression in the ground — a small cellar hole walled with dry stone, where the potatoes and apples and carrots and turnips and cabbages and parsnips and salted meat and fish had been stored for decades of winters. "Is this — ?" I began.

"The Kenestons'," he said. "Uncle Luther grew up here, and your Great-Grampa Benjamin, and the others before him. The well they dug is over that way, so mind your feet when you look around. They tapped the stream that flowed from the pool when they got tired of hauling it up that slope in buckets."

I wandered in the old dooryard. A maple above me stretched out a great branch that must have suspended a swing for the children. I stubbed my toe on an old piece of metal that stuck up through the ground. It looked like the wheel of a cultivator.

My grandfather sat on the doorstep. "I'm sorry to stop," he said. "I know you'd like some coffee and pie. I didn't reckon I'd get so tired." He paused a moment, looking at his hands. "You know when you asked if it was virgin pine?" he said. "Your great-grandfather cut the virgin timber there, in the fifties, before the war. He stumped it with oxen and planted it with potatoes and hired a crew to dig them in the fall, and he hauled them to the old railroad and sold them to a man who took them clear down to Boston, to sell them in the big vegetable market down there. But when the war came he couldn't hire a crew, and the fields grew up with bush, and after the war he just couldn't get started again. He lived so long he sold the pine twice from the land he cleared and stumped himself. I reckon to sell it the third time, come next spring."

I wandered to the other side of the clearing, into a bushy meadow that slanted steeply downward. Under my feet I felt the earth wave like the sea, and I suddenly realized that I was walking on land that retained the ridges my great-grandfather had plowed into it. I came back to my grandfather. He was examining his hands again and did not hear me coming. I saw how old his hands looked. Then he looked over at the yoke. "Do you really feel like carrying that?" he asked.

"Sure I do," I said. I took a swallow of water and then lifted the yoke again and settled it where I liked it on my neck. My grandfather lifted the sap buckets and led the way. We descended the bushy meadow into a strip of forest and then climbed an old stone wall to a road.

My grandfather laughed. "You know where we are?" he said.

"New Canada?" I said hopefully.

"Almost," he said. "Twenty rods down we come to New Canada. This is what they called New Road, and the town keeps it up, though I don't know as anybody's living on it now."

We turned into New Canada and walked downhill all the way home. It was four miles, and my back was sore, but my strength revived when I imagined coffee and pie waiting on the set tubs in the kitchen. We walked quietly past Washington Woodward's camp, for fear he could discover us and want to chat for an hour or more.

At last we turned onto the macadam of the main road, and in a moment I saw the white smoke of our chimney. "Well," I said with sudden gaiety, "we've brought the berries."

"Yes," said my grandfather, "and I don't know when we'll make the trip again. I'm glad I could show you some things to remember."

(From The Reporter)

THE LAST DAY

BY HENIA KARMEL-WOLFE

PIM IS pulling a chair on a long rope. The chair is heavy and twice his size and Pim is perspiring and panting heavily.

"Giddy-up, giddy-up, horsy — giddy-up!" he cries and looks around.

But today nobody pays any attention to him. Mother lies curled up on the bed, Ditta looks out the window, Mama Helka paces up and down the room, and Daddy is drumming with his fingers on the table top. Pim is very disappointed. He is accustomed to being the center of attention and now, unexpectedly, he is left to himself. "Now I am going to plow," he declares loudly, and waits for a reaction. Then, as this too fails, he makes a last attempt.

"Giddy-up, giddy-up, horsy!" he shouts in a very loud voice. "Giddy-up, giddy-up, damn you!"

Now, now it is going to happen. Now Mama will get up, come to him, slap him lightly and there will be sparkles of laughter twinkling in her eyes. "You naughty, naughty boy," she will say. "Who teaches you such words?" And everybody will be laughing.

But today nobody laughs. Mama remains motionless, Ditta stares out the window, and Daddy continues drumming his fingers on the table. Pim sighs with disappointment; one can never know what adults will do next. He shrugs his shoulders resignedly and begins to climb up the chair — first one knee, then the other. Look, everybody, how tall he is! He can even see through the window. He can see the fields, the road, the little chapel, and Marcin the shepherd boy with his cows. How lucky he is, this Marcin. When Pim grows up he too is going to be a shepherd, or maybe "Judenrat" like Uncle Shulim.

Oh, Uncle Shulim, here he comes. From afar Pim recognizes his cap, coat, and high boots. Uncle Shulim is tall, very tall, up to the sky — so tall that he has to stoop and bend his head when he passes through the door. He wears an armband with red letters next to the blue star, and everybody greets him first. He is wonderful, Uncle Shulim. He will open the door and "Pim!" he will call from the threshold, "Pim!" and he will bend down with his pipe smell and be as small as Pim, and then he will lift Pim up and Pim will be as big as Uncle Shulim. "You little monkey," he will say. "You monkey," and he will kiss Pim hard and scratch him a little with his rough cheek.

Pim slips off the chair and trots to the door to open it for Uncle Shulim. But Uncle Shulim does not seem to notice him and when Pim pulls at his trouser leg he pushes him aside as if Pim were not Pim at all but the neighbor's little dog. He goes up to Daddy, leans over him, whispers something in his ear. Daddy's face becomes very white and he looks at Mama and Mama looks at Uncle Shulim and so do Mama Helka and Ditta, and everybody's eyes seem very large. Then they start talking together, disorderly, loud and again softly, in whispers. Heads bend toward one another and draw apart. Mama hides her face in her hands.

Daddy stands up, climbs the ladder to the attic, and looks for something in the straw of the thatched roof. "How could you bury it so deep?" Mama Helka cries out. She seems very upset. "How could you bury it so deep?" Pim repeats after her and laughs. He is holding the ladder. Look, look, everybody, how he is helping his daddy.

But nobody notices.

Now something unexpected is happening. Ditta is dragging the big old trunk into the middle of the room. The same trunk that has traveled with them from Krakow to Lublin, from Lublin to Siedlce, through all the stops of their wanderings. The trunk is seldom opened; it is an enchanted treasure. There are winter clothes smelling of moth balls, old pieces of velvet saved from Grandmother's dress, a broken ivory fan, and many, many more strange things. But, best of all, at the very bottom of the trunk there are the pictures: of Daddy when he was a little boy not

much bigger than Pim, and of Mama from the time when Pim was
not yet here — when he was still "on the roof," as Uncle Shulim
says. Pim is never allowed to touch the pictures. Only sometimes
Mama will take him on her lap, show them to him, and tell funny
stories.

Now here they are scattered over the earthen floor of the hut,
neglected, unnecessary like rubbish. And Pim sits down, picks up
the little cardboard rectangles, looks at them one by one, puts them
together like a pack of cards, and nobody cares that he sits on this
very dirty floor in his freshly washed pants.

Now the door opens and in comes Uncle Mendel with the goatee,
Mr. Adler, and silly Mayer who stutters. They are saying something to Uncle Shulim, and Uncle Shulim becomes red in his face
and shouts at them angrily. Pim has never before heard Uncle
Shulim shout in this way. And, because of this shouting, in comes
Uncle Herschel from the adjoining room. Pim loves Uncle Herschel very much. Uncle Herschel sometimes takes Pim on his lap,
sticks a paper cigarette in his mouth, and teaches him how to puff.
Pim will tug on Uncle's cap and Uncle will take it off and place it
on Pim's head. The big cap will fall down to his nose and cover
his eyes and Uncle and Pim will roll in laughter. "You are already
a grown-up Jew," Uncle Herschel will say. "You must not be without a hat."

But what is wrong with Uncle Herschel now? What is he doing?
Isn't he fully dressed? Why is he putting on one shirt on top of
another, and still another one? He tries to button the shirts and
cannot because his hands are shaking.

The door opens again; it is Hanka with David. She is very excited and her hair is all tumbled as if she has not combed it. She
holds tightly to David's arm and says something to Uncle Herschel
and Uncle Herschel takes a little bundle out of his pocket, gives it
to Hanka, and stretches his hands out to her.

"Don't say good-by, for God's sake don't say good-by!" Hanka
screams suddenly. She runs out the door pulling David after her
and does not look back.

Uncle Herschel remains there, his arms outstretched. He stands
there for a while and then brings them down slowly, very slowly, as
if they were heavy, as if they were not his arms at all but two sticks
attached to his body. When finally he turns around, Pim sees that

Uncle Herschel is crying. But before Pim can ask why he is crying the door opens again and in come Aunt Mita and Lilka and Natalka the peasant girl. Natalka is saying something to Aunt Mita, who does not seem to understand what it is she wants of her. Natalka takes the kerchief off and ties it on Lilka's head.

"Little Miss looks very good indeed," Natalka says. "Little Miss does not look Jewish at all."

She nods approvingly and says some more Pim cannot understand, but through the torrent of words he hears "taken away." And now, for the first time, Pim bursts out crying. That evening before, when Uncle Misha went out and they waited and waited for him with supper, they had also been saying "taken away." And Uncle Misha never came back. Marcin the shepherd boy says Uncle Misha was killed. Pim does not quite know what "killed" means, but he knows that it is something terrible because when he asks about Uncle Misha they don't answer and only grow very still. That is why he is crying.

Now for the first time they notice him.

"The baby, what is going to happen to the baby?" Mama cries out in a terrible voice and she covers her face with her hands.

Everybody looks at Pim, and Daddy looks first at Pim and then at Mama and his lower lip starts trembling and he bites into it. Suddenly everything becomes very quiet. Pim climbs into his mother's lap, pulls away her hands, and tries to look into her eyes.

Mama puts him down gently, goes to the crib, and takes his suit out from under his pillow. Then she kneels before him, takes off his slippers, and kisses his feet, first one then the other. Pim has stopped crying and only sniffles quietly. Through his tears he asks, "Mama, why do you put dirty shoes on me?" The high boots, his prized possession, are muddy and Mama does not seem to notice.

At this moment the door bangs open and the village elder Kowalski with the long curled-up mustache stamps in followed by another man, a very tall man, with an iron hat, beautiful gleaming black boots, and a green coat with shiny buttons. The tall man yells something at Uncle Shulim and shakes a little black thing at him. And Uncle Shulim, big wonderful Uncle Shulim, steps backward and his knees bend and he doesn't seem to be as tall as he used to be. He doesn't even seem to be as tall as Uncle Herschel.

They all go outside and climb into the horse wagon — Mama

and Daddy, Uncle Shulim and Aunt Regina and Putzi and Mimi
and Mama Helka and Ditta and Uncle Herschel. The overloaded
wagon shakes and lurches forward, splashing mud to the side of
the road. Behind, more wagons come, all full of people. Daddy
puts his arms around Mama, Mama holds Pim tightly, Mama Helka
and Ditta sit so close to each other that it is hard to tell where one
stops and the other begins. Only Uncle Herschel is sitting by himself. He lifts his eyes up and moves his lips soundlessly. Uncle
Herschel is praying. Suddenly Pim feels sorry for Uncle Herschel,
and climbing down from his mother's lap he crawls up to Uncle
Herschel and places his cheek on the big dark fist. Uncle Herschel looks at him sadly, shakes his head, and does not interrupt
his prayer. After a while he bends down to Pim and asks him in a
whisper: "Do you remember what Uncle taught you, do you remember how one prays?"

Pim remembers and repeats after Uncle Herschel: "Sh'ma Yisroel
Adonoi Elohaynu Adonoi Echod."

The wagon bounces on the uneven road and splashes mud
around. It is getting colder and colder; it drizzles. Mama wraps
Pim in a blanket; he dozes off. He feels Mama kissing him, at first
quietly and gently, and then harder and harder. He wakes up
crying. He feels these are not the usual kisses. "Mama," he cries,
"why do you kiss so hard? It hurts."

The wagon shakes over the muddy road. It is getting darker
and colder and the drizzle changes to rain. In the distance, dark
against the overcast sky, rise the church steeples of Izbica.

"Where are we going, Mama?" Pim asks.

Mama looks at him and doesn't answer right away. And then she
says slowly, "To the trains. Just to the trains . . ."

(*From The New Yorker*)

IN THE MIDDLE OF THE FIELDS

BY MARY LAVIN

*L*IKE A ROCK in the sea, she was islanded by fields, the heavy grass washing about the house, and the cattle wading in it as in water. Even their gentle stirrings were a loss when they moved away at evening to the shelter of the woods. A rainy day might strike a wet flash from a hay barn on the far side of the river — not even a habitation! And yet she was less lonely for him here in Meath than elsewhere. Anxieties by day, and cares, and at night vague, nameless fears — these were the stones across the mouth of the tomb. But who understood that? They thought she hugged tight every memory she had of him. What did they know about memory? What was it but another name for dry love and barren longing? They even tried to unload upon her their own small purposeless memories. "I imagine I see him every time I look out there," they would say as they glanced nervously over the darkening fields when they were leaving. "I think I ought to see him coming through the trees." Oh, for God's sake! she'd think. I'd forgotten him for a minute!

It wasn't him *she* saw when she looked out at the fields this spring morning. It was the ugly tufts of tow and scutch that whitened the tops of the grass and gave it the look of a sea in storm, spattered with broken foam. That grass would have to be topped. And how much would that cost?

At least Ned, the old herd, knew the man to do it for her. "Bartley Crossen is your man, ma'am. Your husband knew him well."

She couldn't place him at first. Then she remembered. "Oh, yes — that's his hay barn we see, isn't it? Why, of course! I know him well — by sight, I mean." And so she did — splashing past on the road in a big muddy car, the wheels always caked with clay, and the wife in the front seat beside him.

"I'll get him to call around and have a word with you, ma'am," said the herd.

"Before dark!" she cautioned.

But there was no need to tell him. The old man knew how she always tried to be upstairs before it got dark, locking herself into her room, which opened off the room where the children slept, praying devoutly that she wouldn't have to come down again for anything — above all, not to answer the door. That was what in particular she dreaded. A knock at the door after dark!

"Ah, sure, who'd come near you, ma'am, knowing you're a woman alone with small children that might be wakened and set crying? And, for that matter, where could you be safer than in the middle of the fields, with the innocent beasts asleep around you?"

If he himself had to come to the house late at night for any reason — to get hot water to stoup the foot of a beast, or to call the vet — he took care to shout out long before he got to the gable. "It's me, ma'am!" he'd shout. "Coming! Coming!" she'd cry, gratefully, as quick on his words as their echo. Unlocking her door, she'd run down and throw open the hall door. No matter what the hour! No matter how black the night. "Go back to your bed now, you, ma'am," he'd say from the darkness, where she could see the swinging yard lamp coming nearer and nearer like the light of a little boat drawing near to a jetty. "I'll put out the lights and let myself out." Relaxed by the thought that there was someone in the house, she would indeed scuttle back into bed, and, what was more, she'd be nearly asleep before she'd hear the door slam. It used to sound like the slam of a door a million miles away.

There was no need to worry. He'd see that Crossen came early.

It was well before dark when Crossen did drive up to the door. The wife was with him, as usual, sitting up in the front seat the way people sat up in the well of little tub traps long ago, their knees pressed together, allowing no slump. The herd had come with them, but only he and Crossen got out.

"Won't your wife come inside and wait, Mr. Crossen?" she asked.

"Oh, not at all, ma'am. She likes sitting in the car. Now, where's this grass that's to be cut? Are there any stones lying about that would blunt the blade?" Going around the gable of the house, he looked out over the land.

"There's not a stone or a stump in it," Ned said. "You'd run your blade over the whole of it while you'd be whetting it twenty times in another place!"

"I can see that," said Bartley Crossen, but absently, she thought.

He had walked across the lawn to the rickety wooden gate that led into the pasture, and leaned on it. He didn't seem to be look-ing at the fields at all, though, but at the small string of stunted thorns that grew along the riverbank, their branches leaning so heavily out over the water that their roots were almost dragged clear of the clay.

Suddenly he turned around and gave a sigh. "Ah, sure, I didn't need to look! I know it well!" As she showed surprise, he gave a little laugh, like a young man. "I courted a girl down there when I was a lad," he said. "That's a queer length of time ago now, I can tell you!" He turned to the old man. "You might remember it." Then he looked back at her. "I don't suppose you were thought of at all in those days, ma'am," he said, and there was something kindly in his look and in his words. "You'd like the mowing done soon, I suppose? How about first thing in the morning?"

Her face lit up. But there was the price to settle. "It won't be as dear as cutting meadow, will it?"

"Ah, I won't be too hard on you, ma'am," he said. "I can prom-ise you that!"

"That's very kind of you," she said, but a little doubtfully.

Behind Crossen's back, Ned nodded his head in approval. "Let it go at that, ma'am," he whispered as they walked back toward the car. "He's a man you can trust."

And when Crossen and the wife had driven away, he reassured her again. "A decent man," he said. Then he gave a laugh — it, too, was a young kind of laugh for a man of his age; it was like a nudge. "Did you hear what he said, though — about the girl he courted down there? Do you know who that was? It was his first wife! You know he was twice married? Ah, well, it's so long ago I wouldn't wonder if you never heard it. Look at the way he spoke about her himself, as if she was some girl he'd all but forgotten! The thorn trees brought her to his mind! That's where they used to meet, being only youngsters, when they first took up with each other.

"Poor Bridie Logan — she was as wild as a hare. And she was mad with love, young as she was! They were company-keeping while they were still going to school. Only nobody took it seriously — him least of all, maybe — till the winter he went away to the agricultural college in Clonakilty. She started writing to him then. I used to see her running up to the postbox at the crossroads every other evening. And sure, the whole village knew where the letter was going. His people were fit to be tied when he came home in summer and said he wasn't going back, but was going to marry Bridie. All the same, his father set them up in a cottage on his own land. It's the cottage that's used now for stall-feds — it's back of the new house. Oh, but you can't judge it now for what it was then! Giddy and all as she was — as lightheaded as a thistle — you should have seen the way she kept that cottage. She'd have had it scrubbed away if she didn't start having a baby. He wouldn't let her take the scrubbing brush into her hands after that!"

"But she wasn't delicate, was she?"

"Bridie?" She was as strong as a kid goat, that one! But I told you she was mad about him, didn't I? Well, after she was married to him she was no better — worse, you'd say. She couldn't do enough for him! It was like as if she was driven on by some kind of a fever. You'd only to look in her eyes to see it. Do you know what! From that day to this, I don't believe I ever saw a woman so full of going as that one! Did you ever happen to see little birds flying about in the air like they were flying for the divilment of it and nothing else? And did you ever see the way they give a sort of a little leap in the air, like they were forcing themselves to go a bit higher still — higher than they ought? Well, it struck me that was the way Bridie was acting, as she rushed about that cottage doing this and doing that to make him prouder and prouder of her. As if he could be any prouder than he was already and the child getting noticeable!"

"She didn't die in childbed?"

"No. Not in a manner of speaking, anyway. She had the child, nice and easy, and in their own cottage, too, only costing him a few shillings for one of those women that went in for that kind of job long ago. And all went well. It was no time till she was let up on her feet again. I was there the first morning she had the place to herself! She was up and dressed when I got there, just as he was going out to milk.

" 'Oh, it's great to be able to go out again,' she said, taking a great breath of the morning air as she stood at the door looking after him. 'Wait! Why don't I come with you to milk?' she called out suddenly after him. Then she threw a glance back at the baby asleep in its crib by the window.

" 'Oh, it's too far for you, Bridie!' he cried. The cows were down in the little field by the river — you know the field, alongside the road at the foot of the hill on this side of the village. And knowing she'd start coaxing him, he made out of the gate with the cans.

"Good man! I said to myself. But the next thing I knew, she'd darted across the yard.

" 'I can go on the bike if it's too far to walk!' she said. And up she got on her old bike, and out she pedaled through the gate.

" 'Bridie, are you out of your mind?' he shouted as she whizzed past him.

" 'Arrah, what harm can it do me?' she shouted back.

"I went stiff with fright looking after her. And I thought it was the same with him, when he threw down the cans and started down the hill after her. But looking back on it, I think it was the same fever as always was raging in her that started raging in him, too. Mad with love, that's what they were, both of them — she only wanting to draw him on, and he only too willing!

" 'Wait for me!' he shouted, but before she'd even got to the bottom she started to brake the bike, putting down her foot like you'd see a youngster do, and raising up such a cloud of dust we could hardly see her."

"She braked too hard!"

"Not her! In the twinkle of an eye she'd stopped the bike, jumped off, turned it round, and was pedaling madly up the hill again, her head down on the handle bars like a racing cyclist. But that was the finish of her!"

"Oh, no! What happened?"

"She stopped pedaling all of a sudden, and the bike half stopped, and then it started to go back down the hill, a bit as if it skidded on the loose gravel at the side of the road. That's what I thought happened, and him, too, I suppose, because we both began to run down the hill. She didn't get time to fall before we got to her. But what use was that? It was some kind of internal bleeding that took her. We got her into the bed, and the neighbors came running, but she was gone before the night."

"Oh, such a thing to happen! And the baby?"

"Well, it was a strong child! And it grew into a fine lump of a lad. That's the fellow that drives the tractor for him now — the oldest son, Bartley."

"Well, I suppose his second marriage had more to it, when all was said and done."

"That's it. And she's a good woman — the second one. The way she brought up that child of Bridie's! And filled the cradle, year after year, with sons of her own. Ah sure, things always work out for the best in the end, no matter what!" he said, and he started to walk away.

"Wait a minute, Ned," she said urgently. "Do you really think he forgot about her — for years, I mean?"

"I'd swear it," said the old man. And then he looked hard at her. "It will be the same with you, too," he added kindly. "Take my word for it. Everything passes in time and is forgotten."

As she shook her head doubtfully, he shook his emphatically. "When the tree falls, how can the shadow stand?" he said. And he walked away.

I wonder! she thought as she walked back to the house, and she envied the practical country way that made good the defaults of nature as readily as the broken sod knits back into the sward.

Again that night, when she went up to her room, she looked down toward the river and she thought of Crossen. Had he really forgotten? It was hard for her to believe, and with a sigh she picked up her hairbrush and pulled it through her hair. Like everything else about her lately, her hair was sluggish and hung heavily down, but after a few minutes under the quickening strokes of the brush, it lightened and lifted, and soon it flew about her face like the spray above a weir. It had always been the same, even when she was a child. She had only to suffer the first painful drag of the bristles when her mother would cry out, "Look! Look! That's electricity!"

and a blue spark would shine for an instant like a star in the gray
depths of the mirror.

That was all they knew of electricity in those dim-lit days when
valleys of shadow lay deep between one piece of furniture and another. Was it because rooms were so badly lit then that they saw it
so often, that little blue star? Suddenly she was overcome by longing to see it again, and, standing up impetuously, she switched off
the light.

It was just then that, down below, the iron fist of the knocker was
lifted and, with a loud, confident hand, brought down on the door.

It wasn't a furtive knock. She admitted that even as she sat stark
with fright in the darkness. And then a voice that was vaguely familiar called out — and confidently — from below.

"It's me, ma'am! I hope I'm not disturbing you!"

"Oh, Mr. Crossen!" she cried out with relief, and, unlocking her
door, she ran across the landing and threw up the window on that
side of the house. "I'll be right down!" she called.

"Oh, don't come down, ma'am!" he shouted. "I only want one
word with you."

"But of course I'll come down!" She went back to get out of her
dressing gown and put on her slippers and pin up her hair, but as
she did she heard him stomping his feet on the gravel. It had been
a mild day, but with night a chill had come in the air, and, for all
that it was late spring, there was a cutting east wind coming across
the river. "I'll run down and let you in from the cold," she called,
and, twisting up her hair, she held it against her head with her
hand without waiting to pin it, and she ran down the stairs to un-
bolt the door.

"You were going to bed, ma'am!" he said accusingly the minute
she opened the door. And where he had been so impatient a minute beforehand, he stood stock-still in the open doorway. "I saw
the lights were out downstairs when I was coming up the drive," he
said contritely. "But I didn't think you'd gone up for the night!"

"Neither had I!" she said lyingly, to put him at his ease. "I was
just upstairs brushing my hair. You must excuse me," she added,
because a breeze from the door was blowing her dressing gown
from her knees, and to pull it across she had to take her hand from
her hair, so that the hair fell down about her shoulders. "Would
you mind closing the door for me?" she said, with some embarrass-

ment, and she began to back up the stairs. "Please go inside to the sitting room, won't you?" she said, nodding toward the door of the small room off the hall. "Put on the light. I'll be down in a minute."

But although he had obediently stepped inside the door, and closed it, he stood stoutly in the middle of the hall. "I shouldn't have come in at all," he said. "I know you were going to bed! Look at you!" he cried again in the same accusing voice, as if he dared her this time to deny it. He was looking at her hair. "Excuse my saying so, ma'am, but I never saw such a fine head of hair. God bless it!" he said quickly, as if afraid he had been rude. "Doesn't a small thing make a big differ," he said impulsively. "You look like a young girl!"

In spite of herself, she smiled with pleasure. She wanted no more of it, all the same. "Well, I don't feel like one!" she said sharply.

What was meant for a quite opposite effect, however, seemed to delight him and put him wonderfully at ease. "Ah sure, you're a sensible woman! I can see that," he said, and, coming to the foot of the stairs, he leaned comfortably across the newel post. "Let you stay the way you are, ma'am," he said. "I've only a word to say to you, and it's not worth your while going up them stairs. Let me have my say here and now and be off about my business! The wife will be waiting up for me, and I don't want that!"

She hesitated. Was the reference to his wife meant to put her at *her* ease? "I think I ought to get my slippers," she said cautiously. Her feet were cold.

"Oh, put something on your feet!" he cried, only then seeing that she was in her bare feet. "But as to the rest, I'm long gone beyond taking any account of what a woman has on her. I'm gone beyond taking notice of women at all."

She had seen something to put on her feet. Under the table in the hall was a pair of Robert's old shoes, with fleece lining in them. She hadn't been able to make up her mind to give them away with the rest of his clothes, and although they were big and clumsy on her, she often stuck her feet into them when she came in from the fields with mud on her shoes. "Well, come in where it's warm, so," she said. She came back down the few steps and stuck her feet into the boots, and then she opened the door of the sitting room.

She was glad she'd come down. He'd never have been able to put on the light. "There's something wrong with the center light," she said as she groped along the wainscot to find the plug of the reading lamp. It was in an awkward place, behind the desk. She had to go down on her knees.

"What's wrong with it?" he asked, as, with a countryman's interest in practicalities, he clicked the switch up and down to no effect.

"Oh, nothing much, I'm sure," she said absently. "There!" She had found the plug, and the room was lit up with a bright white glow.

"Why don't you leave the plug in the socket, anyway?" he asked critically.

"I don't know," she said. "I think someone told me it's safer, with reading lamps, to pull them out at night. There might be a short circuit, or mice might nibble at the cord, or something — I forget what I was told. I got into the habit of doing it, and now I keep on." She felt a bit silly.

But he was concerned about it. "I don't think any harm could be done," he said gravely. Then he turned away from the problem. "About tomorrow, ma'am!" he said, somewhat offhandedly, she thought. "I was determined I'd see you tonight, because I'm not a man to break my word — above all, to a woman."

What was he getting at?

"Let me put it this way," he said quickly. "You'll understand, ma'am, that as far as I am concerned, topping land is the same as cutting hay. The same time. The same labor cost. And the same wear and tear on the blade. You understand that?"

On her guard, she nodded.

"Well now, ma'am, I'd be the first to admit that it's not quite the same for you. For you, topping doesn't give the immediate return you'd get from hay — "

"There's no return from it!" she exclaimed crossly.

"Oh, come now, ma'am, come! Good grassland pays as well as anything — you know you won't get nice sweet picking for your beasts from neglected land, but only dirty old tow grass knotting under their feet. It's just that it's not a quick return, and so — as you know — I made a special price for you."

"I do know!" she said impatiently. "But I thought that part of it was settled and done."

"Oh, I'm not going back on it, if that's what you think," he said affably. "I'm glad to do what I can for you, ma'am, the more so seeing you have no man to attend to these things for you, but only yourself alone."

"Oh, I'm well able to look after myself!" she said, raising her voice.

Once again her words had an opposite effect to what she intended. He laughed good-humoredly. "That's what all women like to think!" he said. "Well, now," he said in a different tone of voice, and it annoyed her to see he seemed to think something had been settled between them, "it would suit me — and I'm sure it's all the same with you — if we could leave your little job till later in the week, say till nearer to the time of the haymaking generally. Because by then I'd have the cutting bar in good order, sharpened and ready for use. Whereas now, while there's still a bit of plowing to be done here and there, I'll have to be chopping and changing, between the plow and the mower, putting one on one minute and the other the next!"

"As if anyone is still plowing this time of the year!" Her eyes hardened. "Who are you putting before me?" she demanded.

"Now, take it easy, ma'am. No one. Leastways, not without getting leave first from you."

"Without telling me you're not coming, you mean!"

"Oh, now, ma'am, don't get cross. I'm only trying to make matters easy for everyone."

But she was very angry now. "It's always the same story. I thought you'd treat me differently! I'm to wait till after this one, and after that one, and in the end my fields will go wild!"

He looked a bit shamefaced. "Ah now, ma'am, that's not going to be the case at all. Although, mind you, some people don't hold with topping, you know!"

"I hold with it!"

"Oh, I suppose there's something in it," he said reluctantly. "But the way I look at it, cutting the weeds in July is a kind of a topping."

"Grass cut before it goes to seed gets so thick at the roots no weeds can come up!" she cried, so angry she didn't realize how authoritative she sounded.

"Faith, I never knew you were so well up, ma'am!" he said, looking at her admiringly, but she saw he wasn't going to be put down by her. "All the same now, ma'am, you can't say a few days here or there could make any difference?"

"A few days could make all the difference! This farm has a gravelly bottom to it, for all it's so lush. A few days of drought could burn it to the butt. And how could I mow it then? What cover would there be for the 'nice sweet pickings' you were talking about a minute ago?" Angrily, she mimicked his own accent without thinking.

He threw up his hands. "Ah well, I suppose a man may as well admit when he's bested," he said. "Even by a woman. And you can't say I broke my promise."

"I can't say but you tried hard enough," she said grudgingly, although she was mollified that she was getting her way. "Can I offer you anything?" she said then, anxious to convey an air of finality to their discussion.

"Oh, not at all, ma'am! Nothing, thank you! I'll have to be getting home." He stood up.

She stood up, too.

"I hope you won't think I was trying to take advantage of you," he said as they went toward the door. "It's just that we must all make out as best we can for ourselves — isn't that so? Not but you're well able to look after yourself, I must say. No one ever thought you'd stay on here after your husband died. I suppose it's for the children you did it?" He looked up the well of the stairs. "Are they asleep?"

"Oh, long ago," she said indifferently. She opened the hall door.

The night air swept in immediately, as it had earlier. But this time, from far away, it bore along on it the faint scent of new-mown hay. "There's hay cut somewhere already!" she exclaimed in surprise. And she lifted her face to the sweetness of it.

For a minute, Crossen looked past her out into the darkness, then he looked back. "Aren't you ever lonely here at night?" he asked suddenly.

"You mean frightened?" she corrected quickly and coldly.

"Yes! Yes, that's what I meant," he said, taken aback. "Ah, but why would you be frightened! What safer place could you be under the sky than right here with your own fields all about you!"

What he said was so true, and he himself as he stood there, with

his hat in his hand, so normal and natural it was indeed absurd to
think that he would no sooner have gone out the door than she
would be scurrying up the stairs like a child! "You may not believe it," she said, "but I am scared to death sometimes! I nearly
died when I heard your knock on the door tonight. It's because I
was scared that I was upstairs," she said, in a further burst of confidence. "I always go up the minute it gets dark. I don't feel
so frightened up in my room."

"Isn't that strange now?" he said, and she could see he found it
an incomprehensibly womanly thing to do. He was sympathetic
all the same. "You shouldn't be alone! That's the truth of the
matter," he said. "It's a shame!"

"Oh, it can't be helped," she said. There was something she
wanted to shrug off in his sympathy, while at the same time there
was something in it she wanted to take. "Would you like to do
something for me?" she asked impulsively. "Would you wait and
put out the lights down here and let me get back upstairs before
you go?"

After she had spoken, for a minute she felt foolish, but she saw
at once that, if anything, he thought it only too little to do for her.
He was genuinely troubled about her. And it wasn't only the present moment that concerned him; he seemed to be considering the
whole problem of her isolation and loneliness. "Is there nobody
could stay here with you — at night even? It would have to be another woman, of course," he added quickly, and her heart was
warmed by the way — without a word from her — he rejected that
solution out of hand. "You don't want a woman about the place,"
he said flatly.

"Oh, I'm all right, really. I'll get used to it," she said.

"It's a shame, all the same," he said. He said it helplessly,
though, and he motioned her toward the stairs. "You'll be all right
for tonight, anyway," he said. "Go on up the stairs now, and I'll
put out the lights." He had already turned around to go back into
the sitting room.

Yet it wasn't quite as she intended for some reason, and it was
somewhat reluctantly that she started up the stairs.

"Wait a minute! How do I put out this one?" he called out before she was halfway up.

"Oh, I'd better put out that one myself," she said, thinking of the awkward position of the plug. She ran down again, and, going past him into the little room, she knelt and pulled at the cord. Instantly the room was deluged in darkness. And instantly she felt that she had done something stupid. It was not like turning out a light by a switch at the door and being able to step back at once into the lighted hall. She got to her feet as quickly as she could, but as she did, she saw that Crossen had come to the doorway. His bulk was blocked out against the light beyond. "I'll leave the rest to you," she said, in order to break the peculiar silence that had come down on the house.

But he didn't move. He stood there, the full of the doorway.

"The other switches are over there by the hall door," she said, unwilling to brush past him. Why didn't he move? "Over there," she repeated, stretching out her arm and pointing, but instead of moving he caught at her outstretched arm, and, putting out his other hand, he pressed his palm against the doorjamb, barring the way.

"Tell me," he whispered, his words falling over each other, "are you never lonely — at all?"

"What did you say?" she said in a clear voice, because the thickness of his voice sickened her. She had hardly heard what he said. Her one thought was to get past him.

He leaned forward. "What about a little kiss?" he whispered, and to get a better hold on her he let go the hand he had pressed against the wall, but before he caught at her with both hands she had wrenched her arm free of him, and, ignominiously ducking under his armpit, she was out next minute in the lighted hall.

Out there — because light was all the protection she needed from him, the old fool — she began to laugh. She had only to wait for him to come sheepishly out.

But there was something she hadn't counted on; she hadn't counted on there being anything pathetic in his sheepishness. There was something actually pitiful in the way he shambled into the light, not raising his eyes. And she was so surprisingly touched by him that before he had time to utter a word she put out her hand. "Don't feel too bad," she said. "I didn't mind."

Even then, he didn't look at her. He just took her hand and pressed it gratefully, his face still turned away. And to her dismay she saw that his nose was running water. Like a small boy, he wiped it with the back of his fist, streaking his face. "I don't know what came over me," he said slowly. "I'm getting on to be an old man now. I thought I was beyond all that." He wiped his face again. "Beyond letting myself go, anyway," he amended miserably.

"Oh, it was nothing," she said.

He shook his head. "It wasn't as if I had cause for what I did."

"But you did nothing," she protested.

"It wasn't nothing to me," he said dejectedly.

For a minute, they stood there silent. The hall door was still ajar, but she didn't dare to close it. What am I going to do with him now, she thought. I'll have him here all night if I'm not careful. What time was it, anyway? All scale and proportion seemed to have gone from the night. "Well, I'll see you in the morning, Mr. Crossen!" she said, as matter-of-factly as possible.

He nodded but made no move. "You know I meant no disrespect to you, ma'am, don't you?" he said then, looking imploringly at her. "I always had a great regard for you. And for your husband, too. I was thinking of him this very night when I was coming up to the house. And I thought of him again when you came to the door looking like a young girl. I thought what a pity it was him to be taken from you, and you both so young! Oh, what came over me at all? And what would Mona say if she knew?"

"But you wouldn't tell her, I hope!" she cried. What sort of a figure would she cut if he told — her hair down her back, her bare feet! "Take care would you tell her!" she warned.

"I don't suppose I ought," he said, but he said it uncertainly and morosely, and he leaned back against the wall. "She's been a good woman, Mona. I wouldn't want anyone to think different. Even the boys could tell you. She's been a good mother to them all these years. She never made a bit of difference between them. Some say she was better to Bartley than to any of them! She reared him from a week old. She was living next door to us, you see, at the time — " He hesitated. "At the time I was left with him," he finished in a flat voice. "She came in that first night and took him home to her own bed — and, mind you, that wasn't a small thing for a woman who knew nothing about children, not being what you'd call a young girl at the time, in spite of the big family she gave me afterward. She took him home that night, and she looked after him. It isn't every woman would care to be responsible for a newborn baby. That's a thing a man doesn't forget easy! There's many, I know, would say that if she hadn't taken him someone else would have, but no one only her would have done it the way she did.

"She used to have him all day in her own cottage, feeding him and the rest of it. But at night, when I'd be back from the fields, she'd bring him home and leave him down in his little crib by the fire alongside of me. She used to let on she had things to do in her own place, and she'd slip away and leave us alone, but that wasn't her real reason for leaving him. She knew the way I'd be sitting looking into the fire, wondering how I'd face the long years ahead, and she left the child there with me to break my thoughts. And she was right. I never got long to brood. The child would give a cry, or a whinge, and I'd have to run out and fetch her to him. Or else she'd hear him herself maybe, and run in without me having to call her at all. I used often think she must have kept every window and door in her place open, for fear she'd lose a sound from either of us. And so, bit by bit, I was knit back into a living man. I often wonder what would have become of me if it wasn't for her. There are men and when the bright way closes to them there's no knowing but they'll take a dark way. And I was that class of man.

"I told you she used to take the little fellow away in the day and bring him back at night? Well, of course, she used to take him away again coming on to the real dark of night. She'd take him away to her own bed. But as the months went on and he got bigger, I could see she hated taking him away from me at all. He was beginning to smile and play with his fists and be real company. 'I wonder ought I leave him with you tonight,' she'd say then, night after night. And sometimes she'd run in and dump him down in the middle of the big double bed in the room off the kitchen, but the next minute she'd snatch him up again. 'I'd be afraid you'd over-lie him! You might only smother him, God between us and all harm!' 'You'd better take him,' I'd say. I used to hate to see him go myself by this time. All the same, I was afraid he'd start crying in the night, and what would I do then? If I had to go out for her in the middle of the night, it could cause a lot of talk. There was talk enough as things were, I can tell you, although there was no grounds for it. I had no more notion of her than if she wasn't a woman at all — would you believe that? But one night when she took him up and put him down, and put him down and took him up, and went on and went on about leaving him or taking him, I had to laugh. 'It's a pity you can't stay along with him, and that would settle all,' I said. I was only joking her, but she got as red as fire, and next thing she burst out crying! But not before she'd caught up the child and wrapped her coat around him. Then, after giving me a terrible look, she ran out of the door with him.

"Well, that was the beginning of it. I'd no idea she had any feelings for me. I thought it was only for the child. But men are fools, as women well know, and she knew before me what was right and proper for us both. And for the child, too. Some women have great insight into these things! And God opened my own eyes then to the woman I had in her, and I saw it was better I took her than wasted away after the one that was gone. And wasn't I right?"

"Of course you were right," she said quickly.

But he slumped back against the wall, and the abject look came back into his eyes.

I'll never get rid of him, she thought desperately. "Ah, what ails you!" she cried impatiently. "Forget it, can't you?"

"I can't," he said simply. "And it's not only me — it's the wife I'm thinking about. I've shamed her!"

"Ah, for heaven's sake. It's nothing got to do with her at all."

Surprised, he looked up at her. "You're not blaming yourself, surely?" he asked.

She'd have laughed at that if she hadn't seen she was making headway — another stroke and she'd be rid of him. "Arrah, what are you blaming any of us for!" she cried. "It's got nothing to do with any of us — with you, or me, or the woman at home waiting for you. It was the other one! That girl — your first wife — Bridie! It was her! Blame her! She's the one did it!" The words had broken from her. For a moment, she thought she was hysterical and that she could not stop. "You thought you could forget her," she said, "but see what she did to you when she got the chance!" She stopped and looked at him.

He was standing at the open door. He didn't look back. "God rest her soul," he said, and he stepped into the night.

(From The Kenyon Review)

HANGING HAIR

BY JACK THOMAS LEAHY

*T*HE OLD WOMAN lived in a crumpled shack on the high cliff down past the river where the wind came in strong from the end of the ocean and bent the green ocean bush back from the cliff so that the leaves hung in loose shreds over the land. She was a very gentle old woman and the Indians called her Hanging Hair. Even before father had moved to Teahwit and set up a store for the Indians, we had heard of her. The Indians who occasionally came to New Royal, the white town about twenty miles inland where father had another store before he went broke, would talk about her. They thought she was a spirit.

"Bosh!" my mother would say. "There ain't no spirits 'cept one." My mother didn't like the Indians. She thought they stole tobacco and things like that from the store, and so, when Father said we were going to move down to an Indian village on the coast, Mother was very mad and at night I could hear her shouting at Father and much later crying herself to sleep.

After we came to Teahwit and set up the store, the Indians still stopped in to talk about Hanging Hair. They regarded her as they would a spirit whenever she walked down the long road alongside the ocean, her clam-bag hanging by a loose sealskin thong over her shoulder. In the early morning, from my bedroom window above the store, I would watch her gathering clams on the beach that stretched south from the river to the Graveyard of the Giants, the great outcropping of rocks that poked themselves up, full of barnacles, from the ocean.

My grandfather, who had homesteaded the territory and built the school at Teahwit on orders from the governor, came up to my room one moonlit night when the ocean was rolling upon its soft shadows and told me the story of Hanging Hair. Nan, my sister, and Buckety, the Indian half-caste about my own age, sat on the bed and listened to him as he talked on and looked out the window toward Hanging Hair's house on top of the wind-swept cliff past the river.

According to Grandfather, the Indians thought that not only old Hanging Hair was a spirit; in the past, when he had come out here to build the schoolhouse, they believed that everything else was a spirit too. The Graveyard of the Giants was the outstretched arms of men who had drowned, and the End-of-the-Ocean was an evil god who caused the fishing canoes to disappear. Even the riptide, where the pregnant and gleaming ocean rushed in a great embrace around the ugly black shadow of Barebones Island and collided with itself, was the home of Where-It-Sinks, a monster who chewed up canoes as they passed overhead.

In the moonlight, with a soft breeze springing up from the End-of-the-Ocean, it was not hard to see how the Indians could believe such things. It seemed to me that I could already hear the moans coming from the Graveyard of the Giants and the ugly rushing laughter of Where-It-Sinks.

"And she," Grandfather's voice went on, "she is a spirit too, only unlike the rest of them, she is kind."

"Old Haluka says she's a spook," Buckety said. Old Haluka was Buckety's grandfather. He was president of the Tribal Council, and was the son of Calawa, who had been chief of the tribe when grandfather came in to build the schoolhouse.

"That's right," Grandfather said. "All the Indians say that, just as they used to talk about Kwatte, the god of Trickery, and the End-of-the-Ocean and the Graveyard of the Giants, but they don't rightly believe those stories any more." Grandfather stopped talking and stared sadly out past the long sandspit to where the angry flood tide leaped in fury at the sky. Far down the beach the Graveyard of the Giants moaned in the moonlight. The wind began to howl inward from the End-of-the-Ocean and swept back the bush from the top of the high cliff where Hanging Hair lived.

"Do you believe the stories?" I asked Grandfather.

"No," he said simply, turning to look at the wind-blown cliff. "I do not believe them."

In the first few months after we moved to Teahwit, business at the store was not good. The Indians had a poor fishing season and they bought only what they absolutely needed. Father was frantic. He ran around with his hands buried in his bushy hair and bumped into things. There was no use trying to talk to him because he would begin to swear and shout. After a while, he would swing open the heavy door of his private cabinet and get out a bottle. Then it was best to get out of the store. When Father did that, Mother would go into her room and lock the door. That meant that Father would sleep on the vegetable table, or wherever he finally fell down.

Things did not get any better and night after night I would hear Mother slam and lock the door to her room. Then there would be the crashing and staggering about downstairs and the silence as Father collapsed into the carrots and tomatoes or the bang of the door as he stumbled out to the road and careened down toward the beach. When Father drank like that, Grandfather usually came up to my room bringing cookies and milk for Nan and me, since Mother would refuse to cook dinner. We would sit on my bed and listen to the racket from downstairs and at times it got so loud that Nan would get frightened and begin to cry. When that happened, Grandfather told stories to hush her up. Sometimes he talked about how he had come out and homesteaded the territory and how he got married and finally built the first school in Teahwit.

"Your grandmother was the damnedest woman I ever met," he said late one afternoon when Father began throwing oranges at the windows of the store and yelling triumphantly whenever a pane was broken. He chuckled and then put his pipe in his mouth. Father let loose with something heavier than an orange and shattered the showcase window. Ignoring his laughter and Mother's muted scream, Grandfather puffed slowly on his pipe and went on talking. "When I met her she was living in a tent with her parents. Her pa was a misguided philosopher come West to prove something or other and make his fortune along the way. I especially remember Roseline's hair; her long hair that seemed to flow down over her shoulders and hang in a beautiful waterfall over her back. And I remember the way she used to walk through the town all dressed in white. The loggers came out of the bar just to watch her go by and tip their hats to her. You may not believe it, but she always smiled at them, even though half of them fell on their face from the effort of bowing and the other half were struck dumb.

"Well, one day when I was in the store eating crackers, she come in and started ordering groceries and things. When the man flung down a fifty-pound sack of flour I seen my chance and went up to offer my help getting all those things home. I took off my cap and bowed and started to say 'Afternoon, ma'am,' the way the loggers had done it in front of the saloon, and then suddenly I remembered that my mouth was full of crackers. There I was, bowing with a fistful of crackers in one hand and my cap in the other and not able to open my mouth to say a blessed word because — "

There was a tremendous crash downstairs and this time we all ran to look out. Father had slammed the door and broken the window. He had a bottle of whisky in one hand and a carton of eggs perched under his elbow, and every few steps he would somehow balance himself and get an egg out and throw it furiously at the store as he went staggering backward toward the beach. He finally got to a tangled jungle of driftwood logs and, giving a final heave of the whole box of eggs, began to scamper over the logs, the half-filled bottle carefully cradled in his hand. Grandfather puffed on his pipe and went on with his story.

"It would have been the same whether my mouth was full of crackers or not. She had pity, that woman did, and without me even saying, she said it: asking if I would be kind enough to carry the sack of flour home for her."

Down the beach Father was sitting on the big rock and carrying on. He waved his half-empty bottle at the End-of-the-Ocean. The waves swirled in at him and hissed at his feet, but he seemed not to notice them. The sun touched the end of the sea and threw golden spears over the rolling waves. Father stood up on the big rock and swore loudly at it. Down the beach a white blur merged with a blinding glare and came slowly toward him. The dying sun stung and clawed at my eyes as I tried to see beyond the flaring light, making out finally the long flowing wind-blown hair as she came steadily on toward the big rock where Father stood swearing at the sun, the sealskin bag swinging loosely at her side.

"So I done it," Grandfather said. He had walked away from the window as though he didn't want to see what was going on out there. The bed creaked and groaned under his weight as he flung himself down upon it. "I carried that sack of flour home for her, right past the loggers who come out of the saloon to 'Evenin', ma'am' her. I staggered along behind under all that flour and hadn't managed to get myself straightened out when we finally got to the tent where her pa was sitting out in front reading a book. He didn't even look up when we went by. Just sort of grunted, as though he might have been expecting me, or something like me all the time, underneath a fifty-pound sack of flour, to come broken-back past him to go inside and propose to his daughter and marry her."

I was only half listening to Grandfather. The old woman came slowly down the beach toward Father. She was dressed in white flour sacks that billowed like balloons in the wind. Occasionally she would stop and turn over stones with her pointed stick and then scratch in the sand for the tiny butter clams. Father paid her no attention. He sat down on the smooth top of the big rock and began to drink from his bottle. It looked as if Hanging Hair hadn't seen him either, for she kept her head toward the ground, moving slowly and steadily toward where Father sat.

"But it didn't happen just that way. When I got in the tent, damned if Roseline didn't pull out the tent pole and somehow get outside again. That was the last I saw of anything until the old man got me untangled from the god-awful mess that had come down on my head. That took him awhile and when he got me uncovered, and me sitting there with that fifty-pound sack of flour in my lap, I found out why. He still had the book in one hand, opened part way with his thumb marking the spot."

The old woman kept coming down the beach, getting nearer to Father. She would stop every so often and upturn a few rocks. Then she would move on, always getting closer.

"And right behind him was his daughter, peering at me as if I was a bug. All I knew was that I wanted out of there fast because any woman who will pull a tent pole out, especially when it happens to be holding up the tent, is downright dangerous, not to say downright mad."

The sun had disappeared beneath the sea and it was getting dark. The old woman had stopped and picked up a long piece of driftwood, slender and pointed like a spear. She moved a few steps down the beach and then froze suddenly and stood for a long while looking out toward the End-of-the-Ocean. She seemed to be listening to something. Her head was cocked toward the west and every so often she would nod. At the end of the spit, the flood tide made the water erupt in tiny fierce waves that formed a long black angry line clear to Barebones Island. She seemed to stand there for ages as Father went on drinking from his bottle, standing up every so often to swear loudly and then sitting abruptly down again. Finally, Hanging Hair began to move toward Father much more quickly, her long sharp piece of driftwood pointed at his weaving back.

"And so I got. The old man never even took his thumb out of the book. He was already in his chair, getting back to his reading, when I run past him, getting away from that female as fast as I could. I could hear her yelling at me as I ran down the road, and I think she was halfway screaming and halfway crying, but the only thing I could think of was to get to the other side of the saloon as fast as I could. And damn her if she didn't come after me, yelling all the way down the street, so that the loggers come out again. Only this time they didn't bow, except those that was dying from laughter."

The moon had come up over the mountains and was beginning to throw its pale white light across the ocean. Hanging Hair went toward Father, the driftwood like a spear balanced in her hand. She got behind the big rock and then stopped, standing there frozen as a statue. Father stood up to curse at the ocean and went tumbling right over the side of the rock. For a while Hanging Hair didn't move, only stood there, seeming to listen to the pounding of the waves. Then she put down her driftwood and went around to the other side of the rock.

"I finally got away from her, God only knows how I done it, but it took some running. And the next day damned if when I was walking down the street the whole . . ."

Hanging Hair had ahold of Father and was dragging him around to one side of the big rock. She got him propped up and tore off part of her flour-sack dress and soaked it in the waves that were beginning to lap at her feet.

". . . damned Indian tribe didn't come into town with old Calawa the chief carrying an apple pie in front of him like it was a god, and right behind him four Indians carrying that spear-like tent pole, and right behind them it seemed like half the tribe carrying the Indian that had tried to swipe the apple pie from Roseline's tent just as I come marching in carrying my flour sack, and the rest of the tribe singing and chanting along in the rear. Everyone in town hurried out to watch as Calawa came up to the collapsed tent. He stood there staring at it until finally Roseline's father came from the woods across the way — where they'd camped that night under the trees — his book neatly thumb-stuck in one hand. When he seen the pie he yelled for his daughter, and she came out and bowed before old Calawa, her white dress floating to the ground like a collapsed balloon. Old Calawa bowed too and gave her the apple pie, one huge bite missing from it. Then he stepped aside to make room for the four Indians with the tent pole. They laid it on the ground before her. Finally the rest of them, all clamoring together now, dragged up the prostrate Indian. He'd run twenty miles down the long Indian trail through the ocean bush with the pie stuck out straight before him in both hands and the tent pole stuck clean between his shoulder blades, exactly where she'd aimed it. When he got to the village, he collapsed before the big rock, setting the pie just in front of it, and then fell to pin himself on the sand."

Hanging Hair began to caress Father's head with the white cloth. He suddenly sat straight up and began shouting at her and, even at that distance, I could hear his voice booming over the crash of the incoming waves.

"What?" Father was screaming at her, "what do you say?" And then he was trying to stand up and shake her all at the same time. The furious flood tide came in and swamped him clean off his feet, so that for a moment he disappeared under the rushing flow of water, and then emerged all at once, still yelling, as Grandfather went on talking:

"Your grandma was crazy as an owl. If she'd lived past giving birth to your father, she'd be out there trying to drag him out of the surf, just as Hanging Hair is probably doing right now."

Grandfather hadn't moved from the bed, so he couldn't see father yelling at Hanging Hair and stumbling around in the raging water. My face must have shown my surprise, for he said:

"Oh, she always does it. I've watched her haul Lubin out of the water more than once. Would have had to do it myself if she hadn't got there first. Whenever Lubin takes his bottle down to the big rock, you can be sure that sooner or later the surf is going to come up and get him, and he's just going to sit there and yell at it, like the whole thing was unnatural, until it swamps him. Hanging Hair will be there to drag his carcass ashore. Last thing your grandmother said was that somebody was going to have to take care of him. I figured that was me, but the job proved too much."

The job looked to be proving too much even for Hanging Hair right then. Father had ahold of her and was shaking her up and down, yelling so loud that even Grandfather got up from the bed and came over to the window to see what was going on.

"Well, I'm damned," he said. "Lubin's doing it again. Not only wasn't it enough to have come out of his mother sideways, now he wants to start out again with the only other creature that could ever love him or pity him, your mother included." Grandfather was already making for the stairs as I caught a last glimpse of Father trying to shove Hanging Hair's head under water. The both of them were standing knee-deep in the flowing flood tide when Grandfather shot out like an arrow from the store underneath. Farther along the beach, old Haluka and Buckety came tearing out of their fallen-down shack, and then I was running too, down the stairs and out the door, past my pale and frightened mother. Father had Hanging Hair all the way under the water now and it seemed like the whole village was running toward the big rock, but Grandfather got there first. He took hold of Father by the neck and somehow picked him right clean away from the water and Hanging Hair, who billowed and popped to the surface in her torn white dress. Grandfather carried Father like a toy through the surf and roared at him, "By God, boy, you've needed a whipping for some time now." I believe he'd have tried it right then, except that Hanging Hair came shouting straight up out of the surf, and Father yelled at him too. The old man stopped dead and stood there, tall in the moonlight, unsure, his son held struggling and kicking before him, until finally he heard what it was that they were both yelling at him, and then he simply let Father drop and walked off silently toward the store.

"I never could spank your pa," Grandfather said later. "I believe that the only time anyone ever hit him was when the doctor smacked him one to get him breathing, and he probably even resented that." It was a week after Father had tried to drown Hanging Hair. Grandfather had gone back to the store that night, but the next day he'd disappeared, and he stayed away for six days. "On the seventh day, He rested, and by God, so do I," Grandfather said when he came back. Father tried to get him to tell where he'd been, but it didn't do much good. Only when he came up to my room that night did he begin to talk. For a few days, he'd gone up to New Royal, but then he'd come back and stayed at Hanging Hair's house. Grandpa wanted to get straight the yelling he'd heard that night.

"In those years before your father was born, it was better," Grandfather said. "I guess I loved Roseline, and I guess it started when the Indians brought the tent pole back to her, along with the Indian she'd thrown it at. That was a surrender of a sort that's not likely to be seen again. And she, of course, stood there all dressed in white, and gave them back the pie. Then she kissed the Indian she'd damn near killed. Her father was sitting in the background, reading a book, and her mother flitting around, for God's sake, passing out Bibles, but Roseline would have no part of that. I asked her to marry me that evening."

He stopped talking and began to fill his pipe. "There were things before your pa got born that made it worth while. But she was crazy. Like Hanging Hair. Hanging Hair's a spook, all right. She loves your father too, God only knows why. There's something that Roseline said. She didn't believe in the human race. She figured it was coming to an end. At times, she used to say the whole business was a big mistake, and then she got large with your father. My God, I never seen a woman suffer so much. 'It will come,' she said, 'and who's going to take care of him?' 'Come what?' I asked. 'The end,' she said. That was just a week before she killed herself with your father. 'The end,' she said. And she didn't mean hers. She meant more than that, and even then I could see it. She meant the whole business, and then she began to cry and there wasn't much to say. What can you say to something like that?"

Outside, the moon had begun to reflect itself on the incoming tide, the big rock stood stark and ugly, a black movement out of the sand. The End-of-the-Ocean rose up and down, weaving about the pane of my window sill. Down to the south, the Graveyard of the Giants rose great and powerful out of the surf waving its angry old arms at the young moon.

"Which was what Hanging Hair was yelling that night when Lubin tried to drown her: just that simple, 'The end,' was what she was trying to tell Lubin. The end."

Downstairs it was all quiet. Since Father had tried to get Hanging Hair under the ocean and failed, he hadn't drunk anything, not even — so far as I could tell — water. In fact, he was quite pleasant. Father could be that way. At times, he would come up to me as I was tending the store, and look at me for a long while without saying anything. And then move away.

"The end," Grandfather said. "Because Where-It-Sinks is angry. You know the tale. She believes it. She's part of it. And Where-It-Sinks is angry and wants everything this time. He wants the world."

I sat by the window and listened to Grandfather. He lay on my bed and puffed at his pipe. I looked out at the beautiful moon, all dressed in white, beginning to die at the End-of-the-Ocean, and in a blotch of greater whiteness, her hair tumbling down over her back, Hanging Hair came, wandering wildly down the beach, waving her long jagged clam stick at the rushing waves. When the water broke swirling and hissing at her feet and then began its seeping retreat, she would run after it, beating at sinking waves with the stick. At the End-of-the-Ocean, another wave would gather itself to greatness and swell toward the moon. It would come after her, rolling smoothly over itself, getting larger, breaking finally into a towering fountain of foam and spray, and then slide at her like a long sidewinding snake.

It was a strange battle that seemed to be going on, as if Hanging Hair intended somehow to push back the water to the End-of-the-Ocean. Grandfather came and stood behind me and watched as Hanging Hair quickly ran back from the wave and then, as it reached for her with a final line of foam, began to chase it back to the sea.

"She's mad," Grandfather said, "just like your grandma was."

I looked at Hanging Hair, waving her clam stick and chasing the angry dying wave toward the ocean, her torn and dirty flour-bag dress billowing about her, and getting just so far, suddenly stopping and then beginning to run furiously toward the beach as the newly born wave came tumbling and roaring shoreward. In the water off the spit, Where-It-Sinks was angry. He tossed himself upward in churning great anger, rising in blackness toward the sky and then falling back. Hanging Hair moved up the beach in the direction of the great white spit that flung itself toward Barebones Island.

"She's got salmon berries in that bag of hers," Grandfather said. "She's going to try and feed him." Grandfather's voice sounded tired. I turned to look at him, but he was moving away from me, going over toward the bed. "You watch," he said, "she's going to fling berries at the rip tide."

In the moonlight Hanging Hair was moving down the long sandy spit. Where-It-Sinks roared at the moon and then fell in fury upon himself. When Hanging Hair got as far as she could go, she began to throw handfuls of the small red berries at the water. On both sides of her, the waves came rushing in, and I expected her to be swept off her feet. But they stopped short and fell away as though somehow they were frightened. Where-It-Sinks rose to new fury. Even the waves seemed to take courage from his anger. They began to rush at Hanging Hair, swamping her from both sides as she stood at the farthest reach of the spit, flinging the bright sun-red berries in all directions. She flung her clam stick into the water; then she took off her sealskin bag and threw that in too; then, as if that were not enough, she began to tear at her flour-sack dress, ripping at it, shredding it into long ribboned strips. The moon above her was suddenly shattered into tendrils by a ragged cloud that passed in front of it.

"What she's doing is to get Where-It-Sinks quiet," Grandfather said. He had himself stretched out on the bed and was staring absently at the ceiling. It didn't look as if Hanging Hair was going to get away with it because one huge wave had started out at her from the End-of-the-Ocean. It danced and rose. It tottered and fell. It gathered and growled. It came on at Hanging Hair, who stood in shredded whiteness at the end of the spit. The wave grew. It rose. It roared. It seemed higher than the store, the trees, the mountains. It came at her.

Then suddenly it broke and fell, and Hanging Hair, as if drunk, began to sing and chant because the wave had begun to retreat upon itself, taking with it the sealskin basket and the clamming stick and the long white shreds of her dress, going away from the spit with Hanging Hair right behind it shouting and screaming at the retreating wall of water.

"She does that all the time," Grandfather said. "She goes out there and gets swamped. She's trying to beat the ocean, and she can't do it."

"It looks as if she's done it this time," I said.

"What?" Grandfather said sleepily.

"It looks as if she's won," I said. "She's chasing that wave clear past Barebones Island."

"What!" Grandfather shouted, but he was already ahead of his voice, coming at the window and staring out as Hanging Hair was going after the backward flowing wave of water, farther out than I had ever seen a wave go, far enough out so that the water between the end of the spit and Barebones Island was no longer there; farther than that, since Barebones Island was no longer even an island, but simply an outcropping of the land surounded by a lot of fish dying in the moonlight, and Hanging Hair, so far out now that she was only a white splotch on the horizon, as Grandfather stood there and suddenly began to yell.

"Lubin!" he screamed, loud enough to wake the dead, and then he was already out of my bedroom and going down the stairs with me somehow getting carried along.

"Lubin!" Grandfather was yelling, "she's coming!" and then we were outside and in the truck with Grandfather trying to get it started and shouting and blowing the horn all at once. Over his shoulder I could see Father as he tumbled out of the store, trying to pull his pants up. He stared with amazement at the disappearing ocean, and then he began to shout too and disappeared into the store, coming out again almost at once with Nan in his arms and Mother right behind him. Grandfather grabbed me from the cab and threw me into the back of the truck, and we were off with Father shouting and honking and Grandfather yelling "She's coming, she's coming," to the Indians that were popping out of their ramshackle cabins. Suddenly he jumped clean over the back end of the truck, disappeared for a moment in the long moonlit wave of dust that tumbled behind us, and then, as the wind and the broken moon surged around me, reappeared in full gallop, going away from us in a shattering blur of waving arms and legs and dust, shouting so that his words curled back in long splintered echoes: "Hanging Hair! Hanging Hair!" And then Father, gearing and honking and yelling, turned up the long ribbon of road away from the ocean, and the village and the moon were swallowed in blackness.

When it was over, we came back. Grandfather, in his underwear, stood in the middle of what was left of the road, waiting for us. For what seemed miles, we had gone through the torn, ripped, crushed ocean bush that the wave, in its peace and quiet, had moved over. That was the way the wave finally would be. Moving like the other waves would move; not much higher, a black line against the horizon, not even jumping at the moon, not angry, just coming on, showing its silent power by sucking the End-of-the-Ocean toward it, by swallowing Where-It-Sinks, by making all the gods disappear as Hanging Hair went running toward it, shouting what she had already shouted, yelling what Grandfather had known was possible and what Father had known was possible, yelling it so loud and with such violence that when the ocean finally did back up, what was myth and what was memory all came together and made sense: that the big wave was coming in, and wherever the gods may sit, whoever the gods might be, there was nothing that was going to stop this one. When we came through that incredible tangle of bush and mud, the village was no longer recognizable; there was simply nothing left. The store still stood like a broken sentinel, but it had been badly damaged. The only thing that had any meaning or that made any sense was Grandfather, kneeling in the middle of the road as Father came twisting and gearing toward him.

"Pa," my father called. Grandfather got up off his knees and came toward the truck. I looked around me. The waves came crashing in. Only the store stood. Here and there a frantic chicken ran back and forth, pecking its way over the flattened shacks, tapping with a curious bill over the tumbled driftwood planks. There was no road left, but a single cow was making the best of it, coming moaning and tumbling over the incredible mess that the ocean had left so that she could get at us. Grandfather caught her as she galloped by, and she finally came to a halt in the middle of a tangled and grotesque pile of driftwood. Grandfather sat on what had once been a table and began to milk her. Father had gotten out of the truck and run up to him. Here and there Indian heads began to pop up from the midst of the cluttered wreckage. From down the beach I could see Buckety and Old Haluka making their way slowly toward us. Beyond them, out toward Barebones Island, the long sandy spit had been washed away and only a muddy rock-strewn flat lay where Where-It-Sinks had surged toward the sky. On the night of the big wave, our honking and shouting had awakened most of the Indians in time for them to get back to the high plateau that rose behind the village. The few that did not make it in time had simply disappeared.

Grandfather sat milking the cow. The Indians were milling about, trying to salvage what they could. Father was shouting at Grandfather. He wanted to know what had happened and how come Grandfather hadn't got himself killed and what were we going to do now that everything was wrecked.

"Well," Grandfather said, "I guess we're just going to have to start over again." He told us then how he had chased Hanging Hair clear out past Barebones Island and how he had just gotten hold of her when the wave hit him. That was the last thing he remembered until he woke up sitting in the branches of a tree in his underwear. He guessed Hanging Hair had been carried out to sea.

"Damned old fool," Father yelled at him. "You risk your neck running after a crazy woman like that when even the Indians won't touch her. Sometimes I think you're crazy yourself." Father went stomping off through the mud toward the store.

Grandfather went on milking the cow. "I guess maybe I am crazy at that," he said quietly. "I guess maybe that it's not enough to love and it's much too late to really start over again." When he turned to look at me, I saw that his eyes were full of tears.

(From The Kenyon Review)

"TO HELL THE RABBIS"

BY BEN MADDOW

*M*Y *FATHER-IN-LAW*, Mr. Bronnish, had never had the pleasure of meeting Mahatma Gandhi. However, he admired him profoundly, and tried, as well as the cacophonies of Chicago would allow, to live as he lived. Mr. Bronnish was just seventy-five, and I'd been commissioned by my wife to buy him a present, which I carried in a long cardboard tube under my arm.

Mr. Bronnish met me at the airport with a bunch of flowers. "Field flowers," he told me; though the fields from which they had been plucked were covered with eight inches of grimy snow. His great, sad, booming voice, his vegetarian embrace, his enormous white Cossack mustache, his shirt open at the neck to the January winds, all reminded me once again how artificial, how unhealthy I had become, how distant from the purity of nature, and the wild taste of goat's milk, taken with wafers of caraway seed, for the teeth's sake.

Mr. Bronnish, amazed and cheerful as a dog, wanted to watch the jet take off again; it roared, belched and bolted; he put his thumbs in his ears, and said, "Science should be abolished — before somebody is killed!"

"It's too late, Papa Bronnish," I told him.

He shook me by the lapels of my overcoat, and said, "Take the moon for an example. How do they know?"

"Know what, Papa Bronnish?"

"If there is any such a thing as the other side of the moon?"

"They don't," I assured him.

"Aha! Fakers!" he cried.

"How do you know you're living!" I told him.

Drinking hot wax cups of tea out of the dispenser, and arguing this delicate point back and forth, we managed to miss the airport limousine. I insisted upon a taxi; Mr. Bronnish urged upon me the moral imperative to walk: it was a mere twelve miles to his house, and snowing; but I saved myself by assuring him that I, and I alone, would pay for the taxi. He accepted this defeat, rather too easily I thought, rolled down all the windows of the taxi, and inhaled and exhaled with sibilations of pleasure.

"Most people breed with their lungs. Wrong!" he told me. "Breed with your belly. More natural."

"My suits are shrinking," I admitted.

"Lack of exercise," he said. "Take hats, for an example," he went on, with his soft and insinuating logic. "Hats clog up the brain. You know what I mean?"

I said I did, which was a lie.

"It reminds me," he continued, "which in the old country, my uncle, very religious, met me walking on the street, cock-a-doodle-do! I was smart in those days, which I proved by I didn't wear a hat. So he told me, shame yourself, where's your hat, it's against religion to go without a hat, do you understand?"

He paused and laughed. Simultaneously, the taxi began to jolt like a horse, and the driver, a swarthy man with sunglasses, pulled it off into the soft snow and stopped. We all got out and stared at the four tires in turn. The taxi driver leaned forward and spat upon the left rear wheel.

"That's the bugger," he said.

"Don't make yourself sick," said Mr. Bronnish. "It's only flat on one side."

The taxi driver took this as some kind of obscure insult. He refused our help: he claimed it would lead straight on to lawyers and lawsuits. Mr. Bronnish agreed. He walked about, clapping his hands to keep warm. So did I. We applauded a fine landscape of slag, brick chimneys, and an auto graveyard whose black bones, huge and tawny, were strewn under the snow.

"Make a long story short," said Mr. Bronnish, "when he said, against religion, that made me angry. I told my uncle, I said, Uncle, where does it stand written? Where? Where is it written that a man should wear a hat? Which my uncle said, *Abraham*. I said, What? He said, *Abraham! Abraham? Abraham?* What is got to do, *Abraham?* Which my uncle said as follows: Go! Leave your family! Leave your house! Go forth into the world! Now would a person like God let Abraham to go forth into the world without a hat? I ask you?"

He laughed at his own joke, till one could see nothing but the brown stumps of his teeth.

"You've brought something there?" he said, poking at the cardboard cylinder under my arm.

"A surprise," I said. "A present for your birthday."

"You shouldn't go to such trouble with all your other troubles!" he said politely.

"How many times does a man have a seventy-fifth birthday?" I said.

"Yes, old is also natural," he said, sighing. "But frankly I don't care for it."

Mrs. Bronnish, my mother-in-law, was in a panic. There was a bird in the house, and why, of the four flats in this poor old house, the bird had to pick theirs was an aberration of nature she refused to understand. She was a big woman with deep, sad eyes, and a body the shape of an old-fashioned bomb. She wore tight, thin dresses made out of printed gingham, was eternally cold, and kept the windows tightly shut, and the gas oven lit, and wide open. Generations of chickens had been roasted in this flat, iron cavern, and the heat which it breathed forth so generously smelled of distant scorching and forgotten pinfeathers.

"Mrs.! Mrs.!" cried Mr Bronnish to his wife. "Leave the poor creature alone! It's a living thing, it knows what's what better than you nor I! With all our civilization! So-called."

He got a bottle of wine out of the pantry, and set it down on the dining-room table. Mumbling and grumbling, Mrs. Bronnish brought two tiny glasses for the men, and polished them with a corner of the tablecloth. She warned him, "I don't want windows opened in this house!" He poured out the wine, smiling and nodding. Mrs. Bronnish swung a fat forefinger under his white mustache. "This winter is going to be my winter!" she told him.

"Where is the poor creature?" he said at last.

"I don't know, I don't care to know, dirty up the house, that I know!"

"Mrs., please, please! Rather than give myself heartburn, I'll rescue the poor bird. Satisfied?" he told her. He went immediately into the bathroom, and was heard to murmur endearments to a flurry of invisible wings. He came out again with a small, brown finch in his two hands. I opened the front door — one of four identical ones, side by side — and the bird flew off into the air, a blot of black wings against the moving snow. We felt wonderful, we two smug, kindly, nature-loving men. We went back to the table and guzzled our wine, warm and smiling.

Mrs. Bronnish said, "Did you clean up the dirt from that dirty bird? Fat chance."

Mr. Bronnish sipped his wine. "Drink, drink!" he told me. "Pay no attention to remarks."

"Mahatma Gandhi didn't indulge in alcohol, believe me!" Mrs. Bronnish remarked.

"He's not the last word. The world progresses. I believe Darwin was not mistaken," he replied. "So if man perishes, the Norwegian rat will take over very nicely."

"Rats? Why do you bring up rats!" she cried, waving her fat arms dramatically in the dining room. "Just to spite me, that's all! I keep a clean house! There's no rats in my house! Only windows! Only drafts! Only double pinnumonia!"

Mr. Bronnish waited for the conclusion; it was a scene that he knew, enjoyed, and refused to interrupt. At last, Mrs. Bronnish said, "I couldn't locate the bird, where'd you locate the bird, smart aleck?"

"Logic. Simple logic. A bird," said Mr. Bronnish, "is an article of nature. Therefore it seeks out peace and quiet. So where in this house will you find peace and quiet? In the living room? No! In the bedroom? No! In the foyer? No!"

Mrs. Bronnish pulled at my shirt and addressed me personally. "It's true, if my husband goes in the toilet, he disappears. Hours! Hours! People call up. Where is Mr. Bronnish? I am ashamed to tell them. I am an average ignorant nobody, but tell me this, if you please, what can he take pleasure in a bathroom?"

"I can open up the window," he said softly; watching me smile, he struck me jovially on the back. He drank up; his mustachios were tipped with globules of red, sweet wine.

"He takes his enjoyment from other people's suffering," she told me.

The four-family house in which the Bronnishes lived had five white pillars and four green doors. With this, all order and regularity was exhausted. The windows had been punctured through the wall at random, and were of random size and shape, some square, some oblong, some almost, if not quite, circular. This mad design was extended into space by the four separate antennas; they were set at cross angles, on a roof that was itself composed of multitudinous angles; wood, paint, and metal had been bent, blistered, and corroded by Midwest industrial weather. The loftiest and most fanciful antenna of them all, probing outward to suck electromagnetism out of the faintly sulphurous air, drew it down by a tiny ladder, through a back window, and into the Bronnishes' TV set.

This machine was rather unusual. It was enclosed, for example, in a cabinet that was originally intended to display fancy groceries. A blue ceramic leopard stood upon it, chained collar to foot with a gold glazed chain. Mrs. Bronnish loved TV, it was another person in the household, to her way of thinking; she admired its sentiment, was moved by its drama, argued with its politics, and occasionally, during the newscast, became sufficiently enraged to slap it smartly on the front plate glass. She turned it on as soon as she rose in the morning, and stood before it, answering it back and combing her hair at the same time.

Mr. Bronnish, however, regarded the set as unnatural, and probably one of the unrecognized causes of cancer. As a compromise, therefore, the video was left on and the sound shut off. Flickering all day long in this mute state, the TV had a certain ethereal fascination which was possibly not intended by the makers.

Sitting with his back to the machine, Mr. Bronnish drank wine through his mustache, and repeated for me his immense theory of health and disease, of the relation between blood pressure and fruit juice, and the relative merits of various grinders and homogenizers, a problem on which he had apparently spent considerable

time and money in the last ten years. Neither I nor Mrs. Bronnish
listened very carefully. I yawned. She hummed. At last, Mr. Bronnish, well accustomed to this neglect, sighed deeply, and put out
his great square pale hand to touch the cardboard cylinder I had
brought for his seventy-fifth birthday.

"It's time, time," he said at last. "Time to face facts!" With his
right thumbnail, untrimmed, and hard as a spike of horn, he split
the paper covering on the present. Then he unrolled the sheet
and spread it out on the tablecloth.

"Ah, aha," he said, as it unrolled. I smiled at Mrs. Bronnish
and Mrs. Bronnish smiled back at me. The anticipation of happiness for another human being is still one of the special pleasures of
the race. Mr. Bronnish rose, though, rather suddenly, and seized
the present in both hands, tore it apart as though it were a sandwich, swung open the rear door, and hurled it out among the three
empty garbage cans in the cement back yard.

I thought he'd had a stroke and gone entirely mad.

I must explain: I'd become, in the last few years, a passionate
admirer of the painter Chagall, of his mixture of irony and sensuality, of his luminous but also keen and piercing line: I felt the
ancient, almost African wit behind the passionate Semitism of his
paint. At times, even, his sense of things corresponded so closely
to my own that I felt Chagall to be more like myself than I, indeed, was ever likely to be. The gift of this Chagall print, thus,
was wound and interwound with my sense of family and inheri-
tance, which was both guilty and sentimental. When Mr. Bronnish
tore apart my gift, it appalled me, therefore, far more than it
should have.

Now, too, there was a terrible and unaccustomed silence in the
Bronnish house. Mrs. Bronnish moved out to the kitchen and
began to pluck peppermints out of a striped bag, cracking and
chewing them as though they were stolen. Mr. Bronnish sat at the
table, playing with a few grains of salt which he had spilled onto
the cloth as a kind of personal magic. He was flushed and enraged.
Suddenly, with the flat of both hands, he struck the cloth till the
salt jumped into the air, grain by grain. "To hell the rabbis!" he
shouted.

It was true. I had brought him the Chagall print of the Chief
Rabbi, sad, powerful, with the ritual shawl around his shoulders.

"I won't have a rabbi in my house," he told me, and turned as if in horror from my pale, sinful face.

We sat this way for five or ten minutes, a desolation, a real desert of time, until I felt he had grown calm, and would tell me now why I had so outraged him with my gift.

I said, "I'm sure, Mr. Bronnish, I had no intention — " He struck me on the back; it was an unexpected kindness. I went on, "Very likely there's some good reason which explains — "

"I'm very angry. Very angry! Very upset," he told me.

"Look here, Mr. Bronnish!" I answered. "I came fifteen hundred miles to give you a present for your seventy-fifth birthday, and you turn around and tear it up. How am I going to explain it to my wife? She won't think *you've* gone out of *your* mind, she'll think *I've* gone out of *my* mind."

Mr. Bronnish shook his head. "Son, I'll tell you. Actually, it's highly interesting. The fact is," he said, looking around at his wife, who stood in the kitchen doorway, wallowing in waves of peppermint perfume, "the fact is, I was marked out to be a rabbi. Believe it or not."

"Oh, I do, I do!" I said.

"You don't, you can't, it's unbelievable. Why? Because of my inner nature," he went on to explain.

"Of course," I said, a bit too quickly.

"Why of course? Nothing is of course! The actual fact is, they had me in the *Talmitterah,* learning by night and by day, I was all of eleven years old what did I learn?"

"Nothing," I said.

"Wrong again," he said. "I learned nature very well. Imagine a school that has one window for twenty-four boys, plus a rabbi."

"No air," I added.

"Plenty of air — from the rabbi," he told me.

"Ha, fools make remarks," said Mrs. Bronnish; she sounded as though she had a mouthful of glass.

"The rabbi which I mentioned," he went on, "had as a side line, he made shophars, which if you don't know, I'll also explain — "

"Oh, I know about those," I said.

"You know nothing," he told me.

"Isn't it the horn of the ram, made into a trumpet?"

"Darkness and superstition!" he cried. "Nevertheless, that was the environment in which I lived. Who was I? Nobody. I had fourteen brothers, eight sisters, which half of them died before they could chew bread. But I'll tell you something. I survived! I was lucky! I was strong as an ox! Never touched meat from the age of nine! Had an iron will! And I had it in my heart to blow one of these horns, me, myself, the shophar! To see could I wake up the world! Which was naturally forbidden! Everything was forbidden, for that matter! So I waited my chance, understand me? Till the rabbi had to go toilet, which in those days was a hundred yards in a field somewhere."

"More healthy than where we got it now," said Mrs. Bronnish, invisible in the peppermint-smelling kitchen. "Inside toilets, an American invention, not that I'm against the 'Star Spangled Banner,' long may it wave. I hate that butcher Stalin."

"Stalin is dead, my dear," said Mr. Bronnish. "Have you noticed?"

"Khrushchev is better?" said Mrs. Bronnish.

"Philosophy, let's not have philosophy!" cried Mr. Bronnish.

"What about the shophar? The horn! The ram's horn!" I reminded him.

"The horn! The horn! Yessiree, the horn! I stole that horn out of the rabbi's closet, and I went outside, and I blew such a blast, such a note! You could hear it like from here to Cincinnati. That's how I blew it! The trees shivered, actually, for a fact."

"I have a sister in Cincinnati," said Mrs. Bronnish, fumbling in the peppermint paper, "she's so stingy, she never calls up any more. I never hear a word, is she sick, is she dead."

"Again philosophy," cried Mr. Bronnish.

"About the horn!" I said. "The horn!"

"The horn, yes! The horn! Well, the rabbi," he told me, "came back running. He didn't have time to button up, in those days buttons were universal. *Who blew the shophar?* he yelled out like he was having an operation. Nobody said a word. He took the strap out of his pants, the rabbi, God bless him, and he lined us up in that room and he drew out blood, one by one, with the buckle of his belt. But nobody in all those boys said a word against me. But me, me? Imagine! I bust out crying before he even hit me."

"Crying ever since," said Mrs. Bronnish.

"Long story short, I let out such a yell the poor rabbi got soft-hearted and he let me go. A few measly slaps on the behind, nothing more. The next day he went to the toilet, as per usual, he took a key and locked up the shophars in the closet. And the key, he had the key in his pants pocket. And all I had was the passion, the desire!"

"Gone with the wind," mumbled Mrs. Bronnish.

"A desire — to blow that blast again for once more in my life! But how to open a closet without a key, that I didn't know."

"You forced it open?" I said.

"Impossible," he pointed out. "In the first place, I was a coward. In the second place, to break a lock was going too far. No, I went and I took the funnel — you understand? — which the rabbi used when he poured the wine for himself a little drink on the sly? I took this funnel and went outside and put it in my mouth and took a breath like nobody breathed before, believe me! and I blew, I blew! The sun went behind a cloud! The dead people put one foot out of their grave! It was like thunder!"

"I always dreamed to go to Cincinnati," said Mrs. Bronnish.

"Result," said Mr. Bronnish, "when that rabbi heard such a blast, he thought I had swiped the biggest shophar in the world. Again he rushes back, again his pants he didn't have time, again he looks, but the closet is locked! Locked! You devil, he calls me, how did you do it! And he hits me such a klopp on my ear I went black as coal, and they tell me I walked around in circles like a chicken without a head."

"For blowing in a funnel?" I said.

"A plain, two-cents funnel."

"And what then?"

"And then, what then? That's all, what then! Finished. *Shluss.* I went home. I went straight to my father, he was eating soup, I said out loud, 'To hell the rabbis.' He was so amazed, he blew the soup out of his mouth for a quarter of a mile. I said to my father, 'To hell the rabbis. To hell the rabbis, Papa! I want to be a watchmaker!' Dreams! In those days, who had watches? So I became a tailor. So who bought clothes? So I came to America. So what did I do? Spent my life on vests. So who wears vests? So now I'm a landlord, three miserable tenants."

"Thank you, Columbus," said Mrs. Bronnish.

"America is no paradise. But the old country, that was living in hell. I had eye trouble as a boy, they said eat fish, I wouldn't eat fish, what did they do, they took me to a dead man in his coffin, a big rabbi! And put his hand on my eyes. It made me sick for a week." He sloshed out more wine for both of us, and drank his rapidly, sucking his mustache with considerable noise. "Superstition. Neglect of nature. Therefore I say, to hell the rabbis."

"Your own brother is a rabbi," said Mrs. Bronnish.

Mr. Bronnish disregarded this mad objection. "You know, rabbis, for an example," he told me, "I once knew an old lady retired to Miami Beach."

"I wish I could say the same," said Mrs. Bronnish.

"Miami," continued Mr. Bronnish, "it's nice weather, the sun shines, everything very natural, and do they enjoy it? No. The three old ladies, you can find them sitting on a porch. Pinochle? No. Not even pinochle. They sit. Who knows why? Enjoying, they enjoyed. One had a son, a doctor, the other a son, a certified public accountant. So they said to this old lady, what about your son? What does he do, for an example? He's a rabbi, she admitted. So what did they say to her, they said, Poor thing, a rabbi, is this a profession for a nice Jewish boy?"

Mrs. Bronnish came and shook her fist at him. "Anti-Semitic," she told him, "is in my opinion, the worst kind of a Jew."

Mr. Bronnish said, "We'll see about that in heaven, if there is such a place, that is."

Mrs. Bronnish struck both hands together with a resounding clap. "Who wants heaven? I want to live," she cried. The scent of peppermint was overpowering.

Mr. Bronnish waved both hands until it was diluted and dissipated. Meanwhile, over the horizon of decrepit houses, the sun was being swallowed by the earth. It was Friday, and Mrs. Bronnish went back and forth from the kitchen, and lit several candles on top of the TV set, next to the black leopard.

"I call it superstition," he said to me, apologizing for the candles, "but who knows? Who really knows? Nature is a mystery. For that matter, even a bowl of pea soup is a mystery. Am I right?"

I had no answer. It grew darker outside and inside. We sat finishing the sweet wine, and Mr. Bronnish rocked back and forth in his chair, and Mrs. Bronnish sang a gay little familiar song; after a while, I recognized it as a toothpaste commercial, but in her minty mouth it sounded gay and pure; but then, to drown her out, Mr. Bronnish began to sing for me out of the Saturday Service. The sun was wholly gone. His voice was deep and gloomy; the flames of the candles were burning in his narrow eyes, as they might have burned once in that far-off and indomitable boy, who blew a sacred horn to spite the rabbis.

(*From New World Writing*)

DÉJÀ VU

BY MIRIAM McKENZIE

*S*HE STOOD at the hedge, only her head visible, looking more than ever like a wood creature — startled, vulnerable, remote.

Her face was lit by a strange excitement, and there was the suggestion of a smile, but she said very innocently, so still-ly, "Poor Miranda, I believe her mother is dead."

Coffee cup still at her lips, Lucy looked hard at the beautiful child, so like her own that she could read, with care, her mysterious face. Lethargic, as only the obese or insane can be, burdened by her own flesh and slow-oozing blood, Lucy used her eyes alone for the world, and like the blind man's heightened sense of touch, her sight had grown keen with exercise.

Her hand, frozen now on the cup handle, for well she knew that innocent smile, she said, in a cold, tight voice, "Martha, where is your mother?" and the child laughed, in mad, hoarse glee, and answered: "On the kitchen floor." She bounded off, just a head skimming the hedges, with plaits in suspension, as Lucy lurched out of the chaise, cup dropped more than placed on the grass, the opened book sliding noiselessly from her lap.

For a moment she just stood, a short, heavy girl-woman, backed against her chaise, looking about pleadingly, bewilderedly, as if jolted from sleep by a bad dream, and needing to place herself. Sudden movement, sudden feeling, were antipathetic to her nature, and she stood, faint and thick, inert, wounded, disoriented. The May warmth, spring warmth, and air heavy with the scent of damp earth, early flowers, in which she had, only a moment before, been reveling, was transformed into the feel and smell of a sickroom, and she was the patient, abandoned too soon in her convalescence, weak-kneed, frightened, and fragile.

She looked toward the house, even started for it, dazedly, but remembered it was Laura's day off; there was no one else, child or adult, and she ran, in a strange slow-motion, as if through another's will, into her driveway, barefooted, shapeless feet hardened to the large stones that covered it. The drive, overhung by new leaves, covered by dappled light, was like a tunnel seen in sleep, and Lucy, who never ran, felt the surprise of the dreamer, watching herself in an unexpected action. She was in flight, but she knew not from what, where to, and she looked, running so awkwardly, her ponytail still uncombed, in a soiled white shirt of her husband's, tails out, and a blue denim skirt, like the fat little girl she must once have been, running home to a mother who couldn't comfort her.

Though she still dressed like that child, in ruffled calico, Liberty Bell buttons, and corduroy jumpers, she no longer recognized her in her mirrors, taken in by the woman who puffed on her pink powder, drew on the red mouth. Smoking three packs of cigarettes a day, always with a cup of coffee at her elbow, she never recognized that little girl, in her quilted skirt, her denim skirt.

But the slow, clumsy running did what no mirror could, and she sank into a walk, biting her thumb hard, as she remembered her mother, slim in black linen, her tanned arm, jangling in its golden bangles, extended, while she tucked a crisp bill into Lucy's counselor's breast pocket. She remembered how the counselors had gathered about her whenever she came, a court to her beauty and wit, so pleased, in their new adult status, to be included in her little jokes, her quick flippancies. For days after, they would speak of her as if she were their mother and not hers, and as if they shared some wonderful secret with her from which she, Lucy, was excluded.

It took her two minutes to reach the end of her short drive, and emerging from its shade, she crossed the strip of road, bright with sun, that separated the houses, with no awareness of having done so. It was only after she had taken a few steps into the other driveway, still a hundred feet to the house, that she remembered her errand, and she stopped, completely, not moving a muscle, only panting, shallowly, rapidly. She looked at nothing and felt unseen, and stood there, like a large animal, obstinate in its terror, trying to blend in with its surroundings, to take on the shape and color of a rock. Her body was rigid in its withdrawal, her eyes strained with not seeing.

A side of the house was visible from this point, and when she looked (how long later?) and saw that the shades were drawn, she sagged in stunning relief; with the cunning of the practiced self-deceptive, she concluded that Isabel was taking her midmorning nap, and Martha had, after all, only been playing one of her sick little tricks. That child was really a monster, something that had crawled out from under a rock. Isabel had confided that there were days when she couldn't look at her small, hidden face, and Jack would have to take her off somewhere, anywhere, until she regained her composure, always, for this child, a steel-like control. She said she didn't trust herself at those moments, so enraged was she by the very sight of her, and Lucy was swept by an impulse to hunt her out and slap her, an instant's fury that disappeared as she dawdled in the drive, painfully catching her breath. She had an uneasy sense of something being out of place, of the dream continuing, and she lingered, breathing heavily, pinching off the black-green leaves from the hedge detachedly with her left hand.

Perhaps it was the sun on her hand, a strong, past-noon sun, or the kind of hush, not of the morning, or the children's voices, from a distance, muffled but shrill, that shattered her feeble illusion; it was past noon, and she knew that Isabel, efficient housewife, would long ago have been up and at her scheduled tasks. Lolling in her own garden, she hadn't thought of the time, knowing a neighbor, probably Isabel, would feed her children if they didn't turn up.

The shades were drawn to the same point, room to room, and Lucy remembered, nauseous now with fear, the time she had gone to Olive Lane's house, one childhood morning, to ask her to draw more paper dolls, and she couldn't touch the bell because of the ugly gray crape that concealed it. For months after, she was torn between her need for Olive's dolls, so like Olive herself — bow-mouthed, rouged, spit-curled — and her terror of that house in which Olive's grandfather, brown with age, the monkey-man, had died.

She moved forward, involuntarily, almost stealthily, as if she must be on guard; she had a sudden image of an oversized funeral wreath, gaudy flowers stiffly wired, and she looked to the ground, afraid a snake might slither across her path. Now she concentrated on the path, absorbedly, formulating the precise color and shape of its fine gravel, almost counting her steps. She liked the feel of her feet sinking in the gravel, and she stopped a minute to dig her big toe in more deeply.

A crescendo of shrieks, like birds frightened from a cover, sent her scurrying instinctively, head still bent, into the rustic play-house that sat just back from the turn in the drive. She had to duck a little at the door, but once inside she could stand, and she leaned against the log wall, trembling, feeling the beat of her heart in her back.

The room was as trim as one of Isabel's, and though she had always been intrigued by the real windows that pushed out, the child-size rocker, the doll bed, the stove, the tea set, she saw noth-ing, only welcomed the concealment. Standing so, just inside the door, against the wall, she had the posture of a child in hiding, hiding inadequately, and just as sure that a furious mother would storm through the door and discover her. She felt very warm, clammy with fear, and there was that pain, and yet thrill, in her throat. She read *Rock-a-bye, baby,* painted in gold script across the top of the black, lacquered rocker, and she watched a spider make its way slowly, somnambulistically, across the opposite sill.

Their voices were coming from the kitchen, just paces away, a rising and falling, the essence of extreme excitement, phrased by very brief, very breath-holding silences, and she began to mumble, as if telling a rosary, making extravagant promises to God and the possibly deceased, if only she were spared this one time more. She made little spitting sounds with her lips, reviving a long-forgotten defense against the Devil, and her mumbling and spitting mingled with the buzzing of a bee, out of sight, lost somewhere in the raft-ers.

It was David's shout, "You kick her, Mandy" (she had heard no words before, could only take in the rumble), that wrenched her from her hiding place, walking rapidly, pitched forward, the mother, herself, ready to pounce. His voice drew her as red mag-netizes the bull, with the first response always that of rage, and though she felt her fear just behind it, she was up the back steps and at the screen door with a burst of energy that left her, pulsatingly, palpitatingly, as she looked, transfixed, at the tableau within.

Four children, shocked, laughing, anguished, were pinching, kicking, touching, and recoiling from, the dead young woman, face purple and swollen, who lay on the floor. They formed a circle that undulated as one child would suddenly dart forward, daring contact with the dead, the others, nerved, following, and then one by one, pulling sharply back, stricken. Each became the leader, unchallenged — they brought an order to death they had never brought to play — only quickly to relinquish his position to the next brave one. Goliath lay slain, but could one be sure?

The afternoon sunlight, mote-filled, fell on them from the two windows like giant spotlights, carefully angled, and in their brightly colored summer dresses and jerseys, they looked like dwarfed Breughel peasants, dancing in their drunkenness. The gleaming white stove and sink and refrigerator, the snap beans in a colander on the drainboard, the electric clock, with its second hand sweeping around, served as ground to the figures, oblivious, impervious ground. The herd impelled to stampede, a crowd moved to destroy, their pace accelerated; they shrieked and squealed and circled and spun — a merry-go-round of small demons, out of control.

She collapsed against the door, and the dull thud was followed by an immediate hush. For moments, minutes, the four of them were fixed, just where they were, staring at Lucy, an all-seeing monster, two-dimensional and immense, flattened up against the screen. And with glazed, mad eyes, Lucy stared at this pack that had once been young children. The hum of the clock, a large, evil eye, could be heard, but no human sound penetrated this timeless silence.

David spoke first, hushedly: "Isabel's dead, Mom," but Lucy didn't move, didn't hear. He was more shrill, the good boy reporting: "Look, Mom, Isabel's dead." Jennie, just four, the tagalong, began to cry, and ran to the door, but Lucy was unmovable, lifeless. Martha and Miranda hung back, almost bashfully, as if out of modesty — it was so much their show — David with them, prepared for flight, never taking his eyes from Lucy. Unable to get out, Jennie began to scream, and to pound on her mother, scratching her small fists on the screen that separated them, and though none of the others moved, they, like animals, gave small signs of rising panic, and it was these that brought Lucy slowly, con-

fusedly, into consciousness. Faint, on the verge of retching, she
saw the four children, two hers, two Isabel's, and Isabel, neighbor
and best friend, dead, in a checked gingham apron, mustard and
white.

Slack-mouthed, leaning against the door as if deflated, a larger
than life-size Boppo, the clown balloon, aslant and dying on its
cardboard feet, a mute in deep pain, she looked at David, and he
stood, also dumb, his face already concealing, though subtly crossed,
a sensitive surface, by a swift succession of emotions. He waited
for her sign, Fagin's waif watching his master, and finally, with a
hand she couldn't raise, she just visibly, so vaguely, pointed to the
back of him, and he, who could obey no order directly, especially
hers, ran into the hall, glad to begin the long atonement.

Though only six, he could be relied upon to make the call to the
hospital, just as he could have led one to any road in the community at two, told the time accurately at three, and read the newspaper, adult word for adult word, at four; so bleakly lost within,
so mother-lost, he could not risk losing touch without. The in-
congruity of this undersized boy, who looked like a sad Buster
Brown, with his round, dark eyes, and thatch of blond hair, trudging home from the library with his books of facts, amused the
townspeople, who called him a "character," and liked to engage
him in conversation just to hear his serious, little old-head remarks.
The children were still tolerant — he was so gentle in his pedantry
— but they thought he "talked like a book."

The three girls were all at the door, Jennie hysterical, and the
other two, stiffly silent, looking patiently at Lucy, already orphans,
knowing their place. Miranda, the younger, round and sturdy,
secure as the second child in her mother's love, sensed her new
status through Martha, who had been rehearsing this role daily,
all of her seven years. Here, in this moment of final triumph, her
magnificent face was, as always, inscrutable, and her bearing as
tautly erect, but her *raison d'être* was gone, and Lucy saw, even
with the screen between them, a new hollowness in those eyes.

Her throat too tight for more than a cracked whisper, she told
them to come out, stepping back weavingly so they could open the
door. Jennie grasped her leg, almost tumbling her from the steps,
and the two sisters walked into the back garden, Martha stooping
to pick up a broken toy barrow, Miranda just behind, watching

her in silence. Lucy looked back at her friend, always so freshly lovely (honey-blond hair in a high bun; soft, fragrant cotton dresses), now mottled and grotesque, twisted and rigid, and with an involuntary shrug of revulsion, turned away, breaking into a loud hiccup as she stifled a sob, bile filling her mouth. Jennie looked up in alarm, through blurred, tear-filled eyes, and then took up her crying, nuzzling her head deeper into her mother's soft, thick thigh.

She stood a moment longer, struggling with the thought that she should go into the kitchen to see if Isabel were truly dead (Was she dead? Is that death's face?), and then sat down heavily on the top step, her back to the door, trying to shut out what was behind her with all of her body and thought. She pulled Jennie onto her lap, and looked out into the garden with blank, sick eyes, and she sat limply huddled, holding the child in her arms as if she were trying to pull into herself her own escaping entrails, a gesture of self-preservation. She only thought of David, waiting for him to come take up the lead, like a child staving off panic in the dark with one singsong phrase, and she began to rock back and forth, loosely, rhythmically.

Somewhere in her dark web of feelings for David, there was the dependence upon an older brother, hated, envied, and needed, so that mother and son were often brother and sister, taunting, imploring, destroying, supporting. Sometimes she was the big sister, fat and aggressive, shriveling his budding masculinity with a quick, murderous hand on the back of his neck, and sometimes he was the older, triumphant and mocking in answering her needs. The transitions were swift, but each knew his part, recognized his cue.

(With horror and fascination, she had watched Isabel in the same terrible game of destruction with her fist-born, and the irony of the perpetual *déjà vu* did not completely escape her: her neighbor mirror-imaged her own evil. Closest friends after a time, they played Scrabble in the afternoons, locked in one another's homes, their own children shut without.)

The afternoon sun, which dominated this open patch, seemed to hold them like lizards in its grasp, and the only sounds, except for Jennie's chant-like wails, mechanical, fading, were small and very clear: Lucy's hiccups, quieter now, and that of the one good barrow-wheel that Martha was spinning with close attention. Lucy was growing listless, sitting there in the warm sun, hypnotized by her one thought; she was not so afraid sitting there in the warm sun, huddled over — she was never so afraid once she sat or sprawled or curled up.

But the sound of David, running through the kitchen, and the slam of the screen door, exploded the silence, shredded Lucy's cocoon. She turned toward him, but pushing off from her shoulder, he jumped the two steps to the ground, and stood before her, panting, pale, and tense. His lips were quivering, he was close to tears, and mother and son, anxiously scrutinizing each other's faces, were for the first time, deadlocked by panic, complete equals. Each grew more terrified by what he saw in the other's face, and had it not been for Miranda's casual "What are we going to do, Lucy?" they might both have broken into a terrible weeping, two babes in the woods.

Lucy began to bustle, avoiding David's eyes, lifting Jennie, almost asleep, from her lap, and smoothing out her skirt, as she arose, with nervous hands. She announced they were all going to take a walk, and suggested they hurry if they wanted to play on the swings and to get some ice cream. She sometimes slipped into the voice, even the stride, of the senior camp counselor, the quickly assumed voice and demeanor of this moment. She knew that David heard the forced good cheer, the nursery school and "hup-two" rhythms, that he, clearest of all, like the dog that hears the pitch beyond human range, also heard the breathless fear just behind them, and understood that she was determined to get away before the ambulance turned into the drive.

Like the faithful collie, he helped collect, and urge on, the children, pulling away at the head of what looked like a crack-the-whip chain, everyone having reached for everyone else's hand. Miranda was next to David, laughing each time he swung her arm hard, or complained, like a querulous old man, of her pokiness, and Martha was in the middle holding Jennie with her other hand, gently hurrying her along — they practically ran the length of the drive, each knowing some need for haste — talking in her pretend-mother voice, the voice she used for Betsy, her doll and alter ego. Jennie was pleased (she loved attention, and only by chance was not wearing her tutu, her favorite play dress), but wary, never before having been Martha's "baby." She held her mother's hand firmly, while permitting Martha to direct her around a puddle, to murmur "Jennie-sweetie" and "darling baby."

Lucy came last, and looked as though she were unbalancing, pulling back, this fragile line of children, spread ahead, S-shaped, on the steep hill that ran between the houses. She pushed forward, determinedly — in her mind transporting herself over the turnings and byways to the village green, her goal, her haven — struggling up that road she rarely walked, her attention so directed ahead that she ignored her bursting lungs, her audible puffing. The children were growing noisier now that there was a distance between them and the dead, but Lucy said not a word, raptly following their zigzag course.

They were on level ground again, on the road that led past the outdoor Shakespeare theater and the community hall, Tudor setting for the weekly square dances and the meetings of the "guilds." (This was a suburb with a purpose, more cooperative and art-conscious than most, with its woodedness enhancing its narcissism, provincialism.) She hadn't been by here since the Valentine party, and she remembered Isabel, regally beautiful as the Queen of Hearts, sitting next to her, making her terse, acid comments, as she looked on with a jaundiced eye. (My God, Isabel was dead! My God! My God! With whom would she ever talk or laugh again?) She moaned, a low sound of fright, but the sound was swallowed up in the light babbling of the children.

The road was deserted, the hour falling short of meeting time, school dismissal, and Lucy, wanting no delay, no encounter, was remotely grateful for their solitary course. They were scattered across the road, and, followed by two of the many dogs that paraded about, patrolled the town, all day long, they looked like a band of ragamuffins, disheveled and rootless. A bread truck turned out of a drive behind them, and Lucy, absent-mindedly, called everyone into the ditch. She scarcely looked up as it passed, but the children shouted, "Hell-o, Don."

They circled with the road, making only a small noise in the large afternoon silence. The cars on the highway, a half-mile away, could be heard distinctly; there was even the hum of a distant vacuum cleaner. Lucy felt the weight of her usual afternoon melancholy, intensified by the shadow of a terrible thought lurking around its edges, and her face was alive in its new anguish. Later, trying to remember the walk to the green, she could only catch that sadness (like a dread spreading through her body), and a few images: the bread truck, and wild mushrooms, looking obscene, clumped along the roots of an old tree. When had she lost those ten minutes? How many years ago?

There was the green, a patched oblong, with its bald spots of earth, the base of the vacuum into which they had been drawn, irresistibly, sinking, sinking — empty, deserted. The baseball diamond with its markers, the swings in a row, the jungle gym, like an ancient ruin, looked to Lucy like cemetery plots, and sickened by their stamp of death, their loneliness, she quickly turned away from them, following the children into Murphy's "general store" just opposite.

The cowbells on the door jingled loudly, and the children ran to the ice-cream case, throwing open its little black doors, reaching in for popsicles. Murphy was rarely in the front of the store and everyone helped himself, going behind the old-fashioned walnut counter, or into the turn-of-the-century candy case, with its sliding doors and curved glass front. The candy was displayed in small glass dishes (Murphy had all the penny varieties) on dirty shelf paper, and the shelves lining the sides of the room were less than half full, with a few brightly wrapped loaves of bread, cans of soup and beans, bars of soap. There was a grappler hanging to a side, though there was nothing on the top shelves except for a peeling Coca-Cola sign, and a large metal samovar (Murphy had visited Russia in the '20's). One of Murphy's cats was asleep on the counter, and Lucy, seating herself on the one stool, off in a gloomy corner, felt for the first time as if she had wandered into a child's play-store.

She noted the children's choices (Jennie, to infuriate, was copying David again), and thought, with shame, of the double-dip cone she would wait for Murphy to get for her. She looked hungrily, furtively, at the rack of ten-cent cakes and pies, and began to tremble with the push of her compulsion, the anxiety it always gave her in public. She felt a terrible guilt as she thought of Isabel, dead, not yet gently lifted from the kitchen floor, and she wanted all the cake and candy and ice cream in Murphy's store.

Murphy came through the door at the rear, a short man, in his Western shirt, levis, and sandals, with his customary look of slight surprise and empty geniality. He never made conversation unless one insisted on it; Murphy only seemed to come into his own on square-dance night, when he flew about and promenaded-home like a man half his age, always partnering his ugly, suspicious Scottish wife. He gave Lucy her cone, covered with chocolate sprinkles, and wrote the sale on a slip of paper, since Lucy had no money with her; they exchanged no more than the few words necessary for the transaction. The children were teasing Murphy's cat, an orange one, and trooped out after Lucy, comparing how much each had left as they crossed to the swings.

Miranda and Martha were already swinging, and David was taking his last bite, only half on his swing, when the siren splintered the afternoon quiet, growing immediately louder, more loudly immediate, and Jennie, who had just handed her popsicle to Lucy, en route to the low swings, started to cry again, as if she had never stopped. David jumped down, and ran to stand by Lucy, looking wildly at the two sisters, bent toward them, a frantic, angry terrier. He shouted, "Your mother is dead, don't you know your mother is dead?" repeating and repeating, with more fury and agitation, as Martha and Miranda, never looking down, continued to swing, pumping harder, flying higher. Lucy licked at her dripping cone, quickly, expertly, her eyes fixed on her task.

(*From Esquire*)

THE PROPHECY

BY ARTHUR MILLER

*N*OT ALL, but some winters in those parts are almost unendurable. A fog settles into the old Dutch valleys toward the end of November and never really goes away until April. Some nights it suddenly appears on the ridge tops, leaving the lowlands clear, and no one knows why it moves about, but it does, sometimes settling around a particular house for days at a time and nowhere else. Then it goes away and reappears around another house. And some winters the sun never properly comes out for two months at a time. A grayness like water drowns all the views, and the trees drip all day when their branches are not covered with creaking ice.

At the start of winter there is always hope, of course, that it will be a decent one. But when, day after day and week after week, the same monotonous wind sucks the heat out of the house, and there is never even a momentary break in the iron sky, the old people first and then everyone else gradually change their temperaments. There are unaccountable arguments in the supermarkets and at the gas station, lifelong enmities are started, people decide to move away and do, forever, and there is always a rash of unnecessary road accidents. People break arms, hitting trees whose locations they know by heart, there are always one or two who get run over by their own cars rolling back down the driveways, and decisions are made out of desperation which permanently change the course of many lives.

Toward the end of December of such a winter, Stowey Rummel

decided to personally supervise the hanging of his architectural drawings and the display of his models for a permanent exhibition of his work in a new Florida university whose campus he had designed a few years before. He was in his mid-fifties at this time, long past the establishment of his name and the wish to be lionized yet once again, and it was almost a decade since he had sworn off lecturing. There was never a doubt any more how his structures would be received; it was always the same unqualified success now. He could no longer build anything, whether a private residence in his Pennsylvania county or a church in Brazil, without it being obvious that he had done it, and while here and there he was taken to task for again developing the same airy technique, they were such fanciful and sometimes even playful buildings that the public felt assured by its sense of recognition after a time, a quality of authentic uniqueness about them, which, once established by an artist as his private vision, is no longer disputable as to its other values. Stowey Rummel was internationally famous, a crafter of a genuine Americana in foreign eyes, an original designer whose inventive childishness with steel and concrete was made even more believably sincere by his personality. He had lived for almost thirty years in this same stone farmhouse with the same wife, a remarkably childish thing in itself; he rose at half-past six every morning, made himself some French coffee, had his corn flakes and more coffee, smoked four cigarettes while reading last Sunday's *Herald Tribune* and yesterday's Pittsburgh *Gazette,* then put on his high-topped farmer's shoes and walked under a vine bower to his workshop. This was an enormously long building whose walls were made of rocks, some of them brought home from every continent during his six years as an oil geologist. The debris of his other careers was piled everywhere; a pile of wire cages for mice from his time as a geneticist and a microscope lying on its side on the window sill, vertical steel columns wired for support to the open ceiling beams with spidery steel cantilevers jutting out into the air, masonry constructions on the floor from the time he was inventing his disastrous fireplace whose smoke would pass through a whole house, visible all the way up through wire gratings on each floor. His files, desk, drafting board and a high stool formed the only clean island in the chaos. Everywhere else his ideas lay or hung in visible form: his models, drawings, ten-foot canvases in monochromes from his painting days, and underfoot a windfall of broken-backed books that looked as though their insides had been ransacked by a maniac. Bicycle gear-sets he had once used as the basis of the design for the Camden Cycly Company plant hung on a rope in one corner, and over his desk, next to several old and dusty hats, was a clean pair of roller skates which he occasionally used up and down in front of his house. He worked standing, with his left hand in his pocket as though he were merely stopping for a moment, sketching with the surprised stare of one who was watching another person's hand. Sometimes he would grunt softly to some invisible onlooker beside him, sometimes he would look stern and moralistic as his pencil did what he disapproved. It all seemed — if one could have peeked in at him through one of his windows — as though this broken-nosed man with the muscular arms and wrestler's neck was merely the caretaker trying his hand at the boss's work. This air of disengage-ment carried over to his apparent attitude toward his things, and people often mistook it for boredom in him or a surrender to repe-titious routine. But he was not bored at all; he had found his style quite early in his career and he thought it quite wonderful that the world admired it, and he could not imagine why he should alter it. There are, after all, fortunate souls who hear everything, but only know how to listen to what is good for them, and Stowey was, as things go, a fortunate man.

He left his home the day after New Year's wearing a mackinaw and sheepskin mittens and without a hat. He would wear this same costume in Florida, despite his wife Cleota's reminders over the past five days that he must take some cool clothes with him. But he was too busy to hear what she was saying. So they parted when she was in an impatient humor. When he was bent over behind the wheel of the station wagon, feeling in his trouser cuffs for the igni-tion key which he had dropped a moment before, she came out of the house with an enormous Rumanian shawl over her head, which she had bought in that country during one of their trips abroad, and handed him a clean handkerchief through the window. Find-ing the key under his shoe, he started the engine, and while it warmed up he turned to her standing there in the dripping fog, and said, "Defrost the refrigerator."

He saw the surprise in her face, and laughed as though it were the funniest expression he had ever seen. He kept on laughing until she started laughing with him. He had a deep voice which was full of good food she had cooked, and good humor; an explosive laugh which always carried everything before it. He would settle himself into his seat to laugh. Whenever he laughed it was all he was doing. And she was made to fall in love with him again there in the rutted dirt driveway standing in the cold fog, mad as she was at his going away when he really didn't have to, mad at their both having got older in a life that seemed to have taken no more than a week to go by. She was forty-nine at this time, a lanky woman of breeding with an austere, narrow face which had the distinction of a steeple or some architecture that had been designed long ago for a stubborn sort of prayer. Her eyebrows were definite and heavy and formed two lines moving upward toward a high forehead and a great head of brown hair that fell to her shoulders. There was an air of blindness in her gray eyes, the startled-horse look that ultimately comes to some women who are born at the end of an ancestral line long since divorced from money-making and which, besides, has kept its estate intact. She was personally sloppy, and when she had colds would blow her nose in the same handkerchief all day and keep it, soaking wet, dangling from her waist, and when she gardened she would eat dinner with dirt on her calves. But just when she seemed to have sunk into some depravity of peasanthood she would disappear and come down bathed, brushed, and taking deep breaths of air, and even with her broken nails her hands would come to rest on a table or a leaf with a thoughtless delicacy, a grace of history, so to speak, and for an instant one saw how ferociously proud she was and adamant on certain questions of personal value. She even spoke differently when she was clean, and she was clean now for his departure and her voice clear and rather sharp.

"Now drive carefully, for God's sake!" she called, trying to attain a half humorous resentment at his departure. But he did not notice, and was already backing the car down to the road, saying "Toot-toot!" to the stump of a tree as he passed it, the same stump which had impaled the car of many a guest in the past thirty years and which he refused to have removed. She stood clutching her shawl around her shoulders until he had swung the car onto the road. Then, when he had it pointed down the hill, he stopped to gaze at her through the window. She had begun to turn back toward the house, but his look caught her and she stood still, waiting there for what his expression indicated would be a serious word of farewell. He looked at her out of himself, she thought, as he did only for an instant at a time, the look which always surprised her even now when his uncombable hair was yellowing a little and his breath came hard through his nicotine-choked lungs, the look of the gaunt youth she had suddenly found herself staring at in the Tate Gallery on a Thursday once. Now she kept herself protectively ready to laugh again and sure enough he pointed at her with his index finger and said "Toot!" once more and roared off into the fog, his foot evidently surprising him with the suddenness with which it pressed the accelerator, just as his hand did when he worked. She walked back to the house and entered, feeling herself returning, sensing some kind of opportunity in the empty building. There is a death in all partings, she knew, and promptly put it out of her mind.

She enjoyed great parties when she would sit up talking and dancing and drinking all night, but it always seemed to her that being alone, especially alone in her house, was the realest part of life. Now she could let out the three parakeets without fear they would be stepped on or that Stowey would let them out one of the doors; she could dust the plants, then break off suddenly and pick up an old novel and read from the middle on; improvise cha-chas on the harp; and finally, the best part of all, simply sit at the plank table in the kitchen with a bottle of wine and the newspapers, reading the ads as well as the news, registering nothing on her mind but letting her soul suspend itself above all wishing and desire. She did this now, comfortably aware of the mist running down the windows, of the silence outside, of the dark afternoon it was getting to be. She fell asleep leaning on her hand, hearing the house creaking as though it were living a private life of its own these two hundred years, hearing the birds rustling in their cages and the occasional whirring of wings as one of them landed on the table and walked across the newspaper to perch in the crook of her arm. Every few minutes she would awaken for a moment to review things: Stowey, yes, was on his way south, and the two boys were away in school, and nothing was burning on the stove, and Lucretia was coming for dinner and bringing three guests of hers. Then she fell asleep again as soddenly as a person with fever, and when

she awoke it was dark outside and the clarity was back in her eyes.
She stood up, smoothing her hair down, straightening her clothes,
feeling a thankfulness for the enveloping darkness outside, and,
above everything else, for the absence of the need to answer, to respond, to be aware even of Stowey coming in or going out, and yet,
now that she was beginning to cook, she glimpsed a future without
him, a future alone like this, and the pain made her head writhe,
and in a moment she found it hard to wait for Lucretia to come
with her guests. She went into the living room and turned on three
lamps, then back into the kitchen where she turned on the ceiling
light and the switch that lit the floods on the barn, illuminating the
driveway. She knew she was feeling afraid and inwardly laughed
at herself. They were both so young, after all, so unready for any
final parting. How could it have been thirty years already, she wondered? But yes, nineteen plus thirty was forty-nine, and she was
forty-nine and she had been married at nineteen. She stood still
over the leg of lamb, rubbing herbs into it, quite suddenly conscious of a nausea in her stomach and a feeling of wrath, a sensation of violence that started her shivering. She heard the back door
opening and immediately went through the pantry toward it, knowing it must be Alice. The old woman met her, having already entered, and was unhooking her yellow slicker with her stiff white
fingers.

"Something's wrong with my phone," she said, proving at once
that she had come with a purpose and not to intrude.

"What do you want to do?" Cleota asked, not moving from the
center of the pantry, her position barring the way to the kitchen
door. Her anger astounded even her; she would never have dared
bar the way if Stowey were here, and she thrilled at her aggressiveness toward his old sister.

"I'd better call the company, hadn't I?" Alice asked, already indicating in her tone that she recognized the outlandish barrier and
was not prepared to go out at once.

"Well you can certainly use the phone," Cleota said and turned
her back on the old woman and went to her leg of lamb on the
table.

Alice, wearing calf-height rubber boots and a fisherman's
drooping-brim rubber hat, got to the phone and held it away from
her ear, blinking papery eyelids and avidly inspecting the kitchen

as she waited for the operator to come on. Beside the instrument —
between it and a flour canister — stood a Fiji mask, a carved, elongated face. She turned it absent-mindedly.

"*Please* don't, Alice!"

The old lady turned in such quick shock that her deep-brimmed
hat slid and remained sideways on her head. Cleota, her face swollen with feeling, bent to the oven and put in the meat.

"It was facing toward the wall a little," Alice started to explain.

Cleota stood erect, her cheeks red now. The house was hit by
a slap of wind, a push that shuddered it. "I *have* asked you not to
touch my things, Alice. I'm having guests and I've a lot to do. So
will you please do what you have to and let me get on with it!"

She went to the refrigerator, opened it, and stood half bent over,
looking into it, trying to concentrate on what she had thought to
take from it.

The old lady put down the phone. "Yours is out too, I guess."

Cleota did not answer, remaining before the open refrigerator,
unable to think.

For a moment they stood there waiting, one for the other, as they
had waited at odd moments since Alice had moved into the house
down the road nine years before. Now the old woman hooked up
her slicker, her watery eyes glancing hungrily about the kitchen
as though for some new detail she might not have seen before. She
had no thought to ask what the matter was, not because she clearly
knew but because she took for granted she was hated by this woman
with a reasonless hatred that nothing could ever dissolve. In her
autobiography, which she wrote at every day in her kitchen and
in good weather under the apple tree behind her house, she was
developing the concept of human types, unchangeable personalities
created by a primeval spirit, each of which had the function of testing others who were equally unchangeable. Cleota, in her book,
was the Eternally Dissatisfied. She did not blame Cleota for her
personality, indeed she pitied her and knew that nothing she could
say or do would ever mitigate her need for an opponent, an enemy.
Cleota, like so many other perversely incomprehensible phenom-
ena, was Necessary.

Alice dawdled at the pantry door. She would not leave in too
much of a hurry. She had a right, she felt, to have been invited
tonight; certainly she would have been if Stowe had been at home.

Besides she was hungry, having neglected her lunch today, and the few morsels she did eat would hardly matter to the dinner that was to be served. And if there were to be any men here they would certainly be — as they always were — interested in her views, as so many of her brother's guests had told him after they had met her.

She reached the back door and turned back to her sister-in-law. "Good night," she said. The first tremors of her hurt quavered the word and stiffened Cleota, who barely glanced at her to return the farewell. Alice grasped the doorknob. She felt the words rising to her mouth and tried to escape before they came out, but it was too late. She heard herself asking, "Who are you having?"

The ladle in Cleota's hand struck the stove and slid along the floor. "I can't have this, Alice. You know exactly what I am talking about, so there is nothing more to say about it."

The old lady shook her head, just once, turned the knob and went out, softly closing the door behind her.

Cleota picked up the ladle and stood there shaking. Once again the house was no longer hers. The indignity of the visit made her clench her teeth; Alice knew perfectly well that if her phone was out then theirs was too since they were on the same line. She had come simply, purely, to demonstrate that she had the freedom of the premises, to show once again that whatever else he may have become and whoever he might meet or marry, Stowe was her baby brother first.

Cleota, who did not believe in a definite god, looked toward the ceiling despite herself, with a longing for an ear that would hear, and whispered, "Why doesn't she die?" Alice was seventy-three, after all, and was nothing any longer but a smell, a watery pair of eyes, but above all a coiled power secreted in that house down the road which Stowe had bought for her when her husband had died. She felt now, as she often did, that the old woman lived on only to secretly laugh at her. She knew how unreasonable this idea was; the woman survived falls on the ice, broken hips, and colds and pneumonia last winter because she wanted to live for her own sake, but this stubborn refusal to succumb was somehow obscene to Cleota, quite as though the woman had something illicit in her unabashed craving for a life that would never end. Cleota went to the Fiji mask and turned it as it had been before, as though this would cancel out Alice's having moved it. She touched the hard

brown wood, and her finger rested on a rough spot under the lower
lip. This had always felt like a wart and made the image seem
alive, and the touching of the spot recalled her father's hands on
it when he gave it to her. As foolish a man as he had been, he had
known how to disappear from the lives of those he could not help.
She felt a rising pride in her father now; with his own bizarre dignity he had assembled his lunatic expeditions, read the wrong
books, learned outmoded anthropological theories, sailed to the
unmeaningful islands, spent years studying tribes which had been
categorized many times before, and had succeeded only in clutter-
ing the homes of his children with the bric-a-brac of the South Seas.
Now, however, now that he could never return, she sensed from
his career a certain hidden purpose which she felt he must have secretly followed. It had been his will to declare himself even in his
inanity, and to keep on declaring himself until the idiotic end, his
ankle caught in a rope and his bald head in the water, discovered
hanging over the side of his sloop off San Francisco harbor. How
strange it was that this fool had slowly taken on — for many beside
herself — an air of respect! And it was not wrong that this should
be, she thought. He had had a passion, and that, she felt now, was
everything. Returning to her stove she saw that she was separated
from herself as her father had not been from himself. The gaunt
image of Stowey appeared before her, enraging her mind; why
could she not *have* him! They were like two planets circling one
another, held in their orbits by an invisible force that forbade their
juncture, the force coming out of those two watery eyes, those
clawed white fingers, that put-on stupidity, that selfish arrogance
which sat in the house down the road grinning and enthroned. A
burst of wind against the house reminded her that guests would be
here. She turned her mind to the food, and sought once more the
soft suspension of all desire. One of the parakeets flew up from the
floor and perched on her wrist. She stopped working, and moved
it to her lips and kissed its glistening head, and as always it bowed
and plucked at her flesh with its talons.

To Cleota it was faintly ill-mannered to ask biographical data
of a guest. What people did for a living, whether they were married
or divorced, had mistresses or lovers, had been to jail or Princeton
or in one of the wars — the ordinary pegs on which to drape the

growing tapestry of an evening's conversation did not exist for her
mind. Until she was sixteen she had not met, or at least had not
had to cope, with anyone whose background and attitudes were different from her own. Her uncles, aunts and cousins had all been of
a piece and of a place, even if they had gone all over the world to
live, and it was — or seemed — quite the same for the other girls
who attended her schools. Her life had taken her, at Stowe's side,
into many countries, the *palazzos* of financiers, the hovels of artists,
the Harlems of the world, the apartments of *nouveaux-riches* and
university trustees, and the furnished rooms of doped musicians, but
rich or poor, famous or infamous, genius or dilettante, they were all
greeted and listened to with her same blind stare, her inattention to
details, her total absence of discrimination. She seemed not to realize that people ordinarily judged others, not that she liked everyone equally, but so long as they were in some way amusing, or sincere, or something at least definite, she was happy to have them in
her house. What did arouse her was to be put upon — or to ever be
told what to think or to feel. It was simply an absurdity that anyone
should impose on anyone else. Beyond this prohibition, which her
manner made it unnecessary to enforce very often, she was not troubled by people. Unexpectedly, however, she did not disapprove of
moralists. It was simply that moralizing for them was, or must surely
be, somehow necessary, just as some people hated the outdoors and
others never ate peppery food. There were things, of course, of
which she disapproved, and she often appeared to verge on moral
indignation, as toward people being denied passports by the government or being kept out of restaurants because they were colored.
But it soon became clear she was not speaking of any moral situation; it was simply that her sense of her own person had been inflamed by the idea of some blind, general will being imposed upon
an individual. And then it was not indignation she felt so much as
bewilderment, an incomprehension similar to her father's when he
traveled around the world three different times at his own expense
to present petitions to the League of Nations protesting the oppres-
sion of various tribes, one of which had come close to eating him, and
failed to get any response.

Lucretia had called this morning and among other things had
said that John Trudeau had stopped by the night before on his way
to New York from Boston, and when the two women had decided

to have dinner together Trudeau was inevitably included in, along with another guest of Lucretia's, a Madame something who was also visiting her. Cleota had known Trudeau and especially his wife Betty until last year, when he quit his job teaching at Pemmerton School in Hanock, a few miles from her house, and went to live in Baltimore. She had been less impressed with him than with his wife, a tall young beauty, yet sensible. Some six years ago their wedding party had spilled over into the Rummel house and Cleota still connected Trudeau with that evening, when with Betty at his side he seemed a promising, deeply serious fellow who she hoped would become the poet he had set his heart on being. There had seemed to be a touching faith between them like hers in Stowe, when young. They had had four children, but lived poorly in an unremodeled farmhouse near the school, and Cleota had often dropped in there in the hope she could draw them out of a deepening seclusion which gave her the feeling that they were perhaps ashamed of their poverty. She had made sure to invite them whenever there was anything going at her house, and they came more often than not, but toward the end of their years here she could not help seeing that they were cool to one another and that Trudeau had gotten gray quite suddenly, and she could not tell why their failure had left her feeling an angry frustration, especially when they had never been close friends.

So she was not entirely surprised to see Trudeau tonight with a girl who was not his wife, but that it should be a girl like this! He was still a handsome man in a conventional way, tall, white-haired at the temples, a rather long face with a Byronic nose, but — she thought now — somewhat on the weak side over-all. She saw now that she had met his face on many a sailing boat long ago, the perpetual sportsmen who remained Princeton boys forever. How had she misjudged him so! Yet, he still had something serious, some suffering in his eyes, which she fancied looked at her now with a tinge of nervous shame whose cause she quickly concluded was the physical appearance of this girl who obviously was his mistress.

All through dinner Cleota could neither look at her directly nor take her eyes from her profile. The girl hardly spoke, but stared over the others' heads in seeming judgment upon the not-brilliant conversation, straining her brows which were penciled nearly into her hair, blinking her enormous brown eyes whose lids were blackened like a ballerina's in a witches' dance. She wore a black sweater and a black felt skirt, both tightened over enormous breasts and weighty but well-made thighs, and her shoes were spike-heeled and black too. There was no make-up on her olive skin, not even lipstick. Her arms jangled with bracelets and her name was Eve Saint Bleu. Trudeau, incredibly, called her Saint and from time to time tried to draw her into the talk, but she would only turn her morose eyes toward him instead of the walls and windows. At each of his slavish attempts to engage the girl, Cleota would turn quickly to hear what remark would fall from Saint's full lips, to witness Saint when she might leave off with what to Cleota was an incredibly rude attempt to appear bored and disapproving of everything. Or was she merely as stupid as she looked? After twenty minutes of this silent sparring Cleota refused any further interest in Saint and did what she always did with people in her house — left out whoever did not appeal to her and attended to those who did.

She had always liked Lucretia, her friend since their schooldays, and Madame. . . . "I don't think I heard your name, Madame," she said to the woman who sat across the table from her, eating the lamb in large chunks, and chewing with a full mouth.

"Lhevine. Manisette-Lhevine. Ish shpelled with an aish," the lady said, trying to swallow at the same time.

Cleota laughed at her attempt and liked this ugly woman who was so small she had to sit on a cushion at the table. She had the face of a man, the skin of a mulatto, with a blob of a nose that seemed to have been deboned, it hung so unsupported and unshaped. Her eyes were black like her kinky hair, which was bobbed high and showed her manly ears which stuck out from her head. She had a large mouth and well-filled teeth. Her hands were bulb-knuckled and veined and when she laughed, which she did often, deep creases cut parentheses into her tight cheeks. She had asked permission to remove the jacket of her gray suit, exposing her skinny, muscular arms which sprouted from a sleeveless blouse like the twisted branches of an old apple tree. Cleota, as though to compensate Madame for the sensuous form of her other guest, kept placing fresh slices of bread and meat before her alone as they talked.

"I want Madame to do you," Lucretia said, and only now Cleota recalled her having mentioned on the phone that this woman told fortunes. An oddly suspended smile was hanging on Lucretia's face as Cleota turned to her; she sat there as though she were going to brazen out an embarrassing but true confession, for she had always been a severely practical, scientifically minded woman with no patience whatsoever for any kind of mysticism. During the first years of her marriage she had even returned to school for her master's degree in bacteriology and had worked in laboratories until the children came. She knew exactly how many calories, proteins, and carbohydrates there were in every food, used pressure cookers to preserve the vitamins, kept instruments in her kitchen with which she could predict humidity and weather, and dealt with everyone, including her own children, with a well-scrubbed avoidance of sentimentality and muddle.

But there she sat, not half as embarrassed as Cleota thought she would surely be at having admitted this intense interest in fortune-telling, and Cleota could not absorb such a violent contradiction of her old friend's character, and for a moment her mouth went from a smile to a serious expression as she wondered if she were the victim of a joke.

"She's wonderful, Cleota," Lucretia insisted. "I haven't told her anything about you, but you wait and see what she finds out."

Quite suddenly Saint spoke. "I had an aunt who did that." It was her first remark unprompted by a question from Trudeau and everyone turned to her, waiting for more. And she momentarily looked so eager to tell them something, her supercilious air gone, that she seemed merely a shy girl who had been intimidated to find herself in Stowe Rummel's actual house. Trudeau relaxed and smiled for the first time, and encouraged her with happier eyes to go on. She opened her lips to speak.

"Your aunt didn't do *this,* dear," Madame Lhevine cut her off, grinning across the table at her with clear resentment, and giving the table one significant pat.

Saint looked hurt, suddenly detached from her make-up, and Trudeau put a hand on her thigh under the table and said, "Honey . . ." but Madame Lhevine was going on now to Cleota, to whom she looked with softened eyes, as though she shared a secret understanding with her alone. "There's no need to do you," she said.

"Why not?" Cleota blushed.

"You're there already."

Cleota laughed high. "Where?"

"Where it all begins," Madame said, and her persistent calm, absurd to Cleota at first, gave her an authority which now caused all to watch her every movement.

Cleota's high, hawking laugh burst from her; it was followed by a sip of red wine and a wondering glance at Lucretia, for it suddenly swept in upon her that to have become so intensely involved with this woman her long-time friend must be in some great personal trouble. But she quickly turned back to Madame Lhevine.

"I'm not laughing at you, Madame," she said, busying her hands with sweeping crumbs toward herself. "It's just that I don't know where *anything* begins. Or ends." She laughed again, blushing. "Or anything at all."

Madame Lhevine's eyes did not stir. "I know that, dear," she said.

A blow seemed to have struck Cleota from somewhere, she felt herself pierced by the fanatic but oddly kind eyes of the fortune-teller. A new need for this woman's attention and even for her care pressed upon Cleota, who suddenly felt herself lonely. She lowered her gaze to the last crumbs, saying, "I suppose it's just as real as anything else, though."

"Neither more nor less," Madame Lhevine said with the quiet joy of those who believe and are saved.

Cleota could not sit there any longer. "I'll get some coffee," she said and went out into the kitchen.

Her hand unaccountably shook as she held the kettle under the faucet. Her cheeks were hot. The faces in the living room revolved before her until Lucretia's expression hung in her mind, the close-set eyes so strangely eager for Cleota to accept Madame Lhevine. All at once it was obvious to her that Lucretia and her husband had broken.

She stared at the flame, still, quiet. Bud Trussel was home only week ends this year not because he had to be traveling all over the state on business. They were effectually separated.

This knowledge was like something sliding out of her which she had not known was in her at all. How could she have been so blind to what was so obvious! She felt frightened. Her kitchen itself began to seem strange. What else, she wondered, was lying in her mind, unknown to her? Again she thought of Lucretia's new, almost lascivious manner tonight, the same Lucretia who had always sat with one leg entwined about the other, always blushing before she even dared to laugh! And now so . . . immoral. But what had she done or said that was immoral? It was all silly!

A coldness spread through her body and she glanced toward the pantry to see if the door had opened. She sensed Alice outside, listened, but it was quiet out there. Still, it was not beneath Stowe's sister to peek through the windows. She strode to the back door and opened it brusquely, already infuriated. No one was there. The swift wind was wracking the trees and through their waving branches her eye caught a distant, unaccustomed light. She stopped moving, tracing the geography of the roads in her mind until she decided it was Joseph's house, a surprise since he and his wife rarely came up in winter, although he did alone sometimes, to write. Had she known she would have called him tonight.

Already a smile came onto her face as she returned to the stove thinking of Joseph confronting Madame Lhevine. "A fortune-*what?*" he would ask, poker-faced — or some such half-joke which would make her laugh with embarrassment. There was always something on the verge of the inappropriate about what he said, on the verge of . . . of the truth. She went to the phone and held it absently to her ear, waiting for the tone. And still, she thought, visualizing this man, he is also a believer. So many Jews were, she thought for the first time. And his image came strongly to her mind as she stared at the mask beside the phone — he was like her father that way, he had some torturing statement in him that was always seeming to come out, but never quite did. Like Stowe, too! Now she became aware of the receiver's silence and put it down in pique, half blaming Alice for having damaged it somehow. When she turned back to the stove Lucretia walked in, and stood without speaking in the middle of the kitchen, slumping her long, wide-shouldered body onto one hip. And Cleota saw the willed smile on her shy face.

"Is it upsetting you?" Lucretia's voice was deep; she always seemed to imitate a man when she had to perform a duty.

"No!" Cleota laughed, surprised at her own sharpness. And instantly the feeling came over her that for some reason she was being got at by Lucretia tonight — she had brought the fortuneteller for a reason. What? If only they would both leave. Now! Before this dreadful intimacy thickened. It had never been like this, not even in their beds at school when they had talked into the nights — from the beginning there had been an unspoken agreement to leave truly private matters untouched. It had been not a relation through words, but something like the silent passage of light from sun to moon, as when Lucretia had let her hair grow after Cleota stopped cutting hers, or took to wearing rings when Cleota returned with some for herself from Mexico. Facing her lifelong friend now, seeing the oddly broken smile on her face — was it a cynical smile? — she felt the fear of one who has wielded the power of example without having known it, and must now deal with the revolt of the unwittingly oppressed. It flashed through her mind that Lucretia had only moved to the country because she had, and would never never straighten out the chaos of her house because it was only an imitation of this house, and that her chain of projects — starting her shrub nursery, then designing shoes, now breeding horses — were not the good and natural blossoms of her joyous energy, as she always tried to imply, but abortive distractions in a life without a form, a life, Cleota saw now, which had been shaded by her own and Stowe's. Cleota stared at the seemingly guilty and dangerous eyes, sensing — what she had always known! — that a disaster had been spreading roots through her friend's life this last thirty years and now had burst it apart.

Lucretia took a swallow of her drink and said, "Bud's left me, Cleota," and smiled.

Cleota's spine quivered at her prophecy come true. She cocked her head like a dog that has been summoned and does not know whether to approach or flee. "When?" she asked, merely to fill the silence until she could think what to say.

"I don't know when. He's been on his way a long time, I guess." And now she raised her arms, put them around Cleota's neck, and — much the taller — rested her head awkwardly on her shoulders. In a moment Cleota pressed her lightly away, and they looked at one another, changed.

"Are you divorcing?" she asked Lucretia. How dreamily unfeeling that embrace had been!

"Yes," Lucretia said, red-faced but grinning.

"Is it another . . . ?"

"No," Lucretia cut her off. "At least I don't think there's any-body else." And, glancing at the pot, said, "Coffee'll be cold, won't it?"

The coffee? Cleota only now remembered why she had come into the kitchen. She got the cups down and set them on the tray.

"It won't be much of an adjustment, anyway," Lucretia said, behind her.

"You don't seem very upset. Are you?" Cleota turned to her, picked up the tray, thinking that she had never before asked any-one such absurdly personal questions. Some dangerously obscene thing had invaded her person, she felt, and her house, and it must be stopped. And yet Lucretia appeared not to notice. It suddenly seemed ages ago since Stowe had been here.

"I've been miserable for a long time, Clee," Lucretia answered.

"I didn't know."

"Yes."

They stood in the middle of the kitchen under the hanging bulb, looking at one another.

"He's actually moved out?"

"Yes."

"What are you going to do?"

"Look for a job, I guess. I think I've had it up here anyway."

"Oh," Cleota said.

"I'm glad I could tell you alone. Without Stowe."

"Really? Why?"

"He likes Bud so," Lucretia laughed dryly, "I'd feel ashamed to tell him."

"Oh, Stowe won't mind. I mean," she corrected, "he's never sur-prised at anything." She laughed at Stowe's childish insulation of mind, his somehow irritating ignorance of people's relations, and said, "*You* know . . ." and broke off when Lucretia smiled as though celebrating Stowe's trouble-blind charm.

Cleota picked up the loaded tray. "Have you known her long? Madame . . . ?"

"Only since yesterday. She came up to buy the horses. She has a place near Harrisburg or somewhere. She's fabulous, Clee. Let her do you."

Lucretia's persistence again pressed down upon Cleota like some sort of need for her complicity. Trudeau walked in, bowing a little to both women to apologize for interrupting them. "We'll have to leave, Cleota."

He gripped her hand which she offered him under the tray, and held it under some terrific pressure which only leaving her house would evidently alleviate. She felt she could not ask him what the matter was because it was obviously the girl insisting he must take her away even without coffee. Cleota reddened at his embarrassment, telling him, "It was nice to see you again, John. I think the driveway light is still on."

Trudeau nodded thankfully for her unquestioning farewell, but his honor seemed to forbid him to turn away too soon from the openly bewildered look in her face.

"Tell Stowe I left my best," he said, letting go of her hand.

"Yes."

Now he turned away, a slight shift in his eye confessing to her that his life was misery. The three entered the living room together.

Saint was already in her coat, a black pile, and wore a black gauze veil over her head. She was looking out at the driveway through the pane in the door and turned to Trudeau, who immediately got his coat and joined her. She glanced once at Cleota who had hardly time to put the tray on the table when both of them were gone.

"Well!" She laughed, blushing but relieved. "What happened?"

"She got mad at me," Madame Lhevine said.

"Why?" Cleota asked, still tingling from Saint's hatred of her. What a weird night it was! From out of nowhere a strange girl comes to hate her! And yet everything seemed to be somehow in order and as it had to be, all around her the broken cliffs of people's lives sliding so deftly into the sea.

"Her aunt *couldn't* have been a gypsy. A gypsy is a gypsy, not somebody you just call a gypsy. I told her her aunt was not a gypsy."

"Oh," Cleota said, her eyes very wide as she tried to understand what was so serious about Madame Lhevine's point. "Are you a gypsy?" she asked, innocently.

"Me? No, I'm Jewish."

Lucretia nodded in confirmation. Evidently, she also thought these identities important. Cleota felt that the two of them had the secret of some closed world which gave them some assurance, some belonging sense. She swallowed whisky. Madame lit a cigarette and squinted her eyes in the smoke. Lucretia looked at the table and played with a match. A moment passed in total silence. Cleota realized that she was now supposed to ask Madame to tell her fortune. It was, she began to feel, a matter of their dignity that she ask. To refuse to ask would be to question their authenticity. And a feeling rose in Cleota again that she was being put upon, pressured toward a discipleship of some vague sort.

"I can't understand John," she said to Lucretia. "Do you?"

"It's just sex," Lucretia said, implying a surfeit of experience which Cleota knew she did not have. Or did she?

"But that girl . . ." Cleota said. "She's not very pretty, is she?"

Lucretia was strangely excited and suddenly reached across what seemed like half the room to drag a small table over to herself with a pack of cigarettes on it. "What's pretty got to do with sex?" she said.

"Well, I don't understand it. He must have his reasons, but his wife is much more beautiful than this one."

Cleota was perfectly aware that Lucretia was playing toward Madame Lhevine, acting out some new familiarity with degradation, but she still could not help feeling on the outside, looking in at an underwater world. *The* world? She prayed Stowe had forgotten something and would suddenly walk in.

Madame Lhevine spoke with certainty, an elder who was used to waiting for the issue to be joined before moving in to resolve it along the right lines. "The spirit doesn't always love what the person loves," she said.

Oh, how true that was! Cleota sensed a stirring in her own depths, a delight in the quickening of her own mind.

"It's a difficult thing," Madame went on. "Not many people know how to listen to the inner voice. Everything distracts us. Even though we know it's the only thing that can guide us."

She squinted into the ashtray, and truly listened as Cleota spoke. "But how can one hear? Or know what to believe? One senses so many things. . . ."

"How do you know your body? Your hands feel it, your eyes see it every day in the mirror. It is practice, that's all. Every day we inspect our bodies, do we not? But how often do we set time aside to inspect our souls? To listen to what it can tell us? Hardly ever. People," she said with some protest now, "scoff at such things, but they accept that one cannot sit down at a piano and play the first time. Even though it is much more difficult, and requires much more technique, to hear one's own inner voice. And to understand its signs — this is even more difficult. But one can do it. I promise you."

With enormous relief Cleota saw that Madame Lhevine was serious and not a fool.

"She's marvelous," Lucretia said, without any reserve now that she saw the impression made on Cleota.

"I don't tell fortunes," Madame went on, "because there is really no future in the vulgar sense." How kind she was! How her certainty even loaned her a loveliness now! To have lost touch with oneself, Cleota thought, was what made woman seem unattractive.

"I don't understand that," Cleota said, "about the future."

"Perhaps you would tell me more about what you don't understand," Madame said.

Cleota was reached by this invitation; she felt understood suddenly, for she did want to speak of her idea of the future. She settled more comfortably in her chair and sought her thoughts. "I don't really know. I suppose I never used to think about it at all, but . . . Well, I suppose when one gets to a certain point, and there's more behind than ahead, it just somehow . . . doesn't seem to have been quite worth it. I don't mean," she added quickly, for she noted that Lucretia seemed oddly gratified with this implication of her failure, "I don't say that I've had a bad time of it, really. I haven't. It's really got nothing to do — my idea — with happiness or unhappiness. It's more that you . . . you wonder if it wasn't all a little too . . ." she laughed, blushing, "small." And before Madame could speak, she added without any emphasis, "I suppose when the children aren't around any more one thinks of that." It struck her that she would never have shown such doubt with Stowe around, and felt freed by his absence.

"It's more than the children not being around," Lucretia said.

"It's that too," Madame reminded Lucretia. "We must not underestimate the physical, but," she turned back to Cleota, "it is also the climax inside."

Cleota waited. She felt she was being perceived, but not any

longer by a merely curious mind. Madame, she felt, was seeing
something within her which the word *climax* was connected with.

"One sees that there will be no ecstasy," Madame Lhevine said.
"And that is when the crisis comes. It comes, you might say, when
we see the future too clearly, and we see that it is a plain, an endless plain, and not what we had thought — a mountain with a glory
at the top."

"Oh, I never thought of any glory. . . ."

"I am not speaking of accomplishment. I am speaking of oneness. The glory is only the moment when we are at one."

Death burst into Cleota's mind, the complete sense of a dying;
not any particular person, not herself, but some unidentifiable person lying dead. Then her oneness would be in her, and a glory, a
beneficent peace.

A quick joyousness raised her to her feet and she went to the sideboard and got a new bottle of whisky and returned to the table and,
without asking, poured. Then she looked across at Madame Lhevine, her face flushed.

"What do you do?" she asked, forbearing to say "now." She did
not want to impute any formal routine to Madame, any cheap
ritual. Some truth was closing in, some singular announcement
which, she felt, must not be spoiled.

"If you wish, you can simply put your hands on the table."

Stowe would laugh; her father would have looked at the ceiling
and stalked out of the room. She raised her hands, and when she
set them on the table it felt as though they had been thrust into
a cold wind. Now Madame's hands glided and came to rest with
her middle fingers touching Cleota's. They were old hands, much
older than Madame's face. The four hands looked like separate
living animals facing each other on the table. From out of some
ancient concealment four hands had come and had met on this
table.

Cleota awaited her next instruction, but there was none. She
raised her eyes to Madame's.

The woman's great age struck her newly. Her cheeks seemed to
have sunk, she looked Slavic now, her skin cracked like milk skim,
the veins in her eyeballs twisted like a map of jungle rivers.

"Look in my eyes, please," Madame Lhevine said.

Cleota shuddered. "I am," she said. Was it possible the woman had gone blind? Looking more sharply, Cleota saw in fact that she was not seeing, that her gaze had died, gone within. It was too appropriate, and for a moment she thought to break off, but a feeling came that she would lose by mocking; whatever her distrust, she felt she must continue to look into these black eyes if she ever was to hope again for a connection to herself.

Now Madame Lhevine lifted her hands and patted Cleota's, and breathed. Cleota put her hands back in her lap. Madame Lhevine blinked at nothing, seeming to be putting together what she had heard or seen.

"Is there an older woman . . . ?" Madame broke off. "Is there an old woman?" she corrected.

"My husband's sister. She lives near by."

"Oh." Madame raised her chin. She seemed to be steeling herself. "She will live longer than he."

A tremor shook Cleota's head; she looked stupidly at Madame Lhevine, her mind shocked by the picture of Stowe in his casket and Alice standing over it, while she must wait forever by herself in a corner, a stranger again. It seemed to her she had always had this picture in her head and the only news was that now someone else had seen it too.

Cleota was agonized by the relief she felt at the image of Alice outliving Stowe. Simply, it wiped out her entire life with him. She had met him first in the gallery with Alice at his side, the air between them thickened by a too dense, too heavy communication. She had never broken into it herself, never stood alone in the center of his vision. Thirty years vanished, nullified. She was now where she had come in, with nothing to show.

"I'm sorry I had to . . ." Madame broke off as she laid her hand on Cleota's. The touch brought Cleota back to the room and an awareness of Alice hovering somewhere near the house. Anger puffed her eyelids. What Madame and Lucretia saw was the furious look that was sweeping up into her face.

A car, driven fast, squealed to a halt in the driveway. The three women turned together toward the door, hearing the approaching footsteps outside, the steps of a man. Cleota went toward it as the knocking began, and opened it.

"Joseph!" she almost shouted.

The young man threw up his hands in mock fright. "What'd I do?" he called.

Cleota laughed. "Come in!"

Now he entered, grinning at her and speaking the drollery which had always served best between them. "Am I too late?"

"For what!" Cleota heard the girlish crack in her voice.

"Whatever it is," he said, taking off his zipper jacket and tossing it to a chair. "I mean it's late and I didn't want to wake you."

"We're obviously awake," she taunted him, feeling a new cruelty torn loose within her.

He felt hung up, facing the other two women, and so he shouted, "I mean will I be in the way if I come in for a few minutes because I'm not ready to go to sleep yet and I thought it would be nice to say hello! Is what I mean!"

Lucretia also laughed. There was something aboriginal about him, in her opinion, as she had once told Cleota.

"So hello!" he said, and drew a chair up to the table, combed his fingers through his thick brown hair, and lit a cigar.

"Have you had dinner?" Cleota asked.

"I ate once at five and again at nine," he said. Cleota seemed oddly charged up. He did not know if it was because he was intruding or because he was very welcome as the only man.

He glanced toward Madame Lhevine who gave him a nodding smile, and only now Cleota realized, and introduced them.

"How long will you stay up here?"

"I don't know. Few days." He drank what she put before him. "How's Stowey?"

"Oh, all right," and she gave a quick, deprecating laugh. This had always given him a smoky sense of an understanding with her, about what precisely he did not know. But now she added, seriously, "He's having a show in Florida."

"Oh, that's nice."

She laughed again.

"Well, I meant it!" he protested.

Her face turned instantly grave. "I know you did."

To Madame Lhevine and Lucretia he said, "Between us it's always a battle of half-wits."

The women's laughter relieved him; he was some ten years

younger than Cleota and Lucretia, a rolling-gaited, hands-in-pockets novelist whose vast inexperience with women had given him a curiosity about them so intense as to approach understanding. With women, he usually found himself behind any one of various masks, depending on the situation; at the moment it was that of the raffish youth, the younger poet, perhaps, for it was never possible to arrive — especially before Cleota — as himself. She was, he always sensed, an unhappy woman who perhaps did not even know her unhappiness; she therefore sought something, some sensuous reassurance which he could distract her from by stimulating this carefree artist bantering. Not that Cleota herself attracted him; her being a wife was enough to place her in a vaguely sacred area. Unless he should strike out toward another sort of life and character for himself, a life, as he visualized it, of truthful relations. Which is to say personal relations of a confessional sort. But somewhere in his mind he knew that real truths only came out of disaster, and he would do his best to avoid disaster in all the departments of his life. He had to, he felt, out of decency. For the true terror of living in a false position was that the love of others has become attached to it and so must be betrayed if one is to strike for the truth. And treason to others — to Joseph Kersh — was the ultimate destruction, worse even than treason to himself, living with a wife he could not love.

So that by the time he was seated at the table he was already chafing at the boyish role Cleota had thrust upon him these six or seven years of their acquaintance. He made his manner grave and seemingly even troubled, and since, as the only man present, attention centered on him for the moment and he had to speak, he looked directly into Lucretia's eyes and asked, "How's your husband?"

Lucretia lowered her gaze to her cigarette and tapping it impatiently she said, "He's all right."

He heard her door clap shut; women discovered alone, he believed, must have been talking about sex. He believed this since his childhood when his mother's bridge parties had always gone from screaming hilarity to matronly silence as soon as he appeared. He knew then, as he knew now, that there was something illicit here, something prohibited in the air; knowing was no problem to him. It was admitting that he knew. For it tore at his sense of good,

of right, and of the proper nature of things that wives should betray the smallest contempt for their husbands. And yet, he felt,
contempt was around this table now. And he was dismayed that
this flattered him and gave him a joyous feeling of fitness. "Just
a half," he said to Cleota who was pouring more whisky into his
glass. "I've got to get to sleep soon."

"Oh, don't go!" she said strongly, and he saw that she was flushed
with whisky. "Are you writing up here?"

"No." Gratified, he saw how she was waiting for serious news of
him. Lucretia too was curious. "I'm just worrying."

"*You?*"

"Why not?" he asked, genuinely surprised.

"Just that you seem to do everything you want to do."

Her admiration, he believed, was for some strength she seemed
to think he had, and he accepted with pleasure. But a distant alarm
was ringing for him tonight; something intimate was happening
here, and he should not have come.

"I don't know," he answered Cleota. "Maybe I do do what I
want to. The trouble is I don't know I'm doing it." And he resolved, in the name of some distant truthfulness, to reveal a little
of his own bewilderment. "I really go from moment to moment,
despite appearances. I don't know what I'm doing any more than
anybody else."

"Ah, but you do know," said Madame Lhevine, narrowing her
eyes. He looked at her with surprise. "I have read your books.
You do know. Within yourself you know."

He found himself liking this ugly woman. Her tone reminded
him of his mother's when she would look at him after he had
knocked over a vase, and would say, "You will be a great man."

"You follow your spirit, Mr. Kersh," she went on, "so it is not
necessary to know anything more."

"I suppose I do," he said, "but it would save a lot of trouble if I
could believe it."

"But I'm sure you understand," Madame pressed on, "that the
sense you have of not knowing is what makes your art. When an
artist knows what he is doing he can no longer do it, don't you
think?"

This so matched the license Joseph secretly claimed for himself,
and the blessed freedom from responsibility he longed for, that he

could not in good conscience accept it. "Well I wouldn't go that far," he said. "It's romantic to think an artist is unconscious." And now he broadened his shoulders and his right hand closed in a fist. "A work of art must work, like a good machine. . . ."

"But a machine made by a blind man," Madame said in an experienced tone.

"I deny that," he said, shaking his head, helpless to dam up this flood of certainty. "I have to think through a form before I can write, I have to engineer a structure, I have to know what I am doing."

"Of course," Madame cut in, "but at a certain point you must know nothing and allow yourself only your feelings. In fact, that is my only . . . my only reservation about your work."

"What?" he asked. He did not like her. Women ought not to criticize. She was repulsively ugly, like a dwarf.

"They are a bit overconstructed," she said. "I hope you will not think me presumptuous, but I do have that feeling even though I admire enormously what you say."

He hoped that the heat he felt rising in his face would be attributed to the whisky. Crossing his knees suddenly he knocked the table against Madame, and quickly set it back in place, laughing, "I'm sorry, I didn't mean to cripple you."

He saw, with near shock, that Cleota was openly staring at him. With admiration. It was most noticeable. Why was Stowe gone, alone?

Lucretia was deep in thought, looking at the ashtray and tapping her cigarette on it. "But really, Joe," she faced him with her over-puzzled look, "don't you think that people are really much more disoriented than you portray them? I mean . . ."

"My characters are pretty disoriented, Lucretia," he said, and made Cleota laugh.

"No, seriously; your people always seem to *learn* something," she complained.

"Don't you think people learn?" he asked, and wondered what they were secretly arguing about. There was, in fact, something dense about Lucretia, he had always thought. The first time he had met her she had just come from mating two horses and was feverish with her success, and it had seemed so clear that she had had a sexual interest in the procedure herself, yet was unaware of it, and this had given her a dull quality in his eyes, a musky one too, however.

"Of course they learn," she said, and it was clear she was matching intellects with him, which a woman ought not do, he felt, "but they learn geometry and the necessary dates. Not . . ." She sought the word, and Madame supplied it.

"Not spirit."

"Yes!" Lucretia agreed, but deferred to Madame to continue.

"I'm sure you agree," said Madame, "that essentially the spirit is formed quite early. Actually it knows all it will ever know from the beginning."

"Then what's the point in living?"

"Because we must live. That is all."

"I wouldn't call that much of a point," Joseph said.

"Maybe there isn't much of a point," Cleota suddenly put in.

Joseph turned to her, struck by her sad gravity. He wondered now whether Stowe had any idea she was so hopeless.

But he checked himself — she was only talking, and being her usual tolerant self. That was what he could never understand — she and Stowe could feel deeply about some issue and yet be perfectly friendly with people who stood for everything they opposed. Life to them was some kind of game, whereas one ought to believe something to the point of suffering for it. He wished he could find a way of leaving now instead of sitting here with these three crocked lunks arguing about spirits!

"Although I do think we learn," Cleota went on, and with an open glance of support for Joseph. "I don't know if we only learn what we unconsciously knew before, or whether it's all continuously new, but I think we learn."

How admirably direct she was! Joseph caught this flower she had surprisingly tossed him and with it charged against the other two women. "What always gets me is how people will scoff at science and conscious wisdom and the whole rational approach to life, but when they go to the more 'profound' places, like Mexico or Sicily or some other spiritual-type country, they never forget to take their typhoid shots!"

The mocking voices of Madame Lhevine and Lucretia were in the air and he reddened with anger. Lucretia yelled, "That's got nothing to do with . . ."

"It's only the exact point! If you believe something you have to live by it or it's just talk! You can't say we don't learn and then blithely accept the fruits of what we've learned. That's . . . it's . . ." He wanted to say, "Lying."

"Oh, now, Joe," Lucretia drawled, looking at him with toleration — he sounded like her husband proving to her on engineering principles that she was not unhappy — "what we're talking about is simply not on that *plane*. You're ten years behind the times. Nobody's underrating science and conscious wisdom; it's simply that it doesn't provide an inner aim, a point to live for. It still leaves man essentially alone."

"Excepting that the only people I ever met who feel part of an international, a world community, are scientists. They're the only ones who aren't alone."

"Now, Joe, really — what does a sentence like that *mean?*"

He was furious. "It means that they don't live for themselves only, they live in the service of a greater thing."

"*What,* for heaven's sake?"

"What? The alleviation of human pain and the wiping out of human poverty."

"We can't all be wiping out poverty, Joseph. What do *we* do? We're simply not talking about the same *things*." And she turned to Cleota, "Do you sense the difference, Clee?"

"Of course there's a difference," Cleota said, her eyes avoiding Lucretia's, "but why can't you both be right?" And she glanced at Joseph for confirmation of this, to him, total absurdity.

"I don't care about being right," he said, quietly now. But his hopes for Cleota had again subsided; she was a total mystery to him. Nothing ever came to an issue for her. The idea came sharply to his mind that every time he came here it was an anticlimax. This was why he always left feeling he had wasted his time — they were people who simply lived in an oblong hum and did not strive for some apotheosis, some climax in life, either a great accomplishment or a discovery or any blast of light and sound which would fling them into a new speed, a further orbit.

Yet, inexplicably, when he had been fired out of the university for his refusal to disavow the left-wing youth, she had gone on for months indignantly talking about it, phoning to see how he was, and for a while even spoke of living in Europe to protest the oppressive American atmosphere.

Madame and Lucretia evidently felt he had been put down successfully, and the ugly woman allowed him a kind look, and said, "It doesn't matter anyway — you are a very good writer."

This outstretching of a finger instead of a whole hand made Joseph and Cleota laugh, and he said, "I'm not knocking intuition." Cleota laughed louder, but he had meant this as a compromise with Madame, and said to Cleota, "Wait a minute, I'm making up to her," and Cleota laughed louder still. His abruptness always entertained her, but it was something more now; in his passion for his ideas, ideas she understood but did not find irreplaceable, she sensed a fleshed connection with an outside force, an unseen imperative directing his life. He *had* to say what he said, believe what he believed, was helpless to compromise, and this spoke a dedication not different than love in him.

She drank three inches of whisky straight, observing a bright stain of green moonlight through the wet windows over her guests' heads. A planetary silence seemed to surround the continuing argument, she felt herself floating away. Her only alarm was that the talk was dying and they would all soon leave. She poured whisky for Joseph, who was pounding the table with his open hand. "I am not knocking intuition," he was saying again, "I work with it, I make my living by it. . . ." Out of nowhere an idea hit him. "I'll tell you something, Madame Lhevine. I come from a long line of superstitious idiots. I once had an aunt, see, and she told fortunes. . . ."

Cleota exploded, throwing her hands up in the air and turning from the table doubled over in laughter. Lucretia first smiled, trying to resist for Madame's sake, but she caught the infection and then Madame herself unwillingly joined and Joseph, smiling stupidly, looked at the three women laughing hysterically around him, asking, "What? What!" but no one able to answer, until he too was carried into the waves and, as always happens in such cases, one of them had only to look at the other to begin insanely laughing all over again. And when they had quieted enough for him to be heard, he explained to Cleota, "But she did. In fact, she was part gypsy!" At this Cleota screamed and she and Lucretia bent across the table grasping each other's arms, gasping and laughing with their faces hidden by their shoulders, and Madame kept slapping the table and shaking her head and going, "Ho, ho, ho." Joseph, without understanding what it was all about, could not help feeling their hysteria was at his expense. His soberness returned before theirs and he sat patiently smiling, on the verge of feeling the fool, and lit his cigar and took a drink, waiting for them to come to.

At last Cleota explained with kindness that Saint had said precisely the same things, and that . . . But now it was hard to reconstruct the earlier situation, especially Madame's resentment at the girl's presumptuous claim of an aunt who could do what Madame did — at least it could not be explained, Cleota realized, without characterizing Madame Lhevine as being extremely jealous and even petty about her talent for fortunetelling, and, besides, Cleota was aware that Madame was not happy with the title of fortune-teller and yet she did not know what else to call her without invoking words like spiritualist or seer or whatever — words which embarrassed Cleota and might in the bargain again offend the lady. So that the net of the explanation was a muddle, a confusion which confirmed in Joseph his recurring notion that the Rummels were in fact trivial and their minds disoriented, while for Cleota her inability to finally describe Madame left her — however hilariously amused she still appeared — with the feeling that Madame was perhaps a fraud. This was not at all a distasteful idea to Cleota; it was simply Madame's character. What did disturb her under her flushed smile, and prevented her from detaining Madame, who now said it was getting late, was the thought of being left alone. The image surged up of Stowe lying dead in his casket, and it stiffened her a little toward Lucretia as she helped her into her coat, quite as though Lucretia had borne her this prophecy in part, carrying it from her own blasted home where nothing ever went right.

So that by the time Cleota returned from the driveway and removed her Rumanian shawl and poured herself a new drink, she was still enjoying the exhilaration that follows helpless laughter, the physical cleanliness and strength which it leaves behind in healthy people, and at the same time her eyes had the indrawn look that the discomposing news had left there, and Joseph watched her, bewildered by her double mood.

Without asking him she handed him a drink and they faced each other at the fire which she had just fanned to life. "I'll go soon," he said. "I have to work tomorrow."

He saw that she was drunk, much drunker than she had seemed with the other two women present. In one continuous motion she sat down and let her knees spread apart, staring over his head. Then she leaned over heavily and set her drink on the floor between her feet and fell back into the chair again, blowing out air and turning her face toward the fire. Her breathing was still deep and her hands hung limply from the arms of the wicker chair. Her seeming abandon was not a sign of sensuousness to him at first. He thought she was even indicating such trust in him that she need not look composed.

Drunken women made Joseph nervous. He spoke, trying for their customary bantering tone. "Now what was *that* all about?" he asked, grinning.

She did not answer, seemed hardly to have heard. Her staring eyes suggested some vast preoccupation, and finally a despair which he had never before seen in her. An engagement, a moment of personal confrontation seemed to be approaching, and to ward it off Joseph said, "I did have an aunt like that. She read my palm the night before I left home for college and predicted I'd flunk out after one semester."

He had hardly started his remark when it sounded to him like chatter unworthy of the moment. And now Cleota turned her head, still resting on the rim of the chair's back, and looked at him. With a shock he felt the challenge in her eyes. She was looking at him as a man, and for the first time. Her challenge kept growing in him and to throw her off he lazily threw his arm over the back of his chair and turned to the fire as though he too were preoccupied with other thoughts. Was it possible? Cleota Rummel?

"Do you remember John Trudeau?" she asked.

He turned to her, relieved; it would be gossip after all. "I think so. That tall guy used to teach up at . . . ."

"Why . . . do you know why . . . ?" She broke off, her face drawn together in mystification. She was seeing past him and around him, staring. "Why do they all end in sex?"

He was relieved at the genuinely questioning note; she was not being coy. He damned his evil mind of a moment before. "What do you mean?" he asked.

"He has a perfectly beautiful wife. Those children, too. He was here tonight. With a girl. A perfectly ghastly girl." And once again she demanded of him, as though he must certainly know, being a man, "Do you know why that is happening? To everybody?"

Her driving need for an answer pierced him because the question was his obsession these days. It seemed very strange she had reached into him and had grasped precisely what bewildered him.

"It seems to me," she went on, "that almost everyone I know is going crazy. There doesn't seem to be any other subject any more. Any other *thing*. . . ." She broke off again and drew in a long breath and wiped a strand of hair out of her eyes.

Then she turned back to the fire, unable for the moment to continue looking at Joseph's resolute face. She wanted to weep, to laugh, to dance — anything but to sit here at this disadvantage. For an instant she remembered the warmth in Madame Lhevine's eyes, the feeling she was being enfolded by one more powerful, and she longed desperately to be taken up and held.

Her tone of supplication told Joseph that he was moving into a false position, for he dared not betray his own feelings of bewilderment. If they were both at a loss they would join in their miseries and he could not, on even larger grounds, declare himself dumfounded by life. "I know what you mean," he said, careful to direct his mournful tone toward unspecified others and away from himself and Cleota. "I see it myself all the time."

She looked at him from the fire. "Do you?" she asked, demanding he go on.

"I don't know the answer," he said, and only glanced at her with this. "I guess it's that there is no larger aim in life any more. Everything has become personal relations and nothing more."

The blurred sensuousness drained out of her eyes and she seemed alert to him again. "Is there something more?"

"Sure. That is, there might be."

"What?"

"Well . . ." He felt like a schoolboy, having to say that the welfare of mankind, the fight for justice, caring for the oppressed were the something more. But as he began to evoke these thoughts their irrelevancy choked off his words, their distance from the suffering he saw in this woman lying back in the wicker chair with her knees fallen outward and the drink at her feet. She was lusting for a truth beyond what he possessed, yet he had to go on. "It's a law of history. When a society no longer knows its aims, when it's no longer dominated by the struggle to get food and safety, the private life is all there is. And we are all anarchists at heart when there is no greater aim. So we jump into each other's beds." God, what a fraud all ideas were . . . all anyone wanted was love!

"Joseph," she began, her voice very soft, her eyes on the fire, "why is it happening?"

He felt her proposal stretching out its wings, testing the air. He finished his drink and stood up. "I'll go, Cleota," he said.

She looked up at him, blinking lazily. "That woman said Stowe would die before his sister."

He could not speak; her belief in the prophecy shocked and per- suaded him. He saw Stowe dead. He reached down and pressed his hand on hers, awkwardly. "You can't believe that nonsense, can you?"

"Why are you going?" she asked, her simplicity terrifying him.

"I'll have one more drink," he said, and got the bottle and set it on the floor beside his chair and sat again, taking as long as he could with the business. And again he damned his suspicious mind — she was simply frightened for Stowe, for God's sake! He would stay until she either fell asleep or came out of her fright.

Through the warm haze that surrounded her she saw that Joseph had suddenly come to life. How young he really was! His hair was not even graying, his skin was tight, and there was no judgment coming to her from him, no orders, no husband's impatience; her body felt new and unknown. "A larger aim," she said, her words muffled.

"What?" he asked.

She stood up and thrust her fingers into her hair and breathed deeply, walking to the door. He sat still watching her. She stopped at the pane and looked out through the mist, like a pris- oner, he thought. He took a long swallow of his drink, resolved to leave. She stood there ten yards away with her hands in her hair and he admired the angled backthrust of her torso secreted in her gray woolen dress. He saw her in bed, but all he could feel was her suffering. And then Stowe would return sometime, and the three of them in this room? The weedy morass of that scene shuddered him.

Moments went by and she did not turn from the door. She was waiting for him, he saw. Goddam! Why had he stayed? He saw that he had acted falsely, a role, the protector's part. Beneath his character and hers, beneath their very powers of speech was the anarchy of need, the lust for oblivion and its comfort. He sat there reddening with shame at having misled her, his manhood spurious to him and thought itself a pretense.

She turned to him at the door, lowering her arms. The amateurishness of her seduction pained him for her sake as she stood there openly staring at him. "Don't you like me?"

"Sure I do."

Her brows came together densely as she walked to him and stood over him, her hands hanging at her sides, her head thrust forward a little, and as she spoke her open hands turned ever so slightly toward him: "What's the matter with you?"

He stood up and faced her, unable to speak at the sight of the animal fury in her face.

"What's the matter with you!" she screamed.

"Good night," he said, walking around her toward the door.

"What did you stay for?" she screamed at his back.

He turned, seeing her perplexed fury. He was not able to say anything.

She came toward him unsteadily, a smile of mockery spreading on her face. She could feel, almost touch, his trembling and she clenched her teeth together with the wish to tear with them. She felt her own hands opening and closing and an amazing strength across her back. "You . . . ! You . . . !"

She stood up close to him, seeing his eyes widening with surprise and fear. The taste of her stomach came into her mouth, her disgust for him and his broken promise bringing tears to her eyes. But he did not move a hand to her; he was pitiless, like Stowe when he stared through her toward Alice, and like Alice moving in and out of this house. She wept.

Joseph touched her shoulder with his hand, and instantly saw Stowe's laughing face before him. She neither accepted his touch nor rejected it. As though he had no importance for her any more.

So he raised the immense weight of his arms and held her. The stairs to the second floor were a few yards away; he would almost have to carry her. She would be half conscious on the pillow; toward dawn the countryside from the bedroom window would be littered with hair, with bones, with the remnants of his search for an order in his life. Holding her to him, he feared her offering was an accusation of his complicity with her, their equal pointlessness. But he tightened his arms around her to squash out of her any inkling she might feel of his unwillingness to share her world's derangement.

She encircled his waist and pressed her body against him. To love! To know nothing but love!

He took hold of her head and turned her face up to forestall the next moment. Her eyes were shut, and tears were squeezing out of their corners, her skin hot in his hands. Cleota! Cleota Rummel! But without love? he thought, without even desire? He once again saw Stowe in this room, saw himself bantering with him, discussing, felt Stowe's bumbling warmth. How easy to ruin a man! From tomorrow on he could ruin Stowe with their usual handshake and the clap on the back. The power to destroy shaped itself in his mind like a rising rocket, astounding him with its frightfulness and its beauty, an automatic force given to him like a brand-new character, a new power which would somehow finish a struggle against the meaningless of life, joining him at his ease with that sightless legion riding the trains and driving the cars and filling the restaurants, a power to breathe the evil in the world and thus at last to love life. She pressed her lips against his throat, surprisingly soft lips. Disastrous contempt if he should try to leave her now, but to take her upstairs . . . his practical mind saw the engineering that would entail. A willed concussion of skeletons. He knew it was not virtue loosening his embrace, but an older lust for a high heart uncondemned, a niggardly ambition it seemed to him now as he summoned his powers to say, "Good night, Cleota," and in such a tone as would convince her that he did not dislike her in his arms.

She opened her eyes. God! he thought, she could kill! "Whaz a matter with you?" she asked him.

"Nothing's the matter with me," he said, dropping his hands to his sides, but blushing.

"What?" She swayed alone now in the room, peering at him

through bewildered eyes, genuinely asking, "Whad you stay for?"

A good question, he thought, damning his naïveté. "I thought you didn't want to be alone," he said.

"Yez. You don't like me. I'm old. Older and older."

He reached out his hand to her, afraid she would fall, and she slapped it away, sending herself stumbling sideways, banging against the wall where she held herself upright, her hair fallen over half her face. "Whaz a matter with all of you! All of you and all of you!" She sobbed, but seemed not to know it. "And if he dies before she does? Doesn't someone have to . . . have to win before the end?" And she bent over, thrusting out her hands in a strangely theatrical gesture of supplication — how awkward she had become! how false all gracefulness is! And dredging up her arms from near the floor, her fingers wide, she called, weeping, a furious grimace stretching forth the two tendons of her throat, "Don't you have to win before it's over? Before . . . it's *overrrr!*"

He could not stop the tears in his eyes. "Yes," he whispered. The attempt to speak loosened some muscle in his stomach and he fled weeping from the house.

The thumping resounded through his dreamless sleep. Boom, boom, boom. He opened his eyes. Boom. Again. He got out of bed and staggered. The whisky, he thought. He was dizzy and held the window sill. The booming sounded again below. He pulled up the shade. The sun! A clear day at last. The sun was just starting to come up at the far edges of the valley. The booming sounded again below. He pulled the window up and started to lean out but his head hit the screen. Now he saw Cleota's car in the road before the house, parked askew as though it had been left there in an emergency. The booming noise went on, now violently. He called out, "Yes!" then ran to the bed as though it were a dream and he could go back to sleep now that he had realized it.

But it was truly dawn and the noise was a knocking on his door, a dreadful emergency knocking. He called out "Yes!" again and got into his pants, which were lying on the floor, and struggled into his shirt and ran down the stairs barefoot and opened the door.

She was standing there, morning-fresh except for the exhaustion in her eyes. But her hair was brushed and she stood tall, herself again if one did not know that she had never looked so frightened, so pleadingly at anyone in all her life. Suddenly he thought her beautiful with the sparkling air around her head. He was still passing up through the webs of his sleep and she was part dream standing there in his doorway in a fox-collared coat of deep, rich brown, looking at him as though she had sprung from the grass without a history excepting that of earth and the immense trees on the road behind her. He reached out his hand, and she took it and stepped into the hallway. He was freezing in the icy breeze and started to close the door, but she held it, and looked desperately up at him, wanting back what she had given him.

"I beg your pardon for last night," she said.

It was entirely askew to her; he was standing there trying to keep his eyes open, obviously undisturbed, she felt, by what she had done. Obviously, she saw now, he had had many women and her coming here now was idiotically naïve to him. She felt such shame at her naïveté that she turned abruptly and pulled open the partly closed door, but he caught her arm and turned her to him.

"Cleota . . ."

Drawing her to him he caught a scent of cherries in her hair. The sheer presence of her body astounded him in his house. Only now was he drunk. He lowered his lips to her, but was stopped by the surprise in her eyes, a surprise which had something stiff-necked about it, a resistance, a propriety he would have to overcome.

His hesitation, like respect, moved her; but he was unnecessary to her now that at last she could feel his demand. Raising up her hand she tenderly touched his chest, relieved that he wanted her a little. They were accomplices now and she could trust his silence. And she straightened before him, and a smile softened her face as she recognized his open need.

He saw a little of her old stance returning, her self-respect, but it was no longer necessary to obey it. He kissed her cheek. But she was less beautiful to him now that her despair was going, she was Cleota again, bred and clear-eyed and profoundly unapproachable.

"Take care of yourself," he said, meaninglessly excepting for the brittle-shelled tone, the bantering voice they both knew so well. But how alive their simulation had become, how interesting it was now, this propriety!

"Would you like breakfast?" she asked.

The old proper distance was between them again, safe and

sound, like a shore they had finally reached. He said he had to go back to sleep for a while yet.

"Come later then," she said, warmly, deeply satisfied.

"Okay."

She went down to her car and got in and drove away with a wave of one hand through the window, already getting out of her coat with the other. She will be digging in her garden soon, he thought.

He did not go to her later. He lay in bed until the late morning, castigating himself for a fool at one moment, at the next feeling some odd pride that he had been loyal to himself — and, as it turned out, to her as well.

But it never left the background of his mind that every claim to virtue is at least a little false; for was it virtue whose existence he had proved, or only fear? Or both! He wanted very much to believe that life had a virtuous center where conscience could lie down with sensuality in peace, for otherwise everything but sexual advantage was a fraud. He heard her voice again, "What's the matter with you!" It rang. But was there really nothing truthful in her other voice just now, so civilized and reserved, inviting him to breakfast? Once again good order reigned in this countryside. He smiled at a thought — she would probably welcome Stowey more warmly now that she had glimpsed a conquest. He was glad for her. God! — what a ring of fire there always is around the truth!

He lay a long time listening to the silence in his loveless house.

Alice died toward the end of May, falling asleep in her rocker as she looked at the valley view while waiting for dinnertime. Joseph only heard of it accidentally, when he returned after settling his divorce. He had put his house up for sale and discovered he had no key to the front door to give the real-estate agent. Removing the lock, he took it to the hardware store to have a key fitted and the clerk had mentioned the old lady's funeral. He wanted to ask how Stowe was, but caught himself. Returning with the key, he installed the lock and closed the place, got into his car and drove off. Before he could think, he found himself on the road to the Rummel house. He had not seen Stowe since sometime before his trip to Florida, nor had he seen Cleota since the night that her fortune was told.

Realizing he was on their road he reduced speed. In this fine weather they might be outside and would look up and see him passing. But what, after all, had he to be ashamed of? He resolutely resumed speed, aware now that it was Stowe he would rather not face. Unless, he thought — was this possible too? — Stowe was dead?

The car traveled the long turn which straightened onto a view of the Rummel house. Stowe and Cleota were walking idly on the road, he with a stick knocking the heads off daisies and peering into the weeds every few yards, she at his side watching, breathing — Joseph could already see — her breaths of fitness and staring now and then at the newly green valley beyond Stowe's head. They both turned, hearing the car, and, recognizing it, stood still and tall. Stowe, seeing Joseph through the window, nodded, looked at him as he had the first time they had met many years ago, with a cool and perceptive look. Joseph nodded back, angered by his friend's coolness but smiling, and to both of them said, "How are you?"

"Very well," Cleota said.

Only now could he look directly at her and, strengthened by Stowe's unjust condemnation, he dared hold her in his gaze. She was afraid of him!

"Selling out?" Stowe asked, with noticeable contempt.

It dawned that Stowe was condemning him for his divorce; he had always admired Joseph's wife. Only now Joseph realized how correct his estimate of them had been — they were an old-fashioned family underneath, and Stowe despised those who, at the last moment, did not abide by the laws of decency.

"I'm trying to sell it," Joseph said, relaxing in his seat. "But I'll probably be by again before long. Maybe I'll drop in."

Stowe barely nodded.

"Bye," Joseph said. But this time Stowe simply looked at him without moving.

"Have a good summer," Joseph said, turning to Cleota, and he saw, with surprise, that now she was observing him as a stranger, as Stowe was doing. They were joined.

He drove off past them, a laughter rising in his heart, a joy at having seen chaos at last, and good order closing back over it like an ocean that has swallowed a wreck. And he took a deep breath of May, glancing out the side window at the countryside which

seemed now never to have been cold and wet and unendurably
dark through so many months.

When his car had gone and it was silent on the road, Stowe
swung his stick and clipped a daisy. For a few yards neither spoke,
and then he blew his nose and said, "He's not much."

"No," she said, "I suppose he isn't."

"There was always some sneakiness in him, something like that."

"Yes," she said, and took his arm and they walked together past
his sister's empty house. She kissed his shoulder and he looked at
her, grinning and surprised, for she did not make such displays.
He grunted, quite pleased, and she held him tighter, feeling the sun
on her back like a blessing, aware once again of Stowe's deep reli-
ability, and her own. Thank God, she thought, for good sense!
Joseph, she remembered, had wanted her very much that morning
in his hallway. And she walked in silence cherishing a rapture, the
clear heart of those who glimpse they are of the elect whose doors
were made to hold against the winds of the world.

"Still," she said thoughtfully, and with care, "it's rather a shame
about them."

He shrugged, and bent over to part the roadside weeds, reached
in and brought out a young toad whose squeaks made him laugh.
And suddenly he tossed it to her. She shrieked, reddening with anger, but then she laughed. And as sometimes happened with them,
they just stood face to face laughing down at each other with an
enormous heartiness.

(From The Sewanee Review)

THE VINDICATION
OF DR. NESTOR

BY E. LUCAS MYERS

*A*LEX LOVEJOY entered his hotel room about midnight; his possessions lay on the floor in suitcases and boxes. Only that afternoon he had moved from his former hotel in the Rue Saint André des Arts following a quarrel with his *concierge* over a door broken down by late visitors. He felt the bed and found it, like other hotel beds in Paris, exceedingly rocky and uneven — a senseless thing, he reflected, in a city where the beds have such importance. But he fell onto the sheets without getting between them and went off to sleep at once, owing to the wine he had drunk.

What broke his slumber, well after one o'clock, was an unusual sound coming from the vicinity of a little window high in the corner of the room. Alex lay awake for an undetermined time, wondering if he was in fact awake, for the sounds he heard resembled nothing if not the motherly clucks of hens varied by the occasional suppressed crow of a cock or gobble of a turkey. The light from the street, entering a larger window, threw three shadowy bars in parallel succession on the ceiling and wall, and in his sleepy state it seemed that these could be the accoutrements of a poultry coop on which the fowls were roosting and from which they were emitting their exclamations. Perhaps it was curiosity that got him out of bed or perhaps a certain nervousness at lying in such an exposed position below what might have been three hen-and-turkey perches. Once up, the illusion quickly passed and Alex commenced to search out the real source of these communications. He stood on a chair and opened the little window which looked out onto a long, narrow sun-shaft. All was dark outside except another little window, on the opposite side and on the floor below. As his eyes narrowed to the proper pitch and he became accustomed to the dim light he could discern, one by one, those pieces of furniture in the room which were accessible to his view, and, as his ears quickened, the muffled clucks became more and more distinct. There was a lamp, turned to the wall, which threw into large relief two or three cases, a chair, and a large double bed. In the center of the bed a lengthy figure, attired in a white nightgown, was crouching on a pit, a sort of nest as far as Alex could tell, composed of rumpled bedclothes and towels. A nest it must have been because from it, at discreet intervals, the clucks continued to come. This spectacle held Alex's attention for some minutes before the figure stood up, its head almost touching the ceiling, and taking the contents out of the nest to place them with solicitude in one of the cases, disrupted the perch, transformed it once more into a bed, and turned out the light.

When Alex woke in the morning his curiosity had increased rather than abated and he went to the lavatory on the floor below in the hope of discovering some clue which would explain the performance he had witnessed during the night. He was able to determine which room was the scene of all the night's activity and stood at the door for a time, hoping to hear something from within. But he heard nothing — these hens went early out to the barnyard, he remarked inwardly. The room was number nine; this he carefully registered before going out to the main post office to see if there were any letters from prospective employers. At lunchtime he returned to the hotel, but from the window he could see that number nine, an ordinary and neatly kept room by daylight, was empty. Six o'clock provided a similar disappointment and the evening wore on without any emanation from below, without any light from the window. It was after midnight when he heard the clucks again and saw from his window the lamp turned to the wall and the crouching figure on the bed.

In the late morning Alex returned to his room and washed to go out to a restaurant. On the chance, he dallied a little by number nine and went into the lavatory on a pretended errand. He emerged from the lavatory to find two persons remonstrating with one another in front of number nine: a petite, blackheaded *fille de chambre* and a very tall person with close, gray-white hair, a tough lined face with big bones and hollows in leathery evidence, eyes rather bleary as though they had for years stared through falling snow, and a wintry frame for nose. His clothes hung upon him like sacking on a stick. It was plain that this was the lanky figure Alex had seen crouching on the nest.

The croucher was engaged in mime, rubbing his face and the back of his neck with some imaginary implement and repeating to the *fille de chambre* "More towels, more towels!" She in her turn looked perplexed and replied, *"Je m'excuse, monsieur, mais je ne comprends pas ce que vous voulez."* The scene arrested Alex but he had only a moment to gaze on it before the lanky gentleman turned and spoke to him.

"Pardon me, young man, but do you speak any English?"

"Yes, sir," replied Alex, gratified as he was at the turn of events which promised to allay his curiosity. "I speak a good deal more English than French."

"Well, I'm glad to hear that. Perhaps you'll do me a favor and tell this young woman I need some towels."

"About how many should I say?" Alex asked.

"Oh, I think eight would do."

Alex was prepared to be unastonished by any sort of request from the person with whom he was dealing and so communicated his need to the *fille de chambre*. She, however, was not so easy in this matter and replied that, as the hotel provided only one towel to a guest, if each of its clients demanded eight towels, seven hundred and twenty towels would be required, a quantity it did not possess. When the lanky gentleman understood this reply, he gave no evidences of being satisfied, but remained adamant until Alex could prevail on the *fille de chambre* to fetch the *patronne*. The *patronne* proved more tractable and the towels were provided, together with a casual observation that a charge of one thousand francs would be added to the bill. The charge did not disturb the lanky gentleman at all, though it might have done so, Alex thought, if it had been expressed in the language of dollars.

"Come in and sit yourself down," he twanged out, obviously pleased that his difficulties were happily resolved. "I'm glad to find somebody who speaks English in this hotel." Then, facing Alex and offering him a chair, he added, "My name is Asa Nestor, Dr. Asa

Nestor they call me, Professor of Poultry Psychology at Great Neck University, Vermont. What's your name, young feller?"

"Alexander Lovejoy . . ."

"You're from down there below the Mason-Dixon line if I hear you rightly?"

"Yes, I'm from Tennessee," Alex replied. He was casting a quick eye about him for a glimpse of the paraphernalia which he had viewed from the little window in his room the two preceding nights, but the doctor was observant and it was not easy to let the eye wander, or the ear become inattentive, in his company. Alex could find nothing of interest that was not closed in the three cases by the bed or in the bureau drawers.

"I came over here to this confounded conference of psychiatrists and psychologists they are having in the Rue Ecole de Médecine," the doctor continued, "but I can't see that it's doing anybody any good. I came on their invitation, mind you; I can't see why they invite somebody over here and then don't want to listen to what he's got to say. I reckon most of them come here so they can take it off their income tax, the ones from the U.S.A. anyhow. Professional expenses or some such rigamarole."

During all this the doctor had been pouring out a very good vintage wine. He did not invite Alex to have a glass, but poured the wine out without ceremony, assuming that everyone liked good wine as he himself obviously did. And between the two of them notable progress was made in reducing the level of the wine in the bottle. The doctor got up, stretched, and lit an antique pipe which he had prepared.

"I was just thinking of going out to get a little fodder. If you're not going anywhere, I'd be pleased if you'd come out to lunch with me."

Alex accepted gladly; for one thing his finances were far from healthy. The doctor proved to be a good companion and not, as Alex had already seen, a difficult person to come to know. He was vexed and could find no audience to which to express his vexation, for his only acquaintance in Paris was among the psychologists at the conference and, as Alex guessed, it was against them, or those of them responsible for eliminating his name from the speaking agenda, that his grievance lay.

The doctor chose an excellent restaurant.

"You order; I don't speak any French — don't have much use for it in my work," he said, looking at the quick, precise speakers around him, and then, abruptly turning, cackled out, "Poultry don't speak French, you know, but from the way they carry on I think the French must speak Poultry."

The waiter appeared with a long, elegant-looking menu. Alex consulted the menu and asked the doctor's pleasure. The waiter recommended baked chicken. A cloudy look passed over the doctor's face as he declined. Next he suggested roast duck, a specialty of Périgord. "No," the doctor said tersely. If the monsieur was not hungry perhaps an omelette with mushrooms would do? No, that would not do either. Alex began to get the doctor's drift and suggested beefsteak, which was readily accepted. Careful to avoid anything to do with fowl or eggs, he ordered roast lamb for himself. The doctor, who had somehow learned the names of the French wines if not another word of the French tongue, chose a crackling rosé from the wine list, to be brought immediately.

When the wine arrived the doctor, who to that point had shown a sudden taciturnity in the restaurant, seemed to perceive some signal for the recommencement of talk. His large, bony right hand stretched out to decant the wine and he began:

"Let's see . . . I was telling you about this confounded conference. They sent me a letter — some Frenchman who was organizing the thing — back in December and asked me to give a speech on my work. Now I ought to tell you that I'm the foremost poultry psychologist in the field — as a matter of fact I'm the only one, just me and the chickens in that field. My daughter was going to come over, too, to look after me since my wife isn't alive, but along about February it turned out she couldn't come; it seems like she's going to have a baby before long. Well, when I got here I found out the agenda had got too long and had to be curtailed and about the first one they curtailed was me. When they curtail you they curtail your honorarium, too, cut it right off in fact. They're all human psychologists here except me and a few experimental men who spend their time trying to find out why the egret hops around on one leg on the first of May or which monkey in the Calcutta zoo can pull fleas off which other monkey. Now I'm a practical feller, just trying to make the fowls a little happier in Henry Jones's henyard and I come here and have to listen to why a lot of old ladies in London have megalomania, minoromania, or berry obsessions every day till the turkeys roost, all the stuff I heard as a boy at college, though I grant you it's changed some since my day. A feller likes to have his say, you know, and I had a first-rate speech ready for them. 'Dementia Praecox in Domestic Fowls,' it was called. The most ordinary hens feel their eloignment from the wild state. They're just a big bunch of feathers and legs, just egg-laying organisms nowadays. We ought to strive to make them more comfortable in their domestic state; the happier they are the higher their egg-laying potential. I always have to bring in that about the egg-laying potential, you know. The human psychologist just has to please his subject, but the poultry psychologist has to get more eggs laid by hook or by crook. A durn sight harder it is, too, because you can see eggs but you can't see the conquest of child-hood guilt. Of course, I'm really more interested in making the chickens happier but I always stress the eggs. I have to to please my clients, the ones with the dollars, I mean, not the ones with the feathers. Anyhow, my speech went on to examine dementia prae-cox in fowls, the splitting of the emotional life between the needs of enforced domesticity and the deeply buried commitment to the wild state. What gets me is these battery farmers, the ones that lock the hens up in a little coop all day and turn on the light earlier and earlier until the hens think there are eighteen days in the week and they ought to be laying all the time. The trouble is they lay a lot of eggs that way, but the eggs aren't much good — the yolks are nearly white. Besides, it's a degradation that shouldn't have to be endured. Why, I remember once when a big chicken farmer with battery hens called me down in New York State because his hens were pecking the hell out of each other. You never have seen such a sight, a bunch of draggle-tail hens running around in there, clacking to beat the band, and most of them half naked where they had been pecked up so much. I told that farmer they had claustro-phobia and beakomania and the Lord knows what else; I told him he ought to let them out where they could scratch around a little and peck the ground instead of each other's rear ends. He took them out of battery, divided them up some, and in a few weeks they stopped pecking each other and grew their feathers back. Laid about as many eggs, too. But tell me, young feller, what's your business in Paris?" The meal was nearly finished but the doctor called for another bottle of wine before giving ear to Alex.

"I dub the English versions of French films mostly. I've had a couple of bit parts, too — they need Americans sometimes. But it's nearly a month since I've had any work."

"You're not occupied then? Not till you hear from one of those movie men of yours?" Alex replied that he was not.

"That's good. Well, I'm carrying on an experiment, a kind of hobby of mine, these experiments. I like to run off my own breeds of chicks and I get some of the durndest specimens that ever scratched corn — the Philadelphia Philanderer, the Pertinaceous Snapper, Rose-tailed Mithridates, and the Green Pouter, they're all mine, a real prize bunch. Not much good when it comes to eggs, but they're pretty strong on Oedipus complexes and compulsion neuroses. I had a case history on a Rose-tailed Mithridates hen, called her Jocasta, all set for these people at the conference house but I don't guess they'll be hearing about her now. Anyhow, I've got a proposition to make you. I was just getting out a fine new brand of fowl when it came time to fly over here for that confounded conference, so I brought a half-dozen of the eggs along — only partly hatched out. I had to tell that pack of poke-noses at the customs that I always have eggs for lunch when I travel and then here on this end I had to tell them I hadn't been able to eat because I was sick. Ever since I got here I've been trying to get those eggs hatched out but it seems like the chicks are staying in-doors this summer."

"How are you going about hatching them out, doctor?" Alex asked, for whom things were becoming rapidly clearer.

"Well, young feller, when you haven't got a Cadillac, you ride a Ford, and when you haven't got a Ford, you hop the nearest jackass. I've been trying to hatch those eggs out myself."

"I'm afraid I wouldn't be much good at hatching eggs," Alex put in hastily; "maybe we could get that *fille de chambre* . . ."

"No, if those eggs were going to hatch I suppose I would have got them out all right. I don't want to run down the *fille de chambre*, of course, but I'm a professional and she probably never has done much in the egg line. I was thinking that maybe more towels on the nest would do it, but I'm afraid it's going to have to be a sure-enough hen, a broody one. If you'd like to assist me, young feller, I think we can leave the sitting to the hen."

"But tell me, doctor, where do you plan to conduct the hatching?" Alex asked.

"That will have to be in the hotel," the doctor retorted, confirming Alex's anticipations. "What I want you to do is to go to the market with me early tomorrow morning and help smuggle the hen back into the hotel."

The doctor paid the bill and they repaired to the hotel, room number nine, to initiate Alex further into these undertakings.

The doctor opened the smallest of his cases, an unimposing straw bag, and exposed the contents for Alex's inspection. Inside, carefully packed in straw, were six eggs, but the eye of a poultry psychologist was required to detect what scientifically valuable specimentalia lay inside; to Alex they were merely six not unusual hens' eggs. There was little enough time to contemplate them, however; in an instant the doctor was stalking across the room with an antique ledger in his hands, thoroughly eared and big as a table top. He placed it on Alex's lap.

"This is my hen ledger," he informed him in an absorbed way. "It's been going since 1908 when I was a junior in college. That first entry there in the Vermont Flumenophobe, the earliest and one of the most successful of my eighty-three varieties — great big scapulars and hardly any primaries at all. Couldn't take them near a river, though, or they'd squawk like a turkey cock the day before Thanksgiving."

The ledger was full of most precise information: date of laying, length of incubation period, number of chicks reaching the first week, second week, fifth week, weight of hen, size of rooster's wattles and so on, all scrawled out in a hand that looked more Chinese than English, the most jagged and sprawling Alex had ever seen. Below these particulars was a series of alpha-beta-gammas connected by arrows and crosses which denoted the lineage of the breed. Alex's instruction was rapid, for the doctor had to go off to the Rue Ecole de Médecine to hear more speeches with only time for one sip of wine to sustain him through them all. But after the doctor's return that night Alex could see, from the high window in his own room, the now familiar figure crouched on a truly impressive heap of towels, apparently giving its egg-hatching powers one final chance before it was replaced in its office by a sure-enough hen.

A knocking at Alex's door roused him at six o'clock the following morning. It was the doctor, dressed and ready for the expedition to the market, and Alex was obliged to prepare himself in haste. The doctor stood about, waiting for Alex to dress, with a show of impatience, and soon they were moving, as quietly as could be, through the still-dark hallways, past the bedroom of the *patronne,* and so into the street. The market was not far and, once there, the doctor's sense of immediacy left him and he fell into a state of harmony with the birds around him. He stroked the hens and they responded with delighted clucks, he gobbled with the turkeys and they at once were all attention, he quacked with the ducks, and cackled with a pair of exceedingly flattered geese. The dawn progressed and it seemed that the doctor would never be done with his ministrations when quite abruptly something broke his reverie. It was a fine broody hen, white, with a maternal eye and a striking abundance of feathers in the under region of the abdomen. The doctor, with the air of a man whose professional interests have found scope, drew Alex's attention to those excellences which might otherwise have escaped him: the fine color in comb and wattles, the length and quality of neck and saddle hackles, the firm, wide spread of the toes, and a rare justness in the formation of the ear lappets. All search was ended; he had found his fowl. The purchase was effected and they made their way toward the hotel again, the hen, with whom some sort of communication had been set up, nestling in the doctor's arms.

The clocks struck seven-thirty as they approached the hotel entrance; the hopes that the chambermaid and *patronne* would still be abed began to rise in Alex's well-exercised breast. The doctor was wearing a long New England greatcoat, hardly necessary in the June weather but a garment which proved well adapted to the sequestration of hens. Alex entered first and was followed by the doctor who, for all his care, manifested a perceptible bulge on his left side where the hen was cradled. They advanced in a line across the entrance hall to the stairway and up, with gingerly steps, toward the first landing. It was then that they heard the tread of one descending and, in some perturbation glancing up, saw the *patronne* coming toward them as they gained the landing.

"Bonjour, messieurs, vous êtes matinals," she greeted them pleasantly. Alex explained that they had been out for a stroll before breakfast while the doctor edged around behind him, attempting to

hide the protuberance at his left side behind Alex's arm and back. *"Vous voulez vos pétits dejeuners tout de suite alors?"* their hostess enquired. Alex told her that there was no hurry for their breakfasts, trying at the same time to effect a speedy separation of the persons before and behind him. The doctor, he noticed, was attempting a transverse movement toward the stairs, but before the movement could be completed a distinct and audible cluck ruffled the air in the hollow of the stair well. Eyes swerved in the *patronne's* head, Alex coughed loudly, and the doctor, with a sforzando of chicken noises floating behind him, took to the stairs in long-shanked leaps.

"Comment?" ejaculated the surprised woman, looking at Alex for an explanation but he, parting from her without ceremony, only offered a few words about the doctor's provincial American speech and a state of nerves brought on by the demands of his work. With that he hurried up the stairs, followed by her suspicious gaze.

When Alex entered his room, the doctor was already preparing a nest in the straw case, six eggs ready for the hen's attentions. There was no reference to the incident on the stairs, his powers being absorbed by this more immediate business. The hen appeared to have no doubts as to her duties and was quick to settle down to the performance of them. One part of her audience was totally engaged, the connoisseur witnessing a peculiarly fine performance of some ancient classic, the other part, the guest of the connoisseur, attentive as one who must take an intelligent interest in that which he does not fully understand. The spectacle progressed toward a denouement which was obviously still remote; the audience attended. Time elapsed but the doctor was obviously unconscious of its passage until an unwelcome knock on the door interrupted the processes of nature. Startled, he jumped up to pull hen and case out of view, and Alex went to the door. He opened it a crack and in doing so made as much shuffling, coughing, and scraping noise as possible in order to drown emanations from the hen, who had begun to protest. It was Giselle, the *fille de chambre,* come to clean the room, and while she stood before him with ears pricked up and regard all curiosity, explaining her errand, Alex could see from the corner of his eye the doctor doing all he could to calm the displeased bird. Giselle was reluctant but Alex succeeded in persuading her to come back in five minutes and the door was shut again.

"Who was that, young feller?" the doctor instantly asked.

"That was the *fille de chambre,* the one you thought couldn't get the eggs out. She looked mighty interested, though. Anyhow she's coming back in five minutes to do the room."

The doctor's mind was working at a great speed; he rose to put his greatcoat on and addressed Alex in a muted voice.

"Have you got our keys handy?"

"Right in my pocket."

"All right. Now you go outside and beckon me when it's safe." The hall was empty and Alex beckoned; they climbed the stairs, which creaked, very loudly to their sensitive ears, and reached the next floor. A guest was locking his room; they passed behind him and got to Alex's room unnoticed. The doctor sat down rather wearily, caressing the hen and remarking that the city was not the place for a poultry-loving man, but no sooner was the remark out than a knock at this door obliged him to cover the hen with his greatcoat once more. At the door Alex managed to persuade the increasingly astonished *fille de chambre* to return in ten minutes. It was evident that a second transfer had to be effected, and that it had to take place between the time the *fille* finished the doctor's room and the time she began Alex's. They waited three minutes and then crept out on tiptoe; the halls were empty and they passed down the stairs to number nine and listened at the door. A bustle of sheets being smoothed and pillows being arranged indicated the *fille de chambre*'s presence inside; they listened and suddenly a step toward the door announced another important fact. The doctor shot down to the lavatory and turned the doorknob, but to no effect: the lavatory was occupied. Although a look of alarm passed over his face, he did not arrest his movements but disappeared into the shower room just as the chambermaid emerged from number nine. Alex suppressed those expressions of relief which offered to prevail in his face and escape from his throat; unwarranted they were in any case for, as he stood facing the *fille de chambre,* his ears were assailed by new sounds from the interior of the shower room. The events of the last quarter of an hour, mysterious to any bird accustomed only to the predictable life of coop and barnyard, had overcome the doctor's hen and she gave out a series of cackly wails, perhaps mourning her nest, but briefly enjoyed. The doctor's wits had not left him, however, for all his sixty-eight years, and the wails were almost immediately lost in the sound of water rushing out from the showerhead. Alex nodded to the maid as though nothing unusual were taking place and entered the doctor's room. Shortly, the doctor himself entered, his hair somewhat wet from the shower, but evidently satisfied with the outcome of their adventures. Without comment he opened the closet and from its shelves constructed a highboard around the egg case which he had placed on the floor inside. Next, the hen was nested and all seemed well. The two men sat for some time, savoring the pleasure of escape from peril and the relief such escape brings, before they got up and left the hotel, the doctor to go to the conference house and Alex to go to the main post office.

Alex returned to the hotel, rather weary and with no new prospects of a role, in the late afternoon, but found the doctor in an ebullient mood. At the time Alex arrived he was engaged in some sort of intimate communication with the hen, who had settled herself on the nest most peacefully after the occurrences of the morning.

"Chickens have short memories," the doctor remarked, "that's why they are better company than most people I know," and he went on to break some important news to Alex. "Well," he began, "it seems like some people in Paris want to hear more from me than those fellers over at the conference house do. They've got a big vulture from Tanganyika at the zoo here, with a wife for him, too, very rare birds, both of them, the only Vulturidae of their species outside Africa. Seems like she's willing, but the male just flops around all day like the bashful boy who took Jeannie May behind the barn and then didn't know what to do, and the people at the zoo haven't got any vulture chicks to show for their trouble. Sounds like a case of agoraphobia to me. Somehow they heard I was in Paris and they want me to come around next week and see what I can do. Do you figure you can go around with me to keep the language straight?"

"That's all right with me," Alex replied.

On the following morning the doctor put into effect a plan he had evolved for the avoidance of any further encounters between blackheaded *fille de chambre* and hen at room-cleaning time. Keeping an eye on the maid's activities, he retired to the shower before she appeared to tidy his room, with the hen as spectator to his ablutions, and remained there until the bed should be made and the floor swept. This plan was pursued with excellent success through-out the week until it seemed that nothing could prevent the meta-morphosis of egg to chick.

After supper Saturday they were sitting in the "Select" feeling amiable and satisfied. The doctor filled his pipe and turned to Alex.

"Young feller, seems to me like we've done a pretty good week's work. When a feller cuts corn all week, he ought to pull off his brogans Saturday night." The doctor paid the bill and they got into a taxi which took them to a club on Avenue Kléber. They visited several other bars in the vicinity and, later, took a cab to Mont-martre. In a night club there, they fell in with some French actresses and Italian businessmen. The hours went by so pleasantly that neither the doctor nor Alex noticed their passage. Finally, the com-pany thinned and the doctor asked Alex what time it was. Alex looked at his watch incredulously and they jumped up and raced outside. They blinked; it was broad daylight. Alex looked at his watch again. It was a quarter past seven. For ten minutes they could not find a taxi; when they did, they urged him to drive as fast as possible. The streets were not full and their progress was rela-tively quick, but the Sunday morning leisureliness of the atmos-phere in the city jarred on their mood. They crossed Pont St. Michel, turned onto Rue Vaugirard, and in a moment the taxi pulled up. The driver was paid hurriedly and as he drew away Alex realized they had gone several blocks too far. When they got to the hotel door, it was past eight.

Alex was somewhat winded, for the doctor showed himself capable of lengthy strides, as though nothing had been drunk the night be-fore. He bounded up the stairs, with Alex in his trail, as far as the first floor. But what greeted them there was far from reassuring. The hen was sitting on a table in the hallway in a vocal frame of mind and her six hatched-out chicks were scrambling about the floor in front of Giselle, who was trying to gather them up, while the *patronne* and several guests in states of demi-attire looked on with surprise in every feature.

"Well, looks like they hatched out all right," the doctor com-mented, waving the *fille de chambre* away and collecting the chicks in great swoops. He took them through the open door into his room and quickly reappeared to apprehend the hen. Meanwhile Alex was obliged to deal with the *patronne,* whose understanding could

not compass motives that might lead anyone to hatch baby chi
in a hotel.

"Mais pourquoi, monsieur, pourquoi avez-vous emporté
poule?" she kept repeating. There was no answer to that questi
No reasonable explanation could have been made had Alex
tempted it and the *patronne,* whose orderly mind made no ot
requirement of her guests than that their behavior be reasonal
but exacted that as a minimum, set the departure of hen, chic
doctor, and Alex for one hour from that moment.

Meeting the deadline was rendered difficult not by the amount
packing to be done, but because of the disproportionate time
doctor spent examining the new chicks. There was, howev
little to be discovered of the chicks' qualities so early and the doc
eventually deployed them in the straw-filled case and descended
a waiting taxi. Alex followed with the straw-filled case and
patronne saw them off, not unkindly but with relief.

When they were disposed in the taxi, it occurred to Alex th
they had no address to give. The doctor was unconcerned, tak
up entirely with the chickens, but Alex interrupted his ruminatio

"Where are we going, doctor?"

"Some hotel, young feller. You don't take a Sunday drive wi
half the barnyard in your pocket."

"You can't get into a hotel with chickens." The doctor paused
moment and looked thoughtful.

"Maybe not. Seems like these hotels are too full of durn fools
have room for anything else." He paused again, musing. "Loc
like we'll have to board these chickens somewhere."

"Where? On a farm?"

"Well, I don't see any farms around here. I've got to be close
these chickens."

"How about a pet shop, doctor?"

"That's it, young feller," the doctor replied emphatically, in
commendatory tone. "You've hit it."

The cab took them to a pet shop on the Quai de l'Hôtel de Vil
open for the Sunday trade, and Alex went inside to bargain wi
the owner, a large woman whose face looked like a raw side of bee
The doctor paid a week's board in advance, remarking that it co
durn near as much to board a chicken in Paris as a homo sapie
and the cab took them to a hotel a block and a half away. There w

a surcharge on the cab fare for the transportation of the birds, but Alex said nothing about that to the doctor. Both of them slept through most of the remainder of the day.

The morning came, a bright summer morning with a pleasant ruffling wind and high pink clouds, a day which ought to have cheered the dourest and most retired of vultures. When the doctor and Alex arrived at the zoo, the animals were all luxuriating in the warmth of the sun and only the bears showed signs of distress. As they went along they came to a slate-gray heron with a grouchy manner who walked about like an old man. The doctor had only to stand before the fencing to gain the creature's confidence. It approached and he began to reminisce. He had treated a heron of this species in Boston once. There was an emu next, and golden pheasants from China, and finally the vulture cages. A good many vultures were in stock, eyes like the hollows in a skull when viewed straight on, bare skin of a powdery gray-blue or sometimes scarlet and purple color around the head, and collars of a ghastly whitish fuzz-like texture. They walked about in an obscene gait or sat on the perches folding their wings and making foul noises. It did not take the doctor long to identify his patient. One cage held two of the birds, a female who did all the vile things one expects of a vulture and a male in the corner of the cage who was taking no apparent interest in life. He was crouched down in the dust, staring at nothing, with slumping neck, wings folded so as to trail on the ground behind him, and bluish talons stuck forward. He was of a large species but his posture made him appear to be relatively small.

The *directeur,* when they found him, resembled certain of the animals in his zoo, a burrowing mammal or perhaps some quaint desert rodent. But he was cordial and spoke excellent English, to Alex's great relief. He gave them lunch and assured the doctor that he took a great interest in this cure and that anything necessary to effect it would be provided upon request. During the meal such a quantity of bird talk was provided with the meat that Alex felt relieved to go back to the scene of psychotherapy.

"Just as I thought," the doctor said, a professional tone coming into his voice, upon return to the patient. "A case of agoraphobia. That means that the subject has a fear of broad avenues, open spaces, wide prospects, etc. This is complicated a little because the patient is caged up so he doesn't have to cross the open spaces, but he can't help seeing them all the time with these big paths and walks in front of him — that's why he keeps himself down in the corner like somebody's aunt and won't look out of the cage. What we are going to have to do is to get him up into some trees with a lot of foliage."

The cure required several days. On the first afternoon the doctor merely squatted in front of the cage making peculiar noises at the bird and trying "to focus his mind on exterior objects." On the second the vulture and his mate were transferred to a cage which was at once more sequestered and gave the psychologist better access to patient. Already there were signs of success; the vulture ceased his crouchings from time to time and began to hop about and spread his wings. Occasionally the director of the zoo came around to inquire about their progress and the attendants and keepers formed an unfailing audience. But the vulture as yet gave no evidence of interest in his mate; the strains of agoraphobia still swelled his brain so that he was incapable of bestowing attentions elsewhere. In the hope that enforced concentration on the pivotal necessity, meat, a taste for which even agoraphobia had failed to expel from the bird's psychical equipment, might cause him to gather up his faculties with an intensity sufficient to overcome his mental imbalance, the doctor devised a curious plan. He climbed up onto the cage at feeding time, cut the vulture's ration into a number of small bits, and tied them onto the end of a long string. This he let down into the cage and dangled before the bird, leading him around and around in circles and eventually allowing him to seize the bloody morsel. Then he tied another piece to the string and repeated the performance. After this had been done three or four times, the subject began to show signs of anger; his slow waddle gave way to swifter steps and gestures until he flew at the meat and tore it with his beak. That in vultures as in man lassitude is the one hopeless state, and where anger resides love may also stir, the doctor remarked when the day's work was done, and added with conviction that there would be little vultures yet.

In the morning they went first to the office of the *directeur* to arrange another transfer. This was quickly done and as they were going out the *directeur* handed the doctor a letter, postmarked Cambridge and bearing the return address of Trinity College.

"A feller would say I was getting to be an international celebrity," the doctor remarked upon opening it. "Anybody but one of these ostrich-squawkers over at the convention house on Rue Ecole de Médecine would. Says they want me to go to Cambridge University and give a lecture to the faculty of agriculture in full concourse as soon as I can — they've had a bad outburst of chicken pecking all over the British Isles and they can't figure out what to do about it. Durn sight better honorarium than they were going to give me here, too." The doctor fell silent a moment. He was unusually pleased. "Better go over with me, hadn't you, young feller? From the times I've heard them talk I'd say I'll need a translator over there about as bad as I do here."

"Well, I haven't got any roles yet, doctor. It sounds like a good idea to me." The doctor nodded and was lost in obviously agreeable thoughts as they walked toward the aviary.

There was a large domed cage with a number of trees inside and a pond at the center where the eagles were kept with several of the rarer vultures. It was into this cage that the patient and his mate were introduced, and the neurotic male immediately took to the trees. At feeding time the doctor enticed him down and fed him once again with a string. Alex noticed that the doctor placed powder from a little packet in the last chunk of meat he gave the bird.

When they returned on the next morning the patient's demeanor was utterly changed. He strutted about with chest protruding and wings stirring up the dust. Then he extended both wings and flew to a commanding position on the bough of a tree, only to zoom down in his lady's eye and strut again. When he walked he picked up his legs like a soldier and put them down again with a thump. This behavior constituted vulture courtship, and though in the eyes of mammals it might not have been prepossessing, the female vulture was thoroughly taken by it. At feeding time the doctor emptied several packets of powder into the subjects' food.

It was now evident that their duties at the Jardin des Plantes had been successfully brought to an end. Delight reigned among the keepers and the *directeur* came out to say good-by, all gratitude. He promised the doctor to send him news of further developments and both felt confident of good results, reproductively speaking, in a short time.

"Exactly what was the powder you gave the subject, doctor?" Alex asked as they walked out the gates.

"That powder?" the doctor caught him up with interest. "Well, young feller, people who practiced my profession in earlier times didn't hesitate to use what they called a love philter on proper occasions — improper occasions, too — but since they've taken to calling themselves psychologists they've gotten too sophisticated for that. According to my way of thinking it never does a bird any harm to administer a little aphrodisiac when the symptoms call for it."

They had just returned to the doctor's room after supper to refill his tobacco pouch when the telephone jangled. It was for Dr. Nestor. From the earpiece rapid metallic sentences came forth and these were punctuated from time to time by the doctor's one-syllable replies. Then he said, "We'll be right over," and replaced the receiver. Alex waited for him to sit down again and disclose whatever information the conversation had put him in possession of.

"Looks like we'll have to go straight out to the zoo," he told Alex. "That vulture is out of control and he's going after a very chaste lady eagle now. He's already been at that mate of his but it must not be enough for him. Sounds like some people I know. . . ." The doctor sighed. "And the *directeur* is downright flummoxed. 'I did not intend that the cure should be so radical,' he says. I can't say as I did either."

When they drew up at the gates of the zoo, the *directeur* was waiting for them in a nervous condition. "The situation is very grave," he declared. "How could such a situation come about between a vulture and an eagle? There is no precedent for this." Alex walked behind the doctor and the *directeur*. Already shrieks and cries could be heard from the birds in the largest cage and the other animals had become uneasy with the disturbance. An elk stamped and an alligator slid into his pond. At the opening in the wire net five keepers were waiting furnished with enormous electric torches. There was very little moon. Three of the keepers stationed themselves at points around the cage, lights in hand; the other two attended the gate to the cage. The doctor put on a heavy leather coat, leather gloves, and a mask with goggles. Then he entered the enclosure.

In the shifting light it was possible to see swooping forms in the air and dark hulks or hunchbacked shapes situated on the boughs of the trees. High in the foliage a continuous clamor and rustling sound were breaking on the air. None of the birds was below. The doctor threw a large chunk of meat into a corner and went over and stood in the corner opposite. One or two eagles descended to feed, but the disorder above continued without respite. Suddenly, an eagle struck down toward the ground. She cocked her head fiercely and looked about with a glittering eye. Her wings were still half extended; she ruffled them in an attitude of pride. Soon afterwards the author of complications, the doctor's unsatisfactory patient, alighted with an exaggerated flurry of feathers and commenced strutting a few yards away. This was the signal for several other birds to come down from the treetops: his proper mate first, a jealous wife from appearances, and two male eagles who must have thought little of a vulture's demonstrations directed toward one of their own breed. They formed a loose and extended circle, immobile except for the male vulture, whose strutting became ever more foppish and extravagant. One could see that this was a crucial moment, a crucial juxtaposition of birds and the exacerbated birdish emotions which were in play under their several sets of breast feathers. The death or injury of any one of the five specimens in question would be an expensive matter for the zoo and a grievous one for the *directeur,* who was proud of the range of his collection.

The doctor stood with the air of a man who knows that strong forces are best controlled by a slight touch at the very moment one sees them prepared to take a new course, the current which must be diverted, not dammed. On the ground by his feet there was a portable, bell-like cage with an open bottom so that it could be put over a bird as he stood on the ground. He held a piece of meat in his right hand. With a swift movement he pitched it over toward the circle of birds. It landed just between the male eagles. At the same moment he began to make a noise in his throat which had no correlation in words but obviously had a precise one in the ears of vultures. The strutting bird, in whose breast the pendulum of the affections had swung from indifference to reckless lust, left the two females on either side of him and advanced. The doctor came on to meet him and the patient apparently recognized his old friend, but he turned without greeting to seek out the quarter from which the alluring breeding sounds had come. The doctor was quick. He distracted the bird for a moment with a piece of meat. It could not hold his attention long, but it was long enough to clap a hood over his head and the cage over his person (and his persona, too, the doctor observed aloud). The keepers came in now and took him to a private cage where the doctor could consult with him more freely. Confused, angry, and unsatisfied, he gave vent to peculiar vocifera-tions which were muffled in the hood.

The doctor's vigil would be long and the keepers were dismissed. Alex wandered off to stroll in the dark shadows of the alleys and rest on the benches in the lanes; he returned and wandered off again. In the early hours of the morning the doctor called out for him and announced that he and the *directeur* were satisfied that all was well, and the *directeur* escorted them to the big iron gates on the Place Valhubert, opened them, and bid them good night. The next morning early, however, they returned, and the doctor spent several hours with the vulture, but his attention was hardly necessary; a catharsis had taken place and the vulture's behavior was entirely normal. He and his mate were transferred to the cage where they had originally been lodged, and the doctor told Alex he could make reservations on the nine forty-five flight to London the next day. They walked across the Seine together, and Alex went off to a travel bureau, while the doctor spent his afternoon at the pet shop of the Quai de l'Hôtel de Ville. At supper the doctor was gloomy; two of the chicks had died.

The flight was smooth and short and they arrived in time to have lunch and several quarts of bitter at a pub near King's Cross Station before boarding the train. When Alex and the doctor got down from the train at Cambridge, the station clock showed three thirty-five. A good many passengers had got off before them and milled about the ticket barrier and tea stand with bags in their hands. Up the platform, two elderly men of distinguished appearance, and a third, very elegantly dressed, a man of about twenty stood scanning the length of the train as it emptied out through the carriage doors.

"Figure they're looking for us, young feller?" the doctor asked, but did not pause for a reply before he went up to the party. Alex followed him closely.

"How' do," the doctor addressed them. "Were you looking for the poultry professor from Great Neck University, Vermont?"

"Why . . . yes," the elder of the dons replied, a dignified man, balding somewhat, with hair fringing the dome. He gazed at the doctor's rumpled corduroy trousers an instant before he collected himself. "Is it Dr. Nestor?" he asked, now smiling cordially.

"I'm Dr. Nestor. This young feller with me is Mr. Alexander Lovejoy."

The white-headed don introduced his party: himself as Dr. Teritus Champwell, Professor of Animal Husbandry, his colleague as Sir Arthur Grange, Regius Professor of Agronomy, and the young man, an undergraduate up to do some special work during the summer term, as Christopher Nearball, who was to help in showing them about.

"Perhaps you would join me in my rooms for tea," Professor Champwell said when he had made these introductions. "Afterwards if you would like to . . ."

" 'Fraid my gizzard hasn't evolved in the direction of tea, professor," the doctor broke in. "Do you suppose we can have a look at some of those chickens? Maybe Mr. Lovejoy will have some tea with this young feller here who's doing the summer work."

They agreed to meet for dinner in three hours and Christopher Nearball led Alex off to his rooms across a cobbled courtyard in the largest of the colleges, chattering pleasantly and urbanely all the way and pointing out important sights. Christopher Nearball took a bottle of cognac from his closet and poured two tumblers full; they drank, resting comfortably in the arms of upholstered chairs, and refilled the tumblers once or twice. When they rose from the chairs to go out to tea, Christopher Nearball was more relaxed than before and his manner less formal — it had become expansive in fact. They crossed Kings Parade and walked toward a large market place.

"Your universities across the Atlantic aren't on exactly the same plan as ours, are they?" Christopher Nearball began.

"No, they aren't," Alex agreed and commenced to explain the plan of American universities.

"Yes, I had understood this in part," Christopher Nearball interrupted. "You know Cambridge and Oxford accept degrees from only two of your universities. Rather stuffy of them, I think." He guided Alex into a narrow lane which ran off the market square, and began anew before Alex was able to make use of his own tongue. "A friend of mine, a lady who has traveled in the United States a bit, was telling me about games in American universities. Someone took her to a match of American football. Professional players, are they usually? Of course we play a lot of games here, too, but it's a different affair — just for the sport of it sort of thing."

"They aren't exactly professionals . . ."

"Oh, yes, and she showed me one of your horror comics. Extraordinary business. They give them to the children to read in grade schools if I'm not mistaken."

"No, they don't give them to the children in school."

"Oh, they don't then? Well, I've always wanted to visit in America and see it for myself — one can't judge without knowing firsthand. When I told my parents I should like to go, they said, 'Why, Christopher, of all places to want to visit.' They just couldn't understand even when I'd explained. Made it into sort of a family joke."

They entered a building and climbed a flight of stairs to a room almost the size of a ballroom with mobiles hanging from the ceiling, an espresso coffee bar in the center, and tables and chairs around the walls which were decorated with greatly enlarged photographs of peasants at the time of some revolution. Here they spent a lugubrious hour before returning to the college for dinner.

Dinner was served in a high, vaulted hall and they were seated on a dais at one end of a table known as the high table. Throughout the soup and the main course, the utmost decorum prevailed, and the doctor, evidently absorbed in his own thoughts, was exceedingly taciturn, although Professor Champwell on one side and Sir Arthur on the other made polite attempts to draw him out. Alex had become slightly uncomfortable on the doctor's account by the time the dessert was brought in.

Just then, without warning, the doctor started up from his place like Archimedes from the bath. "Young feller, you want to come with me?" he said to Alex. "I think I've got the solution."

"Solution to what?" Alex demanded, but the doctor left the question unanswered and turned to Professor Champwell.

"Professor," he said, "do you know where a man can get hold of a piece of pliable plastic?"

Professor Champwell rose and led them out while the other diners continued the meal, appearing not to notice the disturbance, although the faces of some of them froze. They crossed the courtyard, went out of the gate, and proceeded down to the physical science laboratories. A porter admitted them on a word from Professor Champwell.

"Professor," Dr. Nestor commenced once they were inside, "I think the way to make these poultry stop pecking each other is to stick some spectacles on their beaks."

"Spectacles?" the professor enunciated.

"Yessir, spectacles. I'm not talking about glass spectacles. Mighty few hens have bad vision and even when they do they can still peck a good deal of corn and hold on to their mental balance just about the same as another hen. Wouldn't want to admit a bunch of poultry oculists to the enclosure anyhow — seems to me there're enough people fooling with the hens as it is. No sir, what I've got in mind is opaque plastic spectacles. If you put the specs on their beaks, they ought to act as a guard — their beaks won't sink in past the feathers and you'll have a bunch of poultry acting surprised as a goose on a duck egg. Before you know it they'll cut that pecking out. Won't bother their feeding, though — you know a hen doesn't need to sight down her beak fo feed. She pecks out with her whole head and neck. *De corpore in toto* most of the time."

"That's really admirable, Dr. Nestor. Do you think it will work?" Professor Champwell asked.

"That's what I'm getting ready to see." The doctor made Alex hold the strip of plastic for him while he deftly cut out four pairs of spectacles and filed the edges smooth. Then he heated them in water, fashioned them to the necessary shape, and cooled them slowly.

"Have you got any hens around here?" he asked the professor.

"There are several in the laboratory and a good many more out at the experimental station."

"Well, I only need several. They aren't dosed up or anything like that?"

"No. They were just brought in this afternoon."

"Mean peckers?"

"I understand that they are quite hardy."

In the laboratory the doctor affixed the spectacles to the beaks of four hens and put them in a cage together. The three men stood around waiting expectantly. But the hens only ruffled their feathers and jumped up onto the roost.

"Have you got a bright light?" the doctor asked when it had become apparent that the hens were going to remain somnolent. "And some corn." Alex helped the professor to place a strong light in the cage and the doctor threw corn onto the cage floor. Immediately the hens aroused themselves and, one by one, they descended from the perch. The spectators waited, but not for long; all at once a large, white, glossy hen pecked out viciously at a smaller one feeding by her side. The smaller hen made a motion, as if to jump aside with an outcry, but perceived that she was not hurt and settled herself to feed as before. The large hen pecked tentatively a second time, but there was no proper reaction from her victim, and she emitted a muffled sort of squawk, cocked her head this way and that, and returned to the corn. The spectators continued to watch in silence; two more hens attempted to peck, but after a short time they abandoned their attempts confusedly, and all was calm. The time for the doctor's lecture was drawing near and they turned off the lights and made their departure.

The doctor's audience was small, "select" as Professor Champwell put it in introducing him, and composed mostly of dons since few undergraduates in agriculture came up for the summer term. In the course of his lecture the doctor drank all the water in the pitcher provided for him and Christopher Nearball was sent out to refill it. He stood at a table on a raised platform with one hand on the chicken ledger which lay there and the other free to gesticulate. During the first minutes of his lecture, a journalist photographed him a number of times in this posture, and Alex was given to understand that a celebrated London weekly paper planned to do a sketch of him in the next Sunday's edition. Much of what the doctor said was familiar to Alex, being, in substance, the speech he had prepared for the convention but never delivered.

"It is reasonable to assume, and evident from observation, that dementia praecox in domestic fowls occurs with greatly increased frequency under the increasingly specialized patterns of living modern hens find imposed on them. Any attempt to resist the drift of change in these patterns would be unrealistic and retrogressive — you know any durn fool can start out to paddle upstream against a six-mile current, but that doesn't mean he's going to get to Grand Junction. Still, I could tell you about a friend of mine, a Mrs. Fensterchurch, who used to keep hens in her back yard, like a scrabble farmer's wife — she wasn't one, though — and got a pretty good stack of eggs every evening and no dementia praecox, not even any hysterics, as a matter of fact. In principle, however, we have to assume that contemporary hens are going to live under contemporary conditions, and that we can expect mental imbalance to appear in current modes and proportions. If I were a human psychologist, I would put little confidence in any procedure directed toward the total exorcism of guilt; I would not expect a patient so treated to emerge in a state greatly preferable to that of a patient who revels in guilt feelings. I would endeavor, instead, to have the patient come to the end of his problems in his own manner and, to the greatest degree possible, through his own exertions. I'm a poultry psychologist, though. With poultry there is no question of guilt because they are incapable of excogitation and analysis. Since they can't think (especially the Rose-tailed Mithridates — that's the most irrational bunch of poultry I've ever run across) they need someone to aid them when they fall into neurotic or psychotic states.

"Developing means of treatment and therapy for chickens, therefore, is a much more absolute procedure than it properly can be with homo sapiens. Excluding rationalism frees the poultry scholar from an enormous range of troublesome variables which complicate the lives of just about everyone else. What a poultry man has to have is enough patience to squat down with the hens awhile, long enough to do some sure-enough observation, and then a little canniness to hit on a treatment, the simpler the better. By nature a hen wants to get down and lay; if she isn't doing it, it's not because she's worrying about Uncle Egbert — probably has more to do with the corn or what's happening to her tail feathers. And those feathers always respond to treatment a good bit quicker than Uncle Egbert ever would. That's why the ratio of poultry cures to treatments is so much higher than the sapiens ratio — this is statistics I'm talking about, not any personal claim." The doctor's treatment of theoretical questions continued for the greater part of an hour, but there had been almost no coughing or scraping of chairs when he finished it and went on to purely practical questions.

"Now I'll tell you about some of the poultry I've bred myself. A rooster's a pretty lucky sort of bird," he said, turning over the leaves of the chicken ledger. "He's got most of what it takes to keep a fowl happy, what with a barnyard full of hens turning up their tail feathers at him, so if you're breeding for dementia praecox or catatonics, you've got to deduce a little bit on your roosters — the delicate balance of mind requisite may easily be there in potential, but not, commonly, in its realization. There is no problem, on the other hand, in selecting the hens — sometimes they don't exhibit the impulse to breed at all, and you know something must have moldered the beans — same as you would with anybody else who twiddles around that way."

The doctor continued his remarks through the histories of several of his breeds, and finally came to the third part of his lecture, which concerned the use of spectacles in poultry. He outlined his ideas briefly, telling his audience that he could say no more at the present stage of experimentation, and threw the floor open to questions.

When the applause had finally died down, a precise, nervous young don of about thirty-five rose to speak. "Dr. Nestor," he said, "your concept of spectacles for poultry is indubitably an ingenious one, but I am rather at a loss to see how they can prevent pecking when they are pushed far up on the fowl's beak, as they must inevitably be after the bird has made several attempts to peck."

"No, they must not inevitably be. Not if you make them right. Professor Champwell, would you send the boy out to get those hens at the laboratory?" Christopher Nearball went out to fetch the hens.

The doctor turned back to the audience to answer further questions from the floor. But his hearers were rising, advancing toward the platform, trying to attract his attention, and asking so many questions that he could answer only a fraction of them. By the time Christopher Nearball arrived with the cage of hens the speaker's platform was so thronged he could scarcely make his way to the table. The dons stood about until after midnight watching the birds, discussing the invention of spectacles for them, and questioning Dr. Nestor unremittingly. Finally, Professor Champwell took Alex and the doctor away to guest rooms in the college, thanked them graciously, and said good night. Alex was on the point of going into his room when the doctor stopped him.

"Young feller," the doctor asked, "did you catch the name of that picture-taker at the lecture tonight?"

"No, I didn't get his name, but I know what paper he works for."

"Step in here a minute, young feller." Alex followed the doctor into his room. "Wonder if there's a phone anywhere around here," the doctor said aloud, then noticed one by the bed. "See if you can get that paper on the phone for me."

"What are you going to tell them?" Alex asked when he had placed the call, but just then the connection was made.

"Hello, Circulation Department?" the doctor said, taking the receiver. "Well, give me the Circulation Department. Hello, this is Dr. Nestor, the poultry lecturer. Suppose you could send four or five copies of that article about me to the Psychology Conference in the Rue Ecole de Médecine in Paris?" The doctor replaced the receiver. "Seems to me the proper circulation ought to include those durn fools," he said, and filled his pipe.

(*From New World Writing*)

EVERYTHING THAT RISES MUST CONVERGE

BY FLANNERY O'CONNOR

HER DOCTOR had told Julian's mother that she must lose twenty pounds on account of her blood pressure, so on Wednesday nights Julian had to take her downtown on the bus for a reducing class at the Y. The reducing class was designed for working girls over fifty, who weighed from 165 to 200 pounds. His mother was one of the slimmer ones, but she said ladies did not tell their age or weight. She would not ride on the buses by herself at night since they had been integrated, and because the reducing class was one of her few pleasures, necessary for her health, and *free,* she said Julian could at least put himself out to take her, considering all she did for him. Julian did not like to consider all she did for him, but every Wednesday night he braced himself and took her.

She was almost ready to go, standing before the hall mirror, putting on her hat, while he, his hands behind him, appeared pinned to the door frame, waiting like Saint Sebastian for the arrows to begin piercing him. The hat was new and had cost her seven dollars and a half. She kept saying, "Maybe I shouldn't have paid that for it. No, I shouldn't have. I'll take it off and return it tomorrow. I shouldn't have bought it."

Julian raised his eyes to heaven. "Yes, you should have bought it," he said. "Put it on and let's go." It was a hideous hat. A purple velvet flap came down on one side of it and stood up on the other; the rest of it was green and looked like a cushion with the stuffing out. He decided it was less comical than jaunty and pathetic.

Everything that gave her pleasure was small and depressed him.

She lifted the hat one more time and set it down slowly on top of her head. Two wings of gray hair protruded on either side of her florid face, but her eyes, sky-blue, were as innocent and untouched by experience as they must have been when she was ten. Were it not that she was a widow who had struggled fiercely to feed and clothe and put him through school and who was supporting him still, "until he got on his feet," she might have been a little girl that he had to take to town.

"It's all right, it's all right," he said. "Let's go." He opened the door himself and started down the walk to get her going. The sky was a dying violet and the houses stood out darkly against it, bulbous liver-colored monstrosities of a uniform ugliness though no two were alike. Since this had been a fashionable neighborhood forty years ago, his mother persisted in thinking they did well to have an apartment in it. Each house had a narrow collar of dirt around it in which sat, usually, a grubby child. Julian walked with his hands in his pockets, his head down and thrust forward and his eyes glazed with the determination to make himself completely numb during the time he would be sacrificed to her pleasure.

The door closed and he turned to find the dumpy figure, surmounted by the atrocious hat, coming toward him. "Well," she said, "you only live once and paying a little more for it, I at least won't meet myself coming and going."

"Some day I'll start making money," Julian said gloomily — he knew he never would — "and you can have one of those jokes whenever you take the fit." But first they would move. He visualized a place where the nearest neighbors would be three miles away on either side.

"I think you're doing fine," she said, drawing on her gloves. "You've only been out of school a year. Rome wasn't built in a day."

She was one of the few members of the Y reducing class who arrived in hat and gloves and who had a son who had been to college. "It takes time," she said, "and the world is in such a mess. This hat looked better on me than any of the others, though when she brought it out I said, 'Take that thing back. I wouldn't have it on my head,' and she said, 'Now wait till you see it on,' and when she put it on me, I said, 'We-ull,' and she said, 'If you ask me, that hat does something for you and you do something for the hat, and besides,' she said, 'with that hat, you won't meet yourself coming and going.' "

Julian thought he could have stood his lot better if she had been selfish, if she had been an old hag who drank and screamed at him. He walked along, saturated in depression, as if in the midst of his martyrdom he had lost his faith. Catching sight of his long, hopeless, irritated face, she stopped suddenly with a grief-stricken look, and pulled back on his arm. "Wait on me," she said. "I'm going back to the house and take this thing off and tomorrow I'm going to return it. I was out of my head. I can pay the gas bill with that seven-fifty."

He caught her arm in a vicious grip. "You are not going to take it back," he said. "I like it."

"Well," she said, "I don't think I ought . . ."

"Shut up and enjoy it," he muttered, more depressed than ever.

"With the world in the mess it's in," she said, "it's a wonder we can enjoy anything. I tell you, the bottom rail is on the top."

Julian sighed.

"Of course," she said, "if you know who you are, you can go anywhere." She said this every time he took her to the reducing class. "Most of them in it are not our kind of people," she said, "but I can be gracious to anybody. I know who I am."

"They don't give a damn for your graciousness," Julian said savagely. "Knowing who you are is good for one generation only. You haven't the foggiest idea where you stand now or who you are."

She stopped and allowed her eyes to flash at him. "I most certainly do know who I am," she said, "and if you don't know who you are, I'm ashamed of you."

"Oh hell," Julian said.

"Your great-grandfather was a former governor of this state," she said. "Your grandfather was a prosperous landowner. Your grandmother was a Godhigh."

"Will you look around you," he said tensely, "and see where you are now?" and he swept his arm jerkily out to indicate the neighborhood, which the growing darkness at least made less dingy.

"You remain what you are," she said. "Your great-grandfather had a plantation and two hundred slaves."

"There are no more slaves," he said irritably.

"They were better off when they were," she said. He groaned to see that she was off on that topic. She rolled onto it every few days like a train on an open track. He knew every stop, every junction, every swamp along the way, and knew the exact point at which her conclusion would roll majestically into the station: "It's ridiculous. It's simply not realistic. They should rise, yes, but on their own side of the fence."

"Let's skip it," Julian said.

"The ones I feel sorry for," she said, "are the ones that are half white. They're tragic."

"Will you skip it?"

"Suppose we were half white. We would certainly have mixed feelings."

"I have mixed feelings now," he groaned.

"Well let's talk about something pleasant," she said. "I remember going to Grandpa's when I was a little girl. Then the house had double stairways that went up to what was really the second floor — all the cooking was done on the first. I used to like to stay down in the kitchen on account of the way the walls smelled. I would sit with my nose pressed against the plaster and take deep breaths. Actually the place belonged to the Godhighs but your grandfather Chestny paid the mortgage and saved it for them. They were in reduced circumstances," she said, "but reduced or not, they never forgot who they were."

"Doubtless that decayed mansion reminded them," Julian muttered. He never spoke of it without contempt or thought of it without longing. He had seen it once when he was a child before it had been sold. The double stairways had rotted and been torn down. Negroes were living in it. But it remained in his mind as his mother had known it. It appeared in his dreams regularly. He would stand on the wide porch, listening to the rustle of oak leaves, then wander through the high-ceilinged hall into the parlor that opened onto it and gaze at the worn rugs and faded draperies. It occurred to him that it was he, not she, who could have appreciated it. He preferred its threadbare elegance to anything he could name and it was because of it that all the neighborhoods they had lived in had been a torment to him — whereas she had hardly known the difference. She called her insensitivity "being adjustable."

"And I remember the old darky who was my nurse, Caroline. There was no better person in the world. I've always had a great respect for my colored friends," she said. "I'd do anything in the world for them and they'd . . ."

"Will you for God's sake get off that subject?" Julian said. When he got on a bus by himself, he made it a point to sit down beside a Negro, in reparation as it were for his mother's sins.

"You're mighty touchy tonight," she said. "Do you feel all right?"

"Yes I feel all right," he said. "Now lay off."

She pursed her lips. "Well, you certainly are in a vile humor," she observed. "I just won't speak to you at all."

They had reached the bus stop. There was no bus in sight and Julian, his hands still jammed in his pockets and his head thrust forward, scowled down the empty street. The frustration of having to wait on the bus as well as ride on it began to creep up his neck like a hot hand. The presence of his mother was borne in upon him as she gave a pained sigh. He looked at her bleakly. She was holding herself very erect under the preposterous hat, wearing it like a banner of her imaginary dignity. There was in him an evil urge to break her spirit. He suddenly unloosened his tie and pulled it off and put it in his pocket.

She stiffened. "Why must you look like *that* when you take me to town?" she said. "Why must you deliberately embarrass me?"

"If you'll never learn where you are," he said, "you can at least learn where I am."

"You look like a — thug," she said.

"Then I must be one," he murmured.

"I'll just go home," she said. "I will not bother you. If you can't do a little thing like that for me . . ."

Rolling his eyes upward, he put his tie back on. "Restored to my class," he muttered. He thrust his face toward her and hissed, "True culture is in the mind, the *mind*," he said, and tapped his head, "the mind."

"It's in the heart," she said, "and in how you do things and how you do things is because of who you *are*."

"Nobody in the damn bus cares who you are."

"I care who I am," she said icily.

The lighted bus appeared on top of the next hill and as it approached, they moved out into the street to meet it. He put his hand under her elbow and hoisted her up on the creaking step. She entered with a little smile, as if she were going into a drawing room where everyone had been waiting for her. While he put in the tokens, she sat down on one of the broad front seats for three which faced the aisle. A thin woman with protruding teeth and long yellow hair was sitting on the end of it. His mother moved up beside her and left room for Julian beside herself. He sat down and looked at the floor across the aisle where a pair of thin feet in red and white canvas sandals were planted.

His mother immediately began a general conversation meant to attract anyone who felt like talking. "Can it get any hotter?" she said and removed from her purse a folding fan, black with a Japanese scene on it, which she began to flutter before her.

"I reckon it might could," the woman with the protruding teeth said, "but I know for a fact my apartment couldn't get no hotter."

"It must get the afternoon sun," his mother said. She sat forward and looked up and down the bus. It was half filled. Everybody was white. "I see we have the bus to ourselves," she said. Julian cringed.

"For a change," said the woman across the aisle, the owner of the red and white canvas sandals. "I come on one the other day and they were thick as fleas — up front and all through."

"The world is in a mess everywhere," his mother said. "I don't know how we've let it get in this fix."

"What gets my goat is all those boys from good families stealing automobile tires," the woman with the protruding teeth said. "I told my boy, I said you may not be rich but you been raised right and if I ever catch you in any such mess, they can send you on to the reformatory. Be exactly where you belong."

"Training tells," his mother said. "Is your boy in high school?"

"Ninth grade," the woman said.

"My son just finished college last year. He wants to write but he's selling typewriters until he gets started," his mother said.

The woman leaned forward and peered at Julian. He threw her such a malevolent look that she subsided against the seat. On the floor across the aisle there was an abandoned newspaper. He got up and got it and opened it out in front of him. His mother discreetly continued the conversation in a lower tone but the woman across the aisle said in a loud voice, "Well that's nice. Selling typewriters is close to writing. He can go right from one to the other."

"I tell him," his mother said, "that Rome wasn't built in a day."

Behind the newspaper Julian was withdrawing into the inner compartment of his mind where he spent most of his time. This was a kind of mental bubble in which he established himself when he could not bear to be a part of what was going on around him. From it he could see out and judge but in it he was safe from any kind of penetration from without. It was the only place where he felt free of the general idiocy of his fellows. His mother had never entered it but from it he could see her with absolute clarity.

The old lady was clever enough and he thought that if she had started from any of the right premises, more might have been expected of her. She lived according to the laws of her own fantasy world, outside of which he had never seen her set foot. The law of it was to sacrifice herself for him after she had first created the necessity to do so by making a mess of things. If he had permitted her sacrifices, it was only because her lack of foresight had made them necessary. All of her life had been a struggle to act like a Chestny without the Chestny goods, and to give him everything she thought a Chestny ought to have; but since, said she, it was fun to struggle, why complain? And when you had won, as she had won, what fun to look back on the hard times! He could not forgive her that she had enjoyed the struggle and that she thought *she* had won.

What she meant when she said she had won was that she had brought him up successfully and had sent him to college and that he had turned out so well — good-looking (her teeth had gone unfilled so that his could be straightened), intelligent (he realized he was too intelligent to be a success), and with a future ahead of him (there was of course no future ahead of him). She excused his gloominess on the grounds that he was still growing up and his radical ideas on his lack of practical experience. She said he didn't yet know a thing about "life," that he hadn't even entered the real world — when already he was as disenchanted with it as a man of fifty.

The further irony of all this was that in spite of her, he had turned out so well. In spite of going to only a third-rate college, he had, on his own initiative, come out with a first-rate education; in spite of growing up dominated by a small mind, he had ended up with a large one; in spite of all her foolish views, he was free of prejudice and unafraid to face facts. Most miraculous of all, instead of being blinded by love for her as she was for him, he had cut himself emotionally free of her and could see her with complete objectivity. He was not dominated by mother.

The bus stopped with a sudden jerk and shook him from his meditation. A woman from the back lurched forward with little steps and barely escaped falling in his newspaper as she righted herself. She got off and a large Negro got on. Julian kept his paper lowered to watch. It gave him a certain satisfaction to see injustice in daily operation. It confirmed his view that with a few exceptions there was no one worth knowing within a radius of three hundred miles. The Negro was well dressed and carried a briefcase. He looked around and then sat down on the other end of the seat where the woman with the red and white canvas sandals was sitting. He immediately unfolded a newspaper and obscured himself behind it. Julian's mother's elbow at once prodded insistently into his ribs. "Now you see why I won't ride on these buses by myself," she whispered.

The woman with the red and white canvas sandals had risen at the same time the Negro sat down and had gone farther back in the bus and taken the seat of the woman who had got off. His mother leaned forward and cast her an approving look.

Julian rose, crossed the aisle, and sat down in the place of the woman with the canvas sandals. From this position, he looked serenely across at his mother. Her face had turned an angry red. He stared at her, making his eyes the eyes of a stranger. He felt his tension suddenly lift as if he had openly declared war on her.

He would have liked to get in conversation with the Negro and to talk with him about art or politics or any subject that would be above the comprehension of those around them, but the man remained entrenched behind his paper. He was either ignoring the change of seating or had never noticed it. There was no way for Julian to convey his sympathy.

His mother kept her eyes fixed reproachfully on his face. The woman with the protruding teeth was looking at him avidly as if he were a type of monster new to her.

"Do you have a light?" he asked the Negro.

Without looking away from his paper, the man reached in his pocket and handed him a packet of matches.

"Thanks," Julian said. For a moment he held the matches foolishly. A No Smoking sign looked down upon him from over

the door. This alone would not have deterred him; he had no cigarettes. He had quit smoking some months before because he could
not afford it. "Sorry," he muttered and handed back the matches.
The Negro lowered the paper and gave him an annoyed look. He
took the matches and raised the paper again.

His mother continued to gaze at him but she did not take advantage of his momentary discomfort. Her eyes retained their bat-
tered look. Her face seemed to be unnaturally red, as if her blood
pressure had risen. Julian allowed no glimmer of sympathy to show
on his face. Having got the advantage, he wanted desperately to
keep it and carry it through. He would have liked to teach her a
lesson that would last her a while, but there seemed no way to continue the point. The Negro refused to come out from behind his
paper.

Julian folded his arms and looked stolidly before him, facing her
but as if he did not see her, as if he had ceased to recognize her existence. He visualized a scene in which, the bus having reached their
stop, he would remain in his seat and when she said, "Aren't you
going to get off?" he would look at her as at a stranger who had
rashly addressed him. The corner they got off on was usually deserted, but it was well lighted and it would not hurt her to walk by
herself the four blocks to the Y. He decided to wait until the time
came and then decide whether or not he would let her get off by
herself. He would have to be at the Y at ten to bring her back,
but he could leave her wondering if he was going to show up.
There was no reason for her to think she could always depend on
him.

He retired again into the high-ceilinged room sparsely settled
with large pieces of antique furniture. His soul expanded momentarily but then he became aware of his mother across from him
and the vision shriveled. He studied her coldly. Her feet in little
pumps dangled like a child's and did not quite reach the floor. She
was training on him an exaggerated look of reproach. He felt completely detached from her. At that moment he could with pleasure
have slapped her as he would have slapped a particularly obnoxious
child in his charge.

He began to imagine various unlikely ways by which he could
teach her a lesson. He might make friends with some distinguished
Negro professor or lawyer and bring him home to spend the eve-

ning. He would be entirely justified but her blood pressure would rise to 300. He could not push her to the extent of making her have a stroke, and moreover, he had never been successful at making any Negro friends. He had tried to strike up an acquaintance on the bus with some of the better types, with ones that looked like professors or ministers or lawyers. One morning he had sat down next to a distinguished-looking dark brown man who had answered his questions with a sonorous solemnity but who had turned out to be an undertaker. Another day he had sat down beside a cigar-smoking Negro with a diamond ring on his finger, but after a few stilted pleasantries, the Negro had rung the buzzer and risen, slipping two lottery tickets into Julian's hand as he climbed over him to leave.

He imagined his mother lying desperately ill and his being able to secure only a Negro doctor for her. He toyed with that idea for a few minutes and then dropped it for a momentary vision of himself participating as a sympathizer in a sit-in demonstration. This was possible but he did not linger with it. Instead, he approached the ultimate horror. He brought home a beautiful suspiciously Negroid woman. Prepare yourself, he said. There is nothing you can do about it. This is the woman I've chosen. She's intelligent, dignified, even good, and she's suffered and she hasn't thought it *fun*. Now persecute us, go ahead and persecute us. Drive her out of here, but remember, you're driving me too. His eyes were narrowed and through the indignation he had generated, he saw his mother across the aisle, purple-faced, shrunken to the dwarf-like proportions of her moral nature, sitting like a mummy beneath the ridiculous banner of her hat.

He was tilted out of his fantasy again as the bus stopped. The door opened with a sucking hiss and out of the dark a large, gaily dressed, sullen-looking colored woman got on with a little boy. The child, who might have been four, had on a short plaid suit and a Tyrolean hat with a blue feather in it. Julian hoped that he would sit down beside him and that the woman would push in beside his mother. He could think of no better arrangement.

As she waited for her tokens, the woman was surveying the seating possibilities — he hoped with the idea of sitting where she was least wanted. There was something familiar-looking about her but Julian could not place what it was. She was a giant of a woman.

Her face was set not only to meet opposition but to seek it out. The downward tilt of her large lower lip was like a warning sign: DON'T TAMPER WITH ME. Her bulging figure was encased in a green crepe dress and her feet overflowed in red shoes. She had on a hideous hat. A purple velvet flap came down on one side of it and stood up on the other; the rest of it was green and looked like a cushion with the stuffing out. She carried a mammoth red pocketbook that bulged throughout as if it were stuffed with rocks.

To Julian's disappointment, the little boy climbed up on the empty seat beside his mother. His mother lumped all children, black and white, into the common category "cute," and she thought little Negroes were on the whole cuter than little white children. She smiled at the little boy as he climbed on the seat.

Meanwhile the woman was bearing down upon the empty seat beside Julian. To his annoyance, she squeezed herself into it. He saw his mother's face change as the woman settled herself next to him and he realized with satisfaction that this was more objectionable to her than it was to him. Her face seemed almost gray and there was a look of dull recognition in her eyes, as if suddenly she had sickened at some awful confrontation. Julian saw that it was because she and the woman had, in a sense, swapped sons. Though his mother would not realize the symbolic significance of this, she would feel it. His amusement showed plainly on his face.

The woman next to him muttered something unintelligible to herself. He was conscious of a kind of bristling next to him, a muted growling like that of an angry cat. He could not see anything but the red pocketbook upright on the bulging green thighs. He visualized the woman as she had stood waiting for her tokens — the ponderous figure, rising from the red shoes upward over the solid hips, the mammoth bosom, haughty face, to the green and purple hat.

His eyes widened.

The vision of the two hats, identical, broke upon him with the radiance of a brilliant sunrise. His face was suddenly lit with joy. He could not believe that Fate had thrust upon his mother such a lesson. He gave a loud chuckle so that she would look at him and see that he saw. She turned her eyes on him slowly. The blue in them seemed to have turned a bruised purple. For a moment he had an uncomfortable sense of her innocence, but it lasted only a second before principle rescued him. Justice entitled him to laugh. His grin hardened until it said to her as plainly as if he were saying aloud: Your punishment exactly fits your pettiness. This should teach you a permanent lesson.

Her eyes shifted to the woman. She seemed unable to bear looking at him and to find the woman preferable. He became conscious again of the bristling presence at his side. The woman was rumbling like a volcano about to become active. His mother's mouth began to twitch slightly at one corner. With a sinking heart, he saw incipient signs of recovery on her face and realized that this was going to strike her suddenly as funny and was going to be no lesson at all. She kept her eyes on the woman and an amused smile came over her face as if the woman were a monkey that had stolen her hat. The little Negro was looking up at her with large fascinated eyes. He had been trying to attract her attention for some time.

"Carver!" the woman said suddenly. "Come heah!"

When he saw that the spotlight was on him at last, Carver drew his feet up and turned himself toward Julian's mother and giggled.

"Carver!" the woman said. "You heah me? Come heah!"

Carver slid down from the seat but remained squatting with his back against the base of it, his head turned slyly around toward Julian's mother, who was smiling at him. The woman reached a hand across the aisle and snatched him to her. He righted himself and hung backwards on her knees, grinning at Julian's mother. "Isn't he cute?" Julian's mother said to the woman with the protruding teeth.

"I reckon he is," the woman said without conviction.

The Negress yanked him upright but he eased out of her grip and shot across the aisle and scrambled, giggling wildly, onto the seat beside his love.

"I think he likes me," Julian's mother said, and smiled at the woman. It was the smile she used when she was being particularly gracious to an inferior. Julian saw everything lost. The lesson had rolled off her like rain on a roof.

The woman stood up and yanked the little boy off the seat as if she were snatching him from contagion. Julian could feel the rage in her at having no weapon like his mother's smile. She gave the child a sharp slap across his leg. He howled once and then thrust his head into her stomach and kicked his feet against her shins. "Be-have," she said vehemently.

The bus stopped and the Negro who had been reading the newspaper got off. The woman moved over and set the little boy down with a thump between herself and Julian. She held him firmly by the knee. In a moment he put his hands in front of his face and peeped at Julian's mother through his fingers.

"I see yoooooooo!" she said and put her hand in front of her face and peeped at him.

The woman slapped his hand down. "Quit yo' foolishness," she said, "before I knock the living Jesus out of you!"

Julian was thankful that the next stop was theirs. He reached up and pulled the cord. The woman reached up and pulled it at the same time. Oh my God, he thought. He had the terrible intuition that when they got off the bus together, his mother would open her purse and give the little boy a nickel. The gesture would be as natural to her as breathing. The bus stopped and the woman got up and lunged to the front, dragging the child, who wished to stay on, after her. Julian and his mother got up and followed. As they neared the door, Julian tried to relieve her of her pocketbook.

"No," she murmured, "I want to give the little boy a nickel."

"No!" Julian hissed. "No!"

She smiled down at the child and opened her bag. The bus door opened and the woman picked him up by the arm and descended with him, hanging at her hip. Once in the street she set him down and shook him.

Julian's mother had to close her purse while she got down the bus step but as soon as her feet were on the ground, she opened it again and began to rummage inside. "I can't find but a penny," she whispered, "but it looks like a new one."

"Don't do it!" Julian said fiercely between his teeth. There was a streetlight on the corner and she hurried to get under it so that she could better see into her pocketbook. The woman was heading off rapidly down the street with the child still hanging backward on her hand.

"Oh little boy!" Julian's mother called and took a few quick steps and caught up with them just beyond the lamppost. "Here's a bright new penny for you," and she held out the coin, which shone bronze in the dim light.

The huge woman turned and for a moment stood, her shoulders lifted and her face frozen with frustrated rage, and stared at Julian's mother. Then all at once she seemed to explode like a piece of machinery that had been given one ounce of pressure too much. Julian saw the black fist swing out with the red pocketbook. He shut his eyes and cringed as he heard the woman shout, "He don't take nobody's pennies!" When he opened his eyes, the woman was disappearing down the street with the little boy staring wide-eyed over her shoulder. Julian's mother was sitting on the sidewalk.

"I told you not to do that," Julian said angrily. "I told you not to do that!"

He stood over her for a minute, gritting his teeth. Her legs were stretched out in front of her and her hat was on her lap. He squatted down and looked her in the face. It was totally expressionless. "You got exactly what you deserved," he said. "Now get up."

He picked up her pocketbook and put what had fallen out back in it. He picked the hat up off her lap. The penny caught his eye on the sidewalk and he picked that up and let it drop before her eyes into the purse. Then he stood up and leaned over and held his hand out to pull her up. She remained immobile. He sighed. Rising above them on either side were black apartment buildings, marked with irregular rectangles of light. At the end of the block a man came out of a door and walked off in the opposite direction. "All right," he said, "suppose somebody happens by and wants to know why you're sitting on the sidewalk?"

She took the hand and, breathing hard, pulled heavily up on it and then stood for a moment, swaying slightly as if the spots of light in the darkness were circling around her. Her eyes, shadowed and confused, finally settled on his face. He did not try to conceal his irritation. "I hope this teaches you a lesson," he said. She leaned forward and her eyes raked his face. She seemed trying to determine his identity. Then, as if she found nothing familiar about him, she started off with a headlong movement in the wrong direction.

"Aren't you going on to the Y?" he asked.

"Home," she muttered.

"Well, are we walking?"

For answer she kept going. Julian followed along, his hands behind him. He saw no reason to let the lesson she had had go without backing it up with an explanation of its meaning. She might as well be made to understand what had happened to her. "Don't think that was just an uppity Negro woman," he said. "That was the whole colored race which will no longer take your condescending pennies. That was your black double. She can wear the same hat as you, and to be sure," he added gratuitously (because he thought it was funny), "it looked better on her than it did on you. What all this means," he said, "is that the old world is gone. The old manners are obsolete and your graciousness is not worth a damn." He thought bitterly of the house that had been lost for him. "You aren't who you think you are," he said.

She continued to plow ahead, paying no attention to him. Her hair had come undone on one side. She dropped her pocketbook and took no notice. He stooped and picked it up and handed it to her but she did not take it.

"You needn't act as if the world has come to an end," he said, "because it hasn't. From now on you've got to live in a new world and face a few realities for a change. Buck up," he said, "it won't kill you."

She was breathing fast.

"Let's wait on the bus," he said.

"Home," she said thickly.

"I hate to see you behave like this," he said. "Just like a child. I should be able to expect more of you." He decided to stop where he was and make her stop and wait for a bus. "I'm not going any farther," he said, stopping. "We're going on the bus."

She continued to go on as if she had not heard him. He took a few steps and caught her arm and stopped her. He looked into her face and caught his breath. He was looking into a face he had never seen before. "Tell Grandpapa to come get me," she said.

He stared, stricken.

"Tell Caroline to come get me," she said.

Stunned, he let her go and she lurched forward again, walking as if one leg were shorter than the other. A tide of darkness seemed to be sweeping her from him. "Mother!" he cried. "Darling, sweetheart, wait!" Crumpling, she fell to the pavement. He dashed forward and fell at her side, crying, "Mamma, Mamma!" He turned her over. Her face was fiercely distorted. One eye, large and staring, moved slightly to the left as if it had become unmoored. The other remained fixed on him, raked his face again, found nothing and closed.

"Wait here, wait here!" he cried and jumped up and began to run for help toward a cluster of lights he saw in the distance ahead of him. "Help, help!" he shouted, but his voice was thin, scarcely a thread of sound. The lights drifted farther away the faster he ran and his feet moved numbly as if they carried him nowhere. The tide of darkness seemed to sweep him back to her, postponing from moment to moment his entry into the world of guilt and sorrow.

(*From Partisan Review*)

THE EDUCATION OF A QUEEN

BY THALIA SELZ

*W*HERE IS *that green iron gate, swinging to with an easy clang, hurled carelessly backward by my young hand as if batted by an Amazon?*

I woke precipitously last night, teetering back from the dizzy lip of tuinal sleep, hearing that pipestem gate creak and slam, and the sleeping pill stuck in my throat like a chip of blue and red ceramic tile. For no reason I was afraid as if I were a girl again — an adolescent girl whose periods have just begun and who is panic-struck by the magnitude of her sins.

I did not get up and fling open the french windows to inspect my charming Tyrolean wooden balcony, my geranium box, my compulsive *Seebach* rushing pell-mell and churning up foamy spittle and make-believe racket like a mountain brook in the movies. Or the soft, midnight walls of my valley — in the daytime cropped, domesticated slopes: tilting, hummocky mattresses for cows to lie on. At night cradled in wood — intimate, old-fashioned wooden fences; wooden turnstiles, the spokes crossed with stiff ceremony like arms in a folk dance or children's games (". . . take the key and lock her up, my fair lay-dee-e-e!"); or long, cumbersome wooden gates, slow as a cow.

I knew it was not a cow gate. With a damp, mossy fear born of guilt and drugs I fixed that swift, ominous, metallic *clank* as an intrusion from another world. I curled up icily, trying this gate and that, poking and prying through the rubbish heap of childhood, floating over games and lawns, deep-sea swimming among sidewalks, collie dogs, secret huts, dried skin from once-young faces, old people's coffins. The young never die.

I switched on the bedside lamp. I was clammy-nosed, drunk on sedative, and absurdly terrified because I had abruptly remembered and could not cry for my childhood acquaintance ("friend" is too strong a word) Aggie, whom I had not seen for at least twenty years, who was still in the fifth grade when she was fourteen years old, and who was the simplest, most absolute and apocalyptic Catholic it has ever been my misfortune to meet. A few months before, my mother had mentioned in a moment of brisk reminiscence that Aggie's aunt had told Norbert Leinfelder who had told her that Aggie had died of uterine cancer last summer, having given birth to three living children and one stillborn.

"German Catholic!" snorted my mother. "You'd think they'd learn, but they never do!"

My first thought then and last night, too, was thank — well, just *thank* — for all the children, even the stillborn, for the husband who infused them into that treacherous womb, and even for the mythic Lord who eased Aggie's end by promising her cherubs with pancake make-up on their puffing cheeks to take the places of her children — not to mention of course forgiveness of her awful sins.

I lay on my pillow, seeing her face dying on her dying pillow, not as it really must have looked: clayey and nook-cheeked, puff-eyed, sour-breathed, sweating out her imbecilic immortal soul at the pores. But twenty years ago, smooth-skinned, innocently boyish and square-jawed, fearsomely stupid under her miracle-spinning eyebrows.

I tried to weep, but she was so evil. She was the most evil girl under heaven. She was dumb. Often she smelled of pee, because she was apt to wet herself when her mother hit her with the razor strap or locked her into her room for two days at a time. She cried every passing-time when she did not pass and the others filed proudly, banners blaring, brasses flying, into the next home-room.

What's Aggie to me or me to she, that I should weep for her? "Come on in," said Aggie's loving ma, "and recite to my guests. Aggie don't have no memory at all, but now *her*, she's *fabulous* — " indicating me in my lank pigtails, horrid scarred knees, and scuffed Buster Browns.

With a fierce pride, ignoring the reproach of poor Aggie's ashamed, admiring eyes, I dove with flawless form:

> Up from the meadows rich with corn,
> Clear in the cool September morn,
> The clustered spires of Frederick stand
> Green-walled by the hills of Maryland.

Sixty lines complete with dramatic modulations of tone, inspired gestures, and bell-like enunciation. I had had no other teacher than my mother with her beautifully controlled, schoolmarm voice and her untamed, gothic imagination. Aggie, asking nothing from life, congratulated me solemnly:

"Gee, you sure got a fabalus memry, all right. . . ."

Except for Oliver Twist, she had the most wretched childhood I have ever heard of.

"Weep, damn you," I plead into my frozen featherbed, in the guilt-lit hotel room. And *reeeeek* I hear it once more out on the flowering Tyrolean meadows, the light swing on the Gary, Indiana-manufactured hinges, opening to the gentle, firm touch of Mr. Doom with his soft death's eyes, coming to claim me once and for all.

It was Aggie's gate. No, it was mine — it was Mary Melowski's (*Polish*-Catholic) next door!

I am crying now, without effort, without guilt, into my fragrant pillow smelling sweetly of straw, crying for Mary's lessons in wickedness under her back porch, for her brothers' further lessons in the secret hut, for calling and yodeling at front and back doors, for the drunken Mexicans up by the tracks, for running in the ozone-smelling sunshine — a sudden, mindless, breast-bursting sprint toward the train whistle miles away, for the Dirty Dozen with their flies open, for Aggie's idiot countenance — sorrow and doom dimly smeared across it like a double exposure, for my thirty-four years and the refuse of all our pasts and my own death, for the beautiful, simmering, chocolate eyes of Mr. X — his sweet smile madly calm — his timid, pale, long girl-fingers insanely sure as he delicately places the green pipestem gate in the wooden box and matter-of-factly swings it to.

I first met Mr. Joshua X the way I met anyone worthwhile or peculiar at all — through my family. I loathed my family, of course, but I was shrewd enough even then (I was twelve) to know that rather than sneak off to Hollywood to be adopted by Jeanette Mac-Donald, I'd better hang around the house and see the world come by.

It was 1937 and the war hadn't yet jerked us up out of the Depression. My father was still piping home strays — usually Greek, but sometimes Negro or Jewish: anybody with a real or manufactured right to pity. We had a table with food on it, even if it was in the kitchen. We had a rusty iron cot in the basement, but the blankets were still warm in spite of great age, and they bore our proud, mad, double-family crest like a brand, branding with our mixed blood, irrational phobias, and rash hopes anyone who slept under them. *1833* said the red, white, and pink "Lemon Star" quilt: the year Oberlin was founded and my great-great-grandmother Otis drove a wagon, all alone, from Barnstable on the Cape to the new one-room farmhouse in north-central Ohio. But the harsh, iron-woven blanket with its queer, lowering, iconic colors and its surface like John the Baptist's hair shirt was dated in stilted, twisted, gothic numerals *1897:* my father's mother, Anastasia Karamoulis, had woven it with thumb pricks, tears, and hate for her husband to keep himself warm and uncomfortable with in steerage on his way to make a million grass-green dollars in the States. Green fell for the parched, tawny hills of *Griechenland.* (Not that many of his few hundreds ever traveled back home. The barren slope, the empty pot were all that Anastasia got, which is why I tend to sneer at that Lawrencian image of the sturdy Peasant Woman: poor and sexually satisfied!) Together, these blankets were enough to endow any two-dimensional stray with all the length, breadth, depth, and momentous history he could use, and by God we were there to see that he didn't shirk. All of us, dead and alive, whooping him on. No chance to let go and die happy!

I offer as proof that in all those years from the crash till the war we had only three cases of theft and one instance of bedbugs.

But Mr. X is no ordinary stray. At first, indeed, he looks like one of many usual types of strays. I see him tread hesitantly in the back door after my father, and because he is sure of his shabbiness and unsure of his welcome he sets the heel of one shoe awkwardly down on the toe of the other. This makes him collapse almost to his knees at the next step, and my cruel, insensitive, unfeeling eight-year-old brother laughs. But Jason has a soul like an armadillo's back, anyhow. I am twelve and have not laughed in six months. It is unlikely that anything will ever be able to make me laugh again. I am setting plates for dinner, and I look gravely across the kitchen into those rich, innocent, madman's eyes, as they wash over me without seeing me at all really, only feeling Watchers, Warm, Food, Place.

"This is Joshua X," says my father; "he is an artist." Simple declarative, like a royal sentence of death.

At once I am in love. Without transition, conscious memory, or anticipation. But this has happened so often before that unconsciously I am quite used to it. Gently I set his place between my mother's and mine; deliberately I single out the best piece of everyday California Friarware: without chip or crack, a heraldic orange. My mother and I of necessity — by *rights* — get the two unmatched, most nicked plates. I am subtly aware that my little brother is beginning to be on to me, but I would no more think of setting at his place, and in revenge, my chipped plate with its brown stains along the cracks than I would of letting him ride my new bicycle.

"How do you do," says my mother's mellifluous, slightly strained voice. She is neither tired nor haughty. Her voice is simply stretching to make a place for him, too. "Will you eat with us?" (As if he'd been dragged in here for any other reason!) "Are you Greek perhaps? If you are, you'll like our lamb stew, I'm sure."

She is impossible, I am thinking. Our lamb stew! She's as prissy as a New England preacher (I have met no preachers and only a few priests: Greek Orthodox), and I *hate* those clothes. Years before they become chic on women's campuses she is wearing tight, worn Levis and one of my father's castoff shirts. She wears this costume to make her other clothes last, and I know this, but its shabby unwomanliness and the ludicrous contrast of the long, gray hair piled in loose coils and old-fashioned silvery puffs on her stately head fill me with distaste. She is a walking anachronism, and I have grown sensitive to the artistic verities. Also, I consider her abused and either too proud or too stupid to fight back — for pretty clothes or fewer free guests.

But most of all I detest the Greek routine. She thinks *anything*

Greek is peerless though among peers. At least I think she thinks so.

"But I'm not Greek," Mr. X says helplessly. Like Aladdin, he sees it vanishing — whoosh! the cast-iron kettle of stew, the dinner plates, the whole table fly out the window in a twinkling and skim away, up, up, to take their place with Orion's Belt.

"I'm not either," says my mother comfortingly.

"Never mind!" shouts my father. "You're an artist. You belong to the world!"

He always shouts, indoors or out in the back lot. Parlors or bedrooms or kitchens. I hate it.

"Where will you seat our guest, Daphne?" my mother asks, with this habitual loftiness that is not hauteur so much as the result of her persistent romanticism.

At twelve I consider my mother absolutely the creature of her dreams. She must make a ritual even of our simple, monotonous meals! But faced with exposure I feel my stomach curling up to tap startlingly at my palate. I swallow it back down again, and Jason sniggers the dirty snot-eyed pig behind his smelly paw. I am contemplating him being run over by a railroad train, when my mother quite simply puts Joshua X down beside me, places a napkin between his transparent fingers, ladles stew onto his sunset-colored plate, and tells him not to wait . . .

"We are never *polite* with each other in the family circle." She makes politeness sound like B.O.

Joshua X did not get to sleep on the iron maiden in the basement. (Oh, honor those harsh spikes, corners, and springs smelling of rust and, deliciously, of moist cement; they've pierced courage into many a poor stumblebum!) Mother put him on the parlor couch, but the next morning she would not allow Jason or me to touch anything in the room until he returned with a pink O.K. slip from the chest X-ray unit in the neighborhood clinic. Then she carefully made up the couch herself, tenderly folding her ancestors and my father's and laying them away in the coat closet till evening.

"Anyhow, I *won't* have him sleeping in the basement. He is *much* too frail! Daphne, see that he gets fresh bedding every week, like the rest of us."

"How long is he going to stay, Mother?" My love was already

blooming in bleeding stigmata on my underdeveloped bosom, but she didn't notice.

"Daphne, we never ask a guest how long he is going to stay." She was embarrassed for me: with the Otis and Karamoulis blood in my veins I should have known better *instinctively* than to breathe the vaguest suggestion of a termination to his visit.

At the dinner table, she once said to Jason and me: "Hospitality is the *strongest* of the Greek traditions."

"In Homeric times," roared my father, "we would even send our wives to bed with the guests!" My mother bent over the Brussels sprouts and pursed her lips, but I saw the corners of her mouth twitch.

At one time I had found my father's steady harping on the means and functions of the procreative organs very amusing, indeed. There was an embarrassing family legend that Daphne, aged five, glimpsing her papa making drunken (let us give him the benefit of the doubt) passes at a girl during one of the interminable Karamoulis parties had tripped up to him, crying, "Go to it, Daddy!"

What do you suppose he did then? Coughed, got up, and strode off, looking well over the bridge of his nose — suddenly very much the dignified Mediterranean *paterfamilias?* Probably it cramped his style for the rest of the evening. At any rate, the "bohemian parties," as my mother chose to call them, stopped a few years later. She put an end to them herself, of course. She said, "No more or I walk out." Since no Otis ever uttered a threat without being willing to back it up (the Lord of the Atheists at our right hand), there were no more bohemian parties.

But there continued to be a certain strain, like dangerously stretched rubber-bands, in and around the subject of sex. When I was nine or so my father made some sexual smart crack at which I laughed broadly.

"Mother," I cried, "isn't he funny? Don't you think he's funny, Mother?"

"Daphne," said my mother, "it is my hope that someday you too will grow beyond Rudolph Valentino!"

"Oh Mother," I said, "you're no fun."

My parents belonged to the progressive school of child-rearing, and I was not reproved, but sometime later — I must have been ten or eleven — Mother clarified the subject slightly.

"Grownups, even mothers and fathers, do not always agree about everything."

"When I grow up," said Jason, "I'll always agree with Daphne."

Mother quickly seized his pawn. "When you grow up, I hope, children, that you will no longer kick and scratch like animals — "

"Oh no-o!" We shook our heads. We should live to see the day!

"But you won't *always* agree either. Your father and I don't always agree. . . ."

Jason and I sidled glances. Damn right they didn't!

"But we *resolve* our differences for the sake of the family." Jason was looking puzzled, but Mother bellied on triumphantly down the wind. "Because our family is more important than any one of us, isn't it? Try to remember this, children. . . ."

We nodded solemnly.

"And Daphne, never forget that a woman's first duty — her *privilege* — is to keep her family together."

I sighed. How horrid and prissy it all was!

But of course, in spite of our united family, I found myself making choices. Probably it *wasn't* good to blurt sex-sex-sex all over the place, all the time. I didn't realize that Mother did it, too, that it was the almost ineradicable hallmark of the twenties when she and my father had come to maturity and found their gods (Nature, Freedom, Passion).

"You have the most beautiful young *body!*" she would exclaim, gazing rapturously after the bath at my pipestem shanks, my almost concave belly, and poor funny little breasts. I could have cried, but because I loved her I forgave her and glozed over these unseemly comments.

I did not forgive my father.

It is Sunday and I have on a new pink rayon blouse. My first that clings. I am standing beside the Victrola, winding it up to play the "Anvil Chorus," my favorite piece of music at this time next to "Juanita." I want to play it for Marianne, whom I admire and who, together with her boy friend, Dr. Digger, is having Sunday dinner with us. I don't admire Dr. Digger one bit and he has just tumbled himself into limbo by drunkenly catching me behind the bathroom door, screwing his satyr's grin up to his eyebrows, ecstatically touching his tongue to the tip of his long nose, and whimpering,

"*Oh* what cute little boobies! Jus' like inverted teacups — makes a fella wanna drink out of 'em, I tell *you!*"

I am disgusted and indignant with the outrage that only an adolescent can muster, but I am also strangely flattered. In addition, my mother is bringing me up to be a lady, and I am damn well going to make it up to Marianne.

At just this moment, as I am leaning down to wind the Victrola, I am sent catapulting against it with a stupendous WHAM! on the back that slams the breath through my lips, and my father strides by, bellowing jovially,

"Stop slumping! Stick 'em out and show us what you've got! It may not be much now, but you'll get more someday. . . ."

Dr. Digger snickers.

I try to smile. I could set a tiger on my father.

I really didn't love my father in those days. I adored him, which meant that I fervently hated him too. But I loved Joshua.

I loved him, insufficient body and puerile soul. I loved him tenderly — and hopelessly, except in raging fantasies when he would rescue me from the brink of Niagara or from a burning hotel and press his clean, hard, all-American lips to mine. He really had a wide, thick-lipped mouth — out of place in that otherwise delicate landscape. His face was square, but the pale skin was stretched so tightly over it that the bones looked ready to tear right through. Indeed, the teeth had already burst it and his lips were the swollen flanks of the wound. I used to fancy that in the night they bled of their own accord.

A horrid notion. My periods had come on almost two years before, and though I was used to them I was much taken up with thoughts of bleeding. Was sap tree-blood? (I knew better.) Was fish blood warm or cold? Did bleeding begin *right* under the skin, or how far down did you have to go? I would take these problems to my mother, and when she couldn't answer she would shoo me on to my father.

I took neither of them the night and the prayers. The long, unsteady nights without sleep — several times I lay dizzily awake till breakfast, my ears growing funnels, my heart plopping, my lips in mounds. What was the matter? At times I couldn't imagine. At others I knew at once, with implacable self-judgment, absolute horror:

"Oh God, forgive me for doing dirty things at night and with Mary and Steven and Junior when I was six and eight years old but that was a long time ago and they taught me. Oh gran'ma *please . . .*"

This last was addressed to Grandma Otis whose Christian Science martyrdom I trusted to get me in right again with God. (She had died of cancer of the stomach, refusing to see a doctor — "I'm perfectly well in Science, dear." . . . "B'lieve I'll just stick to my Spirit, thank you! And don't you forget, Daphne, we wouldn't have a speck of pain if 't'weren't for Mortal Mind." But oh what horror at the end, the mindless maggots of the eyes crawling in the sockets, the pretty old-lady mouth screaming for *aspirin* to ease the pain.)

There was no help to be had by invoking my immediate family: they didn't believe in God. Even Jason would declare self-righteously, if asked by an unwary neighbor: "I'm an atheist, like my whole family."

Whereas these days I hedged. "Well, I was *bap*tized Greek Orthodox . . ." And when hard-pressed: "I don't really think we ought to discuss religion; it's more private, like politics, don't you think?"

Then at night, heavily weighted down with my lippy passion for Joshua X, I would plead God's pardon for evading Him. But what were these slender filaments of lips that drove me crazy morning to night and to morning again? Why *there?* I knew — I knew, well enough, without knowing. My parents singly and together (with Jason lately wise-guying it behind the door) had explained to me the whole process of sexual love (oh, the twenties), mating (oh, the thirties), and having babies blah blah blah! I persisted in imagining that babies emerged from the rectum, though when asked directly (as I often was by mates — like poor Aggie — with less progressive parents) I would reply dutifully that of course they came out of your you-know-what, whatja think goofy cross-eyes? Huh, goofy?

Aggie said she didn't think so. Why not? "Our Sister in Cath'lic school says babies come from Heaven."

Aggie, did they come from Heaven when your man stuck them in you and they ripped out again, swollen with life — even that putrid stillborn — leaving placentas and blood and cancer behind them? In you? In your torn, bleeding, pulpous, lippy box?

At night, in foreign quaint-garden Tyrol, I know no better. I have such a horror of what can be put in boxes: children and dead people and cancer and garden gates and palpable, breathing, passionate fantasies.

Joshua was an artist. A story so monotonous as hardly to bear notation. He was on WPA but he had caught pneumonia and WPA could not pay his bills. He needed to live free somewhere for a brief time to save a little money. He lived with us for four months while my mother built up his health and morale and my father helped him find a steady job that left him enough time and energy to make his "objects."

They weren't paintings and they weren't sculptures and at the time and for years afterward (though I never admitted it to anyone but myself) they seemed very queer even to me. Now I know that he was a kind of Surrealist and that he was doing really very original work, though Giacommetti had made related objects a few years before — and Cornell was doing so then but quite without knowledge of Joshua's work. No one came to know Joshua's work.

Usually he used shoe boxes without lids, or he would cut holes or little doors in the lids or sides and sheet them with cellophane so you could peek through. This was in the beginning. When he began earning a few dollars he bought scraps of lumber and hammered together boxes which he fitted with glass tops.

"What's *that?*"

"A platypus."

"What?"

"A clong. A schnoo. A fllmnp. — Daphne!"

It is impossible to *describe* a work of art (which is what these were) without driving out of it that very quality of unexpected, perfect resolution which makes it art. I said these boxes were queer, and they were, but in spite of my adolescent fears, shames, and proprieties I rather liked them. They reminded me of the dollhouse I had played with till I was ten and was ashamed (but yearned) to play with now that I approached, queenly, the years of high school.

In the boxes and in precise, painstakingly considered juxtaposition he placed all manners of madnesses: coils of thin wire and snippets of hair (one of my shorn curls went into a box labeled "Little Side-Dream": I was delighted by the curl but obscurely hurt by the title), fragments of newspaper photographs and print, toothbrush bristles and fingernail parings and empty lipstick cases, shreds of cloth and bits of broken glass or china, pebbles, the insides of watches, pencil stubs, even one of Jason's molars. My mother got to saving all the nondecayable refuse of each day for him to pick over at night.

"I don't like them or understand them," she said, "but he has the *right,* I believe." She could be very romantic about her principles.

At night Jason and I would hurtle down to the basement to watch him work till bedtime. He never complained at our presence though he talked very little while he worked. We jabbered incessantly, boomed and yakked the radio, and even tinkered with his tools and tiny toys. Occasionally Joshua would frown us away from something, and once he said to me,

"Daphne, if you were my little girl I would slam you one on your behind," which made me rush upstairs to my room weeping with humiliation and disappointment. *Little girl,* indeed! when he was the forbidden fruit of my fantasies. I wouldn't blossom forth (Elaine, the lily maid of Astalot) until he came to murmur through my keyhole, "Come on out, sweetheart; I'll make you a special box all your own. O.K.?"

He made us — each member of the family — several boxes, which have been flooded out or burned or lost in the way of most flotsam. I see now that his boxes were more than cute three-dimensional collages or elaborate toys. They were often playful but just as often wistful or downright sad. There was frequently a narrative or descriptive element to them, but neither simple nor temporal: they didn't tell stories like a picturebook.

"Little Side-Dream" was a wooden box almost a foot square. Under the sliding glass lid with its delicately beveled edges lay a whole nest of old-fashioned watches, perhaps a dozen, each telling a different time. He had bought them (all broken) in a lot at a rummage sale. When you slid out the glass and lifted the watch faces you found beneath each, instead of the works, a special scene or object: a used railway ticket; a ship tumbling over the waves; a tiny effulgent city, the neon lights drops of colored enamel; a sidereal landscape; a sleeping maiden; the silky parabola of my curl. Like all his boxes, it revealed in a flash a whole fantasy or fragment of experience.

In short, it was art. If it were to be resurrected today I suppose the museums, ravenous as ever, would stick it in an Extinguished Talent or Old Americans show and then, frail creation, it'd be taken up and touted about by the best fairy gallery in New York. *Requiescat in pace.*

My friend, my secret pet, my slight gentle idol, ignorant companion of my midnight, pre-breakfast and, frequently, surreptitious naptime revels was no fairy himself, however. At first he simply seemed to pull a blank around women. Maybe he was just too tired or discouraged. Maybe he wanted to work more than to chase girls. This disturbed my father. He had not the usual overaggressive male's fear of homosexuals; quite the opposite, in fact. He relegated to them a position as honorable as that of women, only less fortunate.

"There are three species of sexual humans in the world." He hammers his fist on the dinner table for silence, and the knives and forks skip at our places.

"First" (with a broad wink toward my mother) "the least important: women who sleep with Men. Next, fairies who sleep with each other or with Men; and finally, Men who sleep preferably with women, but with fairies if there aren't any women around or if they need a free meal or a little extra cash. These — "

He stops for an instant to swallow: during his harangue he has been cramming food into his mouth with the same breathless insatiability with which he talks.

" — are called the *bulls* [*bools*]; homosexuals and women we call the *cows.*"

Mother is furious. She hacks her food in bits and snaps it off the fork.

Chin arched intellectually — I have recently discovered *Well of Loneliness* wedged in at the end of one of our bookshelves — I inquire where he would place Lesbians in his scale. It is one of the compensations for our peculiar childhood that he almost always considers Jason's and my questions seriously. He stops chewing, thoughtfully clears his sinuses, and replies:

"Upon reflection I can recall only two important Lesbians: Sappho and Queen Elizabeth. And though I have none of the usual prejudices — in fact, I was once in puppy-love [*poppy-lahve*] with with a beautiful Lesbian girl named Rosemary — how is it possible to count a movement [!] which in approximately five thousand years of recorded history has produced only two significant examples? Whereas from Plato to Gide there have existed thousands of important fairies, only here I will distinguish further between fairies and pederasts. . . ."

At this point even I, really interested only in sex these days — even I weary and cease to listen while I toy with Joshua's empty coffee cup at my elbow.

After a quick, seemingly casual inspection my father decided that Joshua (certainly no fairy, and probably not even a pederast) needed nothing so tonic-y as a woman, and accordingly he began to bring them in. It gave him a good excuse to gather pretty girls around him, and my mother, after a grim sigh, pitched in to help with extra meals and occasional parties, though she "would have nothing wild," she stated, darting a menacing glance at my father.

"*Puritana!*" muttered my father, but he stopped hanging out his tongue all the same.

At first they came and went in swift succession, frail blossoms on the gusts of our prince's bored sighs. Grace, who helped with dishes, and Viola, who did not and smeared "I really love Jason best" all over the bathroom mirror with Tangee lipstick. Pretty Nanette with whom I fell briefly in love and to whom we gaily sang all one evening, "No, no Nanette! No, no." Jean — from a dull Iowa family — who had joined the social revolution and tried earnestly to convert Joshua to socially significant art. Sarah, who was Jewish and was really having a hell of a time trying to organize the lady garment workers in her district. He liked her best for a while, but, I heard him tell my father, he just didn't feel like sleeping with her.

"Why *not?*" roared my father.

"Why?" queried Joshua, and there Sarah rested.

Then my father started to round up the Greek girls. Had I

thought, had I been strong and brave and used to offering advice to my father, I would simply have warned him, *"Don't!"* I understood this instinctively, for I had no truck with Greek girls myself, but in those days I didn't know how to examine an intuitive reaction for its validity as a genuine mode of conscious behavior. I was still all instinct and feeling, rushing about with my eyes tight shut and my mouth wide open — panting, greedily swallowing. By the time (very soon) I knew enough to take rational action, I didn't want to act. I wanted calamity. I hated Joshua. I stood like a fence post and let it come down.

Joshua did not nibble at the first two or three "Greek girls" either, and my father grew really worried. But I had seen a spark light up, far back in those sweet wild eyes of his, at the very suggestion of Greekness and *I* was worried. With my customary self-condemnation (Daphne, you mean skinny witch, you!), I attributed this to simple female jealousy, and I tried to scour it out of my heart. *I* couldn't have Joshua (I still had to go to high school and college and become famous and besides, I was just his "little side-dream," wasn't I?) but that didn't mean some Woman (grown up and with breasts) couldn't gobble him up, marry him down, discharge him with babies, and make him blissful or at least quiet in the accepted manner.

It never once occurred to me — till a little later, of course — that I might be seismographically recording a very faint tremor in Joshua's crust which, intensified, could split his delicate world wide open.

That first tremor was in his eyes, but it was not, really. It was in "Little Side-Dream." Stupid Daphne!

The girl's name was Vasiliki (broad *a*, accent on the last syllable). It was the feminine form of Basil: in Greek most of us are merely afterthoughts of the male, as it were: female appendages, like an extra set of nipples, on the male name. It means "little queen."

She was. She was small and she carried herself as if she expected to have both her hands kissed. This in a seventeen-year-old movie cashier is no minor attainment. Perhaps she was merely modeling herself after Norma Shearer or Bette Davis, but within the boundaries of her very limited world she succeeded. Her hands were kissed and fondled. She received orchids for dances at a time when few young men could afford to send orchids. She was sent presents and she took them, except for clothing. Here of course she was already approaching the dangerous no-man's land of the Greek community where no unmarried girl, not even a little queen with a diadem between her thighs, dares to walk abroad. She had been engaged twice and had kept the diamonds and the wrist watches, for which it was already whispered that she was a *poutana* by a very few old hens. But this whisper got no breeze to travel on. Vasiliki carried about in her patent-leather handbag a clear image of herself, to maintain which she was willing to make considerable sacrifices.

She gave the plainest wrist watch to her favorite girl cousin who *needed* it, she pouted to her mother, father, aunts, uncles, and girl friends. She had the diamond prized out of one ring and set in a gold, heart-shaped locket in which she actually wore the beefy, bewildered countenances of Mama and Papa. The other ring she gave with a certain amount of ladylike publicity to St. Dimitrios during a fund-raising drive. She was even included in a group photograph of church "donors" in the *Greek Daily*. By the time Joshua came along she was forging a pretty coat-of-arms in the Greek community for a mere cook's daughter.

I see now that she used Joshua to get to us because she really believed she needed us for the construction of her private palace. I'm not contriving excuses for her; she was wrong from the moment she took it into her shiny, black-helmeted head that it was a shameful thing to be the issue of a poor restaurant cook. But oh Vasiliki, queen bee, grubby infant of a fat, sweaty Macedonian hick who always smelled of other people's food, snorkled in his soup and wiped the grease off on the back of his hand — target for the slings and arrows of portly, be-taffeted, real gold-ed Daughters of Hera with their "teas" and their "luncheons" and their squealing Demotic "minutes" and their infernal money-raising — you with your purse-mouthed pursuit of a cell padded in real Brussels lace and imported Spanish shawls with a grand piano in the middle to play the latest Greek tangos on (they were still tangoing in Athens in 1937) — miscarriage of your environment, lost crown jewel of Byzantium set in village mud, lemon blossom with your soul like the withered lemon rind — let me not judge you.

My father was a lawyer and for all his mixed marriage, free talk, and derision of the church, he was a great prince in this tiny principality in the marches. I could afford to be scornful of Greek girls and go my way: I had an American mother, American girl friends, and an American college waiting for me. My mother had graduated from the same college in 1918 — my grandfather in 1892 — my great-grandmother in 1860. I was a free agent.

Vasiliki was not. She lived in a box; her soul wasn't big enough to break out, so she felt she had to see that her box got furnished right.

Joshua did not appear to nibble the first time. He sat far back on the couch that was his nighttime bed, with his thin legs awkwardly crossed like a boy just beginning to wear long trousers and his skinny, supple hands jammed in his pockets. Maybe he was running. Interior flight. He said little except, challengingly, that he read *PM*, voted for Roosevelt (this was no challenge, everyone Vasiliki knew voted for Roosevelt), and believed that art could best serve the social revolution by following its own organic growth in joyous freedom (hear hear!).

Vasiliki was only seventeen but she was no fool; she was a good Greek girl. She ignored him gently except for an occasional sweet, plump glance full of sisterly laughter and spent her time talking to Mother and me. She was demure with my father. Though she allowed herself, at the end of the evening, to be pinched on the behind, she quickly patted his hand, sped to my mother, kissed her on both cheeks, slipped her arm around my waist and gave me a hug, and drew that imp Jason to her bosom with real affection.

She had a beautiful bosom. I loved it. It was high and full without being distorted like those on the calendar Petty Girls Jason was already collecting. On her second visit, a few nights later, she wore a soft white lace collar folded in a deep V across her breasts — a fichu really. There were a number of uniquely old-fashioned touches about her: she bought long earrings in the dime store and wore them with her black hair, which had never been cut, spiraling in a somber crown round and round the summit of her perfect little head.

What my father had failed to take into account with Viola and Sarah and even Nanette was that an artist usually demands both genuine and unusual beauty in his woman. Not just any pretty girl. But a *different, beautiful* girl. When Vasiliki bent over

Joshua to offer him a snowy box of *loukoum* and a glass of *musti-kah* and her pretty breasts belled downward in her Betsy Ross bodice and her obsidian coronet tilted toward him, like gleaming, curved blades — *then* I saw him leap toward life. His hands and feet jerked, and his face lit like a Roman candle: eyes, lips, teeth, taut incandescent skin. My father saw it, too, and purred deep in his throat like a big cat — rumble of vicarious pleasure in all that fragrant female flesh. Then he sighed and drew his brows together, probably at his own denial.

But I was lost in the second act. What divine revelation was taking place in our makeshift crèche? Such pain, such pleasure! Like my father's really — pleasure in the sudden stimulus to the senses which the spectacle of those two offered us, pain in knowing that I was only in the audience.

Once Jason, who knew a Trojan horse when he saw one, said, "What's he so crazy about that glamourpuss for?"

"Oh, he thinks it's so la-dee-da, being Greek," I sneered.

Years later — only a matter of weeks ago — I saw Joshua's face again as it was at that moment. I was standing in the Uffizi before the central panel of the Portinari Altarpiece: the "Adoration of the Shepherds." And there he is. The third peasant, racing in on the tides of his need, his shepherd's crook clasped to his breast like a crucifix, like the hand of his beloved — his crazy northern face lit and wild with recognition as he stares at the Virgin. Diamond of Judah! Full, bursted melon of the House of David, spilling the secret of all creation from the cornucopia of your womb! Van der Goes, they say, ended his days as a monk in a madhouse — oh mad in that monkeyhouse — of course I stand and stand to stare and muse, why do I love it? where does it hurt so? whom have I seen him become before? It isn't till now, jerking suddenly up on my mattress of geraniums and cuckoo clocks that I remember and am ashamed for the cruel, casual, protective loss of memory that denies us our intensest experiences so that we can go on living.

There was already some slight, subtle footwork between my mother and me on the subject of the boxes.

My father only said, "What th'hell! Let her take him as he is. She's only a woman, isn't she? Good brood mare!"

But we knew better. Their third meeting was a date, so there wasn't any danger then. He took her to see *The Garden of Allah*, and I suppose Vasiliki thenceforward incorporated Dietrich into her rogues' gallery for the composite model: the ironic queen never really possessed, even in the final close-up caress. Joshua came home, contemplated the autographed still of Charles Boyer I had tacked over my own fretted couch, and said cryptically,

"Wait and see."

Then he said, "If you like, Vasiliki will get you all the photos of stars you want. For free. From the movie where she works."

Greedy little beast Daphne! It was clear what she was up to, but I grabbed at my bribe with delight. Pride and personal autographs to the winds! What I hungered for were pieces of Hollywood dream-cake to nibble on. I was only twelve and I didn't hesitate for an instant to toss away the ruby so I could take the glass chip to dream on.

There followed in quick succession a book for my mother, a toy watch for Jason (she favored watches), and two packs of the best Turkish cigarettes for my father. Vasiliki had almost no extra spending money so she had to buy shrewdly, and she bought with taste. The volume for my mother was a stroke of genius: the *complete* poems of Browning. Enormous. Later I learned that she had paid a special visit to her old English teacher in high school simply to ask her what one gave an American lady who had been to college and liked to read. Of course her teacher said Browning (amazing that it wasn't "Bobby" Burns); even so, Vasiliki had the fine good sense not to buy a "collected verse." A delicate point maybe, but she went up fast in my mother's estimation after that.

Really, though, that was so Greek of her — the desire to impress by amassing *all* the riches. While of course my mother mistakenly concluded that Vasiliki had read and liked Browning and had the true poetry lover's distrust of an anthology, "which — Daphne — depends on some *other* reader's taste."

Not much later I became Vasiliki's confidante, and I never betrayed her, till now when all the marbled batter of venom and love pushes up in me like something rising too fast in the oven. I despised her sly maneuvers, but I loved her. Because Joshua wanted her, because she was beautiful, because I longed to *be* her, because with all my mother's brains and education she had never developed such a skill in stratagem to teach to me so I could become a woman like other women.

At their fourth meeting, in spite of all mother's and my delaying tactics, Joshua took Vasiliki down into the dank basement to see his boxes. Mother was a romantic and wanted their idyll to continue a little longer. I was afraid of what might happen to Joshua. Nervously, we traipsed downstairs together after them, peering ahead to see what was going on under the electric light bulb.

"How-do-you-like-them-aren't-they-marvelously-clever?" Mother cried all in one breath.

"Oh yes, they're so cute," said Vasiliki in her pretty, very very faintly accented syllables. "I like *that* one," pointing at random.

"Which? Which?" cried poor Joshua.

"Oh — that one, I guess." It was written all over her face: well, so you're a nut after all; I'm not going to have any nuts in *my* box, thank you!

But Joshua wasn't looking; if he had been I think even he would have understood. Instead, he said with great excitement and satisfaction: "Well, if you *really* like them and don't *mind,* of course, I'll make you one, too."

"Oh, thanks a million!"

"Unless of course you'd rather have *this* one . . ."

"Oh no, no! Thanks *ever.*"

"I'm glad," said Joshua simply. "I would rather make one just for you and give it to you myself." He looked her straight in her black tip-tilted eyes, without a trace of childishness or evasive flirting. His money was plumped there on the line and she could take or leave it. Do I get my ticket or don't I?

Vasiliki's gaze actually fell; she pursed her lips, swiveled on her spike heels and marched off upstairs with her adorable rump switching and her eyes bent thoughtfully on the carpeting.

I was sweating with repressed laughter and nerves. I raced after her, ahead of Joshua and Mother, and confronted her in the parlor.

"What are you going to do?"

She gave me a long, calculating look. "Daphne, what about him? Is he . . . ?"

I stopped being twelve and became a hundred. "*Well . . .*" I smiled compassionately.

Suddenly she slipped her arm around my waist and gave me a tight squeeze. "Daphne, you're *marv!* Why don't we have a regular hen-fest one of these days? We could go to the movies on my free pass and then to Prince Castle after. I *love* Prince Castle, with all that glop they put on top!"

Joshua came into the room. "Who's this prince you love? I'll take him on right now."

"It's like an ice-cream parlor," Vasiliki said, with the faintest trace of stiffness.

"I'll take you there myself."

He's jealous of me, I thought. I could have wept to see things so turned around. But he had seen my face fall, for he walked right over and rubbed his nose in my hair — the tenderest gesture he had ever made toward me. "Don't cry, Betty Boop! You'll get your ice-cream sundae; never fear."

I burst into tears and ran out of the room.

The next afternoon as I came in from school, the phone rang: Vasiliki inviting me to see *Stella Dallas* and go for a sundae afterwards.

I had to ask Mother. "I think that would be *nice*," she said, rolling out cookie dough. "I guess she's interested in Joshua, after all."

I'll fix that, I thought to myself, and dashed back to set the time.

I didn't actually tell any lies behind the white tiled turrets of Prince Castle; I simply let her convince herself of what she already wanted to believe.

"He's really off his rocker, isn't he?"

I blinked.

"Why do your mother and father let him hang around, then?"

I shrugged.

"I don't see how you can stand it," she said, sticking out her tongue to lick her cherry. I proffered her mine, on my spoon.

"Don't ever do that with a fellow, Daphne."

"Why not?"

She stared. Then she hissed, with her face in mine, "*Cherry!* Get it?"

"No. I don't like maraschino cherries; I don't see why I shouldn't give them to somebody who does."

"You *are* a dope. Cherry is what you've got here," gesturing toward her lap with her spoon. "Virginity. Get it?"

"Oh." I thought of all the times Joshua had taken me out for ice cream and gobbled up my cherries greedily. Probably he'd been mocking me all the time. I hated him for it. "What will you do with that box Joshua's going to make for you?"

"Turn him in."

I really don't think I heard her at first. I went on destroying my Double Chocolate Delight until gradually the whipped cream began tasting like cheese. I laid down my spoon.

"What did you say?"

"*I'm* not taking any chances."

"You wouldn't!"

"Oh but definitely! He's probably a sexual pervert or something."

"But he hasn't done anything — "

"How do you know? You don't know anything about him before he came to live with you. All you know is he's from Sioux Falls or someplace. He might be a rapist, even." She paused. "You know, I'll bet he's an Indian."

"Why?"

"Oh, I don't know. Sioux Falls or something. *I* wouldn't let an Indian sleep in my parlor. That's why I don't understand your folks — "

"You're *prejudiced!*" I cried hotly, my voice echoing from the damp, tiled walls, reeking of warm milk and sugar.

She eyed me haughtily. "I don't discuss politics, myself."

I went home feeling sick in my soul and my stomach. I wanted to tell my parents what Vasiliki had said, but they were out. Jason was in bed though awake, of course, the little snoop. I went in and asked him where Joshua was.

"He's in the basement making a box for Vasiliki. Ooo! Lovey-dovey!" Then he began to sing, "Daphne lu-uvs Josh-wa! Daphne lu-uvs Josh-wa!"

I was terrified that Joshua might hear him down the hot-air register, so I snapped, "Shut up or I'll lock your door."

He subsided at once, and I went into the bathroom. I wanted to go right down to warn Joshua but I was afraid of three things. One. That Jason might hear me and set up that yodel again. Two. That Joshua had already heard Jason and now knew my secret shame. Three. That I was going to be horribly sick to my stomach.

I threw up everything: Double Chocolate Delight complete with whipped cream, malt-balls from the movies, supper's lamb chop, even the salted peanuts I'd nibbled after school.

Then I went to bed and cried for a long time.

Eventually I heard Joshua trudge upstairs. He went into the parlor, opened the coat closet door, shut it again, and came back, poking his head in at my door.

"Daphne?"

I considered a moment and then murmured, "Mm-m — "

"I'm going out for a breath of air. Your folks should be home soon. You scared to stay alone?"

"No." This was a lie.

"I won't go far."

"O.K."

"Good night, Betty Boop."

Now is the time. Now — now! Call him in before he gets to the kitchen, before his step crosses the threshold, before he shuts the back door. Sit him on the foot of your bed. Tell him everything in a rush, no matter how it sounds. He is your Joshua and he is in danger.

Instead I sulked silently, listening to his steps crunch down the cinder drive, because in my hideous self-consciousness I was afraid I smelled sour from the vomit and because I was even more afraid of his disbelief. He was crazy — and he was crazy about that piece of fake exoticism, Vasiliki; he wouldn't believe me. He would think I was mean and jealous and he would never call me Betty Boop again.

In addition, there lingered a fantastic apprehension at the back of my memory. Maybe Vasiliki was right. We knew very little about him, after all. He had said *for a breath of air,* but what if he meant something else? I shivered and wriggled farther under the covers.

Sometime later my parents came home. They were arguing as they walked up the drive, and I heard them step into the basement, probably just for a look, and then come upstairs, still arguing. Briefly they were silent while my mother trotted into the parlor and quickly returned toward the kitchen, gently closing Jason's door and mine on the way.

I knew they wanted to be alone to argue so I did not summon

them in to hear my troubles. Instead, I got up and quietly opened
my door to listen. I heard my father say,

"You're up to your old tricks — you want to limit my freedom."

"We must all learn to live within limits," said my mother.

"Man is born free. Woman enslaves him!" He began pacing up
and down the kitchen.

"Nonsense!" snapped my mother. Then she murmured something I couldn't catch.

"Look," he said, "if you want another child, I'll give you one.
We can't really afford it but times are bound to get better. I'll give
you a great, big, walloping belly, and then . . ."

"And then," said my mother in a voice suddenly as lean as bone,
"you'll go chasing after the first pig in skirts you see. No, *thank
you.* I've served my term. No more having my husband fall all
over me *simply* because the mindless slut he slept with couldn't
satisfy him."

I could have thought another woman had spoken, the words
were so strange. She stopped and I could hear her panting sharply
with anger. But when she spoke again it was in a very different
voice. "I'm sorry. I shouldn't have said those things. Only once
in a while I allow myself to feel bitter — I lose control . . ."

"You've made it quite clear what you think already," my father
said with a sound of stiff and terrible pride.

"No," my mother said. "No. — That's only part of it."

I closed the door and slipped back into bed. I was trembling with
disgust but I was puzzled, too. What did she mean, *only part of it?*
Then, quite simply, the way children do, I decided to forget the
whole discussion. Mother was Mother. My father was "difficult"
(Mother's word) but he was "terrific," "awfully smart," and "loads
of fun," too, and though I wasn't then capable of loving him, I certainly worshipped him, and the notion of any other father would
have been heresy.

The next morning I went in to breakfast fully determined to
make my confession to Joshua, but the sight of his red, red mouth
— too red no matter what the weather — made me think of that
breath of air, and I turned mute in adolescent alarm and jealousy.
The more he tried to wheedle out of me what the matter was, the
more I shunned him.

But that evening when he was again in the basement working,

I pricked and poked up my courage and went downstairs. He was fitting a gate made out of green pipestems into a long, wooden box — Vasiliki's.

"Why did you make it green?"

"Why not?" Then, afraid perhaps that he'd been too brusque with his pet, he looked up and smiled with extraordinary sweetness. It shredded to bits my puerile soul, and I could hardly bear the thought of letting him down by telling him the truth.

"What are you going to do now?"

"I'm going to put *her — here.*" He pointed with one hand to a space behind the gate and with the other he picked up and held aloft my — *my* little porcelain mermaid.

I gave an involuntary cry. "You can't!"

"Why not?"

There she was, darling and white and nude with little softly rounded, pink-tipped breasts. Once long long ago she had reclined, exquisitely languid, on the sandy sea-bottom of somebody's goldfish bowl. Then, oh bliss, she had lost an arm (Madame Recamier undergoes surgery) and been given me for my dollhouse. I never played with it any more of course, but the notion of giving her to Vasiliki — try to imagine this gnashing agony. The night-brown walls of the basement turn a sickly mud-yellow with the approaching hurricane. I could kill. In an instant. In the despotic obliquity of youth I perceive that I, who merit all rewards *by right,* am losing one of my possessions to a cook's spawn.

I almost spit. "She's mine!"

"Funny. I found her here on the table. Jason or your mother must have . . . Never mind; it doesn't matter. Here, sweetheart, take her back. You're my best girl of all." Then he utters the ultimate misfortune. "I'll find something better for her."

I was dumb with bitterness and shame. I stumbled back upstairs, clutching my one-armed mermaid, so long outgrown, so much a part of my myriad inadequacies.

What happened during the next two days I have to reconstruct from what my mother has told me.

During the night Joshua must have finished Vasiliki's box. What it looked like in its final form only Mother knew, for she was the only one of us to see it and she recalls a nude female figure of some kind. He was still at his job when I came home from school, and I ran eagerly across the street to call on Aggie, with whom I hadn't played for at least two months. We retired to the ping-pong table in the depths of her basement, and I let her win game after game — anything to avoid going home. At six o'clock her mother, in a rare good humor, invited me to stay for supper, and I eagerly accepted after sending Aggie back across the street to ask permission of Mother.

At seven-thirty Aggie and I wandered upstairs to her bedroom "to read library books" (Aggie read the comics). Meanwhile, Joshua cleaned himself up, put on his *other* suit, wrapped the precious box in tissue dug up somewhere by Mother, and departed to seek out Vasiliki in her cashier's box, longer than a coffin but not much wider. He hadn't called for a date, but he told Mother it didn't matter for he knew her schedule. Mother said he was perfectly at ease.

I am sure it never occurred to Joshua that Vasiliki might laugh; worse yet, might disapprove, be afraid. Why should it? We had adopted and protected him, surrounding him like a wall with our family, our love, our broad shoulders. My mother accepted his boxes as an honor and showed them to all her friends — not because she understood or even liked them, but because she loved Joshua. He can hardly be blamed for not knowing all this.

At eight o'clock my father went off to a professional meeting, and at eight-thirty while I was still buried in *The Red Fairy Book* in Aggie's bedroom, two policemen called at our house and demanded to see the "pornography" in the basement. It was a great pity my father wasn't at home then. Though he seldom handled criminal cases, he was known and respected down at City Hall, and I dare say that with a phone call he could have sent them away, at least temporarily. As it was, they put a large number of "exhibits" in the police car and drove away, shaking their heads over "the crazy guy."

My mother finally managed to reach my father at his meeting, and he went rampaging over to the police station, bailed out Joshua, and brought him home. He did not think, however, to check on the fate of all those "exhibits," and Joshua didn't know about them.

Mother said Joshua looked very queer when he arrived back from the police station. She said he looked the way he did four months before when my father first dragged him home to supper.

She saw to it that he didn't go down to the basement but gave him a sedative with orange juice (Mother didn't really approve of sedatives and thought that swallowing them with the aid of orange juice somehow made them morally acceptable), and sent him to bed on the parlor couch. When I slunk in — at ten o'clock, unheard of during the week — all she said was,

"Oh, where have *you* been?" And then, "What a time we've had!" And shut me in the kitchen with her to tell me all. I sat there on the hospital-white kitchen stool, utterly condemned by myself, but I felt it would be even worse to confess.

Joshua slept through breakfast, and Mother phoned his job to say he was sick and not coming in that day. I took one peek at him, lying there in his faded pajamas like a pauper on his slab, before running off to school and I have never been able really to gloze over that memory. I think right then I died a little without knowing that was what I was doing. I walked to school abstractedly and on the way I decided that "it would be better to forget about it." And by virtue of a prodigious effort I really forgot him off and on during the day.

While I was working at forgetting, my father went to see Vasiliki and quickly persuaded her to drop the case. She appeared eager to talk to him and took both his scolding and advice without a murmur. She said she had been "frightened" and "mistaken," and she cried "pathetically" (his word) on his shoulder. For a lawyer he could occasionally be fairly obtuse. They drove together to the police station, and my father asked for the boxes. The harassed sergeant, glad to make an end of the matter, said he would send them to the house in a patrol wagon. My father then went to his office.

By the time Joshua waked, my mother was able to tell him that everything was all right. He washed, shaved, and ate a good breakfast; he seemed cheerful enough, Mother said, though perhaps still a trifle groggy from the sedative. Then he went into the parlor to watch for the patrol wagon.

When it still had not come at noon Mother telephoned the police station. The sergeant was polite but brief: obviously he had had his fill of this case. One of his men had thrown them boxes in the incinerator, thinking they was just trash. Sorry. Mother shut the kitchen door and phoned my father at his office. I don't know what they agreed to say to Joshua, but whatever it was, wasn't enough.

He listened calmly, "only," Mother said, "tilting his head at me a little and going rather paler, *if* possible . . ." Then he left "without his coat." This fact correctly struck her as ominous, and she waited for him in great apprehension the rest of the day, not even going out into the back yard for fear of missing the telephone.

When I came home from school at three-thirty, there still hadn't been word from or about him. I wandered down to the basement, regarded the dismal scrap heap left behind by the invading policemen, and then I recalled my new resolution to forget it all. I went across the street again to Aggie's, but she was being punished by her mother, so I took a long walk up the railroad tracks toward the country.

At dusk I ambled home to find Mother and Jason crying in the kitchen. Joshua, they said, was in the state hospital. At four he had appeared with a form for Mother to sign, admitting him for treatment. His family was dead; she must sign. In desperation she telephoned my father, and together they stormed at, argued and pleaded with Joshua. Finally, gravely, he rolls up his cuffs to show them the slightly twisted, delicate white twine scarring his skinny wrists.

This scene I have always found it impossible to visualize. My father and mother are real: they cough and more. But there is Joshua, displaying the emblems of his martyrdom as sedately as a saint. Like a schoolteacher he points to the blackboard — no! I can't see him. Once upon a time he had cut his wrists, that's all. He was my Joshua and I done him wrong deliberately and with hatred in my heart. Joshua, I summon you. I resurrect your fleshless narrow delicate most beautiful blanched cutting bones! When did you slash your wrists? Why? *You never told me.*

I was twelve. No one told me much of anything I wanted to know. My father drove Joshua to the hospital and returned, silent with gloom, to his lawbooks. I hung about his study door. Back and forth. Aimlessly pawing the threshold.

"Whatever — why — what do you think . . . ?"

I couldn't get it out, but suddenly he shouted,

"Joshua was too damn weak, that's all! The race is to the swift, the strong, the sonuvvabitching pigs who never even take their brass knuckles off in the bathtub. He — was — too — goddam — *weak,* for Christ's sake, Daphne! Now will you leave me alone and get the hell out?"

I got: embarrassed, frightened, appalled by his tears. But shame-facedly thanking the family gods that we were never, any of us, really, in Joshua's way at least, weak.

Joshua was well treated at the hospital. The chief resident psychiatrist was a friend of my father's law partner and anyhow, he said, Joshua was one of the most amenable patients he had ever had. Very soon we were allowed to visit him. I was frightened the first time, but he took my arm and led me to a bench on the hospital lawn where we talked pleasantly about my school work, how they treated him, and what books I should bring him next visit. When I left he called me Betty Boop.

My mother went to see him regularly once a week. How she found time to add these visits to all the rest of her urgent scurrying, I'll never know. My own appearances were irregular and I did not look forward to them, but once there, with him, my anxiety drained away and I was almost as happy as I had been watching him work in the basement. I no longer believed I loved him; in a way of course I didn't — I never had.

We talked about everything except the boxes. He said of Vasiliki that "it was a kind of insanity even to have fallen for her."

I worked the toe of my oxford in the gravel, feeling I was hearing something too old for me.

"Dangerously immature," he continued, like a pupil who wants to please Teacher by giving the correct answer.

"Still . . ." He paused with an expression of stunned wonder on his face. ". . . what happened to me? What a dreamer I was! What pitiful, magnificent visions they personify!"

"They?" I asked myself. "They *who?*"

On another, very different day we were walking through the gardens loosely holding hands when suddenly he turned to look closely at me, his face right up against mine — as if he were nearsighted, I remember thinking at the time.

"I should have waited for you to grow up, Daphne. But of course you wouldn't bother with someone like me. Why should you?" And he laughed deprecatingly.

I could have said right then, "Yes I *will* bother." I was thirteen now — almost a woman — but I was too startled and besides I didn't want to. The moment spilled on really unnoticed, for Joshua had from the beginning been relegated to dreamland.

As time passed I began to feel that growing up was learning not to care. I decided that in removing myself from Joshua — from my dreams — I had begun to grow up.

After Joshua was released and took a job teaching handicrafts in a trade school (work for which he was conspicuously unsuited), we continued to visit back and forth, but gradually and almost consciously I forced our relationship into a new pattern in which I was the elder, the big sister, the girl-mother. He played along with it although sometimes I used to catch him watching me with the quirk of a smile. I think that by trying to dominate him I was trying to keep my dreams under control.

We had of course to see that he didn't meet Vasiliki at our house. This was not easy, for she was always running in "just to say hello" but really to find a good husband at our hands. At first my mother would barely speak to her, but gradually even her principles were caught and enervated by Vasiliki's wiles. Vasiliki and I were quite comfortable together. We agreed about very little except the unspoken mutual tact which absolutely prohibited any mention of that conversation at Prince Castle, and this bound us together in easy familiarity.

As time went on, I was occasionally made the recipient of her discarded boy friends, gifts which I accepted without any false pride. Sometime, I don't know exactly when, I had decided that I wasn't above taking what I could get where I could get it. By and by, one of these rejects (the dullest, of course; isn't it always that way?) made me. The seduction was mutual — both pantingly determined. The act took place in our garden hammock: no mean accomplishment. Because of the lurching, swaying hammock, he couldn't scramble out of his clothes, and I never got to see what he really looked like, but it didn't much matter. I was made, initiated, deflowered, uncherried: no longer a silly, giggling virgin like most of my friends, surreptitiously passing around dirty paragraphs about creamed bananas, but a woman, a queen, or at least a princess.

The boy, somewhat to my surprise, had got genuinely excited; he

wanted to meet again. I held up my chin, gazing off into the delicious landscapes beckoning me on, and said no thank you. I was a
princess, wasn't I? Casual dispenser of ladies or tigers. Sometimes
ladies (myself) but quite frequently tigers, too.

I was wise enough not to sleep around. Some tatter of dream
remained around my shoulders like a leash, and I was also aware
that I must protect my reputation. The world couldn't get too familiar with a princess, or she would lose her power. I learned that
Vasiliki permitted the most extraordinary liberties without ever
"going the whole way." I didn't despise her. She was a good Greek
girl: just didn't have the soul of a princess. It wasn't her fault.

One day when I went to drop off at Joshua's a box of cookies
Mother had packed for him — she was always putting up extra
batches of cookies for other people: "our Joshua" or "our Marianne" — I found two small canvases propped against the sofa-back
in his one-room apartment. They were still tacky: I could smell
the turpentine. I was relieved that he didn't look at me as I stared
at them, because I didn't like them.

But when I dropped in again, perhaps two weeks later, he was
openly at work on some boxes. The top of his only table looked as
if he'd just turned the wastebasket upside down on it.

I said, "Joshua!" I was so excited I bent down and kissed his
cheek.

Again he didn't look up, but he said with his smile — "Then this
one will be for you."

He brought it round the following week, and it was "Little Side-
Dream," exactly as it had been, even to the black curl.

I said, "Where did you get the hair, Joshua?" I think I was actually jealous again for the breath of an instant.

He laughed. "What did you think? That I'd kept only one of
your curls?"

But there were no more good boxes. Whatever it was that had
made them good was gone. Vanished. Blitzed. I think he realized
this — I am sure he did from a remark he made to me sometime
later about failure. But slowly he continued to turn them out. Frequently he went back to see his psychiatrist, and they held long
discussions together. Perhaps they talked about his boxes. I don't
know. Joshua was a very patient man, but he was no longer either
talented or mad. I think his talent blew out at the same time as

that lovely wildness in his eyes. This was hardly the psychiatrist's fault. Please understand that I am not repeating "artists are madmen" or "psychoanalysis removes the desire to create" — those glib catch-phrases of our blind times. Joshua was not The Artist. He was a particular human being in a special set of circumstances. I think the light in Joshua's eyes was a conviction of immortality — mistaken, maybe, but necessary to *his* continuance as an artist. That light was quenched when he realized that the striking of a match had — not *could,* but *had* — destroyed his fantasies. Killed his boxes. That is dreams had proved to be as casually ephemeral as his mere life.

At about the time I went off to college he got a much better job and moved to another city, but we corresponded with some regularity. It was 1943 and he was glad, he wrote, to be ruled 4-F (shirker! draft-evader! people said) because of those weeks in the state hospital. He had a small lath-and-plaster bungalow with a garden, and he would much prefer, he remarked in a letter to me, killing weeds than people.

I was having a rousing good time at college. There were almost no male civilians left on campus, but the air force, in its infinite wisdom, had seen fit to set up a base in the next town — eight minutes by bus, every hour on the hour. I liked the air force uniforms, and the sense of dash and urgency their lives imparted to the "boys" excited me, too.

Why was it that there was nothing so sexy as frolicsome Mr. Bones, jauntily tap dancing around the corner? Flyers were killed all the time in routine training flights, and with each crash we coeds pursued the survivors ever more hotly. It was more than grab-pleasure-while-you-can. More than the youthful romantic desire to give ourselves to potential heroes. It was as though we were trying to get through, into the very crashes, to immolate our own young bodies on those exploding gasoline pyres. We wanted to die, too, consumed by our sex, the violence of the times, the frightful rape of flame and history. We wanted to kill and be killed in one glorious holocaust — to become both the raper and the raped in the red womb of our crazy collective suicide. And we would do strange things to express our excitement. A certain memory recurs.

I am lying flat on my back between the lectern and the altar in the Church of the Holy Trinity. I have not a stitch on and the young gentleman on top of me, pumping sweatily away, hasn't either. We have earlier in the day rejected both the Baptist and the First Congregational as not provocative enough in their imagery, and as I lie there afterward staring thoughtfully up at the medium-high church Episcopalian stars in the modest plaster firmament above me, I reflect (in that moment of awesome clarity which always follows a climax with someone you in no way love) — I *understand* that what we have really been looking for up there is a good, old-fashioned, implacable Byzantine Pancreator like those I have seen in slides of Monreale and Daphne (yes!).

Of course I am not ashamed. I use the Church of the Holy Trinity the way I use the "boys," to excite me with the spectacle of my own prodigious power. And to see if I can't get caught, somehow, and be made to die for it all. Oh, sweet death, with your infinitely wet kisses.

Even Vasiliki has got her husband (acquired, of course, through us) killed in the Battle of the Bulge, and now my family finally shuns her. Even Jason won't speak to her when he meets her on the street. It is as though they suspect she is a witch, has the Evil Eye, and so at last she can be allowed to pay (lucky Vasiliki) for what she did to Joshua.

Am I never to pay? Later my boy takes me to a forbidden road-house with an imitation log-cabin bar. Not beer, but whisky, for the boys have money to squander in the quaint, rusticated ante-chambers of doom. I have two scotch-on-the-rocks that I remember and then probably more. Suddenly I am insisting that I must see Joshua.

"Who?"

"My uncle."

"A-a-ah!"

My boy is getting too familiar: he questions my word. I sway up the bar — has anybody got enough gas coupons to drive me to Cleveland?

"You bet I'll drive you to Cleveland, baby! Me and my buddy here — NOW?"

Since I do not believe in mass fornication (princesses are particular), I catch the ten o'clock bus alone.

I have a distant suspicion — all my suspicions are distant now — that Joshua is a little displeased by my condition when he opens his lath-and-plaster front door. But I also suspect that he is genuinely delighted to see me. He takes off my shoes, makes me coffee, and turns up the thermostat.

"Now," he says, "now, Betty Boop, what the devil have you been up to?"

I gaze over the rim of my cup into his sweet, fond, innocent, patient face, and I decide to give it to him straight. He's asking for it, isn't he? Betty Boop, indeed!

And I do. In spite of a certain drunken tendency to dump all my words into one pot, like a goulash, I begin with the hammock, progress through Uncle Sam's boys, and conclude chapters later with the Church of the Holy Trinity. I get to liking the sound of my own voice and describe actors and scenes in rapturous, epic catalogs. When I run out of true confessions, I make them up and since, in spite of everything, I am not really so wicked as I like to believe, some of the most inspired episodes in my saga are fictitious. Perhaps he understands this. I never really stop, however; I just drivel off to sleep in his armchair.

When I waken he forces more coffee on me, washes my face, and bundles me into his car for the sixty-mile drive back to college. It must use up a month's gasoline ration; he can't have a very high priority. Before letting me out at my dormitory, he takes me sternly by the shoulders. His thin fingers dig through the wool of my coat.

"Listen! Can you understand me? If your parents ever hear any of this — from *anyone* — I'll slap that stupid smirk right off your face myself! O.K. Now go on up to bed and try sleeping by yourself for a change. What do you think you look like: coming to me like a slut tonight?"

In the morning I was fortunately still drunk enough to write him a letter of apology. My rhetoric was high-flown schoolgirl, but I don't remember what I said except for two things. *One.* That I would die if he didn't answer me. *Two.* P.S. That I loved him. Now this was not really true, of course, but I was still in the grip of an arsenic-green hangover: the asphalt billowed puckishly as I crossed the street to the mailbox.

My answer came the next afternoon, by special delivery, and since I still have it, like all the other letters he wrote me, I'll transcribe a little of it.

"You do not disgust me. Don't say that! Nothing you ever do can disgust me, and I'm sorry if I said some hard things. I was furious. At first I felt I had failed you, somehow, for you to do these things, as I have failed in other ways. Later on I remembered that you are grown and a free agent and must make your own choices. But I think you can't really know anything about death, though you talked so much about it the other night, or you wouldn't try so hard to hurt yourself in these ways. It is simply not pleasant or sexy or even easy to die — so don't." There followed a humorous paragraph about the garden and then a "P.S. Yes, Daphne, I love you."

By the time I got his letter I was sober, twenty years old, and yellow with embarrassment. As far as I let myself reflect on the matter, I perceived that by traipsing drunkenly into his parlor to confess I appeared to have been issuing another invitation. Probably I had only our old friendship to thank for the fact that Joshua hadn't made me right in that overstuffed armchair. Then I remembered Sarah and Nanette and Vasiliki, and scornfully concluded that nothing would have happened anyhow. For of course it never had.

Just the same, I vowed to reform and put the letter away to answer when I could face it. But I never had to. The next week he caught pneumonia hoeing in that damned garden and, even with sulfa, died in a few days. Perhaps if penicillin had been released for civilian use — but I don't think so. There is destiny.

Mother and Jason traveled three hundred and fifty miles for the funeral. I did not write them that I was in the infirmary, though I was tempted. I went with them to the funeral and forced myself to look into Joshua's box and I promised that fearsome, unnatural face . . . what? I don't know. To love, maybe. Simply to love.

I was sincere, but it is not so easy to keep promises. Love what? Whom? I like my work as an art critic very much, and I love my family. Perhaps that's enough. The promiscuity stopped, of course, and of course I quickly became a very steady character. Sometimes, I suspect, a bit of a bore.

Before leaving for Europe this summer I spent a week with all of them — my parents, Jason, his wife, their four-year-old Daphne Otis — in a cottage on one of the lakes where we go, where we've always gone.

Little Daphne said to me: "When will you be married, Aunty? Will you be married tomorrow?"

"No."

"I'm very sorry," she answered with genuine regret.

"But Daphne, I don't really want to marry anyone I know."

It is true, but their obvious disbelief — all of them with apologetic eyes — unnerves me. When we fall to discussing Joshua, as we inevitably do, I can no longer sustain my objectivity. He rides up to greet me — that smiling skeleton beating time on his brass steed — and I become annoyed and questioning.

"I mean, why didn't he do good work after that?"

"Weak. He was too weak, I tell you!" My father shrugs. For him Joshua will always be a shrug. There he lost a battle, not with Joshua but with fate, who leers and snatches back even from the grip of kings.

"He took himself in and out of a state institution. Singlehanded. He laid hold of his life and lived it reasonably through to the end. I don't call that *weak*," says Jason.

"Just the same, his relationships with women . . ." I proceed caustically. They have made me wince today, and I am going to kill Joshua over again if I have the chance.

"What *about* his relationships with women?"

My mother is bristling. Hands on hips, shoulders thrust forward pugnaciously, she glares at me. The white tower of her hair, still ramped and turreted like the Tower of Babel, trembles down its proud spiral with the passion of her defense. "Just because he didn't sleep with Sarah and break her *heart!* Well, Nanette was crazy about him and they had *quite* an affair together later on, I can tell you. Also, there were *several* other girls before he moved away, and then that married woman he lived with later . . . Oh, I was his confidante all right, and I used to say to him, 'Settle *down*, Joshua! Settle on *one* of them before it's too late!' And you see? I was right."

I am thunderstruck and some of it must show, for Jason roars with laughter and claps me a brother's clap on the shoulder. "Did you think he was going to carry the torch forever?"

"Carry the torch for whom?"

We are all confused and stare at one another and then off in several directions toward the somber black pines and the passive, sky-colored lake.

So that I no longer have even that leg to stand on.

Later that night I paced beside the lake, upon the round smooth pebbles the glaciers had broken and caressed down from rocks and left behind in their vast, magnificent passage, and I tried to understand and thaw that secret, hard core of my anger.

Absurd! I tossed into the charcoal dust of night, settling, like an invisible, infinitely soft fall of black snow, on the invisible, tender surface of the summer lake.

Absurd, but why not? I argue now, sitting stiffly upright in the icy sharp cold, arguing with Joshua who smiles into my eyes, as always, with an air of infinite relinquishment.

I observe him this time in earnest annoyance. My determination. My passionate nature. I am so used to getting my way because I know what I want. If he hadn't been so evasive I could have helped him do really good work again, as he did in our basement. Perhaps that's only conceit, but my mother and father seem to help each other work somehow; they still spar over sex, but as Mother said, "that is only part of it." I wouldn't really have been afraid to bear Joshua's children; I think all together we could have thrown up that magic ring of fire to protect our immortality.

I had a kind of share of immortality once. As always, my soul un-withers when I remember it. So did Joshua. Within that fiery iron ring of Family — internecine passions, false pride, bitter resentments, pointless loyalties — in that magic area we were for a while doomed to live, not to die. If we had held tightly together, I think that no one, not even Vasiliki, could have hurt him.

But I suppose it's always the oldest child who breaks the ring first. One has to get out, go beyond, become a free agent. And it's probably woman's greatest single delusion that she can save a man from his destiny.

I am not crying now in Tyrol for Aggie, but for death, the still-born life — that monstrous foreclosure of the mortgage after nine months of hard work and promises — the cancer at the bottom of the box, my own death at twelve years of age, my murder of Joshua. After all, he could never have loved me if he had known about the

Prince Castle, could he? (But I dare say, wistful ghost, you could have performed even that miracle.)

There was only one thing he couldn't do. He couldn't raise himself from the dead. The absolute, imponderable quality of extinction surrounded him all in a breath, and he just wasn't able to ignore that awful Presence. I believe that every time he lifted his hand to paste some bauble in a new box, he felt it moving slowly through the ether of final outer space, and he simply didn't have the energy to push his way through it all alone. None of us do.

But I had so much energy, and I could have helped him. Had I been older, less selfish; had I understood; had I not been me.

(*From Esquire*)

LOVE ON A DARK STREET

BY IRWIN SHAW

*T*HE NIGHT is the time for calls across the ocean. Alone in the hours past midnight in a foreign city, a man's thoughts center on another continent, he remembers loved voices far away, he calculates differences in time zones (*it is eight o'clock in New York, the taxis are bumper to bumper, all the lights are lit*), he promises himself that there will be a general saving on such things as cigarettes, liquor, and restaurants to make up for the sweet extravagance of several moments of conversation across the three thousand miles of space.

In his apartment on the narrow street behind the Boulevard Montparnasse Nicholas Tibbell sat, holding a book in his hand, but not reading. He was too restless to sleep, and although he was thirsty and would have liked a beer, he was not resolute enough to go out once more and find a bar that was still open. There was no beer on ice in the apartment because he had neglected to buy any. The apartment, which he had rented from a German photographer for six months, was an ugly, small place, with only two badly furnished rooms, the walls of which were covered by blown-up photographs of emaciated nude women whom the German had posed in what Tibbell considered rather extreme positions. Tibbell spent as little time and thought on the apartment as possible. At the end of six months, the company for which he worked, a large organization which dealt in chemicals on both sides of the Atlantic, would decide whether he was to be kept in Paris or sent somewhere else. If his base was to be permanently in Paris, he would have to find more comfortable quarters for himself. In the meantime, he used the apartment merely for sleeping and for changing his clothes, and tried to keep down the waves of self-pity and homesickness which assailed him at moments like this, late at night, trapped among the unfleshed contortionists of the German's living room.

From the stories he had heard from other young Americans in Paris, it had never occurred to Tibbell that he would have to face so many nights of loneliness and vague, unformed yearning once he had established himself in the city. But he was shy with girls and clumsy with men and he saw now that shyness and clumsiness were exportable articles that passed from country to country without tax or quota restrictions and that a solitary man was as likely to find himself alone and unremarked in Paris as in New York. Each night, after a silent dinner with only a book for companion, Tibbell, with his neat American haircut, his uncreased, neat Dacron suit, his naïve, questing, blue, polite American eyes, would go from one crowded *terrasse* of St. German des Près to another, drinking as little as he dared, waiting for the one brilliant night when he would be noticed by some glorious, laughing band of young people who, with the legendary freedom of the capital, would seize upon him, appreciate him, sweep him along with them in their expeditions among the joyous tables of the Flore, the Epi Club, the Brasserie Lipp, and out to the gay and slightly sinful inns in the smiling green countryside beyond Paris.

But the one brilliant night never arrived. The summer was nearly over and he was as alone as ever, trying to read a book, near the open window, through which the warm night breeze carried an erratic distant hum from the traffic of the surrounding city and a thin fragrance of river water and dusty September foliage. The thought of sleep, even though it was after midnight, was intolerable.

Tibbell put down the book (it was *Madame Bovary*, to improve his French) and went over to the window and looked out. He found himself looking out the window a good deal of the time when he was in the apartment. There wasn't much to see. The apartment was one floor up, confronted by tightly locked shutters and flaky soot-gray stone walls. The street was narrow and looked as though it were waiting to be bombed or torn down to make way for a modern prison and at the busiest of times carried very little traffic. To-night it was silent, and deserted except for two lovers who made a single, unmoving shadow in a doorway diagonally across from him.

Tibbell peered at the lovers with envy and admiration. What a thing it was to be French, he thought, and experience no shame in the face of desire and be able to display it so honestly, on a public thoroughfare. If only he had gone to Paris during his formative years instead of to Exeter!

Tibbell turned away from the window. The lovers kissing in the arch of the doorway across the street disturbed him.

He tried to read, but he kept going over the same lines again and again — *"Une exhalaison s'échappait de ce grand amour embaumé et qui, passant à travers tout, parfumait de tendresse l'atmosphère d'immaculation ou elle voulait vivre."*

He put the book down. He felt much sorrier for himself than for Emma Bovary. He would have to improve his French some other night.

"The hell with it," he said aloud, making a decision, and picked up the phone from its cradle on the bookcase full of German books. He dialed the overseas operator and asked for Betty's number in New York, in his careful, accurate, though unimproved French, which he had learned in two years in Exeter and four at Swarthmore. The operator told him to hold on, saying that there was a possibility that she could put the call through immediately. He began to sweat a little, pleasurably, at the thought of talking to Betty within the next two minutes. He had a premonition that he was likely to say something original and historic tonight and he turned out the light because he felt he could express himself more freely in the dark.

But then the operator came on the line again to say that the call would take some time to put through. Tibbell looked at the radium dial of his watch and told her to try anyway. He pushed the phone to one side and leaned back in his chair with his eyes half closed, and thought of what Betty's voice would sound like from the other side of the ocean, and how she would look, curled on the sofa of her tiny apartment, twelve stories above the streets of New York, as she spoke into the telephone. He smiled as he remembered the familiar, lovely, small image. He had only known Betty eight months and if the Paris trip hadn't come up two months before, he was sure that a propitious moment would have presented itself in which to ask her to marry him. He was nearly thirty and if he was ever going to get married it would have to be soon.

Leaving Betty behind had been a sorrowful experience and it had only been by the exercise of the stoniest self-control that he had managed to get through their last evening together without risking everything then and there and asking her to follow him on the next plane. But he prided himself on being a sensible man and arriving to take up a new and perhaps temporary job in a new country with a new wife at his side was not his idea of how a sensible man should act. Still, the combination of pleasure and longing with which, hour by hour, he thought of her, was something he had never experienced before and tonight he wanted to make powerful and naked statements to her that until now he had been too timid to voice. Up to now, Tibbell had contented himself with writing a letter or two plus a call on Betty's birthday. But tonight he was irresistibly moved to indulge himself in the sound of her voice and in his own avowal of love.

He waited, impatiently, for the phone to ring, trying to make the time seem shorter by imagining what it would be like if Betty were beside him now, and what they would be saying to each other if they were hand-in-hand in the same room instead of divided by three thousand miles of humming wire. He had closed his eyes, his head leaning back against the chair, a little smile on his lips as he remembered old whispers of conversation and imagined new exchanges, when he heard voices, harsh and excited, coming through the open window. The voices were passionate, insistent. Tibbell stood up and went to the window and looked down.

Below him, outlined in the light of the street lamp stood three people, tensely together, arguing, their voices sometimes hushed, as though they were trying to keep their quarrel to themselves, and sometimes, in bursts of anger, carelessly loud and brutal. There was a man of about sixty, with gray hair and a bald spot, clearly visible from Tibbell's post at the window, and a young woman who was sobbing into a handkerchief, and a young man in a windjacket. The young woman had on a gay, flowered-cotton dress and her hair was blond and piled high on her head in the inevitable Brigitte

Bardot style of the season, the ensemble making her look like a stuffed, cleansed little piglet. The old man looked like a respectable engineer or government official, robust and vaguely intellectual at the same time. They were grouped around a Vespa that was parked in front of the building. During the most heated exchanges the young man kept stroking the machine, as though reassuring himself that *in extremis* a means of escape was still available to him.

"I repeat, monsieur," the old man was saying loudly, "you are a *salaud*." His speech had a rotund, self-important ring to it, almost oratorical, as if he were accustomed to addressing large audiences.

"I repeat once more to you, Monsieur Banary-Cointal," the young man said, equally loudly, "I am not a *salaud*." His speech was street-Parisian, rasping, rough, formed by twenty-five years of constant argument with the fellow citizens of his city, but his over-all air suggested the student or laboratory assistant or pharmacist's clerk.

The young woman wept, her hands trembling on a large patent-leather purse she was carrying.

"But you are," the old man said, his face close to the other man's face. "The worst kind. Do you wish proof?" It was an oratorical question. "I will give you proof. My daughter is pregnant. Due to your attentions. And what do you do now that she is in this condition? You abandon her. Like a serpent. And to add to the injury, you propose to get married tomorrow. To another woman."

Undoubtedly, the conversation would have had a different ring to it for a Frenchman who happened to overhear it, but to Tibbell's Exeter-cum-Swarthmore ear all spoken French was translated automatically into English that was constructed like a schoolboy's version of excerpts from Racine and Cicero. To Tibbell, all Frenchmen seemed to have a slightly archaic and elevated vocabulary and they always sounded to him as though they were making a speech to a group of senators in the forum or exhorting the Athenians to kill Socrates. Far from annoying Tibbell, it gave an added, mysterious charm to his contacts with the inhabitants of the country, and on the rare occasions when he understood accurately a few words of argot it supplied a piquancy to his relations with the language, as though he had discovered a phrase of Damon Runyon's in Act III of *Le Cid*.

"I will leave it to the opinion of the most neutral observer," M.

Banary-Cointal was saying, "if that is not the action of a man who deserves to be termed a *salaud*."

The young woman, standing stiffly upright, not yet looking pregnant, wept more loudly.

In the shadow of their doorway, the lovers shifted a little; a bare arm moved, a kiss was planted on an ear rather than on lips, a muscular arm took a new hold — but whether that was due to the commotion around the Vespa or to the natural fatigue and need for variation of prolonged *amour* Tibbell could not tell.

Farther down the street a car approached, with bright lights and an Italian roar of motor, but it stopped near the corner, swinging in to park in front of a closed laundry shop, and the lights were extinguished. The street was left to the disputants.

"If I'm getting married tomorrow," the young man said, "it's her fault." He pointed accusingly at the girl.

"I forbid you to go on," said M. Banary-Cointal with dignity.

"I tried," the young man shouted. "I did everything I could. I lived with her for a year, didn't I?" He said this righteously, with pride and self-pity, as if he expected congratulations all round for his sacrifice. "At the end of the year it became clear to me — if I ever wanted a worthy home for any children I might have, I would never get it from your daughter. It is time to speak frankly, monsieur. Your daughter conducts herself in an impossible manner. Impossible. In addition, her character is abominable."

"Be careful in your choice of words, young man," the father said.

"Abominable," the young man repeated. He waved his arms in emphasis and his long black hair fell over his forehead into his eyes, adding to the effect of blind and uncontrollable rage. "As her father, I will spare you the details, but I will permit myself to say that never has a man had to bear such treatment from a woman who in theory shared his home for twelve months. Even the phrase makes me laugh," Raoul said, without laughing. "When you say 'share a home,' you imagine that it means that a woman is occasionally physically present in the foyer — for example, when a man comes home to lunch or when he returns for an evening of peace and relaxation after a hard day's work. But if you imagine that in the case of your daughter, Monsieur Banary-Cointal, you are sadly mistaken. In the last year, Monsieur Banary-Cointal, I assure you I have seen more of my mother, of my maiden aunt in Toulouse, of the woman who sells newspapers opposite the Madeleine, than I have seen of your daughter. Ask for her at any hour of the day or night — winter or summer — and where was she? Absent!"

"Raoul," the girl sobbed, "how can you talk like that? I was faithful from the first day to the last."

"Faithful!" Raoul snorted contemptuously. "What difference does that make? A woman says she is faithful and believes that excuses everything from arson to matricide. What good did your fidelity do me? You were never home. At the hairdresser, at the cinema, at the Galéries Lafayette, at the Zoo, at the tennis matches, at the swimming pool, at the dressmaker, at the Deux Magots, on the Champs Elysées, at the home of a girl friend in St.-Cloud — but never home. Monsieur" — Raoul turned to the father — "I do not know what it was in her childhood that formed your daughter's character, but I speak only of the results. Your daughter is a woman who has only the most lively detestation of a home."

"A home is one thing, monsieur," the old man said, his voice trembling with parental emotion, "and a clandestine and illicit ménage is another. It is the difference between a church and a . . . a . . ." The old man hesitated, searching for the proper crushing comparison. "The difference between a church and a racecourse." He permitted himself a wild smile at the brilliance of his rhetoric.

"I swear to you, Raoul," the girl said, "if you marry me I will not *budge* from the kitchen."

"A woman will promise anything," Raoul said, "on the night before a man is due to marry somebody else." He turned brutally to the father. "I will give you my final judgment on your daughter. I pity the man who marries her, and if I were a good citizen and a good Christian, I would send such a man an anonymous letter of warning before he took the fatal step."

The young woman cried out as though she had been struck and threw herself against her father heartbrokenly, to sob against his shoulder. Her father patted her distractedly, saying, "There, there, Moumou," while the girl brokenly repeated, "I love him, I love him, I can't live without him. If he leaves me I'm going to throw myself in the river."

"You see," the father said accusingly, over his daughter's bent, tragic head, "you serpent of ingratitude, she can't live without you."

"That's just too bad," Raoul said, his voice high with exasperation. "Because I can't live *with* her."

"I warn you," the father said, speaking loudly, to be heard above the thunder of his daughter's sobs, "I hold you personally responsible if she throws herself in the river. I, her father, am saying this. Solemnly."

"The river!" Raoul laughed in harsh disbelief. "Call me when it happens. I will personally accompany her. Anyway, she swims like a fish. I'm surprised that a man your age can be innocent enough to be taken in by female guff like that."

Somehow, this last statement enraged Moumou more than anything else Raoul had said. With a sound that was a kind of mixture of growl and air-raid siren, Moumou leapt from the shelter of her father's arms and flung herself on Raoul, hurling him out into the middle of the street, whacking him ferociously with the huge leather bag, holding it by the handle, swinging it again and again like an Olympic hammer thrower. From the noise it made as it smashed against Raoul's head and shoulders Tibbell calculated that it weighed about ten pounds and was filled with glass and metalware. Raoul raised his arms to protect himself, shouting, dancing backwards, "Moumou, Moumou, you're losing control of yourself!"

To halt the brutal, arching blows of the bag, which were coming in at all angles, he lunged forward and grappled with Moumou, but she continued her attack with her sharply pointed shoes, kicking him pitilessly in the shins and grinding her high, needle-sharp heels into the soft suede of his moccasins. To Tibbell, watching bemused from his window, the couple seemed to be performing some eccentric tribal dance, with their shadows, thrown by the near-by lamppost, whirling around them and up and down the face of the buildings opposite in an elongated African pattern.

"Moumou, Moumou," Raoul shouted hoarsely, as he clutched her and at the same time kept up his painful, jigging dance, to try to avoid the cruel pert heels that dug into his toes, "what good does this do? It solves none of our problems. Moumou, stop it!"

But Moumou, now that she had started, had no mind to stop it. All the indignities, deceptions, and false hopes of her life were welling up in her, finding ecstatic expression in the blows and kicks with which she was belaboring her defaulting partner. The grunts and muffled growls that accompanied her efforts had a note of triumph and wild, orgiastic release in them, hardly fitting, Tibbell thought, for a public performance on a public street. Foreign and American as he was, he was uneasy at the thought of intervention. In New York City, if he had been the witness of a fight between a man and a woman, he would have rushed to part the combatants. But here, in the strange land of France, where the code of behavior between the sexes was at best a titillating mystery to him, he could only wait and hope for the best. Besides, by any system of scoring, the woman was clearly winning by a large margin, delivering all the blows, gaining many points for what is approvingly called aggressiveness in the prize ring and only suffering such incidental damage as came her way when Raoul's head bumped her forehead as she tried to bite him.

The father, who might have been expected to be disturbed by the spectacle of his pregnant daughter locked in hand-to-hand combat with her faithless lover at this odd hour of the morning, never made a move to stop the action. He merely moved along the street with the struggle, circling it warily, keeping a keen eye on the principals, like a referee who is loath to interfere in a good fight so long as the clinching is not too obvious and the low blows unintentional.

The noise, however, had awakened sleepers, and here and there along the street, shutters opened a crack on dark windows and heads appeared briefly, with that French combination of impartiality, curiosity and caution which would lock the shutters fast on the scene of violence with the approach of the first gendarme.

By this time, Moumou had stamped and hammered Raoul some fifteen yards away from the point of the original attack and they were swaying and panting in front of the lovers who had been tranquilly kissing all this time in the shadow of the doorway on the other side of the street. But now, with the noise of battle on their very doorstep, as it were, and the contestants threatening invasion at any moment, the lovers separated, and the man stepped out protectively in front of the figure of the girl he had been crushing so cozily and for so long against the stone doorway. Tibbell saw that the man was short and burly and dressed in a sports jacket and an open-necked shirt. "Here, here," the man in the sports jacket said authoritatively, seizing Raoul by the shoulders and pulling at him, "that's enough of that. Go home and go to sleep."

His appearance distracted Moumou for an instant. "Go back to your doorway fornication, monsieur!" she said. "We don't need your advice." At that moment, Raoul slid away from her and pounded up the street. "Coward," Moumou shouted, and took off after him, swinging her bag menacingly, running with surprising speed and agility in her high-heeled, pointed shoes. She seemed actually to be gaining on Raoul when he came to the corner and ducked around it, closely followed by Moumou.

The street seemed strangely quiet now and Tibbell could hear the discreet clicking of shutters being closed, now that the principals had departed the scene.

But the father was still there, staring with melancholy, weary eyes at the corner around which he had last seen his daughter disappear, brandishing the patent-leather handbag. He turned his glance on the young man in the sports jacket, who was saying to his girl, "Well, there's a pair for you. Barbarians."

"Monsieur," the father said gravely, "who asked you to meddle in other people's affairs? It is the same all over this poor country. Nobody minds his own business any more. Privacy is a thing of the past. No wonder we are on the edge of anarchy. They were on the point of agreement when you destroyed everything."

"Listen, monsieur," the man in the sports jacket said belligerently, "I am by nature a simple, honorable man. I do not stand by idly while a man and a woman beat each other in my presence. It was my duty to separate them and, if you were not old enough to be my grandfather, I would say that you should be ashamed of yourself for not having separated them sooner."

M. Banary-Cointal examined the simple, honorable man with scientific detachment, as though he were weighing the last statement judiciously, without prejudice. But instead of answering, he turned to the girl, still discreetly in shadow and arranging her ruffled hair with little pats of her hand. "Young woman," the old man said loudly, "you see what's ahead of you? The same thing will happen to you as happened to my daughter. Mark my words, you'll find yourself pregnant and that one" — the old man pointed like a prosecuting attorney at the sports coat — "that one will disappear like a hare in a cornfield."

"Simone," the man in the sports coat said, before the girl had a chance to reply, "we have better ways of spending our time than listening to this old windbag." He pushed a button on the wall next to him and the door against which he and the girl had been leaning opened with an electric buzzing. With dignity, he took the girl's arm and escorted her into the deeper shadow of the inner court. The old man shrugged, his duty done, his warning to a careless generation delivered, as the huge wooden door clicked shut behind the interrupted lovers. Now the old man seemed to be looking around for another audience for his views on life, but the street was deserted, and Tibbell pulled back a bit from the window, fearful of being harangued.

Deprived of further targets for his wisdom, M. Banary-Cointal sighed, then walked slowly toward the corner around which his daughter had vanished in pursuit of Raoul. Tibbell could see him standing there, caught in the dark stone geometry of the city crossroads, a solitary and baffled figure, peering off in the distance, searching the lonely street for survivors.

Now there was the click of shutters again below Tibbell and old women's voices, seeming to rise from some underground of the night, made themselves heard, from window to window.

"Ah," one voice said, "this city is becoming unbearable. People will do anything on the street at any hour. Did you hear what I heard, Madame Harrahs?"

"Every word," a second old voice spoke in a loud, hoarse, accusing, concierge's whisper. "He was a thief. He tried to snatch her purse. Since De Gaulle a woman isn't safe after dark any more in Paris. And the police have the nerve to demand a rise in pay."

"Not at all, madame," the first voice said irritably. "I saw with my own eyes. She hit him. With her bag. Thirty or forty of the best. He was bleeding like a pig. He's lucky to be alive. Though only got what's coming to him. She's pregnant."

"Ah," said Madame Harrahs, "the *salaud.*"

"Though to tell the truth," said the first voice, "she didn't seem any better than she should be. Never at home, flitting around, only thinking about marriage when it was too late, after the rabbit test."

"Young girls these days," said Madame Harrahs. "They deserve what they get."

"You can say that again," said the first concierge. "If I told you some of the things that go on in this very house."

"You don't have to tell me," said Madame Harrahs. "It's the

same on both sides of the street. When I think of some of the people I have to open the door to and say Monsieur Blanchard lives on the third, to the right, it's a wonder I still have the courage to go to Mass at Easter."

"The one I feel sorry for is the old man," said the first concierge. "The father."

"Don't waste your pity," said Madame Harrahs. "It's probably all his fault. He is obviously lacking in authority. And if a man hasn't authority, he has to expect the worst from his children. Besides, I wouldn't be a bit surprised if he didn't have a little thing on the side himself, a little poupette in the Sixteenth, like that disgusting lawyer in Geneva. I got a good look at him. I know the type."

"Ah, the dirty old man," the first voice said.

Now Tibbell heard footsteps approaching from the corner and he turned to see the dirty old man approaching. The shutters clicked tight again and the old ladies subsided after their choric irruption, leaving the street to the weary sound of the old man's shoes on the uneven concrete and the asthmatic sighs he emitted with every other step. He stopped below Tibbell's window, looking sorrowfully at the Vespa, shaking his head, then sat down uncomfortably on the curb, his feet in the gutter, his hands dangling loose and helpless between his knees. Tibbell would have liked to go down and comfort him, but was uncertain whether M. Banary-Cointal was in any condition that night to be consoled by foreigners.

Tibbell was on the verge of closing his own shutters, like the two concierges, and leaving the old man to his problems on the street below, when he saw Moumou appear at the corner, sobbing exhaustedly, walking unsteadily on her high heels, the bag with which she had so vigorously attacked Raoul now hanging like a dead weight from her hand. The father saw her too and stood up, with a rheumatic effort, to greet her. When she saw the old man, Moumou sobbed more loudly. The old man opened his arms and she plunged onto his shoulder, weeping and clutching him, while he patted her back clumsily.

"He got away," Moumou wept. "I'll never see him again."

"Perhaps it is for the best," the old man said. "He is far from dependable, that fellow."

"I love him, I love him," the girl said wetly. "I'm going to kill him."

"Now, now, Moumou . . ." The father looked around him uneasily, conscious of witnesses behind the shuttered windows.

"I'll show him," the girl said wildly. She broke away from her father and stood accusingly in front of the parked Vespa, glaring at it. "He took me out to the Marne on this the first time we went out together," she said in a throbbing voice, meant to carry the memory of ancient tenderness, betrayed promises, to unseen and guilty ears. "I'll show him." With a swift movement, before her father could do anything to stop her, she took off her right shoe. Violently, holding the shoe by the pointed toe, she smashed the sharp heel into the headlight of the scooter. There was the crash of breaking glass and a tinkling on the pavement, closely followed by a shriek of pain from Moumou.

"What is it? What is it?" The old man asked anxiously.

"I cut myself. I opened a vein." Moumou held out her hands, like Lady Macbeth. Tibbell could see blood spurting from several cuts on her hand and wrist.

"Oh, my poor child," the old man said distractedly. "Hold your hand still. Let me see . . ."

But Moumou pulled her hand away and danced unevenly on her one shoe around the Vespa, waving her arm over the machine, spattering the wheels, the handle bars, the saddle, the back pillion, with the blood that sprayed from her wounds. "There!" she shouted. "You wanted my blood, take it! I hope it brings you good luck!"

"Moumou, don't be so impetuous," the old man implored her. "You will do yourself a permanent harm." Finally he manged to grab his daughter's arm and inspect the cuts. "Oh, oh," he said. "This is dolorous. Stand still." He took out a handkerchief and bound her wrist tight. "Now," he said, "I will take you home and you will get a good night's sleep and you will forget about that serpent."

"No," Moumou said. She backed against the wall of the building on the opposite side of the street and stood there stubbornly. "He will come back for his Vespa. Then I will kill him. And after that I will kill myself."

"Moumou . . ." the old man wailed.

"Go home, Papa."

"How can I go home and leave you like this?"

"I will wait for him if I have to stand here in this place all night,"

Moumou said, her words awash with tears. She gripped the wall behind her with her hands, as if to keep her father from taking her away by force. "He has to come here sometime before the church. He won't get married without his scooter. You go home. I will handle him myself."

"I can't leave you here alone in this condition," the old man said, sighing. Beaten, he sat down again on the curb to rest.

"I want to die," Moumou said.

The street was quiet again, but not for long. The door behind which the two lovers had taken refuge opened and the man in the sports jacket came out, his arm around his girl. They passed slowly beneath Tibbell's window, ostentatiously ignoring Moumou and her father. The old man looked balefully up at the linked couple. "Young lady," he said, "remember my warning. Profit by the events you have witnessed tonight. If it is not too late already. Re-enter into your home. I speak as a friend."

"See here, old man," the man in the sports jacket pulled away from his companion and stood threateningly in front of Moumou's father, "that's enough out of you. I do not permit anybody to speak like that in front of . . ."

"Come on, Edouard," the girl said, pulling the man in the sports jacket away. "It is too late at night to become enraged."

"I ignore you, monsieur," Edouard said, then let the girl lead him away.

"Permit, permit . . ." M. Banary-Cointal said loudly, getting in the last word, as the couple rounded the corner and disappeared.

Tibbell watched the old man and his daughter for another moment, wishing that the two of them would move away from their stations of affliction on his doorstep. It would be difficult to sleep, Tibbell felt, knowing that those two grieving, dissatisfied, vengeful figures were still outside his window, waiting for some horrid, violent last act of their drama.

He was just about to turn away when he heard a car door slam far down the street. He looked and saw a woman in a green dress striding swiftly toward him, away from the car that he had earlier noticed being parked near the far corner. Now the car lights switched on, very bright, and the car followed the woman as she half walked, half ran, in the direction of Moumou and her father. She was obviously in flight. Her dress shone a violent, electric lime color in the headlights of the pursuing car. The car, which was a bright red, new Alfa Romeo Giulietta, stopped abruptly just before it reached the old man, who was still sitting on the curb, but with his head turned suspiciously in the direction of the woman bearing swiftly down on him, as though he feared that she was bringing with her, stranger though she was, a new burden of trouble to load onto his bowed and tortured shoulders. The woman darted toward a doorway, but before she could press the button for entry, a man in a black suit leaped out of the car and seized her wrist.

Tibbell watched without surprise. By now he felt that the street below him was a preordained scene of conflict, like Agincourt or the pass of Thermopylae, and that clash would follow clash there continually, like the performances in a twenty-four-hour-a-day movie house.

"No, you don't!" the man in the black suit was saying, pulling the woman away from the door. "You don't get away that easily."

"Let me go," the woman said, trying to escape. She was breathless and she sounded frightened and Tibbell wondered if now, finally, was the time for him to run down the stairs and enter into the night life of the street in front of his window, a tardy Spartan, a belated recruit for Henry's army.

"I'll let you go when you give me my three hundred francs," the man in the black suit said loudly. He was young and slender and Tibbell could see, by the light of the automobile headlights, that he had a small mustache and long, carefully brushed hair that fell over the back of his high, white collar. He reminded Tibbell of certain young men he had seen lounging in various bars in the neighborhood of Pigalle, and he had the kind of face which looks fitting in newspaper photographs that accompany the stories of the arrest of suspects after particularly well-planned jewel robberies and payroll thefts.

"I don't owe you any three hundred francs," the woman said. Now Tibbell heard that she had an accent in French, probably Spanish. She looked Spanish, too, with luxuriant black hair swooping down over her exposed shoulders, and a wide, shiny black leather belt around a very narrow waist. Her skirt was short and showed her knees every time she moved.

"Don't lie to me," the man in the dark suit said, still holding the woman's wrist and shaking her arm angrily. "It was never my intention to buy them."

"And it was never my intention to let you follow me to my home," the woman snapped back at him, trying to pull away. "Let me go, you've annoyed me enough tonight!"

"Not until I get my three hundred francs," the man said, gripping her more firmly.

"Unless you let me go," the woman said, "I'll call for the police."

The man glared at her and dropped her wrist. Then he slapped her hard across the face.

"Here, here!" said Moumou's father, who had been watching the affair with mournful interest. He stood up. Moumou, lost in the egotism of her own unhappiness, took no notice of what was happening.

The man in the dark suit and the Spanish woman stood close to each other, breathing heavily, looking curiously undecided, as though the slap had brought some new and unexpected problem into their relationship which for the moment confused them and made them uncertain about further action. Then the young man, his white teeth gleaming under his mustache, slowly raised his hand again.

"Once is enough," the woman said and ran over to Moumou's father for protection. "Monsieur," she said, "you have seen him strike me."

"The light is bad," the old man said, even in his sorrow instinctively extricating himself from possible formal involvement with the police. "And at the moment, I happened to be looking the other way. Still," he said to the young man, who was advancing menacingly on the Spanish woman, "let me remind you that striking a woman is considered in certain quarters to be a most serious offense."

"I throw myself on your protection, monsieur," the woman said, stepping behind M. Banary-Cointal.

"Don't worry," the man with the mustache said contemptuously. "I won't hit her again. She is not worth the emotion. All I want is my three hundred francs."

"What do you think of a man," the woman said, from the shelter of the old man's bulk, "who buys a lady flowers and then demands to be reimbursed?"

"To keep the record clear," the man with the mustache said, "let me say once and for all that I never bought her any flowers. When I went to the toilet she took the violets from the basket and when I came back the woman asked me for three hundred francs and rather than make a scene I . . ."

"Please," the old man said, interested now despite himself, "this is all very confusing. If you would be good enough to start from the beginning, perhaps I can be of service."

Tibbell was grateful to the old man for this request for clarification, since without it he was sure he would be kept awake most of the night trying to figure out just what the sequence of events had been which had resulted in this midnight chase and punishment. Tibbell had never hit a woman in his life and could not imagine ever doing so, and certainly never for three hundred francs, which was, after all, worth just about sixty cents.

"Let me reconstruct," the man in the dark suit said immediately, presenting his side quickly, before the Spanish woman could roil the crystal waters of truth. "I saw her sitting at a bar, waiting to be picked up."

"I was not waiting to be picked up," the woman said hotly. "I was on my way home from the cinema and I stopped in to have a glass of beer, before going to bed."

"Enfin," the man in the dark suit said impatiently, "you allowed yourself to be picked up. If we are going to quibble about terms, we will be here all night."

"I allowed you to pay for one glass of beer," the woman said. "I am not responsible for any sordid interpretation you choose to put on it."

"You also allowed me to pay for three hundred francs' worth of violets," the man in the dark suit said.

"I allowed it as a small gesture of gallantry," the woman said haughtily. "In Spain one is used to gentlemen."

"You also allowed yourself to get into my car," the man in the dark suit said, "and you furthermore allowed yourself to inflame the emotions by kissing on the lips."

"That, now," the woman said dramatically to Moumou's father, "is a superb lie."

"If it's a lie," said the man in the dark suit, "what about this?"

Violently, he seized the point of his white collar and pulled it away from his neck to show M. Banary-Cointal.

The old man peered at it nearsightedly, bending close to the man in the dark suit. "What is it?" the old man asked. "It's awfully dark here. I can't see anything."

"Lipstick," said the man in the dark suit. "Look." He took the old man's arm and pulled him over in front of the headlights. Both men leaned over low so that the old man could inspect the collar. M. Banary-Cointal stood up. "There's no doubt about it," he said. "Lipstick."

"Ah," said the man in the dark suit, casting a look of angry triumph at the Spanish woman.

"It is not mine," she said coldly. "Who knows where this gentleman has been spending his time and who knows how many times a week he changes his shirt?"

"I warn you," said the man in the dark suit, his voice thick with rage, "I regard that as insulting."

"What difference does it make whose lipstick it is?" the woman said. "You do not please me. All I want is to be allowed to go home alone."

"Ah," said Moumou, her attention finally caught, "if that were only possible — to go home alone."

Everybody, including Moumou's father, looked puzzledly for a moment at the somber figure against the wall, as though it had been a statue that had given cryptic utterance.

"My dear man," said M. Banary-Cointal reasonably, addressing the man in the dark suit, "certainly this lady has made herself very clear." He made a slight bow in the direction of the Spanish woman, who nodded politely in answer. "She doesn't demand very much. Just to go to her own home in peace. Surely, this is not too much to ask."

"She can go wherever she damn pleases," said the man in the dark suit, "as soon as she gives me my three hundred francs."

A look of censure creased the old man's face. "Monsieur," he said, with some asperity, "I am a little surprised that a man like you, the possessor of an automobile of this quality and price" — he touched the gleaming hood of the little Italian car — "could really need three hundred francs enough to make such a . . ."

"It is not a question of three hundred francs," said the man in the dark suit, his voice beginning to be edged, too, at this imputation of miserliness. "It would not even be a question if the sum were fifty thousand francs. It is a question of principle. I have been led on, I have been inflamed, as I mentioned before, I have been induced to spend my money — the amount has nothing to do with the matter, I assure you, monsieur — all corruptly and under false pretenses. I am a generous and reasonable man but I do not like to be cynically made a fool of by a *putain!*"

"Here, now," the old man said sternly.

"What's more, look at her hand!" The man in the dark suit seized the woman's hand and held it in front of M. Banary-Cointal's eyes. "Do you see that? The wedding ring? By a *putain,* who, on top of everything else, is married!"

Tibbell, listening, fascinated, could not discover why the girl's marital condition added so powerfully to the rage of the man in the dark suit, and concluded that perhaps it was something in the man's past, some painful disappointment with some other married woman that had left him tender on the subject and which now served to pour fuel on the fire of his wrath.

"There is nothing more disgraceful than a Spanish whore with a wedding band," the man in the dark suit shouted.

"Here, that's enough of that," M. Banary-Cointal said with authority, as the woman unexpectedly began to sob. The old man had had enough of women's tears for the night, and this new flood made him testy. "I will not allow you to talk in such terms in front of ladies, one of whom happens to be my daughter," he said to the man in the dark suit. "I suggest you leave immediately."

"I will leave when I get my three hundred francs," the man said stubbornly, crossing his arms.

"Here!" M. Banary-Cointal dug angrily in his pocket and pulled out some coins. "Here are your three hundred francs!" He threw them at the man in the dark suit. They bounced off his chest and onto the pavement. With great agility, the man in the dark suit bent and scooped up the coins and threw them back into M. Banary-Cointal's face. "If you're not careful, monsieur," the old man said with dignity, "you are going to get a punch in the nose."

The man in the dark suit raised his fists and stood there, in the pose of a bare-knuckle English fighter of the early part of the eighteenth century. "I await your attack, monsieur," he said formally. Both women now wept more loudly.

"I warn you, monsieur," M. Banary-Cointal said, taking a step backwards, "that I am sixty-three years of age, with a faulty heart, and besides, I wear glasses, as you can see. The police will be inclined to ask you some very searching questions in the event of an accident."

"The police!" said the man in the dark suit. "Good. It is the first sensible suggestion of the evening. I invite you all to get into my car and accompany me to the commissariat."

"I am not getting into that car again," said the Spanish woman.

"I am not budging from here," Moumou said, "until Raoul gets back."

There was a ringing behind Tibbell, and he suddenly became conscious that it had been going on for some time, and that it was the telephone. He stumbled across the dark room and picked up the instrument, the voices outside his window becoming a blurred buzzing on the night air. He wondered who could be calling him at this time of the night.

"Hello," he said, into the mouthpiece.

"Is this Littré two-five-seven-six?" an impatient female voice crackled through the receiver.

"Yes," Tibbell said.

"On your call to New York," the operator said, "we are ready now."

"Oh, yes," Tibbell said. He had forgotten completely that he had put the call in for Betty. He tried to compose himself and put himself back into the tender and rosy mood that had swept over him an hour before, when he had decided to call her. "I'm waiting."

"Just a minute, please." There were some Atlantic, electric howls on the wire and Tibbell pulled the telephone away from his ear. He tried to hear what was being said outside, but all he could distinguish was the noise of a car starting up and surging down the street.

He stood next to the German's bookcase, the telephone held loosely along his cheek, remembering that he had wanted to tell Betty how much he loved her and missed her, and perhaps, if the conversation turned irrevocably in that direction, as indeed it might in the three allotted minutes, to tell her that he wanted to marry her. He found himself breathing heavily, and the ideas churned confusedly in his head, and when he tried to think of a proper opening phrase, all he could think of was, "There is nothing more disgraceful than a Spanish whore with a wedding band."

"Just a moment, please," said an American voice. "We are ringing."

There was some more electrical scratching and Tibbell switched the phone to his other ear and tried to make out what was being said downstairs and at the same time to push from his mind the remark about the wedding band.

"Miss Thompson is not home," the American voice said, with great crispness and authority. "She has left word she will come back in an hour. Do you wish us to put the call in then?"

"I . . . I. . . ." Tibbell hesitated. He remembered the old man's admonition to the girl who had been kissing in the doorway — "Profit by the events you have witnessed tonight."

"Can you hear me, sir?" the crisp New World voice was saying. "Miss Thompson will be back within an hour. Do you wish to place the call then?"

"I . . . no," Tibbell said. "Cancel the call, please. I'll make it some other time."

"Thank you." America clicked off.

Tibbell put the phone down slowly. After a moment, he walked across to the window, and looked down. The street was empty and silent. Thermopylae had been cleared of corpses. Agincourt lay waiting for the plow. Unfinished, unfinishable, unresolved, unresolvable, the conflict, the inextricable opponents, had moved off into the darkness, and now there were only fleeting admonitory echoes, ghosts with warning fingers raised to vanishing lips.

Then Tibbell saw a figure stealing furtively down the other side of the street, keeping close to the walls. It was Raoul. He came out into the light of the lamppost to inspect the scooter. He kicked once at the broken glass on the pavement. Then he waved at the corner. A girl came running out toward him, her white dress gay and dancing and bridal on the dark street. As she sat on the pillion behind Raoul and put her arms lovingly around his waist, she laughed softly. Her laughter rose lightly and provocatively to Tibbell's window. Raoul started the Vespa, with the usual loud, underpowered, falsely important snarl. The Vespa, without headlight, sped down the street, the white dress dancing in the wind, slanting out of sight at the far corner. Tibbell sighed and silently wished the bride luck.

Downstairs, there was the creak of a shutter.

"Spaniards," the night voice said, "what can you expect from Spaniards?"

The shutter creaked again and the voice ceased.

Tibbell closed his own shutters. As he stepped back into the dark room he was thankful for the first time that he had gone to Exeter and Swarthmore for his education.

(From The New Yorker)

PIGEON FEATHERS

BY JOHN UPDIKE

*W*HEN they moved to Firetown, things were upset, displaced, rearranged. A red cane-back sofa that had been the chief piece in the living room at Olinger was here banished, too big for the narrow country parlor, to the barn, and shrouded under a tarpaulin. Never again would David lie on its length all afternoon eating raisins and reading mystery novels and science fiction and P. G. Wodehouse. The blue wing chair that had stood for years in the ghostly, immaculate guest bedroom in town, gazing through windows curtained with dotted swiss at the telephone wires and horse-chestnut trees and opposite houses, was here established importantly in front of the smutty little fireplace that supplied, in those first cold April days, their only heat. As a child, David had always been afraid of the guest bedroom — it was there that he, lying sick with the measles, had seen a black rod the size of a yard-stick jog along at a slight slant beside the edge of the bed, and vanish when he screamed — and it was disquieting to have one of the elements of its haunted atmosphere basking by the fire, in the center of the family, growing sooty with use. The books that at home had gathered dust in the case beside the piano were here hastily stacked, all out of order, in the shelves that the carpenters had built low along one wall. David, at fourteen, had been more moved than a mover; like the furniture, he had to find a new place, and on the Saturday of the second week tried to work off some of his disorientation by arranging the books.

It was a collection obscurely depressing to him, mostly books his

mother had acquired when she was young: college anthologies of
Greek plays and Romantic poetry; Will Durant's *Story of Philosophy;* a soft-leather set of Shakespeare with string bookmarks sewed
to the bindings; *Green Mansions,* boxed and illustrated with wood-
cuts; *I, the Tiger,* by Manuel Komroff; novels by names like Galsworthy and Ellen Glasgow and Irvin S. Cobb and Sinclair Lewis
and "Elizabeth." The odor of faded taste made him feel the ominous gap between himself and his parents, the insulting gulf of
time that existed before he was born. Suddenly he was tempted to
dip into this time. From the heaps of books around him on the
broad old floorboards, he picked up Volume II of a four-volume set
of *An Outline of History,* by H. G. Wells. The book's red binding
had faded to orange-pink on the spine. When he lifted the cover,
there was a sweetish, atticlike smell, and his mother's maiden name
written in unfamiliar handwriting on the flyleaf — an upright,
bold, yet careful signature, bearing a faint relation to the quick
scrunched backslant that flowed with marvelous consistency across
her shopping lists and budget accounts and notes on Christmas cards
to college friends from this same, vaguely menacing long ago.

He leafed through, pausing at drawings, done in an old-fashioned
stippled style, of bas-reliefs, masks, Romans without pupils in their
eyes, articles of ancient costume, fragments of pottery found in
unearthed homes. The print was determinedly legible, and smug,
like a lesson book. As he bent over the pages, yellow at the edges,
they were like rectangles of dusty glass through which he looked
down into unreal and irrelevant worlds. He could see things slug-
gishly move, and an unpleasant fullness came into his throat. His
mother and grandmother fussed in the kitchen; the puppy, which
they had just acquired, "for protection in the country," was cowering, with a sporadic panicked scrabble of claws, under the dining
table that in their old home had been reserved for special days but
that here was used for every meal.

Then, before he could halt his eyes, David slipped into Wells's
account of Jesus. He had been an obscure political agitator, a kind
of hobo, in a minor colony of the Roman Empire. By an accident
impossible to reconstruct, he (the small *h* horrified David) survived
his own crucifixion and presumably died a few weeks later. A religion was founded on the freakish incident. The credulous imagination of the times retrospectively assigned miracles and super-

natural pretensions to Jesus; a myth grew, and then a church, whose theology at most points was in direct contradiction of the simple, rather communistic teachings of the Galilean.

It was as if a stone that for weeks and even years had been gathering weight in the web of David's nerves snapped them, plunged through the page, and a hundred layers of paper underneath. These fantastic falsehoods (plainly untrue; churches stood everywhere, the entire nation was founded "under God") did not at first frighten him; it was the fact that they had been permitted to exist in an actual human brain. This was the initial impact — that at a definite spot in time and space a brain black with the denial of Christ's divinity had been suffered to exist; that the universe had not spit out this ball of tar but allowed it to continue in its blasphemy, to grow old, win honors, wear a hat, write books that, if true, collapsed everything into a jumble of horror. The world outside the deep-silled windows — a rutted lawn, a whitewashed barn, a walnut tree frothy with fresh green — seemed a haven from which he was forever sealed off. Hot washrags seemed pressed against his cheeks.

He read the account again. He tried to supply out of his ignorance objections that would defeat the complacent march of these black words, and found none. Survivals and misunderstandings more farfetched were reported daily in the papers. But none of them caused churches to be built in every town. He tried to work backward through the churches, from their brave high fronts through their shabby, ill-attended interiors back into the events at Jerusalem, and felt himself surrounded by shifting gray shadows, centuries of history, where he knew nothing. The thread dissolved in his hands. Had Christ ever come to him, David Kern, and said, "Here. Feel the wound in My side"? No; but prayers had been answered. What prayers? He had prayed that Rudy Mohn, whom he had purposely tripped so he cracked his head on their radiator, not die, and he had not died. But for all the blood, it was just a cut; Rudy came back the same day, wearing a bandage and repeating the same teasing words. He could never have died. Again, David had prayed for two separate photographs of movie stars he had sent away for to arrive tomorrow, and though they did not, they did arrive, some days later, together, popping through the clacking letter slot like a rebuke from God's mouth: *I answer your prayers in My way, in My time.* After that, he had made his prayers less definite, less susceptible of being twisted into a scolding. But what a tiny, ridiculous coincidence this was, after all, to throw into battle against H. G. Wells's engines of knowledge! Indeed, it proved the enemy's point: Hope bases vast premises on foolish accidents, and reads a word where in fact only a scribble exists.

His father came home. They had supper. It got dark. He had to go to the bathroom, and took a flashlight down through the wet grass to the outhouse. For once, his fear of spiders there felt trivial. He set the flashlight, burning, beside him, and an insect alighted on its lens, a tiny insect, a mosquito or flea, so fragile and fine that the weak light projected its X-ray onto the wall boards: the faint rim of its wings, the blurred strokes, magnified, of its long hinged legs, the dark cone at the heart of its anatomy. The tremor must be its heart beating. Without warning, David was visited by an exact vision of death: a long hole in the ground, no wider than your body, down which you are drawn while the white faces above recede. You try to reach them but your arms are pinned. Shovels pour dirt into your face. There you will be forever, in an upright position, blind and silent, and in time no one will remember you, and you will never be called. As strata of rock shift, your fingers elongate, and your teeth are distended sidewise in a great underground grimace indistinguishable from a strip of chalk. And the earth tumbles on, and the sun expires, and unaltering darkness reigns where once there were stars.

Sweat broke out on his back. His mind seemed to rebound off of a solidness. Such extinction was not another threat, a graver sort of danger, a kind of pain; it was qualitatively different. It was not even a conception that could be voluntarily pictured; it entered you from outside. His protesting nerves swarmed on its surface like lichen on a meteor. The skin of his chest was soaked with the effort of rejection. At the same time that the fear was dense and internal, it was dense and all around him; a tide of clay had swept up to the stars; space was crushed into a mass. When he stood up, automatically hunching his shoulders to keep his head away from the spider webs, it was with a numb sense of being cramped between two huge volumes of rigidity. That he had even this small freedom to move surprised him. In the narrow shelter of that rank shack, adjusting his pants, he felt — his first spark of comfort — too small to be crushed.

But in the open, as the beam of the flashlight skidded with fright-ened quickness across the remote surfaces of the barn wall and the grape arbor and the giant pine that stood by the path to the woods, the terror descended. He raced up through the clinging grass pur-sued not by one of the wild animals the woods might hold, or one of the goblins his superstitious grandmother had communicated to his childhood, but by specters out of science fiction, where gigantic cinder moons fill half the turquoise sky. As David ran, a gray planet rolled inches behind his neck. If he looked back, he would be buried. And in the momentum of his terror, hideous possibilities — the dilation of the sun, the triumph of the insects — wheeled out of the vacuum of make-believe and added their weight to his impending oblivion.

He wrenched the door open; the lamps within the house flared. The wicks burning here and there seemed to mirror one another. His mother was washing the dishes in a little pan of heated pump water; Granmom fluttered near her elbow apprehensively. In the living room — the downstairs of the little square house was two long rooms — his father sat in front of the black fireplace restlessly folding and unfolding a newspaper.

David took from the shelf, where he had placed it this afternoon, the great unabridged Webster's Dictionary that his grandfather had owned. He turned the big thin pages, floppy as cloth, to the entry he wanted, and read:

soul . . . 1. An entity conceived as the essence, substance, ani-mating principle, or actuating cause of life, or of the individual life, esp. of life manifested in physical activities; the vehicle of individ-ual existence, separate in nature from the body and usually held to be separable in existence.

The definition went on, into Greek and Egyptian conceptions, but David stopped short on the treacherous edge of antiquity. He needed to read no farther. The careful overlapping words shingled a temporary shelter for him. "Usually held to be separable in existence" — what could be fairer, more judicious, surer?

Upstairs, he seemed to be lifted above his fears. The sheets on his bed were clean. Granmom had ironed them with a pair of flat-irons saved from the Olinger attic; she plucked them hot off the stove alternately, with a wooden handle called a goose. It was a wonder, to see how she managed. In the next room, his parents made comforting scratching noises as they carried a little lamp back and forth. Their door was open a crack, so he saw the light shift and swing. Surely there would be, in the last five minutes, in the last second, a crack of light, showing the door from the dark room to another, full of light. Thinking of it this vividly frightened him. His own dying, in a specific bed in a specific room, specific walls mottled with wallpaper, the dry whistle of his breathing, the murmuring doctors, the nervous relatives going in and out, but for him no way out but down into the funnel. Never touch a doorknob again. A whisper, and his parents' light was blown out. David prayed to be reassured. Though the experiment frightened him, he lifted his hands high into the darkness above his face and begged Christ to touch them. Not hard or long; the faintest, quickest grip would be final for a lifetime. His hands waited in the air, itself a substance, which seemed to move through his fingers; or was it the pressure of his pulse? He returned his hands to beneath the covers uncertain if they had been touched or not. For would not Christ's touch *be* infinitely gentle?

Through all the eddies of its aftermath, David clung to this thought about his revelation of extinction: that there, in the outhouse, he had struck a solidness *qualitatively different,* a rock of horror firm enough to support any height of construction. All he needed was a little help; a word, a gesture, a nod of certainty and he would be sealed in, safe. The assurance from the dictionary had melted in the night. Today was Sunday, a hot fair day. Across a mile of clear air the church bells called, *Celebrate, celebrate.* Only Daddy went. He put on a coat over his rolled-up shirtsleeves and got into the little old black Plymouth parked by the barn and went off, with the same pained, hurried grimness of all his actions. His churning wheels, as he shifted too hastily into second, raised plumes of red dust on the dirt road. Mother walked to the far field, to see what bushes needed cutting. David, though he usually preferred to stay in the house, went with her. The puppy followed at a distance, whining as it picked its way through the stubble but floundering off timidly if one of them went back to pick it up and carry it. When they reached the crest of the far field, his mother asked, "David, what's troubling you?"

"Nothing. Why?"

She looked at him sharply. The greening woods crosshatched the space beyond her half-gray hair. Then she turned her profile, and gestured toward the house, which they had left a half mile behind them. "See how it sits in the land? They don't know how to build with the land any more. Pop always said the foundations were set with the compass. We must try to get a compass and see. It's supposed to face due south; but south feels a little more *that* way to me." From the side, as she said these things, she seemed handsome and young. The smooth sweep of her hair over her ear seemed white with a purity and calm that made her feel foreign to him. He had never regarded his parents as consolers of his troubles; from the beginning they had seemed to have more troubles than he. Their confusion had flattered him into an illusion of strength; so now on this high clear ridge he jealously guarded the menace all around them, blowing like a breeze on his fingertips, the possibility of all this wide scenery sinking into darkness. The strange fact that though she came to look at the brush she carried no clippers, for she had a fixed prejudice against working on Sundays, was the only consolation he allowed her to offer.

As they walked back, the puppy whimpering after them, the rising dust behind a distant line of trees announced that Daddy was speeding home from church. When they reached the house he was there. He had brought back the Sunday paper and the vehement remark "Dobson's too intelligent for these farmers. They just sit there with their mouths open and don't hear a thing he's saying."

David hid in the funny papers and sports section until one-thirty. At two, the catechetical class met at the Firetown church. He had transferred from the catechetical class of the Lutheran church in Olinger, a humiliating comedown. In Olinger they met on Wednesday nights, spiffy and spruce, in the atmosphere of a dance. Afterward, blessed by the brick-faced minister from whose lips the word "Christ" fell like a burning stone, the more daring of them went with their Bibles to a luncheonette and smoked. Here in Firetown, the girls were dull white cows and the boys narrow-faced brown goats in old men's suits, herded on Sunday afternoons into a threadbare church basement that smelled of stale hay. Because his father had taken the car on one of his countless errands to Olinger, David walked, grateful for the open air and the silence.

The catechetical class embarrassed him, but today he placed hope in it, as the source of the nod, the gesture, that was all he needed.

Reverend Dobson was a delicate young man with great dark eyes and small white shapely hands that flickered like protesting doves when he preached; he seemed a bit misplaced in the Lutheran ministry. This was his first call. It was a split parish; he served another rural church twelve miles away. His iridescent green Ford, new six months ago, was spattered to the windows with red mud and rattled from bouncing on the rude back roads, where he frequently got lost, to the malicious satisfaction of many. But David's mother liked him, and, more pertinent to his success, the Haiers, the sleek family of feed merchants and innkeepers and tractor salesmen who dominated the Firetown church, liked him. David liked him, and felt liked in turn; sometimes in class, after some special stupidity, Dobson directed toward him out of those wide black eyes a mild look of disbelief, a look that, though flattering, was also delicately disquieting.

Catechetical instruction consisted of reading aloud from a work booklet answers to problems prepared during the week, problems like "I am the ——, the ——, and the ——, saith the Lord." Then there was a question period in which no one ever asked any questions. Today's theme was the last third of the Apostles' Creed. When the time came for questions, David blushed and asked, "About the Resurrection of the Body — are we conscious between the time when we die and the Day of Judgment?"

Dobson blinked, and his fine little mouth pursed, suggesting that David was making difficult things more difficult. The faces of the other students went blank, as if an indiscretion had been committed.

"No, I suppose not," Reverend Dobson said.

"Well, where is our soul, then, in this gap?"

The sense grew, in the class, of a naughtiness occurring. Dobson's shy eyes watered, as if he were straining to keep up the formality of attention, and one of the girls, the fattest, simpered toward her twin, who was a little less fat. Their chairs were arranged in a rough circle. The current running around the circle panicked David. Did everybody know something he didn't know?

"I suppose you could say our souls are asleep," Dobson said.

"And then they wake up, and there is the earth like it always is, and all the people who have ever lived? Where will Heaven be?"

Anita Haier giggled. Dobson gazed at David intently, but with an awkward, puzzled flicker of forgiveness, as if there existed a secret between them that David was violating. But David knew of no secret. All he wanted was to hear Dobson repeat the words he said every Sunday morning. This he would not do. As if these words were unworthy of the conversational voice.

"David, you might think of Heaven this way: as the way the goodness Abraham Lincoln did lives after him."

"But is Lincoln conscious of it living on?" He blushed no longer with embarrassment but in anger; he had walked here in good faith and was being made a fool.

"Is he conscious now? I would have to say no; but I don't think it matters." Dobson's voice had a coward's firmness; he was hostile now.

"You don't?"

"Not in the eyes of God, no." The unction, the stunning impudence, of this reply sprang tears of outrage in David's eyes. He bowed them to his book, where short words like Duty, Love, Obey, Honor were stacked in the form of a cross.

"Were there any other questions, David?" Dobson asked with renewed gentleness. The others were rustling, collecting their books.

"No." He made his voice firm, though he could not bring up his eyes.

"Did I answer your question fully enough?"

"Yes."

In the minister's silence the shame that should have been his crept over David; the burden and fever of being a fraud were placed upon *him*, who was innocent, and it seemed, he knew, a confession of this guilt that on the way out he was unable to face Dobson's stirred gaze, though he felt it probing the side of his head.

Anita Haier's father gave him a ride down the highway as far as the dirt road. David said he wanted to walk the rest, and figured that his offer was accepted because Mr. Haier did not want to dirty his bright blue Buick with dust. This was all right; everything was all right, as long as it was clear. His indignation at being betrayed, at seeing Christianity betrayed, had hardened him. The straight dirt road reflected his hardness. Pink stones thrust up through its packed surface. The April sun beat down from the center of the afternoon half of the sky; already it had some of summer's heat. Already the fringes of weeds at the edges of the road were bedraggled with dust. From the reviving grass and scruff of the fields he walked between, insects were sending up a monotonous, automatic chant. In the distance a tiny figure in his father's coat was walking along the edge of the woods. His mother. He wondered what joy she found in such walks; to him the brown stretches of slowly rising and falling land expressed only a huge exhaustion.

Flushed with fresh air and happiness, she returned from her walk earlier than he had expected, and surprised him at his grandfather's Bible. It was a stumpy black book, the boards worn thin where the old man's fingers had held them; the spine hung by one weak hinge of fabric. David had been looking for the passage where Jesus says to the one thief on the cross "Today shalt thou be with me in paradise." He had never tried reading the Bible for himself before. What was so embarrassing about being caught at it was that he detested the apparatus of piety. Fusty churches, creaking hymns, ugly Sunday-school teachers and their stupid leaflets — he hated everything about them but the promise they held out, a promise that in the most perverse way, as if the homeliest crone in the kingdom were given the prince's hand, made every good and real thing, ball games and jokes and big-breasted girls, possible. He couldn't explain this to his mother. Her solicitude was upon him.

"David, what are you doing at Granpop's Bible?"

"Trying to read it. This is supposed to be a Christian country, isn't it?"

She sat down on the green sofa that used to be in the sun parlor at Olinger, under the fancy mirror. A little smile still lingered on her face from the walk. "David, I wish you'd talk to me."

"What about?"

"About whatever it is that's troubling you. Your father and I have both noticed it."

"I asked Reverend Dobson about Heaven and he said it was like Abraham Lincoln's goodness living after him."

He waited for the shock to strike her. "Yes?" she said, expecting more.

"That's all."

"And why didn't you like it?"

"Well; don't you see? It amounts to saying there isn't any Heaven at all."

"I don't see that it amounts to that. What do you want Heaven to be?"

"Well, I don't know. I want it to be *something*. I thought *he'd* tell me what it was. I thought that was his job." He was becoming angry, sensing her surprise at him. She had assumed that Heaven had faded from his head years ago. She had imagined that he had already entered, in the secrecy of silence, the conspiracy that he now knew to be all around him.

"David," she asked gently, "don't you ever want to rest?"

"No. Not forever."

"David, you're so young. When you get older, you'll feel differently."

"Grandpa didn't. Look how tattered this book is."

"I never understood your grandfather."

"Well, I don't understand ministers who say it's like Lincoln's memory going on and on. Suppose you're not Lincoln?"

"I think Reverend Dobson made a mistake. You must try to forgive him."

"It's not a *question* of his making a mistake! It's a question of dying and never moving or seeing or hearing anything ever again."

"But" — in exasperation — "darling, it's so *greedy* of you to want more. When God has given us this wonderful April day, and given us this farm, and you have your whole life ahead of you — "

"You think, then, that there is God?"

"Of course I do" — with deep relief that smoothed her features into a reposeful oval. He was standing, and above her, too near for his comfort. He was afraid she would reach out and touch him.

"He made everything? You feel that?"

"Yes."

"Then who made Him?"

"Why, Man. Man." The happiness of this answer lit up her face radiantly, until she saw his gesture of disgust.

"Well that amounts to saying there is none."

Her hand reached for his wrist but he backed away. "David, it's a mystery. A miracle. It's a miracle more beautiful than any Reverend Dobson could have told you about. You don't say houses don't exist because Man made them."

"No. God has to be different."

"But, David, you have the *evidence*. Look out the window at the sun; at the fields."

"Mother, good grief. Don't you see" — he gasped away the roughness in his throat — "if when we die there's nothing, all your sun and fields and what not are all, ah, *horror?* It's just an ocean of horror."

"But David, it's not. It's so clearly not that." And she made an urgent opening gesture with her hands that expressed, with its suggestion of a willingness to receive his helplessness, all her grace, her gentleness, her love of beauty gathered into a passive intensity that made him intensely hate her. He would not be wooed away from the truth. *I am the Way, the Truth —*

"No," he told her. "Just let me alone."

He found his tennis ball behind the piano and went outside to throw it against the side of the house. There was a patch high up where the brown stucco that had been laid over the sandstone masonry was crumbling away; he kept trying with the tennis ball to chip more pieces off. Superimposed upon his deep ache was a smaller but more immediate worry that he had hurt his mother. He heard his father's car rattling on the straightaway, and went into the house, to make peace before he arrived. To his relief, she was not giving off the stifling damp heat of her anger but instead was cool, decisive, maternal. She handed him an old green book, her college text of Plato.

"I want you to read the Parable of the Cave," she said.

"All right," he said, though he knew it would do no good. Some story by a dead Greek just vague enough to please her. "Don't worry about it, Mother."

"I *am* worried. Honestly, David, I'm sure there will be something for us. As you get older, these things seem to matter a great deal less."

"That may be. It's a dismal thought, though."

His father bumped at the door. The locks and jambs stuck here. But before Granmom could totter to the catch and let him in, he had knocked it open. Although Mother usually kept her talks with David a confidence, a treasure between them, she called instantly, "George, David is worried about death!"

He came to the doorway of the living room, his shirt pocket bristling with pencils, holding in one hand a pint box of melting ice cream and in the other the knife with which he was about to divide it into four sections, their Sunday treat. "Is the kid worried about death? Don't give it a thought, David. I'll be lucky if I live till tomorrow, and I'm not worried. If they'd taken a buckshot gun and shot me in the cradle I'd be better off. The *world*'d be better off. Hell, I think death is a wonderful thing. I look forward to it. Get the garbage out of the way. If I had the man here who invented death, I'd pin a medal on him."

"Hush, George. You'll frighten the child worse than he is."

This was not true; he never frightened David. There was no harm in his father, no harm at all. Indeed, in the man's steep self-disgust the boy felt a kind of ally. A distant ally. He saw his position with a certain strategic coldness. Nowhere in the world of other people would he find the hint, the nod, he needed to begin to build his fortress against death. They none of them believed. He was alone. In a deep hole.

In the months that followed, his position changed little. School was some comfort. All those sexy, perfumed people, wisecracking, chewing gum, all of them doomed to die, and none of them noticing. In their company David felt that they would carry him along into the bright, cheap paradise reserved for them. In any crowd, the fear ebbed a little; he had reasoned that somewhere in the world there must exist a few people who believed what was necessary, and the larger the crowd, the greater the chance that he was near such a soul, within calling distance, if only he was not too ignorant, too ill-equipped, to spot him. The sight of clergymen cheered him; whatever they themselves thought, their collars were still a sign that somewhere, at some time, someone had recognized that we cannot, *cannot,* submit to death. The sermon topics posted outside churches, the flip hurried pieties of disc jockeys, the cartoons in magazines showing angels or devils — on such scraps he kept alive the possibility of hope.

For the rest, he tried to drown his hopelessness in clatter and jostle. The pinball machine at the luncheonette was a merciful distraction; as he bent over its buzzing, flashing board of flippers and cushions, the weight and constriction in his chest lightened and loosened. He was grateful for all the time his father wasted in Olin-

ger. Every delay postponed the moment when they must ride together down the dirt road into the heart of the dark farmland,
where the only light was the kerosene lamp waiting on the dining-
room table, a light that made their food shadowy, scrabbled, sinis-
ter.

He lost his appetite for reading. He was afraid of being am-
bushed again. In mystery novels people died like dolls being discarded; in science fiction enormities of space and time conspired to
crush the humans; and even in P. G. Wodehouse he felt a hollowness, a turning away from reality that was implicitly bitter and became explicit in the comic figures of futile clergymen. All gaiety
seemed minced out on the skin of a void. All quiet hours seemed
invitations to dread.

School stopped. His father took the car in the opposite direction,
to a construction job where he had been hired for the summer as a
timekeeper, and David was stranded in the middle of acres of heat
and greenery and blowing pollen and the strange, mechanical humming that lay invisibly in the weeds and alfalfa and dry orchard
grass.

For his fifteenth birthday his parents gave him, with jokes about
his being a hillbilly now, a Remington .22. It was somewhat like a
pinball machine to take it out to the old kiln in the woods, where
they dumped their trash, and set up tin cans on the kiln's sandstone shoulder and shoot them off one by one. He'd take the
puppy, who had grown long legs and a rich coat of reddish fur —
he was part chow. Copper hated the gun but loved David enough
to accompany him. When the flat acrid crack rang out, he would
race in terrified circles that would tighten and tighten until they
brought him, shivering, against David's legs. Depending upon his
mood, David would shoot again or drop to his knees and comfort
the dog. Giving this comfort to a degree returned comfort to him.
The dog's ears, laid flat against his skull in fear, were folded so in-
tricately, so — he groped for the concept — *surely*. Where the dull-
studded collar made his fur stand up, each hair showed a root of
soft white under the length, black-tipped, of the metal color that
had given the dog its name. In his agitation Copper panted
through nostrils that were elegant slits, like two healed cuts, or
like the keyholes of a dainty lock of black, grained wood. His whole
whorling, knotted, jointed body was a wealth of such embellish-

ments. And in the smell of the dog's hair David seemed to descend through many finely differentiated layers of earth: mulch, soil, sand, clay, and the glittering mineral base.

But when he returned to the house, and saw the books arranged on the low shelves, fear returned. The four adamant volumes of Wells like four thin bricks, the green Plato that had puzzled him with its queer softness and tangled purity, the dead Galsworthy and "Elizabeth," Grandpa's mammoth dictionary, Grandpa's Bible, the Bible that he himself had received on becoming a member of the Firetown Lutheran Church — at the sight of these, the memory of his fear reawakened and came around him. He had grown stiff and stupid in its embrace. His parents tried to think of ways to entertain him.

"David, I have a job for you to do," his mother said one evening at the table.

"What?"

"If you're going to take that tone perhaps we'd better not talk."

"What tone? I didn't take any tone."

"Your grandmother thinks there are too many pigeons in the barn."

"Why?" David turned to look at his grandmother, but she sat there staring at the orange flame of the burning lamp with her usual expression of bewilderment.

Mother shouted, "Mom, he wants to know why?"

Granmom made a jerky, irritable motion with her bad hand, as if generating the force for utterance, and said, "They foul the furniture."

"That's right," Mother said. "She's afraid for that old Olinger furniture that we'll never use. David, she's been after me for a month about those poor pigeons. She wants you to shoot them."

"I don't want to kill anything especially," David said.

Daddy said, "The kid's like you are, Elsie. He's too good for this world. Kill or be killed, that's my motto."

His mother said loudly, "Mother, he doesn't want to do it."

"Not?" The old lady's eyes distended as if in horror, and her claw descended slowly to her lap.

"Oh, I'll do it, I'll do it tomorrow," David snapped, and a pleasant crisp taste entered his mouth with the decision.

"And I had thought, when Boyer's men made the hay, it would be better if the barn doesn't look like a rookery," his mother added needlessly.

A barn, in day, is a small night. The splinters of light between the dry shingles pierce the high roof like stars, and the rafters and crossbeams and built-in ladders seem, until your eyes adjust, as mysterious as the branches of a haunted forest. David entered silently, the gun in one hand. Copper whined desperately at the door, too frightened to come in with the gun yet unwilling to leave the boy. David stealthily turned, said, "Go away," shut the door on the dog, and slipped the bolt across. It was a door within a door; the double door for wagons and tractors was as high and wide as the face of a house.

The smell of old straw scratched his sinuses. The red sofa, half hidden under its white-splotched tarpaulin, seemed assimilated into this smell, sunk in it, buried. The mouths of empty bins gaped like caves. Rusty oddments of farming — coils of baling wire, some spare tines for a harrow, a handleless shovel — hung on nails driven here and there in the thick wood. He stood stock-still a minute; it took a while to separate the cooing of the pigeons from the rustling in his ears. When he had focused on the cooing, it flooded the vast interior with its throaty, bubbling outpour: there seemed no other sound. They were up behind the beams. What light there was leaked through the shingles and the dirty glass windows at the far end and the small round holes, about as big as basketballs, high on the opposite stone side walls, under the ridge of the roof.

A pigeon appeared in one of these holes, on the side toward the house. It flew in, with a battering of wings, from the outside, and waited there, silhouetted against its pinched bit of sky, preening and cooing in a throbbing, thrilled, tentative way. David tiptoed four steps to the side, rested his gun against the lowest rung of a ladder pegged between two upright beams, and lowered the gunsight into the bird's tiny, jauntily cocked head. The slap of the report seemed to come off the stone wall behind him, and the pigeon did not fall. Neither did it fly. Instead it stuck in the round hole, pirouetting rapidly and nodding its head as if in frantic agreement. David shot the bolt back and forth and had aimed again before the spent cartridge stopped jingling on the boards by his feet. He eased the tip of the sight a little lower, into the bird's breast, and took care to squeeze the trigger with perfect evenness. The slow contraction of his hand abruptly sprang the bullet; for a half second there was doubt, and then the pigeon fell like a handful of rags, skimming down the barn wall into the layer of straw that coated the floor of the mow on this side.

Now others shook loose from the rafters, and whirled in the dim air with a great blurred hurtle of feathers and noise. They would go for the hole; he fixed his sights on the little moon of blue, and when a pigeon came to it, shot him as he was walking the ten inches or so of stone that would carry him into the open air. This pigeon lay down in that tunnel of stone, unable to fall either one way or the other, although he was alive enough to lift one wing and cloud the light. It would sink back, and he would suddenly lift it again, the feathers flaring. His body blocked that exit. David raced to the other side of the barn's main aisle, where a similar ladder was symmetrically placed, and rested his gun on the same rung. Three birds came together to this hole; he got one, and two got through. The rest resettled in the rafters.

There was a shallow triangular space behind the crossbeams supporting the roof. It was here they roosted and hid. But either the space was too small, or they were curious, for now that his eyes were at home in the dusty gloom David could see little dabs of gray popping in and out. The cooing was shriller now; its apprehensive tremolo made the whole volume of air seem liquid. He noticed one little smudge of a head that was especially persistent in peeking out; he marked the place, and fixed his gun on it, and when the head appeared again, had his finger tightened in advance on the trigger. A parcel of fluff slipped off the beam and fell the barn's height onto a canvas covering some Olinger furniture, and where its head had peeked out there was a fresh prick of light in the shingles.

Standing in the center of the floor, fully master now, disdaining to steady the barrel with anything but his arm, he killed two more that way. He felt like a beautiful avenger. Out of the shadowy ragged infinity of the vast barn roof these impudent things dared to thrust their heads, presumed to dirty its starred silence with their filthy timorous life, and he cut them off, tucked them back neatly into the silence. He had the sensations of a creator; these little smudges and flickers that he was clever to see and even cleverer to hit in the dim recesses of the rafters — out of each of them he was making a full bird. A tiny peek, probe, dab of life, when he hit it, blossomed into a dead enemy, falling with good, final weight.

The imperfection of the second pigeon he had shot, who was still lifting his wing now and then up in the round hole, nagged him. He put a new clip into the stock. Hugging the gun against his body, he climbed the ladder. The barrel sight scratched his ear; he had a sharp, bright vision, like a color slide, of shooting himself and being found tumbled on the barn floor among his prey. He locked his arm around the top rung — a fragile, gnawed rod braced between uprights — and shot into the bird's body from a flat angle. The wing folded, but the impact did not, as he had hoped, push the bird out of the hole. He fired again, and again, and still the little body, lighter than air when alive, was too heavy to budge from its high grave. From up here he could see green trees and a brown corner of the house through the hole. Clammy with the cobwebs that gathered between the rungs, he pumped a full clip of eight bullets into the stubborn shadow, with no success. He climbed down, and was struck by the silence in the barn. The remaining pigeons must have escaped out the other hole. That was all right; he was tired of it.

He stepped with his rifle into the light. His mother was coming to meet him, and it amused him to see her shy away from the carelessly held gun. "You took a chip out of the house," she said. "What were those last shots about?"

"One of them died up in that little round window and I was trying to shoot it down."

"Copper's hiding behind the piano and won't come out. I had to leave him."

"Well, don't blame me. *I* didn't want to shoot the poor devils."

"Don't smirk. You look like your father. How many did you get?"

"Six."

She went into the barn, and he followed. She listened to the silence. Her hair was scraggly, perhaps from tussling with the dog. "I don't suppose the others will be back," she said wearily. "Indeed, I don't know why I let Mother talk me into it. Their cooing was such a comforting noise." She began to gather up the dead birds. Though he didn't want to touch them, David went into the mow and picked up by its tepid, horny, coral-colored feet the first bird he had killed. Its wings unfolded disconcertingly, as if the creature had been held together by threads that now were slit. It did not weigh much. He retrieved the one on the other side of the barn; his mother got the three in the middle, and led the way across the road to the little southern slope of land that went down toward the foundations of the vanished tobacco shed. The ground was too steep to plant or mow; wild strawberries grew in the tangled grass. She put her burden down and said, "We'll have to bury them. The dog will go wild."

He put his two down on her three; the slick feathers let the bodies slide liquidly on one another. He asked, "Shall I get you the shovel?"

"Get it for yourself; *you* bury them. They're your kill," she said. "And be sure to make the hole deep enough so he won't dig them up."

While he went to the tool shed for the shovel, she went into the house. Unlike her, she did not look up, either at the orchard to the right of her or at the meadow on her left, but instead held her head rigidly, tilted a little, as if listening to the ground.

He dug the hole, in a spot where there were no strawberry plants, before he studied the pigeons. He had never seen a bird this close before. The feathers were more wonderful than dog's hair; for each filament was shaped within the shape of the feather, and the feathers in turn were trimmed to fit a pattern that flowed without error across the bird's body. He lost himself in the geometrical tides as the feathers now broadened and stiffened to make an edge for flight, now softened and constricted to cup warmth around the mute flesh. And across the surface of the infinitely adjusted yet somehow effortless mechanics of the feathers played idle designs of color, no two alike, designs executed, it seemed, in a controlled rapture, with a joy that hung level in the air above and behind him. Yet these birds bred in the millions and were exterminated as pests. Into the fragrant, open earth he dropped one broadly banded in shades of slate blue, and on top of it another, mottled all over with rhythmic patches of lilac and gray. The next was almost wholly white, yet with a salmon glaze at the throat. As he fitted the last two, still pliant, on the top, and stood up, crusty coverings were lifted from him, and with a feminine, slipping sensation along his nerves that seemed to give the air hands, he was robed in this certainty: that the God who had lavished such craft upon these worthless birds would not destroy His whole Creation by refusing to let David live forever.

BIOGRAPHICAL NOTES

FRIEDA ARKIN was born in Brooklyn, but raised in a small village in upper New York state. She received her B.A. from the University of Chicago and her M.A. from Columbia University, in the field of anthropology. She taught this subject at Hunter College for seven years before deciding to devote herself thereafter to her husband, two children, and the writing of short fiction. She has published, to date, several anthropological articles and four short stories.

WAYSON S. CHOY was born in Vancouver and attended schools in British Columbia and Ontario. He is presently at the University of British Columbia, majoring in English, creative writing, and sociology. His past occupations have all been summer jobs: working in a restaurant, frying fish and chips at the beach, doing general office work, digging ditches, working as an editorial assistant and as a sociological research assistant, and finally as Managing Director of Prism.

"The Sound of Waves" in his first published story. Another story will soon appear in Exchange and several others will appear in future issues of Prism.

EDWARD DAHLBERG was born in Boston, but raised in Kansas City, Missouri. His first novel, Bottom Dogs, was published in England in 1929, with an introduction by D. H. Lawrence, and in the United States the following year. Subsequent novels have been From Flushing to Calvary (1932), Those Who Perish (1934), Do These Bones Live (1940), The Sorrows of Priapus (1957) and The Flea of Sodom (1950). Mr. Dahlberg received a grant in 1960 from the Institute of Arts and Letters to complete his autobiography, Because I Was Flesh. Truth Is More Sacred, the literary correspondence between Mr. Dahlberg and Sir Herbert Read, appeared last year. He has also received an award from the Longview Foundation. Mr. Dahlberg has written a great deal of verse and published many literary essays.

BORDEN DEAL's first published short story, "Exodus," was reprinted in The Best American Short Stories 1949 while he was still in college. Since then he has published over a hundred short stories. His latest novel, The Spangled Road, was published this spring. His previous novels were Dragon's Wine, The Insolent Breed, Dunbar's Cove, and Walk Through the Valley. Among other honors, Mr. Deal has been awarded a Guggenheim Fellowship. His books have been translated into more than a dozen languages. His work has been adapted for movies, television, radio, and the Broadway stage.

Mr. Deal was born in 1922 in Pontotoc, Mississippi, and was raised near New Albany, Mississippi. After Navy service in World War II, he attended the University of Alabama, graduating in 1949, and lived in Mexico for several years. He lives now in Tuscaloosa, Alabama, devoting his entire time to writing. He is married to the novelist Babs H. Deal.

STANLEY ELKIN was born in New York City and raised and attended public schools in Chicago. He attended the University of Illinois "for seven hundred years and received at its hands a Bachelor's, Master's and Ph.D. degree in English." He has taught English at Illinois and is now an Assistant Professor at Washington University in St. Louis. His stories have appeared in Epoch, Views, Perspectives, Accent, Chicago Review, and Southwest Review. Last year he received a Longview Foundation Award for two of his stories, "Among the Witnesses" which appeared in Accent and "In the Alley" from Chicago Review. He has been given a leave of absence by Washington University for the coming academic year and with his wife and son will leave for Rome, where he plans to work on a novel.

SEYMOUR EPSTEIN has lived in and around New York City all his life, except for a period of overseas service. He took night courses at C.C.N.Y. and N.Y.U. and was trained in meteorology by the U.S. Army Air Force during the war. He has worked as a salesman, factory manager, and personnel interviewer. Mr. Epstein's work was first published in Antioch Review. Six of his short stories were included in the collection Short Story 1, and his stories and novelas have also been published in Esquire and Redbook. Mr. Epstein has written two novels, Pillar of Salt and The Successor, and is now devoting his time to the completion of a third. He is married and has two sons.

GEORGE GARRETT is the author of three collections of poems, The Reverend Ghost, The Sleeping Gypsy, and Abraham's Knife, two collections of short stories, King of the Mountain and In the Briar Patch, and two novels, The Finished Man and Which Ones Are the Enemy? Two of his plays have been produced by the Alley Theater of Houston, Texas, during the past year: Sir Slob and the Princess (a play for children) and Garden Spot U.S.A. Currently a visiting lecturer at Rice University, he will teach next year at the University of Virginia. His story "An Evening Performance" appeared in The Best American Short Stories 1960. The story included here is part of a recently completed collection, entitled More Geese Than Swans.

WILLIAM H. GASS was born in Fargo, North Dakota, in 1924, but lived most of his life in Warren, Ohio, and other parts of the Midwest. He holds degrees from Kenyon College and Cornell and presently teaches philosophy at Purdue University. With his wife and their three children, he now lives in Brookston, Indiana.

SISTER MARY GILBERT, SNJM, is the author of Springs of Silence (1953), an autobiographical account of convent life. She has contributed poems to about a dozen literary quarterlies during the past three years and has a collection of verse in preparation. Her second full-length prose work is soon to be published.

Born Madeline De Frees in Ontario, Oregon, she attended high school at St. Mary's Academy in Portland. She received the Bachelor's degree from Marylhurst College (Oregon), the Master's degree in journalism from the University of Oregon, and an honorary degree of Doctor of Letters from Gonzaga University, Spokane. For the past eleven years she has been on the faculty of Holy Names College in Spokane.

DONALD HALL was born in Connecticut, received his B.A. from Harvard and a B.Litt. from Oxford. He was a Junior Fellow of the Society of Fellows at Harvard from 1954 to 1957. Now an Associate Professor of English at the University of Michigan, he has published two books of poems: Exiles and Marriages (Lamont Poetry Selection, 1955) and The Dark Houses (1958). "A Day On Ragged" appeared in String Too Short to Be Saved (1961). Mr. Hall is married and has two children.

HENIA KARMEL-WOLFE was born and brought up in Poland, where her schooling was interrupted by the war. She was in various ghettos and concentration camps and started writing, mainly poetry, while in Buchenwald. A book of her poems in Polish was published in America under the title The Song From Behind the Barbed Wire. Soon thereafter she arrived in America. She now lives in Riverdale, New York, with her husband and two children. Her first story was published in The Reporter and a second will soon appear in Harper's.

MARY LAVIN, the author of many short stories, lives on a farm in County Meath, Ireland, and has recently bought and converted a derelict coach house in Dublin. A widow with three daughters, Miss Lavin was born in East Walpole, Massachusetts. After attending elementary school there, she was sent to Ireland to be educated and received her M.A. from the National University of Ireland in Dublin. In 1943 she was awarded the Black and Tan Memorial Prize and in 1960 was the holder of a Guggenheim Fellowship. A collection of her stories, Selected Stories, many of them taken from her previous books, was published in 1959. Miss Lavin holds another Guggenheim this year.

JACK THOMAS LEAHY was born in Seattle, Washington, in 1930. He attended public schools in Seattle and received a B.A. and an M.A. from the University of Washington in English, the latter in 1957. Previous to this, he served with the Navy Air Force in the Korean War. After taking his M.A., Mr. Leahy taught for a year in a private high school in Hawaii. Since 1959, he has been teaching in the Humanistic–Social Studies Department at the University of Washington. During the summers, Mr. Leahy and his wife frequently work as lookouts for the Forest Service.

His first novel, *Shadow on the Waters*, was published by Knopf in 1960. Since that time, his short stories have appeared in *The Kenyon Review*, *San Francisco Review*, *Northwest Review*, *Perspective*, *The Magazine of Fantasy and Science Fiction*, *Descant*, and *Prism*. He is now working to finish a collection of short stories.

BEN MADDOW is the author of the novel *44 Gravel Street*. As a film writer and director, he is known for *Steps of Age*, and *The Savage Eye*, winner of four international prizes. *Affair of the Skin* is a film now in preparation. Mr. Maddow's most recent short stories have been published in *New World Writing*, *Harper's*, and *Hudson Review*. He includes among his avocations painting, photo-collage and "automatic poetry."

MIRIAM McKENZIE was born in Wilmington, Delaware. Her undergraduate studies were in English at the University of Delaware. She received an M.A. from Columbia University and a Ph.D. from New York University in psychology. A clinical psychologist, Miss McKenzie has been a faculty member at Sarah Lawrence College. Married to a theater director, she lives in New York City and is currently at work on a novella.

E. LUCAS MYERS was born in Sewanee, Tennessee, and educated at the University of the South and at Downing College, Cambridge. He spent one year as a merchant seaman, a year teaching English in Rome, and two and a half years teaching English to Frenchmen and anthropology to students in the University of Maryland extension in and around Paris. This past year he taught English at the University of the South. Several of his poems, stories, and reviews have been published in this country and in England, and his poetry has been anthologized in England. Now a field representative for CARE in Cyprus, Mr. Myers is married and has a daughter.

ARTHUR MILLER was born in New York City and attended the University of Michigan. He is the author of many plays including *All My Sons*, *Death of a Salesman*, *The Crucible*, and *A View from the Bridge*. His novel, *The Misfits*, was made into a motion picture. The author of numerous short stories, Mr. Miller has also been the recipient of many prizes, including the New York Drama Critics Circle Award, the Antoinette Perry Award, and the Pulitzer Prize.

FLANNERY O'CONNOR was born in Savannah, Georgia. She graduated from Georgia State College for Women and spent two years studying creative writing at the State University of Iowa. She now lives in Milledgeville, Georgia. She has published stories in literary quarterlies and in *Harper's Bazaar*. Her first novel, *Wise Blood*, was published in 1952. A collection of her short stories, *A Good Man Is Hard to Find*, appeared in 1955.

THALIA SELZ was born in Chicago and studied art history at Oberlin College. She received a Master's degree in English from the University of Chicago. She has taught English literature at the Illinois Institute of Technology and at Pomona College. Her short stories have appeared in *Partisan Review*, *Virginia Quarterly Review*, and *Chicago Review*, and her articles on art and film criticism have been published in film and art quarterlies. Miss Selz is presently at work on a novel.

IRWIN SHAW was born in New York in 1913 and was graduated from Brooklyn College in 1934. He has written many plays, short stories, and novels. His last novel was *Two Weeks in Another Town*, and he has just finished a play entitled *Children from Their Games*. He now lives in Europe, dividing his time between a village in the Alps and the city of Paris.

JOHN UPDIKE was born in Shillington, Pennsylvania, in 1932, attended the Shillington public schools, Harvard College, and the Ruskin School of Drawing and Fine Art in Oxford, England. He has worked for *The New Yorker* and now lives in Ipswich, Massachusetts, with his wife and two children. He has published in book form *The Carpentered Hen*, poems, *The Poorhouse Fair*, a novel, *The Same Door*, a collection of short stories, and *Rabbit, Run*, a novel. "Pigeon Feathers" was recently published in a collection entitled *Pigeon Feathers and Other Stories*.

ROLL OF HONOR
1961

I. *American Authors*

ARKIN, FRIEDA
The Light of the Sea. Colorado
Quarterly, Summer.
Summer Sunday. Mutiny, Summer.

BAILEY, NORMAN
Man of Destiny. Ararat, Winter.
BOLES, PAUL DARCY
Unwritten Love Song. Saturday Evening Post, October 7.
BRENNAN, MAEVE
The Beginning of a Long Story. New
Yorker, February 4.

CHEEVER, JOHN
The Brigadier and the Golf Widow.
New Yorker, November 11.
CHESTER, ALFRED
In Praise of Vespasian. The Second
Coming, July.
CHOWNING, J. R.
Elaine. The Noble Savage, Spring.
CHOY, WAYSON S.
The Sound of Waves. Prism, Summer.
COLTER, CYRUS
Overnight Trip. Epoch, Fall.
COMBS, PRENTISS
The Man with the Shine on His
Shoes, Ladies' Home Journal, September.
COX, JAMES TRAMMEL
That Golden Crane. MSS, Spring.

DAHLBERG, EDWARD
Because I Was Flesh. Prairie Schooner, Spring.

DEAL, BORDEN
Antaeus. Southwest Review, Spring.
DONOHUE, H. E. F.
The Man Who Knew What Ethiopia
Should Do about Her Water Table. Carleton Miscellany, Fall.
DOUGLAS, ELLEN
On the Lake. New Yorker, August 26.

EASTLAKE, WILLIAM
A Bird on the Mesa. Harper's Magazine, October.
ELKIN, STANLEY
Criers and Kibbitzers, Kibbitzers and
Criers. Perspective, Winter.
EPSTEIN, SEYMOUR
Shed One Honest Tear. (Wheat
Closed Higher, Cotton Was Mixed.)
Redbook, June.

GARRETT, GEORGE
The Old Army Game. Sewanee Review, July–September.
GASS, WILLIAM H.
The Pedersen Kid. MSS, Spring.
Order of Insects. Minnesota Review,
April.
GILBERT, SISTER MARY
The Model Chapel. Virginia Quarterly Review, Autumn.
GOLDMAN, MIRIAM
The Lost. Massachusetts Review,
Autumn.
GRAU, SHIRLEY ANN
The First Day of School. Saturday
Evening Post, September 30.

GREENE, GEORGE
The Shape of Jesus. Minnesota Review, Fall.

HALL, DONALD
A Day on Ragged. New Yorker, August 12.
The Wild Heifers. New Yorker, September 2.

HAMMONS, BIGE
The Breath of a Man. Virginia Quarterly Review, Spring.

HANDELMAN, SAUL
Gravity. Canadian Forum, November.

HEISERMAN, ARTHUR
The Castle at Arundel. Harper's Magazine, March.

HEMENWAY, ROBERT
Take It Easy, Irma. New Yorker, September 9.

HERMANN, JOHN
The Piranha. Northwest Review, Spring.

HUBBELL, ALBERT
The Glimpse of Pathos. New Yorker, December 2.

JACKSON, DAVID
The English Gardens. Partisan Review, March–April.

JOHNSON, NORA
A Phrase in the Music. McCall's, November.

KARMEL-WOLFE, HENIA
The Last Day. The Reporter, December 1.

KESSLER, JASCHA
The Detective. Partisan Review, January–February.

KRAUSE, ERWIN D.
The Fall. Prairie Schooner, Summer.

LARSEN, ERLING
Hi, Ho Fidelity. Carleton Miscellany, Summer.

LAVIN, MARY
In the Middle of the Fields. New Yorker, June 3.

LAYTON, IRVING
A Game of Chess. Tamarack Review, Winter.

LEAHY, JACK THOMAS
Hanging Hair. Kenyon Review, Autumn.

LOVERIDGE, GEORGE
Mirrors. University of Kansas City Review, June.

MCKENZIE, MIRIAM
Déjà Vu. New World Writing, Number 18.

MCKINLEY, GEORGIA
The Short Rope. Kenyon Review, Autumn.

MCPHEE, JOHN
The Fair of San Gennaro. Transatlantic Review, Winter.

MADDOW, BEN
"To Hell the Rabbis." Kenyon Review, Summer.

MATTHEWS, JACK
Gift from a Silent Lover. University of Kansas City Review, Autumn.
Cavendish Country. Epoch, Winter.

MILLER, ARTHUR
The Prophecy. Esquire, December.

MYERS, E. LUCAS
The Vindication of Dr. Nestor. Sewanee Review, Spring.

NIERENBERG, EDWIN
Rare and Precious Wares, Kenyon Review, Autumn.

NOWLAN, ALDEN
At the Edge of the Woods. Prism, Summer.
Cynthia Loves You. Vanadian Forum, August.

O'CONNOR, FLANNERY
The Partridge Festival. The Critic, February–March.
Everything That Rises Must Converge. New World Writing, Number 19.

O'CONNOR, FRANK
The American Wife. New Yorker, March 25.

O'HARA, JOHN
The Man with the Broken Arm. New Yorker, April 22.

OLIVE, JEANNIE
The Divided Stream. Colorado Quarterly, Spring.

PEARCE, JOHN EDWARD
Homecoming. Southwest Review, Spring.

PETERS, ROBERTA ENGLE
The Oasis. Colorado Quarterly, Spring,

PRICE, REYNOLDS
The Warrior Princess Ozimba. Virginia Review, Summer.

REBSAMEN, FREDERICK
Margot and the Gargoyle. Kenyon Review, Summer.

REEVES, KATHERINE
The Balance of Nature. Virginia Quarterly Review, Spring.

RUSHING, JANE GILMORE
Against the Moon. Virginia Quarterly Review, Summer.

SANDBURG, HELGA
The Other One. Georgia Review, Fall.

SELZ, THALIA
The Education of a Queen. Partisan Review, Numbers 5-6.

SHARMAN, VINCENT
Any Game You Want. Prism, Winter.

SHAW, IRWIN
Love on a Dark Street. Esquire, March.

SHORE, WILMA
The Thin Duck. Antioch Review, Spring.

The Indifferent Guest. Woman's Day, September.

TAYLOR, PETER
A Love Story. New Yorker, February 25.

TOPKINS, KATHERINE
Repeat the Sounding Joy. Epoch, Spring.

UPDIKE, JOHN
Lifeguard. New Yorker, June 17.
Pigeon Feathers. New Yorker, August 19.
Packed Dirt, Churchgoing, Dying Cat, a Traded Car. New Yorker, December 16.
The Crow in the Woods. Transatlantic Review, Winter.

VANETTI, I. W.
Saul. Venture, Volume 4, Number 1.

WILDMAN, JOHN HAZARD
Take It Off. Arizona Quarterly, Autumn.

WILSON, WILLIAM E.
A Simple Heart. University of Kansas City Review, Autumn.

II. *Foreign Authors*

COPE, JACK
The Man Who Doubted. Harper's Magazine, August.

EDISFORD, ROSEMARY
A Highly Inbred Species. New Yorker, November 4.

FRIEL, BRENDAN
Foundry House. New Yorker, November 18.

HAZZARD, SHIRLEY
Vittorio. New Yorker, June 17.

HUGHES, TED
Miss Mambrett and the Wet Cellar. Texas Quarterly, Autumn.

JHABVALA, R. PRAWER
Wedding Preparations. Kenyon Review, Summer.

KIELY, BENEDICT
A Journey to the Seven Streams. New Yorker, May 6.

A View from the Treetop. New Yorker, August 26.

MEGGED, AHARON
The Sabbath. Atlantic Monthly, November.

MORRIEN, ADRIANN
Hijo de Puta. Literary Review, Winter.

MULISCH, HARRY
What Happened to Sergeant Masuro? Hudson Review, Spring.

SINGER, ISAAC BASHEVIS
The Beggar Said So. Esquire, May.

SPARKS, MURIEL
The Prime of Miss Jean Brodie. New Yorker, October 14.

STRETTON, HUGH
Nugatory Notes. Massachusetts Review, Autumn.

DISTINCTIVE SHORT STORIES IN
AMERICAN MAGAZINES
1961

I. *American Authors*

ADAMS, THOMAS E.
  The Sled. Sewanee Review, Winter.
ALDERMAN, LOIS
  The Young People Next Door. University of Kansas City Review, Spring.
ARKIN, FRIEDA
  The Light of the Sea. Colorado Quarterly, Summer.
  Summer Sunday. Mutiny, Summer.
ATHAS, DAPHNE
  Provender's Tale. New World Writing, Number 18.

BAILEY, NORMAN
  Man of Destiny. Ararat, Winter.
BARTA, ROBERT
  The Pelican Market. Minnesota Review, April.
BECK, WARREN
  Woman's Work. Country Beautiful, September.
BERRY, JOHN
  Flight of White Crows. Noble Savage, Spring.
BERWICK, DONALD
  The Dark Room. Colorado Quarterly, Summer.
BINGHAM, SALLY
  Moving Day. Atlantic Monthly, November.
BIRD, DICK
  Blossom Time. San Francisco Review, Volume I, Number 9.
BLUESTONE, GEORGE
  A Basket for the Needy. Virginia Quarterly Review, Summer.
  Mindyah. Antioch Review, Winter.

BLUM, RALPH
  The Day of the Lion. New Yorker, January 14.
BOLES, PAUL DARCY
  Unwritten Love Song. Saturday Evening Post, October 7.
BONGARTZ, ROY
  Dirt. New Yorker, September 9.
BRADSHAW, GEORGE
  My Uncle — Romantic Forger of Paintings. Vogue, March 15.
BRENNAN, MAEVE
  The Beginning of a Long Story. New Yorker, February 4.
BROWER, BROCK
  Peacetime. New World Writing, Number 19.
BUNCH, DAVID R.
  In the Empire. Shenandoah, Spring.
  Our House. Southwest Review, Spring.

CASPER, LEONARD
  Silent Outcry, Sleep. Southwest Review, Spring.
CASSITY, TURNER
  Distances from Berlin. Kenyon Review, Spring.
CHAPIN, VICTOR
  Time Will Take Care of It. Colorado Quarterly, Winter.
CHAY, MARIE
  Hitch Your Horses to a Star. Southwest Review, Autumn.
CHEEVER, JOHN
  The Chimera. New Yorker, July 1.
  The Seaside Houses. New Yorker, July 29.

The Angel of the Bridge. New Yorker, October 21.

The Brigadier and the Golf Widow. New Yorker, November 11.

The Traveler. New Yorker, December 9.

Christmas Eve in St. Botolph's. New Yorker, December 23.

CHESTER, ALFRED
The Victory. Evergreen Review, May–June.

In Praise of Vespasian. The Second Coming, July.

Behold Goliath. Provincetown Review, Summer.

CHOWNING, J. R.
Elaine. Noble Savage, Spring.

CHOY, WAYSON S.
The Sound of Waves. Prism, Summer.

COLTER, CYRUS
Overnight Trip. Epoch, Fall.

COMBS, PRENTISS
The Man with the Shine on His Shoes. Ladies' Home Journal, September.

COOK, WHITFIELD
Home to Mother. Virginia Quarterly Review, Winter.

COX, JAMES
That Golden Crane, MSS, Spring.

CULLEN, ROBERT
Irish Black. Venture, Volume 4, Number 1.

CULLINAN, ELIZABETH
The Power of Prayer. New Yorker, January 7.

The Reunion. New Yorker, February 18.

DAHLBERG, EDWARD
Because I Was Flesh. Prairie Schooner, Spring.

DAVIDSON, AVRAM
Where Do You Live, Queen Esther? Ellery Queen's Mystery Magazine, March.

Traveler from an Antique Land. Ellery Queen's Mystery Magazine, September.

The Dragon-Skin Drum. Kenyon Review, Winter.

DAVIDSON, BARBARA
Say Goodbye. Epoch, Spring.

DEAL, BORDEN
Antaeus. Southwest Review, Spring.

DEALEY, TED
Horse Wrangler. Southwest Review, Spring.

DEJONG, DAVID CORNEL
Second Journey on the Um. Minnesota Review, January.

Midnight to Afternoon. Transatlantic Review, Winter.

DELATTRE, PIERRE HENRI
A Trip to the Country. Atlantic Monthly, December.

DEVEGH, ELIZABETH
The Gardner of Quinta Maria. Southwest Review, Spring.

DE VRIES, PETER
Heart. New Yorker, November 18.

DONOHUE, H. E. F.
The Man Who Knew What Ethiopia Should Do about Her Water Table. Carleton Miscellany, Fall.

DOUGLAS, ELLEN
On the Lake. New Yorker, August 26.

DOWNEY, HARRIS
Grandfather, We Hear You. Epoch, Fall.

EASTLAKE, WILLIAM
A Bird on the Mesa. Harper's Magazine, October.

ELKIN, STANLEY
Criers and Kibbitzers, Kibbitzers and Criers. Perspective, Winter.

EPSTEIN, SEYMOUR
Shed One Honest Tear. (Wheat Closed Higher, Cotton Was Mixed.) Redbook, June.

FAURE, RAOUL C.
Hounds of Heaven. Virginia Quarterly Review, Autumn.

FAUST, IRVIN
Into the Green Night. Carleton Miscellany, Winter.

FETLER, ANDREW
Loaves and Fishes. Perspective, Winter.

FLAGG, KENNETH
Hello, Miss Annie Oakley. Ararat, Autumn.

FONTANA, BERNARD L.
The Green Dog. Arizona Quarterly, Spring.

FREITAG, GEORGE H.
The Burial of a Friend. Atlantic Monthly, January.

GALLANT, MAVIS
Crossing France. The Critic, January.
Two Questions. New Yorker, November 11.
My Heart Is Broken. New Yorker, August 12.

GARDNER, JOHN
A Little Night Music. Northwest Review, Spring.

GARRETT, GEORGE
The Old Army Game. Sewanee Review, July–September.

GASCAR, PIERRE
The Cistern. New World Writing, Number 19.

GASS, WILLIAM H.
Order of Insects. Minnesota Review, April.
The Pedersen Kid. MSS, Spring.

GEESLIN, HUGH, JR.
Salesmeeting. Georgia Review, Summer.

GILBERT, SISTER MARY
The Model Chapel. Virginia Quarterly Review, Autumn.

GLEN, EMILIE
Wonderful. Four Quarters, January.

GODFREY, DOWE
River Two Blind Jacks. Tamarack Review, Spring.

GOLD, HERBERT
I Wanta Sunday Kind of Love. Hudson Review, Autumn.

GOLDMAN, WILLIAM
Till the Right Girls Come Along. Transatlantic Review, Winter.

GOODMAN, PAUL
The Old Knight. Fresco, Volume 1, Number 2.

GRAU, SHIRLEY ANN
Eight O'Clock One Morning. Reporter, June 22.
The First Day of School. Saturday Evening Post, September 30.

The Lovely April. Shenandoah, Autumn.

GREEN, BRADFORD
The Nazi Helmet. Saturday Evening Post, May 27.

GREENBERG, JOANNE
Two Annas. University of Kansas City Review, June.

GREENE, GEORGE
The Shape of Jesus. Minnesota Review, Fall.

GRUETTI, JAMES
Claude. Epoch, Spring.

HALL, DONALD
A Day on Ragged. New Yorker, August 12.
The Wild Heifers. New Yorker, September 2.

HAMMONS, BIGE
The Breath of a Man. Virginia Quarterly Review, Spring.

HANDELMAN, SAUL
Gravity. Canadian Forum, November.

HEISERMAN, ARTHUR
The Castle at Arundel. Harper's Magazine, March.

HELDMAN, IRMA PASCAL
Created Equal. University of Kansas City Review, Autumn.

HEMENWAY, ROBERT
Take It Easy, Irma. New Yorker, September 9.

HERMANN, JOHN
The Piranha. Northwest Review, Spring.

HILL, ELIZABETH
A Walk in the Evening. Colorado Quarterly, Spring.

HILL, ELIZABETH STARR
The Old Dog. New World Writing, Number 19.

HILTY, PETER
Rain Down on Me. Saturday Evening Post, May 6.

HOFFMAN, A. C.
A Family Portrait. Epoch, Fall.

HOOD, HUGH
Three Halves of a House. Tamarack Review, Summer.

HORWITZ, JULIUS
The Day I Smashed the Pushka. Midstream, Autumn.

HUBBELL, ALBERT
  The Glimpse of Pathos. New Yorker, December 2.
HURST, JAMES
  A Cup of Trembling. Southwest Review, Spring.

INGLER, JAMES
  The Mirror of Reason. Southwest Review, Spring.

JACKSON, DAVID
  The English Gardens. Partisan Review, March–April.
JOHNSON, NORA
  Phrase in the Music. McCall's, November.

KARCHMER, SYLVAN
  The Winter World. Southwest Review, Winter.
KARMEL-WOLFE, HENIA
  The Last Day. The Reporter, December 21.
KEEFE, FREDERICK L.
  Wanda Havley and the Flight of Time. New Yorker, February 11.
  The Field Glasses. New Yorker, May 6.
KESSLER, JASCHA
  The Detective. Partisan Review, January–February.
KLEIN, NORMA
  Declaration of Independence. Canadian Forum, December.
KNAPP, DANIEL
  The Canal. Prairie Schooner, Spring.
KOUMJIAN, VAUGHN
  The Quilt. Minnesota Review, Fall.
KRAUSE, ERWIN D.
  The Metal Sky. Prairie Schooner, Summer.
  The Fall. Prairie Schooner, Summer.
  The Snake. Prairie Schooner, Summer.
KREISEL, HENRY
  Annerl. Prism, Summer.

LADAS, ALEXIS
  A Corner of a Foreign Jail.
LAMBERT, EMILY WHITTY
  The Excortication. Provincetown Review, Summer.

LANDY, SUSAN
  An Absolute Monarchy. Mutiny, Spring.
LANNING, GEORGE
  The Bones in the Long Room. Sewanee Review, July–September.
LARDAS, KONSTANTINOS
  The Devil Child. Atlantic Monthly, July.
LARSEN, ERLING
  Hi, Ho Fidelity. Carleton Miscellany, Summer.
LAVIN, MARY
  In the Middle of the Fields. New Yorker, June 3.
LAYTON, IRVING
  Osmeck. Canadian Forum, February.
  A Game of Chess. Tamarack Review, Winter.
LEAHY, JACK THOMAS
  Hanging Hair. Kenyon Review, Autumn.
LEBOWITZ, ALBERT
  Another, Another You. Mutiny, Spring.
LEVINSON, RICHARD, and LINK, WILLIAM
  The Convalescent. University of Kansas City Review, Spring.
  Small Accident. University of Kansas City Review, Autumn.
LOVERIDGE, GEORGE
  Mirror. University of Kansas City Review, June.
LOWREY, P. H.
  The Great Speckled Bird. Sewanee Review, Autumn.
LOWRY, ROBERT
  Ten Questions. Carleton Miscellany, Winter.
  The Girl with the Big Pocketbook. Carleton Miscellany, Winter.
  Hello, Margaret, Hello. Fresco, Volume 1, Number 2.
LUBKA, NANCY
  Emmet Stark. Mainstream, October.

McCONKEY, JAMES
  A Night Stand. Perspective, Winter.
McFADDEN, FRANCES
  The Other Home. Atlantic Monthly, December.
McKELWAY, ST. CLAIR

Again Deeply Worried. New Yorker, November 25.

McKenzie, Miriam
Déjà Vu. New World Writing, Number 18.

McKinley, Georgia
The Short Rope. Kenyon Review, Autumn.
Christmas Trees Are White in Texas. Southwest Review, Winter.

McMurtry, Larry
Horseman, Pass By. Southwest Review, Spring.

McPhee, John
The Fair of San Gennaro. Transatlantic Review, Winter.

Maddow, Ben
"To Hell the Rabbis." Kenyon Review, Summer.

Marsh, William
A Grandfather's Gift. Saturday Evening Post, November 4.

Meehan, Thomas
A Burnt-Out Ace. New Yorker, August 26.

Matthews, Jack
Gift from a Silent Lover. University of Kansas City Review, Autumn.
Cavendish Country. Epoch, Winter.

Miller, Arthur
The Prophecy. Esquire, December.

Moeckel, Fred
The Drowning. Minnesota Review, July.

Moorse, George
The Hat. New World Writing, Number 19.

Moseley, Edwin
Off Duty. Shenandoah, Winter.

Moser, Edna
For Fitzpatrick's Future. Arizona Quarterly, Summer.

Myers, E. Lucas
The Vindication of Dr. Nestor. Sewanee Review, Spring.

Nierenberg, Edwin
Rare and Precious Wares. Kenyon Review, Autumn.

Nissenson, Hugh
The Well. Harper's Magazine, January.

Norman, Colin
A Matter of Small Importance. Prism, Spring.

Nowlan, Alden
At the Edge of the Woods. Prism, Summer.
Cynthia Loves You. Canadian Forum, August.

O'Connor, Flannery
The Partridge Festival. The Critic, February–March.
Everything That Rises Must Converge. New World Writing, Number 19.

O'Connor, Frank
The Weeping Children. New Yorker, January 21.
The American Wife. New Yorker, March 25.

O'Hara, John
The Cellar Domain. New Yorker, February 11.
Sterling Silver. New Yorker, March 11.
The Man with the Broken Arm. New Yorker, April 22.
The Weakness. New Yorker, July 8.
Mary and Norma. New Yorker, August 5.
The Trip. New Yorker, September 23.
The Father. New Yorker, October 28.
Two Turtle Doves. New Yorker, December 23.

Olive, Jeannie
The Divided Stream. Colorado Quarterly, Spring.

Oliver, Smith
Theodore. Sewanee Review, July–September.

Ortovitz, Gil
The Brass Plaque. Minnesota Review, July.

Ozick, Cynthia
The Butterfly and the Traffic Light. Literary Review, Autumn.

Packer, Nancy Huddleston
Night Guard. Kenyon Review, Winter.

PAUKER, JOHN
  The Somes Saga. San Francisco Review, September.
PEARCE, JOHN EDWARD
  Homecoming. Southwest Review, Spring.
PETERS, ROBERTA ENGLE
  The Oasis. Colorado Quarterly, Spring.
PETRARKIS, HARRY MARK
  The Passing of the Ice. Atlantic Monthly, April.
  The Little Store on Bleecker Street. Saturday Evening Post, July 19.
  A Knowledge of Her Past. Saturday Evening Post, September 2.
PFAFFMAN, LOUISE
  La Folie. Southwest Review, Spring.
POLK, DWAN
  Skirmish at Beaver Creek. Saturday Evening Post, August 26.
PRICE, REYNOLDS
  The Warrior Princess Ozimba. Virginia Quarterly Review, Summer.
PYNCHON, THOMAS
  Under the Rose. Noble Savage, Spring.

REBSAMEN, FREDERICK
  Margot and the Gargoyle. Kenyon Review, Summer.
REEVES, KATHERINE
  The Balance of Nature. Virginia Quarterly Review, Spring.
RIFKIN, SHEPARD
  Liverpool Is Brooklyn. Atlantic Monthly, April.
ROBINSON, R. O.
  Teacher Jones Discusses Race and Color. Canadian Forum, June.
ROGIN, RICHARD
  In the Company of Runners. Harper's Magazine, November.
RUSHING, JANE GILMORE
  Against the Moon. Virginia Quarterly Review, Summer.

SALISBURY, RALPH J.
  On the Old Santa Fe Trail to Siberia. Northwest Review, Spring.
SANDBURG, HELGA

The Other One. Georgia Review, Fall.
SAROYAN, WILLIAM
  Paris Is the Place for You. Saturday Evening Post, September 30.
SAVARESE, JULIA
  The Keeper. University of Kansas City Review, June.
SCHILLER, MARVIN
  The Sheep's in the Meadow. Antioch Review, Fall.
SCHOR, SANDRA MOSKMAN
  The Snows of Fujiyama. Saturday Evening Post, June 3.
SELZ, THALIA
  The Education of a Queen. Partisan Review, Numbers 5–6.
SHARMAN, VINCENT
  Any Game You Want. Prism, Winter.
SHAW, IRWIN
  Love on a Dark Street. Esquire, March.
  A Year to Learn the Language. Redbook, November.
SHORE, WILMA
  The Thin Duck. Antioch Review, Spring.
  The Indifferent Guest. Woman's Day, September.
SIMMONS, CHARLES
  The Substitute Pleasure Theory. Noble Savage, Spring.
SKIDMORE, HOBERT
  The Voice in the Willows. Saturday Evening Post, May 20.
SPARSHOTT, F. E.
  Franciscus, A Dialogue in Riddles. Tamarack Review, Spring.
SPETTIGUE, DOUG
  The Truck. Tamarack Review, Winter.
STEWART, NATACHA
  What Sadness. New Yorker, November 25.
STORTI, FRANK
  The Last Reunion. San Francisco Review, Volume 1, Number 9.
STURHAHN, LAWRENCE
  The Horse That Got Caught on Barbed Wire. Literary Review, Autumn.
SULLIVAN, RICHARD
  The Wake. The Critic, January.

TAYLOR, PETER
  A Love Story. New Yorker, February 25.
TEKEYAN, CHARLES
  An Armenian Is Now a King. Massachusetts Review, Summer.
THOMAS, MACK SHELDON
  Magnolia. Evergreen Review, May–June.
  The Coat. Perspective, Autumn.
TOPKINS, KATHARINE
  "Vista del Sol." Minnesota Review, January.
  Repeat the Sounding Joy. Epoch, Spring.

UPDIKE, JOHN
  The Doctor's Wife. New Yorker, February 11.
  The Astronomer. New Yorker, April 1.
  Lifeguard. New Yorker, June 17.
  A & P. New Yorker, July 22.
  Pigeon Feathers. New Yorker, August 19.
  Packed Dirt, Churchgoing, a Dying Cat, a Traded Car. New Yorker, December 16.
  The Crow in the Woods. Transatlantic Review, Winter.

VANETTI, I. W.
  Saul. Venture, Volume 4, Number 1.
VIVANTE, ARTURO
  A Basket of Peanuts. New Yorker, August 26.

WEBB, LELAND
  Bricktop: He Rambled. New World Writing. Number 19.
WEINBAND, SHIRLEY
  Next Stop the Salton Sea. San Francisco Review, March.
WESTON, CHRISTINE
  Summer Is Another Country. Harper's Magazine, July.
WHITE, EDWARD M.
  The Presence of Pain. Carleton Miscellany, Fall.
WHITE, ROBIN
  Foreign Soil. The Reporter, May 25.
WILDMAN, JOHN HAZARD
  Take It Off. Arizona Quarterly, Autumn.
WILLEFORD, CHARLES
  The Machine in Ward Eleven. Playboy, March.
WILSON, WILLIAM E.
  A Simple Heart. University of Kansas City Review, Autumn.
WOTTON, MARIAH
  The Errand. San Francisco Review, March.
WOODFORD, BRUCE P.
  The Dark Room. Four Quarters, January.

ZILBER, JACOB
  The Price of Admission. Prism, Summer.
ZIMPEL, LLOYD
  Through the Floor. Perspective, Autumn.

II. *Foreign Authors*

AGNON, S. Y.
  Forevermore. Commentary, August.
AKBAL, OKTAY
  Lost Thing. Literary Review, Winter.
AMICHAI, YEHUDA
  Love in Reverse. Midstream, Autumn.
AYME, MARCEL
  Knate. Harper's Magazine, February.

BABEL, ISAAC
  Regards to Odessa. Midstream, Autumn.
BALIKCISI, HALIKARNAS

  The Resurrection of the Unknown Soldier. Literary Review, Winter.
BOLL, HEINRICH
  In This Country of Ours. Evergreen Review, November–December.
BORGES, JORGE LUIS
  Thon, Wqbar, Orbis Tertius. New World Writing, Number 18.

CARY, JOYCE
  The Ball. Texas Quarterly, Autumn.
CLEEVE, BRIAN
  Run with Your Heart. Saturday Evening Post, September 9.

COENCA, YVONNE
  Story. Transatlantic Review, Winter.
COPE, JACK
  The Man Who Doubted. Harper's
  Magazine, August.

DELTEIL, CAROLINE
  Where There Is Love, the River
  Goes. Prairie Schooner, Fall.
DUGGAL, KARTAR SINGH
  Rain God and the Radio. Literary
  Review, Autumn.

EDISFORD, ROSEMARY
  A Highly Inbred Species. New
  Yorker, November 4.
EGGLESTON, R. M.
  The Day before Tomorrow. Trans-
  atlantic Review, Winter.

FAIK, SAIK
  The Mirror at the Beach. Literary
  Review, Winter.
FRIEL, BRENDAN
  Foundry House. New Yorker, No-
  vember 18.
  My True Kinsman. New Yorker, De-
  cember 2.

GORDIMER, NADINE
  The African Magician. New Yorker,
  July 15.

HAZZARD, SHIRLEY
  Vittorio. New Yorker, June 17.
  Villa Adriana. New Yorker, August 5.
HIGGINS, AIDAN
  Winter Offensive. Evergreen Review,
  May–June.
HUGHES, TED
  Miss Mambrett and the Wet Cellar.
  Texas Quarterly, Autumn.

JHABVALA, R. PRAWER
  Wedding Preparations. Kenyon Re-
  view, Summer.
  The Award. Kenyon Review, Winter.

KIELY, BENEDICT
  A Journey to the Seven Streams. New
  Yorker, May 6.
  A View from the Treetop. New
  Yorker, August 26.

LOWRY, MALCOLM
  The Forest Path to the Spring. New
  World Writing, Number 18.

MALAQUAIS, JEAN
  The Hitch-Hiker. Carleton Miscel-
  lany, Summer.
MEGGED, AHARON
  The Sabbath. Atlantic Monthly, No-
  vember.
MICHAL, MIRA
  Nursie. Virginia Quarterly, Winter.
MOOKERJI, TAPATI
  The Quarrel. Literary Review, Au-
  tumn.
MORRIEN, ADRIANN
  Hijo de Puta. Literary Review, Win-
  ter.
MULISCH, HARRY
  What Happened to Sergeant Masuro?
  Hudson Review, Spring.
MURO, AMADO
  My Aunt Dominga. New Mexico
  Quarterly, Winter.

NESIN, AZIZ
  The House on the Border. Literary
  Review, Winter.

O'FAOLAIN, SEAN
  The Sugawn Chair. Atlantic
  Monthly, August.
O'NEILL, SEAMUS
  The Boy from the Village. Trans-
  atlantic Review, Winter.

PATON, ALAN
  Sponono. Esquire, April.
PAZ, OCTAVIO
  The Blue Bouquet. Evergreen Re-
  view, May–June.
POEHLER, KLAUS
  Bubul. New World Writing, Novem-
  ber 18.
PRITCHETT, V. F.
  Noisy Flushes the Birds. New Yorker,
  September 23.

REUBEN, B.
  The Professional Mourners. New
  World Writing, Number 19.
RIBNIKAR, JARA
  Copperskin. Noble Savage, Number 3.

ROLLNICK, SONIA
Pandora's Boxes. New Yorker, December 16.

SINCLAIR, ANDREW
To Kill a Loris. Texas Quarterly, Autumn.

SINGER, ISAAC BASHEVIS
The Shadow of a Crib. Mademoiselle, March.
The Beggar Said So. Esquire, May.

SPARKS, MURIEL
A Member of the Family. Mademoiselle, February.
The Prime of Miss Jean Brodie. New Yorker, October 14.

STRETTON, HUGH
Nugatory Notes. Massachusetts Review, Autumn.

TAYLOR, ELIZABETH
Girl Reading. New Yorker, July 29.
In a Different Light. New Yorker, October 8.

VAN HET RENE, GERARD KORNELIS
The Decline and Fall of the Boslowits Family. Literary Review, Winter.

VESTDIJIK, SIMON
The Stone Face. Literary Review, Winter.

VON DODERER, HEIMITO
The Magician's Art. Literary Review, Autumn.

VUYK, BEB
All Our Yesterdays. Literary Review, Winter.

WARNER, SYLVIA TOWNSEND
A Dressmaker. New Yorker, May 20.
Ah, La Jeunesse. New Yorker, October 21.
Truth and Fiction. New Yorker, December 2.

WEST, ANTHONY
The Fairy Midwife. Colorado Quarterly, Winter.

WILSON, ANGUS
My Husband Is Right. Texas Quarterly, Autumn.

YIZHAR, S.
A Warm Hike. Atlantic Monthly, November.

YUCEL, TAHSIN
Haney Must Live. Literary Review, Winter.

ADDRESSES OF AMERICAN AND CANADIAN
MAGAZINES PUBLISHING SHORT STORIES

Antioch Review, 212 Xenia Avenue, Yellow Springs, Ohio
Ararat, 250 Fifth Avenue, New York 1, New York
Arizona Quarterly, University of Arizona, Tucson, Arizona
Atlantic Monthly, 8 Arlington Street, Boston 16, Massachusetts
Audience, 140 Mount Auburn Street, Cambridge 38, Massachusetts
Between Two Worlds, Inter American University, San Germán, Puerto Rico
Canadian Forum, 30 Front Street West, Toronto, Ontario, Canada
Canadian Home Journal, 71 Richmond Street, Toronto, Ontario, Canada
Carleton Miscellany, Carleton College, Northfield, Minnesota
Carolina Quarterly, P.O. Box 1117, Chapel Hill, North Carolina
Catholic World, 180 Varick Street, New York 14, New York
Charm, Glamour, 420 Lexington Avenue, New York 17, New York
Chicago Review, Reynolds Club, University of Chicago, Chicago, Illinois
Coastlines, 2465 North Beachwood Drive, Hollywood 20, California
Colorado Quarterly, University of Colorado, Boulder, Colorado
Commentary, 165 East 56th Street, New York 22, New York
Commonweal, 386 Park Avenue South, New York 16, New York
Contact, 749 Bridgeway, Sausalito, California
Contemporary Fiction, Box 1323, Milwaukee, Wisconsin
Cosmopolitan, 57th Street and Eighth Avenue, New York 19, New York
Country Beautiful, Elm Grove, Wisconsin
Critic, 210 Madison Street, Chicago, Illinois
Descant, Texas Christian University, Fort Worth, Texas
Ellery Queen's Mystery Magazine, 527 Madison Avenue, New York 22, New York
Epoch, 252 Goldwin Smith Hall, Cornell University, Ithaca, New York
Esquire, 488 Madison Avenue, New York 22, New York
Evergreen Review, 64 University Place, New York 3, New York
Exodus, 239 Thompson Street, New York, New York
Fantasy and Science Fiction, Box 271, Rockville Centre, New York
Four Quarters, LaSalle College, Philadelphia 43, Pennsylvania
Gentlemen's Quarterly, 488 Madison Avenue, New York 22, New York
Good Housekeeping, 57th Street and Eighth Avenue, New York 19, New York
Harper's Bazaar, 572 Madison Avenue, New York 22, New York
Harper's Magazine, 49 East 33rd Street, New York 16, New York
Holiday, Independence Square, Philadelphia, Pennsylvania
Hudson Review, 65 East 55th Street, New York 22, New York
Husk, Cornell College, Mount Vernon, Iowa
Inland, P.O. Box 685, Salt Lake City, Utah
Kenyon Review, Kenyon College, Gambier, Ohio

Ladies' Home Journal, Independence Square, Philadelphia, Pennsylvania
Literary Review, Fairleigh Dickinson University, Teaneck, New Jersey
McCall's, 230 Park Avenue, New York 17, New York
MacLean's, 481 University Avenue, Toronto, Ontario, Canada
Mademoiselle, 575 Madison Avenue, New York 22, New York
Mainstream, 832 Broadway, New York 18, New York
Massachusetts Review, University of Massachusetts, Amherst, Massachusetts
Midstream, 515 Park Avenue, New York, New York
Minnesota Review, Box 4068, University Station, Minneapolis, Minnesota
MSS, 670 East Fifth Avenue, Chico, California
New Mexico Quarterly, University of New Mexico, Albuquerque, New Mexico
New World Writing, 521 Fifth Avenue, New York 17, New York
New Yorker, 25 West 43rd Street, New York 36, New York
Noble Savage, 12 East 22nd Street, New York 10, New York
Northwest Review, Erb Memorial Union, University of Oregon, Eugene, Oregon
Paris Review, 45–39 171 Place, Flushing 58, New York
Partisan Review, 22 East 17th Street, New York 3, New York
Perspective, Washington University Post Office, St. Louis, Missouri
Prairie Schooner, Andrews Hall, University of Nebraska, Lincoln, Nebraska
Prism, University of British Columbia, Vancouver, British Columbia, Canada
Provincetown Quarterly, P.O. Box 473, Provincetown, Massachusetts
Quarterly Review of Literature, Box 287, Bard College, Annandale-on-Hudson, New York
Queen's Quarterly, Queen's University, Kingston, Ontario, Canada
Redbook, 230 Park Avenue, New York 17, New York
Reporter, 660 Madison Avenue, New York, New York
San Francisco Review, San Francisco, California
Saturday Evening Post, Independence Square, Philadelphia, Pennsylvania
Second Coming, Columbia University, New York 22, New York
Seventeen, 488 Madison Avenue, New York 22, New York
Sewanee Review, University of the South, Sewanee, Tennessee
Southwest Review, Southern Methodist University, Dallas, Texas
Tamarack Review, Box 157, Postal Station K, Toronto, Ontario, Canada
Texas Quarterly, Box 7527, University Station, Austin 12, Texas
Transatlantic Review, 821 Seconl Avenue, New York 17, New York
University of Kansas City Review, University of Kansas City, Kansas City, Missouri
Venture, P.O. Box 228, Old Chelsea Station, New York 11, New York
Virginia Quarterly Review, 1 West Range, Charlottesville, Virginia
Weird Tales, 9 Rockefeller Plaza, New York, New York
Western Review, University of Iowa, Iowa City, Iowa
Yale Review, P.O. Box 1729, New Haven, Connecticut
Yankee, Dublin, New Hampshire